ACCLAIM

"*By Blade and Blood* is mystifying and powerful, every page filled with emotion and authenticity, showing the kind of courage needed to truly love and be loved. Augustine delves deep into difficult topics with grace and compassion, offering hope to the hurting and ashamed, and giving readers the chance to know what love is by experiencing it with Dhamar and Inara."

—ERIN PHILLIPS, author of *A Crown of Chains*

"A breathlessly romantic tale of courage and healing. Enter the vibrant, twisted world of Taletha and you're sure to fall in love with its broken characters and their fight to stand up for what's right."

—MEGAN MCCULLOUGH, author of *We Could Be Villains*

"Almost from the first page, we are enraptured by Inara's struggle for belonging and Dhamar's desire to do what is good and right. Set against a colorful and vibrant backdrop that comes alive on every page, we find ourselves centered around the stories of two characters whose desire to love and to be loved is palpable. As the threat of war looms on the horizon, the shining heart of *By Blood and Blade* is the characters' unshakable devotion - to themselves, to each other, and to what is really and truly right."

—BRIAN MCBRIDE, award-winning author of *The Mamoth Series*

"A timeless love story frought with struggle and the beauty that rises from fighting those struggles together."

—AJ SKELLY, bestselling author of *The Wolves of Rock Falls* series and *Magik Prep Academy* series

A Taletha Novel

BY Blood AND Blade

ANNA AUGUSTINE

Also By Anna Augustine

Novels

When You Found Me

A Love Like Ours

Teletha

By Light & Love

By Blood & Blade

Anthologies

The Depths We'll Go To

Fool's Honor

Aphotic Love

Casting Call: Havok Season Six

Animal Kingdom: Havok Season Seven

A TALETHA NOVEL

BY

Blood

AND

Blade

Quill & Flame
PUBLISHING HOUSE

ANNA AUGUSTINE

Quill & Flame
PUBLISHING HOUSE

By Blood and Blade

Copyright ©2023 by Anna Augustine

Chapter Heading Artwork Copyright ©2023 Abigail Augustine

Published by Quill & Flame Publishing House, an imprint of Book Bash Media, LLC.

www.quillandflame.com

This is a work of fiction. Names, characters, and incidents are products of the author's imagination or are used ficticiously. Any similarity to actual people, living or dead, organizations, business establishments, and/or events is purely coincidental.

Cover design by Emilie Haney, www.EAHCreative.com

Dedicated to mothers everywhere:

Whether you know it or not, we see you.

Your joy.

Your tears.

Your struggles.

Your triumphs.

Thank you for giving us life.

For giving us love.

For fighting for us.

You've shown us what motherhood means.

We love you.

And for Grandpa Jack Bechtol

Though you never got to read this book, you were always so supportive. Until we meet again.

Rana
The North Sea
Mordova
capitol of Taletha
Saleem
Hasan
Taletha
Zara
Nasaria
Šeri
home of the Tribesmen

The Palace of
the Malek
Lower City
Middle City
High City

GLOSSARY

Names & Titles

Taletha

Ameer—Prince

Amira—Princess

Malek—King

Rania—Queen

Šeri

Majka—Mother

Kćerka—daughter

Otac—Father

Princezo—princess

Šefe—chief

Teyze—aunt

Dayi—uncle

Clothing

Kaftan—A long flowing dress with trailing sleeves.

Kameez—An overdress that has loose-fitting pants underneath. Dress falls to the knees.

Kurta—Loose, long-sleeved, ankle-length garment. The neck and front can be embroidered and decorated with beads.

Maang teeka—Head locket.

Salwar—Cotton or silk pants worn under the kurta.

Food

Baklava—Layered pastry dessert made of filo pastry. Filled with chopped nuts and sweetened with syrup or honey.

Barazek—Sesame seed cookies served with a thick syrup.

Falafel—Balls of cooked chickpeas, usually fried in oil. Often flavored with garlic/onion, cumin, coriander, and pepper.

Faloodeh—A frozen dessert with semi-frozen rice noodles that has a blend of sweet and sour flavors and punctuated with rosewater.

Foul—Dip made with fava beans. Typically flavored with garlic, lemon juice, tomato, onions, and parsley.

Kofta—Balls of minced lamb or beef with a spicy onion kick.

Manakeesh—Flat bread with sauce, meats, cheese, and herbs.

Samoon—A stone baked bread, brushed with egg whites and vinegar on top. Typically served with jelly.

Shawarma—Spicy, slow-roasted chicken and pita bread.

Za'atar—An herb that is usually seen with a blend of toasted sesame seeds, dried sumac, often salt, as well as other spices.

Instruments

Oud—A short-necked fretless lute.

Ney—A long, end-blown flute.

Mizmars—An oboe-type reed instrument.

CHAPTER ONE

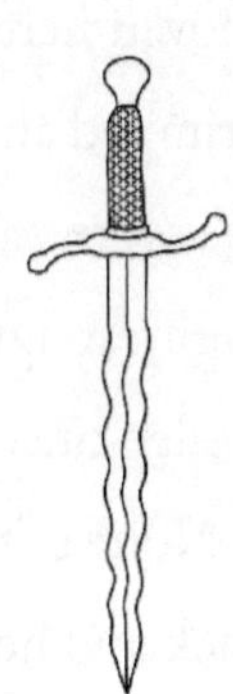

Inara

The Wife Market of Taletha was open for business, and I was up for sale. I smoothed my trembling hands across my white satin kaftan as the short sleeves of the gown chafed against my upper arms. I stood on my block with twenty-nine other women. Straight backed, hands at our sides, eyes gazing ahead at nothing, we appeared like the beautiful marble statues of our goddess, Nicar. If only we had the power she possessed.

The large, domed ceiling kept it pleasantly cool in the large, dimly lit room. There were no windows to let in a cooling breeze or fresh air. There were only three doors: one let prospective buyers in, one allowed the men to take their brides out, and one led to our living quarters. It was the first door we all faced at the moment, although I wanted to escape out of the third door—to curl up into the blessed nothingness of sleep.

It took all my strength to remain serene and poised—*as a wife ought to be.* But inside of me raged a deep-rooted fury. No one deserved this, least of all me. I had been plucked from my home and shoved here for a couple hundred gold coins. Now we all stood, primped and pressed and molded into fake versions of perfection. We were paraded for men to gawk at and buy without even the slightest agreement from us. I was being manipulated and controlled once more.

None of this showed on my face. No, I stood with my shoulders back and head held high as another nobleman strolled by. He was dressed in the style of all young Talethans, with an embroidered vest of black covering his red kurta, flowing salwar cuffed at the ankle, and head bare of any hat. His tan skin and thick black hair displayed his heritage as perfectly Talethan—unlike my own blonde hair and blue-green eyes. The bells on the tips of his pointed shoes rang through the warehouse with every step, curling the nerves in my stomach tauter with each jingle.

He reached my block and glanced me over from the top of my head to the tips of my toes. Being first was the worst sort of punishment. It meant I had been here the longest, rejected over and over again. He stepped up on the block and stretched out his hand, fingering a strand of my blonde hair before the back of his hand caressed my jaw and then my lips. It took a staggering amount of self-control to not bite his wandering fingers, but I could see my owner, Omar, out of the corner of my eye and so I refrained.

I regretted my restraint almost instantly when the man's lip curled in an arrogant sneer. "You're a pretty thing, but it's too bad you look so *northern*." I wanted to flinch as his hand trailed down my bare arm. But seeing Omar's narrowed gaze still focused on me,

I remained staring ahead, even as the noble's hands wandered to places they shouldn't. I tried to think of happy memories from my childhood, but it was nearly impossible.

Eventually, the young noble grew bored of me and moved on, slowly dismissing each girl in turn. At last, it came down to just me and Maram, one of the few girls I considered a friend. Nerves bloomed in my stomach. Like all the women, I did long to be chosen. Even a marriage against my will was preferable to Omar's harping, primping, and meddling. Any one noble would surely be better than enduring the fondling and petting of dozens of men per day, preferable to being treated like livestock. This wasn't the first time it had come down to me and one other woman, and I knew what to expect.

The young man ogled me again, his eyes practically undressing me as he stepped closer. His hands settled on my waist, and I yearned to pull away. Walling up my heart in an icy cage, I closed my eyes, not wanting to see his face.

"Look at me," he ordered, his hot breath blanketing my face and causing me to gag. I had no choice but to obey, my hands shaking at the predatory gleam of victory in his gaze. His hands roamed over me, poking and fondling once more. He took his time, enjoying my body without my leave, like I was a heifer and he a prospective buyer.

Suddenly, his hands fell away, and the look of disgust returned. He turned and walked to Maram, repeating the process with her. But unlike me, she did what was expected of her. She returned his pursuit, settling her hands on his sides, leaning in and accepting his touch, his look, his kiss. She was what he wanted. She fit the world in which we lived. With her flawless olive complexion, dark hair and eyes, she was the perfect Talethan daughter. She was exactly what the patrons of the Wife Market valued in a bride.

It was common practice in Taletha for a rich man to buy a wife—often more than one. The Market stretched across the nation, a warehouse in every major city in Taletha. I had been sold to the Market in Mordova—the city of my birth. Now, I found myself a day's journey northwest in the city of Rana.

Not that it mattered what city we were in. Kept confined to the warehouse until we were chosen, groomed, powdered, and bathed. Our sole focus, our only job, was to be bought by a man. We had to sell ourselves in whatever way necessary.

Some of the wealthier girls were trained from infancy to be the perfect wife, sold by their fathers as young as fourteen in order to secure a match. Those girls were gorgeous, the very picture of the ideal Talethan wife. They were doted on, their parents sending gifts of clothes and jewels weekly—if not daily.

In no way was I one of those girls. My father sold me and never looked back, quickly returning to the seas with my half-brothers. I hadn't heard from any of them in years and often wondered if they were even alive.

The young noble returned to my stand yet again, and I struggled to keep my breathing steady as he traced my jaw with his clammy fingers. My body shook involuntarily when he cupped the back of my neck and leaned in close. Unable to hold his gaze, I dropped my eyes, a single tear leaking from my eye.

"I choose this one," the lord proclaimed, using his free hand to point at Maram, who smiled coyly as he turned from me and extended his hand toward her, his chosen bride.

Omar clapped. "An excellent choice, my lord. Let me call our priest, and we shall deal with the necessary paperwork and ceremony. Are you planning a larger affair later?" He guided the new couple out the far door—the wedding door, as we called it—and I finally allowed myself to sag when the click echoed through the great market room.

The rest of the girls relaxed, and a small wave of conversation began as they moved toward our rooms. As my legs began to tremble, I lowered myself to the platform and buried my head in my hands.

Don't let them know that it bothers you, I ordered myself, trying to maintain the cage of ice around my heart. It had been my constant companion, my only defense, since the tender age of four when I first felt the pain of my father's fist.

Saif, my guard, knelt beside my block and offered me his hand. "I'm sorry, Inara."

"I'm fine, Saif."

The look on his face told me he didn't believe me, but he didn't press the issue. Of everyone in the warehouse, Saif was the only person I trusted. He had been assigned to me since my first day, and for six years never wavered in his devotion.

He pulled me to my feet now and tucked my hand into the crook of his elbow as he guided me back toward the wife wing. "What did you think of that man?"

It had become a game with us. What did we think of each man who spurned me on the buying block? Some were too fat, others too skinny. Some were outrageously dressed, some not dressed enough—as had been the case the day before when a palace guard had come swaggering into the Market in nothing but his under clothes. He'd promptly been escorted out.

"This one seemed like an arrogant, pompous bore."

Saif smiled, his teeth bright against his dark skin. "Yes, and Nicar knows you need someone who can admit when he's wrong."

"Yes, and he has to match my wit." I smiled up at him, thankful for the levity our conversation brought to an otherwise humiliating moment. Saif had one of the few keys to my heart, and I prayed that Omar never learned of it. If he did, he'd remove Saif as my guard, and I would die the day that happened. "Speaking of wit, how is Ranya?"

"Doing well." His eyes danced with love as he spoke of his wife. "I felt the babe kick again last night."

"Oh, how wonderful!" My smile slowly slipped as he continued on and on about Ranya, their unborn child, and their happily wedded bliss. I could never have what they did. Happiness, love, mutual respect—it was a lie I fed myself in the night. When I was lonely, I played with the *what ifs*. What if I wasn't a Market Bride? What if someone would love me for who I was as a woman and not just as a thing to be possessed? What if someone saw the raw bleeding mess that was my heart and chose to stay?

But it was only that—a lie. For I was a Market Bride, and that meant I was an object, a thing to be bartered for and sold to the highest bidder. No one would ever truly see me as a person, as a woman worthy of love and affection. The most I could hope for was a considerate man who would meet my basic needs and not force himself on me. I shivered as my imagination conjured up vivid images far too easily. The fondling I experienced on the block would be nothing to fulfilling my wifely duties, especially with a man I knew nothing about and who likely only bought me for my body. A gag choked me, and my hand rose to my throat as I struggled to think of something pleasant.

We reached the common room where the other twenty-eight women sat on cushions, munching foul and hummus on pita bread. The savory spices made my stomach churn, and I curved an arm across it.

"Oh, look girls. It's the worthless northerner." Kittim, a new arrival, sneered. "Can't seem to get a man to want you, Inara? I can give you some tips."

"Because you've been here for so long." Tirsa rolled her eyes. "I've been here a month, and I'll have you know Inara has never tried to get a man to buy her." She tossed her sleek black hair. "Have you ever returned a prospect's kiss when it's down to you and another?"

"No," I whispered, wrapping my other arm across my middle before sitting.

"No?" Kittim scoffed. "No wonder you can't get a man to choose you."

"She's too sweet," Zivah stated. Henna covered her hands, swirling and scrolling and drawing attention to her smooth, flawless skin. "She doesn't work on standing out."

Kittim giggled. "She stands out enough with that hair! Have you ever thought about dying it?"

"You can't do that!" Tirsa protested. "It's one of the laws of the Market."

"It's also against the law for the men to kiss us, but Omar allows it." Zivah shrugged her slim shoulders.

"Inara?" One of the newest girls—she couldn't have been a day over fourteen—slipped to my side, her eyes glassy.

"What is it, Talora?" I asked, weariness pressing down on me.

"I think..." she glanced down, and I noticed blood on her leg. Her monthly cycle. A sob caught in her throat, tugging on my heart as I turned toward her.

"It's all right." I cupped her cheek. "Has this happened before?"

Her head shook, tears trailing down her cheeks. "What's happening?"

My heart pinched as I remembered my own experience. My mother had been out working when my cycle first began. I thought I was dying and had curled into a ball on my bed all day with my stomach cramping terribly. It wasn't until Mother had returned the following morning and explained what was happening that I learned I would, in fact, live to see another day.

"Come on, dearest. I'll help you clean up and get ready for bed. I'll explain it all."

She sniffed, dashing away the tears with the back of her hand. "I won't be standing up tomorrow at the Market, will I?"

I knew she wouldn't. Omar didn't want anything to hinder a buyer. A man may not want us if he knew it was our time of the month.

I wrapped my arm around Talora and guided her down to our rooms. "Everything will be fine. It only lasts a few days."

Talora's room was identical to mine. Soft embroidered rugs covered the cool tiled floor while a pile of pillows and blankets served as a bed. With a small window on the far wall to let some air flow, it wasn't quite a cell, but the bars on the small opening were a constant reminder that we were indeed stuck here until some man found us worthy.

I helped Talora clean up and then tucked her into bed. Brushing her hair with my fingers, I settled into a rhythm that relaxed my shoulders and pleasantly numbed my mind.

"Have you really been here six years?" Talora asked, breaking the spell of calm.

"Yes."

Six long years of lust and leers. Six years of being almost perfect—but still lacking. Six years of seeing hundreds of others chosen and yet having rejection after rejection tossed my way. Six years of loneliness, isolation, and fear. Fear of never being good enough, never being wanted, never being loved. Once, long before the Market, there had been someone who said they loved me, but he too had rejected me. If he could so casually toss me aside, why would someone who didn't even know me ever want me?

Yet, I couldn't tell Talora that. She wouldn't understand, and I didn't want to worry her. So instead, I leaned over and pressed my lips to her forehead. "But you, my dear, are a beautiful daughter of Taletha. A man will see you and fall madly in love."

"That's a fairytale," she whispered, her eyes already half closed. "I'd be happy if he simply took care of me and fed me."

My throat felt thick, my body heavier than normal as I closed the door to Talora's room and leaned against it. I closed my eyes, trying to will the energy into my limbs to walk the fifteen doors down to my room.

"Inara?" Saif studied me, worry wrinkling his forehead. "What happened?"

"Nothing. I'm fine."

He held his arm out to me, and I was only too glad to lean on it as he escorted me to my room.

"Thank you, Saif. I will see you tomorrow."

"Inara." He didn't let go of my hand until I dragged my eyes up to meet his gaze. "If you ever need anything, let me know. You're like a sister to me, and all I want is for you to find happiness."

A tear snaked down my cheek, and I let it. I wanted to feel again, to not be so terrified of being hurt by everyone that I lived in a constant state of numbness. I let Saif in, if only a bit. But even he could be used against me. Though he was right. Even in this living hell, I wasn't alone. Inhaling sharply, I whispered, "I know."

Saif squeezed my hand before letting me slip into my room. I slumped against the door, having no desire to change my clothes and climb into my bed. Somehow, I managed to shrug out of the white kaftan and into my plain brown nightdress. Curling up on the pillows and blankets, I let the ice thaw and drip down my cheeks. I cried for Talora and her already broken view of love and marriage. For Maram—now married to a stranger who would and could do whatever he wished to her. For my mother, dead for seven years now. And I cried for myself. For the life in which I was trapped. I was a slave. A slave to the Wife Market. And I wasn't sure I'd ever be rescued from it.

Chapter Two

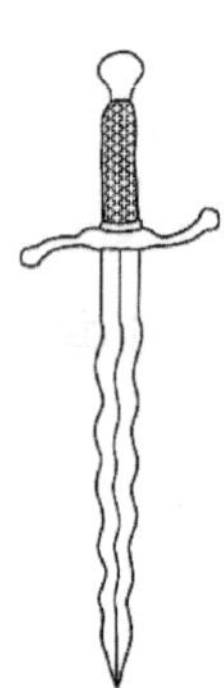

Dhamar

"**P**ardon me, Ameer Dhamar, but your father, the exalted Malek Nadar, requests your presence at the gathering of the council."

I glanced up from the parchment I'd been reading and raised my brow at my guard. "You're now my father's messenger, Zahir?"

His face didn't break from its blank expression, but laughter danced in the depths of his eyes. After twenty years of being my constant shadow, I knew Zahir almost better than I did myself.

"Did the malek say why he wanted me at the meeting?" I asked.

"No, only that he wanted you at his side right away."

With a sigh, I pushed to my feet. Whenever Father *requested* to see me, it meant he was in a foul mood and not to be trifled with. I grimaced and shoved my hands through my black curls as we stepped into the hall. I hated the council. Hated having to appear before them like I was beneath their status. They lorded their position over everyone with great pomp and arrogance despite the fact that a word from my father would relieve them of their heads.

I slid my sweaty palms against my tunic, trying to build up enough courage to enter the council chamber once we reached it. As much as Zahir was my shadow, the council chambers were the one place where guards were forbidden. I would have to enter alone.

Panic began to claw at my throat the longer we walked. I wasn't called to this room often, but when I was, it meant nothing good. The last time I'd been here, I'd been berated for my second divorce. For whatever reason, the council wanted an heir secured from me, and they were less than pleased with my ability to carry out my husbandly duties. I was blessed by Nicar that they hadn't forced the issue. If they had, it would mean an arranged marriage at best. Or royal concubines at worst.

"Will you be all right, my ameer?" Zahir asked, hand on his scimitar and eyes slanting sideways to watch me.

Helplessness swallowed my rational thoughts as I considered a council appointed match. "I can't go in there unawares, Zahir," I choked out.

"Rumors are that this council meeting is about the issues with Šeri." Zahir shrugged, turning his gaze forward once again. Most of the nobility disliked a guard at their side, preferring for them to walk either before or behind. But I liked the steady presence of my friend next to me. He'd been more of a guide to me through life than anyone else, and I valued his insight.

"What about Šeri?" I asked. "I have heard no such rumors."

"Of course not." Zahir smirked. "You're above the common gossip found in the kitchens and training yards."

I managed not to wince at the comment. Zahir meant nothing by it, but I couldn't help feeling guilty about my title and status—a discomfort that was becoming more and more familiar. I wished to do more for my people, but being ameer meant I had to obey the malek. His word was law. I could do nothing without Father's approval and that was something I rarely obtained. All I had been able to do was marry and divorce a handful of women to earn them their freedom.

Shaking away my sour thoughts, I asked, "Well, what about the gossip?"

"The towns near the border claim that they're being raided, that Šeri is stirring up trouble by stealing livestock and produce."

"But the tribesmen are herders. Why would they be stealing livestock? Nicar knows they have enough animals to tend to without stealing more." I scratched my chin, bile coating my tongue when I caught sight of the council chamber doors.

"They are only rumors, Dhamar. Gossip tends to only hold a sliver of truth—if any at all. The wise man searches for that truth before believing what he is told."

"Especially when it doesn't seem logical." I chuckled before sighing. I forced my hands to unclench as we reached the towering doors of the council chambers.

They loomed ominously over us. Carved from ebony, they were easily three times my height. Panels of a lighter wood hung on them and were etched with stories of the exploits of the people of

Taletha. Battles, mostly. Bloody, death-ridden pictures of war and the lives lost to it.

I hated these doors almost as much as the room behind them, and they did nothing to calm the roiling of my stomach. I tasted blood on my tongue and only then realized I was biting it. Forcing my jaw to unclench, I took a deep breath and schooled my features into stony indifference—my mask of choice for most occasions having to do with my father and his council. Then, I stepped through the doors of death.

The space beyond was dim, smelling of dust and sweat. With no windows to let sunlight and fresh air in, it was suffocating in the narrow room. Every few feet along the roughhewn rock walls hung lanterns. They lent their meager glow to the room, illuminating the lords that sat on red cushions. I said each of their names to myself as I walked past but didn't grace their arrogance with the honor of my gaze upon them.

Lord Hakeem, Lord Mostafa, Lord Yamin, Lord Arqa, Lord Shaeen, and Lord Mulazim. They all had beards that fell to their stomachs with various shades of gray streaked in them, and their eyes glinted in the faint light as they watched me walk to the platform that held my father's throne. It was lined with blue and white tiles, the design an intricately twisted desert bloom of some kind. It was too bright and beautiful for this room shrouded with deception and filled with conniving men after their own gain.

When I am malek, this throne will replace the golden monstrosity in the throne room. I will never step foot in this room. The council can meet me in the study or—

"So, you finally decided to grace us with your presence." Father's gravelly voice barked as I knelt and fisted my hand over my heart in submission. Yet another thing I hated. This man deserved no one's respect, least of all mine.

"I came as soon as I received your message, oh my malek." I tactfully refrained from saying Zahir's name. Nicar knew my guard had taken beatings for me on more than one occasion.

"I'm sure." Father's tone was dry and had my jaw clenching. "Stand up, boy. We have news to discuss and plans to make."

Boy. Twenty-five years, and yet I was still *boy*. My teeth ached as I stood and moved to the side of the throne, hands clasped behind my back. It had been this way for years—me silently enduring his belittling to protect the people who mattered to me. I couldn't stop the malek, but I could try to contain him.

"Now to business. We have to decide what to do about these Šerian scum. They cannot be allowed to plunder our borders without consequences. I won't hear of it!" Father banged his meaty fist against the arm of his seat, spittle flying from his lips in his rage.

Lord Shaeen steepled his fingers, tapping each one in turn as he spoke. "Do we know these rumors to be true?" He looked over at my father, his black eyes shining like onyxes in the light of the lantern by his head. His voice was raspy, reminding me of the hiss of an angry cobra.

"We do," Lord Hakeen boomed, shaking his meaty fist in the air. His jowls quivered as he shouted, "I warned of this, did I not? They've been too free in crossing between our land and their own.

We should have hammered them into the sand of their godforsaken wilderness long ago!"

"Come now, Hakeen. Calm yourself. They are far more lucrative than we often credit them." Lord Mostafa said. His arms were crossed, and he leaned against the stones with closed eyes. "Surely you haven't forgotten that our rania blessed us with Ameer Dhamar. She bore a son when none of the malek's other wives were fruitful."

I struggled not to gag. My family didn't have great fortune with marriages, and my father was by far the worst. While he had remained married to my mother and claimed her to be the rania of Taletha, he still had his previous wives as well as a number of concubines in the harem. It made me ill. He kept my mother confined in her room, only calling her out when his flesh was hungry. My mother never complained, never uttered a word of anger or sadness, but I could tell she was unhappy. It wasn't how I wanted to live my life. If I ever married for a fifth and final time, I wanted it to be for love, to have a partner to live through the highs and lows with.

"Enough about my wife." Father batted away the comments as if they were a fly. "There are more pressing issues. What are we going to do about Šeri?"

"Have they attacked our people?" I dared to ask, drawing the gazes of all seven men.

"No," Lord Arqa—the head of our military—finally muttered, his gray eyes dull, and his overly-puffy lips turned down in a frown. "Unfortunately."

"Then I suggest we wait. We cannot attack until provoked." I cut a glance at my father and inwardly winced at the ice-cold glare. The stuffy room choked me, and I fell silent, fixating on the bead of sweat sliding between my shoulder blades.

"Lord Arqa, what is the state of our soldiers?" Father barked.

The man shrugged. "General Beeran's last report stated that there are fifteen hundred men able to fight within Mordova—or thereabouts—with another two thousand in Rana and Nasaria. In the smaller towns, there are around five hundred men each."

"It will take time to call up the men from all the towns, even Mordova." I spoke up again, ignoring the growl emanating from my father. "I counsel caution, oh my malek, until we know the numbers of the tribesmen."

"They are nomads, worthless." He spat to the side and growled again. "But I do agree in part. Before we go to war, there is one small matter we must see to."

All eyes swiveled to me, and I unconsciously took a step back, blood going cold.

I was right. Nothing good ever comes from this room. Nothing at all.

"The matter we must see to, as your father has stated, is the issue of your marital status, Dhamar." Lord Shaeen—the vilest of all the lords—smiled, and my mouth went dry. It was rumored that he had over twenty women he frequently bedded, but as Zahir had reminded me, it was only a rumor. Yet the predatory gleam in his brown eyes lent some credence to them.

"Yes, is it true you've divorced yet another woman?" Lord Mulazim scoffed. "Why not start your own harem? You've been married four times now."

"And all from the Wife Market, if I'm not mistaken." Lord Mostafa raised a brow, no judgment in his gaze. Of all the lords here, he was the wisest. Level-headed and fair. Perhaps the only one who would understand.

"Yes." I clasped my hands behind my back and met each of the six gazes, ignoring my father at my side. "I don't wish to have a harem. I only wish for the right woman."

"Well, you have one final chance to pick the *right* woman." Father spat again. His gray mustache quivered as he frowned, the flickering light making the oils on his black beard gleam. Sweat beaded on his olive skin. "Or I will pick one for you."

"What?" I glance at him in disbelief.

"We need an heir!" Hakeem smacked his fist into his palm. "We cannot wait much longer, especially if war is on the horizon. You will be going into war, Ameer Dhamar, like it or not. If you were to die, where would that leave us?"

I'm sure I have plenty of half-sisters hidden away. Surely one of them has a son by now. I bit my tongue and focused on the sweat on my back once more. Anything to escape this horrible conversation.

"What do you suggest?" I manage to choke out, feeling blackness edging my vision.

"One last chance at the Markets." Shaeen began tapping his fingers again. "Only this time, it will be a spectacle. You shall visit

Rana's Markets as well as ours. You will observe many women until you settle on one."

"You will marry her there." Mostafa smiled, and it was almost kind. "And then a litter will bring you both back where the formal, three-day ceremony will be performed."

"It will be a holiday for Mordova." Arqa huffed. "A waste of a workday."

No one paid him any mind as they began to talk among one another, ignoring Father and me. My father grasped my arm tightly, sending tingles up into my shoulder from the pressure. "You will consummate this marriage, boy."

"What?" Surely, I heard wrong. Heat that had nothing to do with the temperature of the room flooded through me.

"I know the truth of those other marriages. You will marry this one in all ways, and you will produce an heir. If the woman you marry fails to give you a son quickly enough, you will find someone who can."

Disgust curled my lips at the implication, and I wasn't quick enough to hide it. Father stood, looming over me, his brown eyes as cold as the ice that we brought in from the east. The conversations hushed, all eyes on us.

"This is not open for discussion, Dhamar. This is a command not only from your father, but your malek."

And the malek's word is law. I squeezed my eyes shut, balling my hands at my side. Rage bubbled in my chest, but I didn't let it crack my indifferent veneer. "May I go?" I asked.

"Yes." Father stepped back, smoothing his hands over his ample stomach. He flicked his fingers toward the door dismissively. It took every ounce of my self-control to walk, instead of run, down the aisle.

"Oh, and Dhamar?"

I paused, hand on the knob and turned toward my father once again. His face was shrouded in shadows that almost seemed to dance over him in his black kurta and salwar.

"Remember. If you fail to do what I say, your mother will suffer the consequences."

My blood turned to ice. I nodded and stepped through the ebony doors. They grated closed behind me with a thud of finality. I leaned against the tiled wall, burying my face in my hands.

Zahir gripped my shoulder. "Ameer? What happened?"

"War," I choked out.

Zahir swore. When I still didn't move, he asked, "And?"

"And a wife from the Market." I looked up, fear etching its way across my heart. "A real marriage this time. I can't do that, Zahir. I don't know how."

"Well, you better start learning and soon." Zahir stood, hand settling on his scimitar as he scanned the hall. His gaze cut back to me. "Because it looks like you're going to be a husband, like it or not."

CHAPTER THREE

Inara

My eyes were puffy and filled with grit as I stretched the next morning. The bustle of the town hadn't yet started, and the sun was barely new. Rolling to my side, I let my mind drift, not yet ready to face more men and their leering gazes. I couldn't stand the thought of being petted and pawed and then humiliated when I was passed over yet again. Omar and the Market could wait another hour.

The lowing of cattle and bleating of sheep heading to the temple began to carry through my small window. It had been a long time since I'd made an offering to Nicar—goddess of all. Frankly, I hadn't seen her work all that much in my life. My father had been at sea more than at home, and when he was home, it was hell on earth. My mother had loved me, but she worked herself to death to try and provide for me. All my half-siblings hated me—for I looked more like my mother than my father. The man who said he loved me, only to leave me when I was no longer useful to him. No, the temple wasn't holy to me. It was a mockery of all that was good and kind in the world.

Without warning, the door flew open, banging off the wall with a crash.

I leapt up, nearly toppling as the blankets tangled around my feet.

Saif rushed to my side. "Up! Up! Hurry, Inara!"

"What's wrong? Is the warehouse on fire? Is someone sick?"

"No, no! Nothing like that!" Saif grabbed up my kaftan and shoved it at me. "Get dressed and hurry."

"Why?" I sat back onto my bed and threw a blanket over my head. "So I can get pawed and petted and then spurned all over again?"

Saif yanked the blanket away. "Ameer Dhamar is coming!"

I paused, staring up at Saif in disbelief. "He lives in Mordova. Why is he coming here?"

"I don't know, but this is your chance!" He walked over to the low table under the window and picked up a jar of sweet-smelling lotion. Tossing it from hand to hand, he smirked at me.

"You think that I can catch the eye of the ameer of all Taletha?" I crossed my arms and glared at him, but since I was lying on my back, it lost some of the effect.

"Why not?" Saif sat the jar down and planted his hands on his hips, a gesture he'd picked up from Ranya. "You're a beautiful woman, Inara. If he cannot see that then—"

"Then he's smarter than every other man who comes to this goddess-forsaken stock house!" Fury burned in my veins, and I threw a pillow at Saif. "Get out! I'm tired of trying. Tired of never being good enough."

"It doesn't matter what you want, Inara. Omar wants you ready in an hour." Saif's mouth drooped as he knelt beside my bed. He clasped my hand, ignoring me when I dug fingernails into it his palm, trying to free myself. "Please don't despair. You are a shining light here in the Wife Market. What you did for Talora last night? Would anyone else here have helped her?"

I paused in my struggle and sighed.

"No," Saif answered his own question, "no one else would have. She would have been alone and scared. You have a beautiful heart and someday someone is going to see that and crave it for themselves."

"I know." I tugged free, hugging my arms across my aching stomach. Panic and hope warred for supremacy, and I wasn't sure which I wanted to win. I desired hope—hope that someone would choose me for me, that someone would desire to work on a marriage of love, not just of flesh. But the realistic side of me was leaning closer to panic at the thought of being a wife and all it entailed and of leaving the Market with a man I knew nothing about. I grabbed hold of my icy shield, slamming it around my heart as I met my guard's steady gaze. "I know, and that's why I'm afraid, Saif."

He pulled me to my feet and smiled his brilliant grin. "Stop being afraid. You're a bold soul. Let that courage out today, and don't back down. Show Ameer Dhamar what makes Inara of Mordova so very brave and beautiful."

He'd never spoken so frankly, and it made my stomach swirl with nervous anticipation. Perhaps marriage to the ameer was what I was here for. I'd been waiting long enough. Perhaps this was my chance to change my life.

"Do you really think I can catch his eye?" I asked. *And do I even want that?*

Saif smiled. "I think you have the best chance, Inara. You only have to choose to fight for what you want."

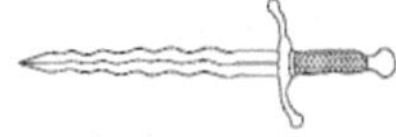

I fidgeted with the ends of my hair as I paced around the edge of my box. Five steps to the left, turn, five steps forward, pivot, another five, around and around as we waited for the signal that *he* was coming. Excited conversations swirled around the other blocks, a few nervous giggles, too. Loudest of all was Kittim. Her voice reverberated around the vaulted ceilings of the gray stone room as she tossed her hair, a smirk on her face as she said, "Bow now, girls. I am your future amira."

Tirsa rolled her eyes. "Well, if he's looking for a humble wife, you're certainly out."

Kittim opened her mouth to reply, but a trumpet blast silenced her. We all hurried to take our places on our blocks, straight and tall and all eyes forward.

As the doors began to open, I glanced over my shoulder, my eyes meeting Saif's.

Be yourself, he mouthed, and I nodded, turning forward as trumpets blared again.

Omar stepped through the doors with a grand sweep of his hand. "Girls, welcome Ameer Dhamar, son of the exalted Malek Nadar, ruler of all Taletha!"

Show your fierceness. Be bold and brave. I swallowed the dryness in my mouth and strained to catch a glimpse of the man who still stood in the shadows without turning my head. *Do you want this, Inara? Will it be better than the Market, or just another hell?*

With only moments to make my life-altering choice, I sucked in a steadying breath and turned to face Ameer Dhamar. Over a black kurta, he wore a purple vest embroidered with red flowers. Flowing red salwar with a tight cuff at the ankle swished with every step. His golden slippers—blessedly without bells—scuffed softly across the stone floor. His shoulders were broad, his brown eyes sharp. On his head was a silver turban, but even that couldn't hide all his black curls. He was stunningly handsome, and my mouth went dry once more.

The ameer met my gaze, and his eyes widened ever so slightly as he studied me. It was against the laws of the Market for the prospective brides to look the buyer in the face, and I felt strange satisfaction in breaking that rule. The reaction from the ameer emboldened me. Clasping my hands behind my back, I dared to rock onto the balls of my feet before tipping back on my heels. All the while, I held the gaze of the ameer.

"Who is that?" He pointed at me and stepped closer.

I abruptly halted and snapped my head forward when Omar turned toward me with a sniff. "Inara of Mordova. Her father sold her to the elite Mordovaian Market six years ago. We acquired her not long after. Her strange looks make her hard to sell."

Ameer Dhamar turned toward my owner, his jaw tight with what appeared to be displeasure. "I will speak to the woman."

"If that is what you wish, my ameer," Omar agreed—as if he had a choice in the matter—before bowing and stepping off a few paces, eyes never leaving the ground.

The ameer stepped onto my box, like every other man who had ever taken interest in me. He dropped his voice to a whisper and asked, "Is what he said true?"

"Yes." I couldn't force out another word as he studied me. I was more aware than ever of my blonde hair and blue eyes, of my pale northern skin and the fact that I didn't belong in Taletha—despite being born here. But Ameer Dhamar's eyes were warm, without the predatory gleam that many who came through the Market contained. He was simply looking, seeing what was before him with no thought of the benefit and enjoyment he might extract from it.

"Do you want to leave here?" he asked at last.

"Doesn't everyone?" The question slipped from my lips before I even fully thought it through.

"Yes." He smiled, and I couldn't stop the corners of my mouth as they twitched in response. "Even me."

"With a bride though." My stomach soured, and I dropped my gaze to my clasped hands. "You should go look at some of the others, my ameer."

"Why?"

"They're the perfect Talethan daughters. They will make a worthy amira." Why did those words taste so wrong on my tongue? I didn't want to be his amira. I didn't want to *be* anyone's. What I longed for was freedom and safety, to be wanted and treasured and adored. But an amira? Kittim would gladly take that job.

His brows rose. "You don't want to be amira yourself?"

"I am nothing worthwhile, my ameer. I'm—tainted by the past." I ducked my head and heard Omar suck in a breath of frustration. We weren't supposed to move as the prospective men eyed us, touched us, and decided if we were worthy.

This felt all too familiar to another time and place, with someone I thought I could trust. Someone who said they loved me.

Dhamar hummed, and I glanced up with my eyes. He scratched at his jaw before turning and moving on down the line. Omar glared, but I was just glad the ameer was looking at someone else with those unfathomably deep eyes of his.

"Did you mean that?" Saif whispered from behind me.

"Mean what?" I asked.

"That you're not worthy to be an amira?" Saif sighed when I nodded, my gaze following Dhamar as he continued down the line of twenty-seven girls. "Oh, Inara."

He said nothing more as Dhamar paused and talked with Kittim, who batted her long brown lashes. It struck me then that he didn't reach out and stroke them. He didn't eye our bodies or our faces. Rather, he spoke to the girls, asked them questions, and smiled kindly. I smoothed my hands against my skirt.

He wouldn't be an awful husband. Too bad you ruined your chance. I closed my eyes, struggling to rein in the swirling emotions that had leaked out of the cage of my heart. *Hold it together for a bit longer.*

"Inara?" The smooth voice jerked me back to the present, and I opened my eyes to find that Dhamar had stepped onto my block again, much closer than he had been before. I could feel the heat of his body and color flamed in my cheeks. He smiled, and I couldn't help but think that it was a pleasant thing. One I could get used to, given the chance.

Shaking away that particularly disturbing thought, I dropped my gaze and whispered, "Yes, my ameer?"

"I talked to the other girls," he stated in a teasing tone that my traitorous heart found endearing.

"I noticed."

He chuckled, and I thought I might melt into a puddle at his feet. Why did the first man that I was attracted to have to be an ameer? And not just any ameer, but the future malek of all Taletha?

Stop it! You're not attracted to him.

"You said I should find the perfect amira, yes?" His brow shot up under some of the curls that had escaped his turban.

I was only able to nod.

"Well, as ameer, I think I get a say in what the perfect amira for my people and me will or won't be." He held his hand out to me. "And I choose you, Inara of Mordova."

A couple gasps rippled around, amplified by the high ceilings and stone walls and floor. I let my gaze meet Dhamar's head on, looking for a hint of teasing on his face, of that cruel sneer I was all too used to. But there was only openness in the expression he wore. He appeared...sincere.

Still, I couldn't help but ask, "Are you certain?"

"Yes. There's something different about you." A slight dimple appeared on the left side of his mouth, and my pulse tripped. Why did he have to be so handsome?

Panic erupted in my mind at *that* thought, and I turned toward Saif, who had stepped to my side. My one friend in this whole place and support over the last six years. Before I could take Dhamar's hand, I needed to ask one thing of him.

"Ameer Dhamar, I—" I took a calming breath. "Might I be allowed to make one request?"

Omar's eyes bugged out, and he slashed his hand across his throat. I knew his meaning, but I kept my focus on the ameer.

His hand was still outstretched, and his smile never wavered. "What request, Inara?"

A shiver slipped down my spine at my name on his lips, and I cleared my throat. "May I bring my guard with me?"

"You have a guard?" he asked, his hand falling as he turned to Omar. My owner quickly tucked the hand he'd been using to silence me behind his back. As close as he was to me, I could feel Dhamar's posture going absolutely rigid as my owner hurried forward. "Why does this woman have a guard?"

Omar laughed nervously. "They all have guards, my ameer. It's to keep them safe from the less scrupulous men that may come into the Market. And—" He hesitated for the barest of seconds.

"And?" The ameer prompted.

"Ah, well, and to keep them from running away."

"I see." Ameer Dhamar's voice had gone cold, and when he turned back to Saif and me, all traces of his smile were gone. "Yes, your guard will be hired by the palace staff as your personal body-guard as Zahir is for me." He gestured to the giant of a man that stood a few paces behind him.

"Thank you, my ameer." I dipped my head in deference.

"Dhamar," he gently corrected. "We are to be wed today, after all." He held his hand out once more, and this time I clasped it, signaling my acceptance. A strange heat traveled up my arm as Dhamar helped me off the platform. I licked my lips in nervous re-alization of what was coming, in disbelief at what was happening.

I am getting married. I will be a wife in less than an hour.

What will he expect? What if—?

I cut off those thoughts as fright began to dull my senses.

Omar clapped his hand like he had done with Maram the day before. "Oh, wonderful, wonderful! Another happy couple!"

Happy couple? No, you're the only happy one here. Happy to be rid of the Talethan who looks too northern for her own good, and who has been a thorn in your side for six years. I laid my free hand against my chest, willing myself to breathe. I prayed that Dhamar couldn't hear the frantic pace of my heart, that he couldn't feel the sweat gathering in the palm of my hand cupped around his arm.

"Are you planning on a ceremony here, Ameer Dhamar?" Omar rambled on, and it took all my will to force my feet to follow as Dhamar led me on his arm to the wedding door.

After years of waiting, hoping, dreading, I would finally walk through and see what was on the other side. Part of me wanted to turn and run back to the comfort of my little room, to stretch and wake up from this dream—nightmare? Was there a difference? This couldn't be real. I glanced up at the face beside me. His olive complexion, high cheekbones, chocolate-brown eyes, and curly black hair were all too precise to be a dream. No, this wasn't a dream. I was really and truly about to marry a complete stranger. The heir to the throne, Dhamar, the ameer of all Taletha, was to be my husband.

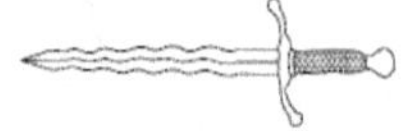

Chapter Four

Dhamar

Inara was shaking. I could feel it in her ever-tightening grip on my arm as we neared the wedding door. A glance at her showed a sheen of perspiration on her forehead, and her eyes darted nervously, as if she were looking for an escape.

She didn't have to accept. I resisted the urge to scratch my jaw, instead fisting my free hand at my side and focusing on the owner of the Market as he continued to speak.

"Now, I'm sure you know the process of a Market wedding, my ameer," Omar was saying, "but I'm going to say it again for the benefit of Inara."

I didn't miss the way his lip curled when he said her name. What was so bad about this woman that even the man who owned her hated her? She was beautiful, with her blonde hair falling around her shoulders, her pale complexion, and the glimpse I'd caught of her brightly colored eyes. She was unlike any other woman in

Taletha, stunning against the olive tones, brown eyes, and black hair of all the others.

The owner of the market began to ramble off all the paperwork that would need signing, the oaths we would take, the witnesses we needed, of which we had plenty, with both mine and Inara's guard following behind us. With all the information being flung at me, and the distraction that was my wife-to-be on my arm, it took me a moment to process the final question.

"Are you going to need a room here for the evening, my ameer?" Omar's brow raised suggestively.

I pulled on my stony mask. This was for real. This was a marriage that I had to make work—or I was going to be subjected to whatever humiliations the council could think up. They wanted an heir, and they would get it.

When I hesitated, Inara whispered, "Omar..." She straightened her spine, and I watched with a strange pang of sorrow as a mask slid over her mortified expression, shuttering it from everyone. I wondered, wondered why she was walling herself off like I so often did. What was she protecting herself from?

Her pale face had grown whiter, and her eyes dropped to the ground.

Sour bile coated my tongue as I turned back to the man in front of us. His ample stomach shook as he chuckled, a cruel sound that matched the sneer on his face.

I don't know how to do this. Do I get a room then try to calm her? She's hiding already. How do I coax her out? I glanced over at Zahir, but my guard was no help. He stared straight ahead, much like the remaining girls on the platforms behind us. *Nicar above, will it always be this hard?* With a small nod, I turned back to Omar. "Yes, the best room you have. We will also require food for after the ceremony."

Inara stiffened further but kept following as we stepped through the door and into a circular room. The swirling orange and yellow patterns on the tiles gave it a dizzying effect. The domed ceiling had a window in the very center, letting in the mid-morning light. The grate over it made a mosaic pattern of circles and swirls on the round table that sat underneath. On top of it sat a peacock quill in a bottle of ink with a stack of parchment beside it. On the other side of the room, a horseshoe-arched doorway with a pointed top led into a long hall.

My heart beat more quickly as a man with a bald head and yellow robes, a priest of the order of Nicar, stepped forward, waving a stick of incense around as he motioned us further into the room. My heart hammered in my ears so loudly I was certain Inara's guard—who hadn't left her side—could hear it. Desperate for affirmation that I was doing the right thing, my gaze found Zahir as he circled the room to stand at the far entrance as he had done at all my weddings in Mordova.

But this time was different. Now I stood in Rana's Market, marrying for real. This time, there would be no backing out, out of this marriage, out of the commitment I made. If I did, then I would be stuck with whatever women my father and the council would foist on me. My throat nearly closed at that thought. I would live with a stiff, cold marriage with the equally frosty woman at my side before I let them subject me to that.

But I need an heir and to do that I have to win her affections. I turned to face Inara, begging her to raise her eyes from my chest to my face as the priest began to chant the wedding blessing. *I won't force myself on her. I'll show her that she's safe with me, and then she'll soften. I can be gentle and kind, everything that Father isn't. That will work, won't it?*

As if she sensed my thoughts, Inara slowly dragged her gaze up to meet mine. This close, I noticed that her eyes were the most peculiar shade of blue. Or perhaps they were green. It was hard to tell, as every blink seemed to shift their depths. The overwhelming urge to tuck her hair over her shoulder hit me, and I tightened my hold on her hands to keep mine from straying. That would only make her uncomfortable, and I needed her to know she was safe, safe to let the mask fall, safe to trust me.

"Ameer Dhamar, do you swear by blood and blade to love this woman to whom you are pledging yourself?" The priest intoned, clearly bored with his job. "Do you promise to cherish her, body and soul, until the day Nicar ushers you both into her heavenly dwelling?"

Yes, Nicar above, I want to learn to love you, Inara. The thought hit me so hard my chest tightened. I nodded in reply to the priest before pushing out, "I do."

He handed me a dagger and I pricked my first finger. I let the blood pool into a bead on my finger before pressing it to Inara's forehead and swiping from left to right. She somehow managed to grow stiffer at the contact, her jaw tightening. I finished my vow to her. "By blood and blade, I am yours. I swear to love you, serve you, and guide you as a husband ought, and to be faithful," the word came out choked as my father's warning rang in my ears, "to you alone until Nicar calls us from this life."

I found it ironic, the vow to be *faithful*. None of the men in the palace were faithful to their wives. The harem was a free for all—except for the women still married to my father. The lords often visited, choosing one woman after another to satisfy their flesh. It nauseated me, the thought of those women and what they suffered. But once again, I was powerless to stop it. Powerless to change anything about their lives or even my own.

The priest turned to Inara, and she dropped her eyes to our clasped hands. "And you, Inara. Do you swear by blood and blade to love this man to whom you are pledging yourself? Do you promise to obey him, body and soul, until the day Nicar ushers you both into her heavenly dwelling?"

I hadn't missed the change in wording for Inara. *Obey*. Women were called to obey, not be faithful. Forced to bend to the wills of their husbands. To do whatever was ordered of them. If I wanted to take Inara this very night, she would be bound by this oath to do so or suffer the consequences. Would she vow this? Would she dare bind herself to me when she had no certainty what marriage to me would be like? And why did I want so desperately to prove to her that I would be a good husband?

"By blood and blade, I am yours." She trembled as she took the knife and pricked her finger. "I swear to love you, serve you, and follow you as a wife ought, and to be obedient to you alone until Nicar calls us from this life." Her voice cracked at the end of her vow, and I noticed the hunch of her shoulders. With her head still ducked, she pressed her finger to my forehead. I felt the warm, sticky sensation of blood against my skin as she swiped it from my hairline down to the bridge of my nose.

The priest swirled the incense around us, the scent of amber and frankincense seeping into my clothes and making my eyes water. "In the sight of these witnesses, let the papers be signed, binding them in the sight of the law. Tonight, they shall be bound by flesh. What is joined this day, let no man break."

Inara still wouldn't look at me as she shakily signed her name at the bottom of the page. She crossed her arms over her stomach as I took the quill and signed with a flourish. It was done. I was married. There was no going back this time.

My hand was clammy as I offered it to Inara. I wanted to catch a glimpse of those stunning eyes again, but she kept her head ducked as Omar guided us down the hall and into the room at the very end. A large mattress, covered in pillows and blankets of various shades of reds and oranges, sat between two arching windows set with glass. A gauzy canopy was draped around the bed, the burnt orange offsetting the cream color of the rock walls. Tapestry rugs coated the gray stone floor, the pattern dizzying if one stared at them for too long. A door to the left led to what I assumed was a private water closet.

"Is the room satisfactory?" Omar asked, bowing after I nodded. "If you have need of anything, my ameer, don't hesitate to send Inara's guard to fetch it. My market is at your disposal."

"Thank you." I glared at the man, arms crossed, as he bowed his way out of the room and shut the door with a click. I turned the lock, then braced my hands against the cool metal filigree melded into the wood, not ready to turn and face the woman—my wife all of fifteen minutes—who stood behind me. I couldn't formulate any cohesive thought. She was stunning, I didn't regret choosing her. But if she knew what the council was demanding, she would hate that she had bound herself to me.

With a sigh I began. "I want to be honest with you, Inara."

"What?" Her tone bit into me. Cold as ice, sharp as a knife, and as blank as a fresh piece of parchment. It shouldn't have stung as much as it did. What did she know about me, besides that I was her ameer? If she had heard the rumors about my family, she would rightly be worried that she was one more body for me to enjoy at my leisure.

I roughed my hand over my face. "You are my—fifth wife."

A strangled sound of shock escaped her. "You have *four* other wives? And you felt you needed a fifth?"

The disbelief and anger in Inara's words had me turning to face her as I shook my head. "No! No, I don't have five wives. Only you are my wife. I divorced the others a few months after marrying them."

"After you used them?" Inara's eyes flashed with venom. She still had that mask in place, that anger in her eyes that was protecting her from me. The others had done the same. It was part of life in the Market, as I'd learned years ago from my first marriage. But that was all I knew. Most of those women hadn't wanted to talk to me about the Market or anything else. It was easier for me to remain coolly detached, so I had kept my distance from them.

But Inara was different; she had to be. I had to win her trust enough to be her husband and all that implied.

"No, I didn't *use* them." My tone darkened and Inara winced, turning away from me. "I never even slept in the same bed as my other four wives, if you must know."

Her head snapped back, and she blinked several times as she processed that information. "Then why...?" Distrust laid in her eyes as they flicked around the room.

I winced, dragging my turban off and throwing it onto the bed. "The Malek's Council ordered me to marry again. They said I need an heir before possible disaster befalls us."

"In other words, what you didn't do with your first four wives, you're going to do with me." That had the cold mask returning to her face.

My head was shaking before I fully comprehended the motion. "I will not force you to do anything, Inara. You are a person worthy of the choice to say yes or no to whatever you wish."

"I swore to obey you." She sunk onto the edge of the bed, arms still over her stomach. But a bit of her boldness returned, her head raised to study me. "If you ordered me to, I would have to obey."

She would obey. I scratched my jaw, watching her as she stared at me. What did she see in me? What did I *want* Inara to see? I wanted her to see me as a man rather than the boy my father treated me as. I wanted her to see a husband who would do everything he had vowed and a soul who longed to love and be loved—in word, in action, in connection. That was who I was, and who I strove to be.

Hesitantly, I sat beside her, far enough to not accidentally brush against her, but close enough to hear her breathing and feel the heat rolling off her body. "I won't order you to do anything. But I want you to be aware of what my father and the council are demanding. They want an heir. If you do not produce one quickly enough for them, they will force others to..." I trailed off, my face flaming as I plucked at the fabric of my pants. "I want to uphold my vow to be faithful to you alone. But if you don't want to do this, we don't have to."

"Do you want me to do it?" Her blue-green gaze collided with mine, and I couldn't deny the attraction I felt. She was strikingly beautiful. But I knew well that beauty wasn't enough to build a marriage on. My mother was gorgeous, a daughter of Šeri, the land to the south of us with whom war was looming on the horizon. She married my father after my grandfather's council had demanded he needed to have an heir. Yet for all her beauty, it wasn't enough to keep Father faithful. I couldn't remember the last time I'd seen Mother smile, seen her with the light I remembered her having when I was a child.

I didn't want to snuff the light out of Inara. It was shuttered from me, shielded by her stony veneer. But if I wanted it and truly fought for it every day, could I win her trust? I wanted to nurture the faint light that I sensed in her and to be the reason it flourished. Was I even capable of building a marriage that was more than a means to satisfy my flesh?

"Ameer Dhamar?" Inara drew back at my silence.

I shook my head. "I would be faithful."

"And you said for that to happen, I need to produce an heir." Her eyes dropped to her clenched hands. "Therefore, it is my duty as your wife to serve you, my husband."

"I don't want duty, Inara." I dared to reach across the expanse and clasp my hand over hers. She flinched, but I didn't pull away. "Not at the expense of your heart. If consummating our marriage hurts you, who you are inside, then it's not worth it."

She stood and walked to the window, gesturing toward the bed as she did so. "You said you saw me as a worthy amira. An amira does what is best for her people and that often does have a cost."

"It's not a cost you have to pay," I insisted, watching her look out at whatever lay beyond this room. Her shoulders shook, and I wondered if she was crying.

Am I already failing to be what she needs?

A light tap sounded against the door, and I strode over to it. A serving girl bobbed a curtsy and carried in a tray laden with food. The savory smells only tightened my churning stomach, but I nodded my thanks before shutting and locking the door once more.

Inara had turned to face me, her hands clasped before her. She stared at the food, her tongue darting out to moisten her lips. Then she took a hesitant step closer, her eyes glancing from me to the food like she wasn't certain if she were welcome at the table.

"Come, sit." I motioned to the low, round table. "I must speak with Zahir for a moment."

She nodded, already lowering herself onto a yellow cushion and plucking up a falafel.

I opened the door and stepped out. Zahir stood on the right side of the door, Inara's guard on the left. Mine raised his black brow. "Shouldn't you be in there?"

"Yes, yes. I'm going back but—" I cleared my throat. "I thought perhaps that Inara needs new garments."

Both of Zahir's brows rose.

"Do you remember the navy and gold kurta and salwar I have? With the bird?"

"Yes."

"Have one made for Inara. It must be delivered tomorrow before our journey home."

Zahir nodded. "It shall be done, my ameer."

"Thank you." I turned back to the door and inhaled sharply before stepping through.

Inara looked up but didn't say anything as I lowered myself across from her, my arms resting on my crossed knees. "How is the food?"

"It's good." Her chin hit her chest. "More flavorful than the foul and bread I'm used to for meals."

"Is that all they feed you?"

She shook her head. "Once a week we get a bit of kofta. And there is hummus instead of foul at times."

Shock coursed through me. "That's it?"

"It's how Omar keeps us...thin." She cleared her throat and took another bite of her falafel. "I like foul and hummus, so it was no great hardship. Growing up, I often went with less."

I had no words as I picked up a piece of kamoon and slathered it with cream and jelly. I couldn't imagine that—foul and hummus on bread for meals. Probably not three meals, if what Inara said about Omar keeping the girls thin was true.

Another knock sounded as we finished our meal and stared awkwardly at each other. Opening it, I found the priest standing there, Zahir behind him with a wide-eyed look of shock on his face. The expression was so unusual for my normally stoic guard that I gaped a little before remembering myself.

"Can I help you, your grace?"

"By the command of Malek Nadar, I am to observe." His face was carefully blank.

Surely not. I'm hearing him wrong. "Observe?"

"Yes." He raised a brow. "The consummation of your marriage as your father commands."

He thrust a piece of parchment at me, and I scanned it, stomach souring more with every word. The first few lines were about my father's thankfulness to Nicar for the priest's services. It mentioned compensation for his assistance and then listed what my father wanted the priest to do. *Watch* as I took Inara. I shoved it back at the priest, my rage making my vision blurry. "This is barbaric! It's a ritual that we have not observed in decades. Why now would he—"

"I don't know why, Ameer Dhamar. But I do know the malek's word is law. This"—he waved the notice at me—"binds me to this room until you do what you're ordered to do."

Ordered. I didn't have a choice and neither did Inara. I turned to where she stood. Her already pale skin was ashen, her eyes wide.

I turned back to the priest. "Give me a moment with my wife."

He was still inclining his head as I slammed the door in his face.

"I'm sorry." I choked on the words and had to ball my fists at my side to keep them from shaking as I stepped to her side.

I didn't think it was possible, but her face grew stonier. Harder. Colder. Her gaze flicked to the door. "Let's just get the humiliation over with."

My gaze caught on the canopy. On the light fading out the window and the shutters on the windows. I glanced at the oil lamp on the table, and an idea began to form in my mind.

"Inara. I think we can fool him," I whispered, gesturing to the bed. "It will take some doing, but I think the canopy can hide the act itself."

"But he'll know—"

"He won't know any more than us what goes into consummating a marriage. Priests of Nicar are not allowed to do such things."

Her jaw locked. "It has never stopped them before."

I was taken aback by her words, but she didn't elaborate.

Rather, she stepped to the bed, smoothing her hand over the white spread that covered it. "Do you really think we can fool him?"

"Yes." I stepped up to her, close but not touching. "Trust me. I'll keep you safe from him."

"What about from you?" she whispered, her eyes not meeting mine.

"Yes." I reached out, lifting her chin up so that her eyes met mine. She flinched at the touch and stepped back, pulling free from my hand. But she kept her gaze on mine. "I promise that I will do everything in my power to protect you. I want—I desire to be a worthy husband."

"Worthy?" she choked out the word. The rawness in her tone broke a bit of my heart. This meant something to her, something deep and painful.

I nodded, holding out my hand to her. "Please, Inara. Trust me to keep our marriage ours alone, away from prying eyes and councils that wish to dictate the pace."

"Is that truly what you wish, my ameer?" She spread her hands out, palms up. "For I am yours to do with what you wish."

"No." I swore, turning away and tearing my hand through my hair. "Nicar above, woman. You're yours. You—" I turned around so quickly that Inara stumbled back against the mattress, sitting down hard. "Is that what happens here?"

"Here?" Her eyes drifted to the door then back to me.

"Do they—?" Yet another knock interrupted me, and I growled under my breath. Inara inched further onto the bed, curling her legs up under her, and began to fiddle with a tassel on one of the pillows.

The priest stood there as I flung open the door. His were arms crossed, eyes narrowed. "No more stalling. It is time for this to begin."

Zahir raised a brow, and I shook my head as the priest sailed into the room and settled onto the cushions by the table and the leftover food.

Closing the door, I took a deep breath. Time to fake being a husband.

Chapter Five

Inara

Dhamar closed the curtains, his eyes urging me to trust him. But I didn't. Couldn't. He could just as easily change his mind, stake his claim, and humiliate me before this priest.

I hated the so-called holy men of Taletha. The priests flaunted virtue and devoutness, all the while hurting those they claimed to serve. I pressed my hand against my stomach, remembering my mother coming home, tired, clothes rumpled, eyes vacant. I didn't want that. I would rather die than become a shell of a person like she had.

Trust me to keep our marriage ours alone.

I swallowed as the curtains closed around me. I heard a squeak, the shutters of the windows closing, further blocking the light of the room.

"Is that really necessary, my ameer?" The priest's nasally voice caused fear to coil tighter. I hugged the pillow to my chest, choking back a sob of dread. I couldn't do this. I wasn't bold and brave. I was broken and beyond terrified of both men on the other side of the curtains.

"It's my wedding night, your grace. If you don't like it, you can leave. I will not keep you here."

"You know I can't do that." The priest sniffed, and I heard the soft steps of Dhamar as he approached the bed.

"Then you can deal with what *I* want."

The rustle of fabric sounded before the curtains parted. Dhamar had removed his vest and kurta. The strong muscles of his chest flexed as he crawled onto the bed and to my side. I tightened my hold on the pillow, my chest aching horribly. Tears—something I'd long ago mastered into submission—pushed against the corners of my eyes as he loomed over me. He placed his hands on either side of me and leaned his cheek against mine.

"Trust me," he whispered.

I don't have much of a choice. My voice failed me as he pulled back the blankets and then pulled them over both of us. I stopped thinking, too afraid to process what was happening. Was he lying to me? Would he take advantage of the situation and my vow to him?

But Dhamar simply held me, occasionally rustling the sheets, and making a grunt or two. He brushed a strand of my hair away from my face and I gasped.

He leaned closer and whispered, "We have to make it believable."

I could only stare, not believing him. Was this really all he would do on our wedding night? After what felt like an eternity, he turned, miming pulling his salwar on before slipping off the bed.

"It's done," his voice rumbled, and even I could hear the displeasure in his tone.

"Good." The priest sniffled. "Sounded like you had fun."

Bile coated my tongue, and I grabbed another pillow, holding it close to my chest.

"Whether I enjoyed my marriage bed is none of your business, your grace." He spat the title as if it were dung on his tongue. "You were witness to the consummation, and I'd thank you to leave my chambers. Now!"

"Of course, my ameer." The shuffle of steps sounded and then the door clicked closed.

The curtain rustled, and Dhamar slipped back under the sheets.

"Thank you," I whispered to his back as he curled onto his side.

For a long moment he said nothing, then sighed. "Get some sleep, Inara."

I rolled away, my back to his and, surprisingly, succumbed to sleep's tender hold.

A hand shook my shoulder, and I rolled away from it. "Five more minutes, Saif."

"We have to rise, Inara."

I jerked at the strange voice, clutching a fistful of blanket to my chest as my eyes flew open. Dhamar's handsome face stared down at me, and with it the events of the day before came flooding back. Heat flooded my cheeks, and I dropped my gaze to my hands that were strangling the blanket.

"We have to journey back to the palace today, and the wedding celebration takes place the day after tomorrow." Dhamar shoved his hand through his black curls, ruffling them even further as he propped his elbow against his knee. My eyes flicked to his well-defined chest, and the blush in my cheeks grew. I had noticed it the night before, but my terror and the shadows of the dark room had obscured just how fit my husband truly was.

My brain caught up to his words. "Wedding celebration? To celebrate our marriage?"

He shook his head. "It will be a full ceremony with the customary three-day party afterwards."

"Why?" I asked.

I sat up, turning to face Dhamar, who grimaced. "They think it will keep me from divorcing you like the others."

"Will it?"

"I never planned on divorcing you to begin with." Dhamar turned and smiled, though it wasn't the heart skipping one from the day before. This one seemed pinched, not quite reaching his eyes.

"Why—?"

A pounding on the door halted my question. Dhamar rose, moving with fluid grace to the door, and cracked it only enough to peek his head through. He exchanged words with whomever was on the other side before closing the door and padding back to the bedside. A bundle was in his hand. "This was delivered for you."

"For me?" I reached for the package, my other hand still tangled in the sheet.

Dhamar gave the bundle to me and gestured toward the water closet. "I am going to ready myself for our trip. I'll be back after you're dressed for the day."

I nodded, and he disappeared through the door. I undid the twine that held the brown paper, and the package fell open to reveal a beautiful dark blue kameez, with golden embroidery along the sleeves, front, and neck. It was finer than anything I had ever owned before. I held it up. The kameez fell to my knees, while the salwar would cuff at my ankle, lined with a gold trim. I quickly tugged off my itchy Market gown and pulled on the salwar, running a hand over them before I wiggled the kameez over my head. The sleeves reached my wrists, and I was thankful for that. The less skin that showed, the better.

The door to the water closet creaked open. "May I come in?"

My heart warmed at Dhamar's careful consideration, and I replied, "Yes."

He stepped through the door, and I gaped at what he wore. The tunic was the same dark blue as mine. The gold embroidery on it was far fancier, with a swooping swallow, the symbol of royalty in Taletha, on his left shoulder.

Dhamar's eyes glanced over me, sweeping from my head—with my loose hair trailing around my shoulders—down my body to my bare feet curled against the carpets. His face was carefully neutral, and I couldn't tell what he thought of me. Desire for him to find me pretty welled up within me, but I quickly squelched it. There was no use hoping for the impossible.

Still, I spun in a slow circle for his perusal. "Well?"

"You look lovely." He smiled, but it was the same pained one from earlier.

Biting back my disappointment—even though I had expected that he would find me lacking—I smoothed my hand against the soft fabric. "Who gave this to me, my ameer?"

Dhamar cleared his throat. "I had Zahir send for it. I thought we could make a statement like this."

Political. For the council and his father. All this to make them happy and to secure an heir.

I forced a smile, drawing myself up as he offered me his arm. Once my fingers were clasped against his forearm, he guided me to the door.

Pausing before opening it, he turned to me. "Thank you, Inara."

"For?" I forced myself to study the trim along the front of his shirt and not his face.

"For trusting me last night."

"I don't want to talk about it." Heat flamed up my neck at the memory. He had barely touched me last night, only enough for the illusion of shadows to trick the priest. But as much as I hadn't wanted him to claim me as his wife, another part of me wondered if I truly was that undesirable. Would I always be lacking in his eyes? Would he ever see me as more than an assignment from his father? But if that's all I was, why had he chosen me, and not a woman who mirrored the beauty of Taletha in their bodies?

Dhamar's clammy fingers clamped over my cold ones. "I won't speak of it again if you don't wish it. I simply wanted you to know that you are going to be an excellent amira. I have no doubt."

Because an amira sits on her ameer's arm, all beauty and grace with no power. She does what she's told to do, regardless of the request. It's bondage in the form of a gilded cage. I swallowed back my bitter thoughts and gave Dhamar a stiff nod.

He swung the door open. Both Saif and Zahir stood there and turned when we exited. I felt Saif's gaze run over me, and the insufferable man smirked. "You're looking lovely today, my amira."

I glared at him and that only widened his grin.

"Saif, do you have a family?" Dhamar asked, his hand clasping over mine on his arm again, anchoring me to his side.

"Yes, my ameer. My wife is expecting our first child." The pride in his voice stabbed at me. Would Dhamar be that proud of any children I bore him? Heat climbed into my face at the mere thought of what that would mean. And still, I couldn't picture Dhamar in Saif's place. Perhaps it was because half of the pleasure in Saif's voice was his love for his wife shining through. And that was what was lacking from my marriage. There was no love, only duty, no trust, only hesitant acceptance. There was no joy, no contentment, no bliss. We were forced together by chance, and there was no escaping this prison.

One cage for another.

"We shall prepare a house for you on the palace grounds, if you wish," Dhamar offered Saif. "Your meals would be provided by the kitchen, and I'm sure we could find your wife a job at the palace."

Saif hesitated. "If it pleases the ameer, Ranya is very near her time. I would prefer she not work until the babe is born."

"And even then, she shouldn't be on her feet." I protested, biting my tongue when Dhamar turned to me. "A woman should enjoy a few months with her child, my ameer."

Dhamar didn't say a word for a long moment. His warm brown eyes studied me, his lips slowly tipping up before he nodded in agreement. "I suppose the service Saif renders the crown will cover the housing of his family." He scratched his jaw with one finger, continuing to watch me, though he addressed Saif as he said, "You alone will work for us. Your wife can live on the palace grounds with you. You will have three nights off a week, and it will be whenever Zahir is on duty. I want to know we have one loyal guard with us at night."

"Of course, my ameer. That is quite generous of you." Saif bowed toward the ameer and still Dhamar's gaze stayed locked on me. My heart fluttered, and I hated myself for it. But Dhamar had cared for a person I loved—considered family. He couldn't have known that. I barely admitted it to myself. And yet here I was, finding that I trusted my husband a bit more with each passing hour.

"Come." Dhamar tugged me the way we'd passed the day before.

We met Omar in the circular room where our vows had been exchanged. He patted his ample stomach and waggled his brows. "I trust you had an enjoyable night, my ameer?"

I couldn't help the gagging noise that came from my throat. Dhamar shot me a strange look, a smirk tugging on his lips. "Oh, it was quite enjoyable. A perfect night for sleeping."

I laughed, slapping a hand over my mouth at the sound that hadn't escaped my lips in ages. "Beg pardon."

Dhamar smiled as if I had handed him the world. "Your laugh is beautiful."

If he had said it with a wag to his brows like Omar, or if he had gotten a slightly lovesick glaze to his eyes, I wouldn't have believed him. But the matter-of-fact way Dhamar stated it—as if my laugh could only be seen as beautiful—made me pause and look into his dark brown eyes. Did he really find me beautiful, even just my laugh?

"Well, if that will be all." Omar cleared his throat, causing us to blink back to reality. "Let me show you to your litter, your highnesses."

"Yes, of course," Dhamar said.

"A litter?" I asked.

"Yes, the council demanded a grand reentrance to Mordova with my bride of choice." He scowled. "I prefer ambiguity on most of my journeys, but the malek's word is law."

The way he said the last phrase was too coated with bitterness to miss. I tucked it away to ponder later and followed him out into the blazing sunlight.

For six years, I had lived indoors, within the darkness of stone and bricks and stifling guards. The touch of warm rays kissing my cheeks nearly brought me to tears, but then the sun crested the horizon, blinding my sensitive eyes. I buried my nose in the crook of my elbow, tears welling at the burn.

"Inara?" Dhamar asked, tugging on my hand when I dug in my heels. "What's wrong?"

"It's too bright." I tried to peek out, but my eyes instantly watered again. "I'm sorry. Give me a moment"

He sighed. "No, I should have thought of that."

"I'll be fine in a moment." But even as I said it, more tears blazed their way down my cheeks.

"May I pick you up?" Dhamar had moved closer, lowering his head to whisper in my ear like he had the night before. Gooseflesh spread along my arms, stealing my breath as Dhamar's caressed my ear. Nicar above, he was an intoxicating presence, and I found myself nodding before I thought too hard about it.

I shrieked as my feet left the ground, his strong arms wrapping around my back and legs. He adjusted his grip before striding forward.

"I'm sorry," I said again as I squeezed my eyes shut and leaned my forehead against his shoulder.

"I already told you, I should have thought about it. Six years is a long time to not see the sun at full strength." His voice lowered. "You have no reason to apologize."

"I'm—" I bit my tongue to keep from doing exactly that again. Dhamar set me down onto something soft, and the light lessened considerably as I sank into warm, sun-kissed pillows. I cracked one eye open as I tucked my legs under me. Varying shades of red and purple surrounded me. Light purple silk pillows were positioned near the narrow parts of the litter. The canopy was a royal purple, while the mattress under us was a ruby red. A sheer, lighter red fabric was draped around the inside of the canopy, presumably to keep out the insects. While it was still bright within the litter, it wasn't the same as the glare of the sun against the sand. I wiped away the remainder of the tears as Dhamar climbed in behind me.

Only then did I realize—I was no longer a slave of the Wife Market. I was out, not free exactly, but no longer a thing to be fondled by whomever wished. I was married, yes, and perhaps that would also be another sort of slavery I would have to endure. But I wouldn't have to wonder who would claim me as theirs. The man I belonged to sat beside me now, his hip brushing mine.

I blushed and scooted as far as I could to the right side of the litter. If Dhamar hadn't been staring at me with a curious expression, I would have shoved a pillow between us.

Silence settled awkwardly around the small space. I traced the pattern sewn into the hem of my kameez, wondering if I should break the tension or let him.

At last, my husband spoke. "Well, I would like to get to know my bride." He reclined, tucking his hands behind his head, and stretching his legs out as we waited to depart.

"What would you like to know, my ameer?" I forced my fingers to splay along my thighs, stilling their nervous fidgeting.

"Why won't you call me Dhamar?" He propped his head in his hand, rolling to his side to study me. He looked far too casual and comfortable, like he belonged among the pillows and finery all around us.

And he did, I realized, with startling clarity. I was the outsider, the woman thrown into the life of an amira and wife without any help whatsoever. How was I supposed to navigate this when my mother had only begun preparing me for the role of wife before she died? She hadn't been a wonderful example. I knew little of wifely duties and what a man expected, but being an amira was something else entirely, another complicated layer that I knew nothing about. Panic choked me, and I struggled to breathe in the stuffiness of the litter.

"Inara?" Dhamar snapped me back to the present, to his question.

"I suppose it's because—"

I gasped as the litter rose, knocking me off balance from where I crouched. The sudden shift caused me to tumble headlong across Dhamar's chest. His hands gripped my arms, easing me back. Bracing my hands against his chest, I realized how very close we were. I felt the solidity of that well-defined chest of his, the rise and fall of it, and the beat of his heart. His eyes seemed to drink me in, and he reached one hand up as if to cup my cheek.

I jerked back, glad the litter had leveled out into a gentle sway. Dhamar's face was a strange mixture of satisfaction and confusion. Heat rose into my cheeks.

"Sorry," I said, blushing again when Dhamar sighed. Before he could reprimand me for apologizing, I hurried on. "To answer your question, I suppose I feel like I don't know you well enough to use your proper name. You're still my ameer, regardless of our relationship."

"But I want you to feel comfortable with me."

Because you care, or because you want something? I pressed my lips into a thin line. All my life I'd learned that people had angles. Some were long and complicated, a maze you'd never unravel until they had you thoroughly trapped. Others were painfully obvious. Two turns to the truth. And still others carefully masked the turn, hid it so you didn't see it until it was too late, and you were too broken to turn around and retreat.

"Ask me a question," Dhamar demanded, pulling me from my sullen thoughts.

Every question I had for him flew from my mind, and it took me a minute to come up with one. The whole time, Dhamar remained silent, waiting, with his hands behind his head. He was more distracting than a swarm of bees.

I asked the first question to return to my head. "Why have you had four wives?"

Dhamar exhaled slowly. "I wondered how long it would take for you to ask that."

"I was going to ask this morning, but Zahir interrupted."

"He has impeccable timing." Dhamar grinned, but it didn't reach his eyes. He scratched at his jaw for a moment. "I married four times because I wanted to help someone."

"Help them?" I crossed my arms, a shiver stealing through me. "Or use them?"

Dhamar glared at me. "I already told you, we didn't even sleep in the same bed. Please don't accuse me of that again."

I swallowed and nodded.

"I truly wanted the first woman as my wife. But she was terrified, angry, and ready to kill me to be free. It was then I discovered that she had been at the Market for some time, and because of that, men entering the Market found her—lacking. Since then, I've been able to rescue three others. All of them were the same—they had been there for some time, and men didn't want them because of that."

They're all like me. The stupid, reckless part of me that had hoped Dhamar chose me for my uniqueness stung with jealousy at his words. I was nothing special. I was simply the fifth in the line of women he had *helped*.

"I married them, took them home, and then quietly divorced them a few months later. I was able to give them new lives with good jobs, and they're very appreciative."

"Good for them." I bit my tongue and turned away.

"Did I say something wrong?" His hand brushed my thigh.

Though butterflies stirred in my stomach, I flinched away. "No. Nothing at all."

"You are a horrible liar," he stated with a smile, but when he was rewarded with my icy silence, he didn't push. "Rest, Inara. It's going to be busy once we reach the palace."

I nodded and curled onto my side, the swaying of the litter soothing my frayed nerves.

Keep your feelings down. It's safer that way. If he knows how much you long for love, he'll use it to hurt you and then leave you even more broken. Just like everyone else.

Chapter Six

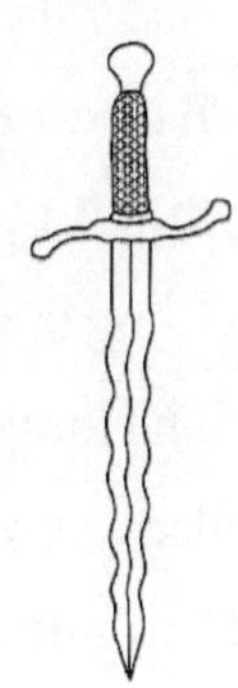

Dhamar

If we could stay here forever, I wouldn't mind it. I stared up at the fluttering top of the litter as Inara's steady breathing filled my ears. She had rolled to her side in her sleep, her face far closer to mine than she would probably have liked. I took the time to study her as she slept. It brought out the youthfulness of her face. Omar's papers said she was twenty-two years old, but looking at her in sleep, she appeared so much younger. Her features were even lighter in the sunshine filtering through the canvas of the litter, giving her an ethereal appearance next to the olive complexions and dark hair and eyes of most Talethans. Was that why Omar had struggled to marry her off? I brushed away a strand of hair that was wafting up and down against her lips as she breathed. Those lips looked...very kissable.

Stop it! I rolled over, staring at the purple fabric of the litter instead of my wife. I wouldn't do that to her. Not after vowing to protect her, even if that meant from myself.

But she is your wife. That means you have the right to kiss her.

Not if she doesn't want it.

You own her.

"No." I growled the word out loud, banishing the thoughts swirling in my head with finality. "There will be no kissing."

The longer I lay beside Inara, the harder it was to ignore her. I rolled to my side again, careful to not brush up against her. Instead of imagining kissing her, I imagined what her life was like before me, before the Market, before pain made her hide herself from the world.

What would it be like to see her smile again, to hear that laugh I'd coaxed out this morning? How I yearned to win her trust so completely that I would be the one she ran to with joy and sorrows, the one she wanted to hug and kiss. Was that even possible to obtain?

I dozed as the hours passed, jerking awake when the litter was lowered to the ground with a gentle thump. Inara sat up, crossing her legs under her as she eyed me warily. "Where are we?"

"I'm not certain, but Zahir will tell us shortly." I rose into a sitting position, running my hand through my hair and smiling at her. "He usually scouts before letting me wander."

"Is that the life of an ameer then, constantly looking over your shoulder for trouble?"

"That is the life of anyone with power." I shrugged. "I've grown accustomed to it, having lived with it all my life. Danger is ever near at hand, even for the safest person."

Inara's brow furrowed, but before she could speak again, Zahir stuck his head inside. "The Nagar River is up ahead. I thought you and the amira might like to stretch your legs."

I nodded, glancing at Inara. "Would you like that?"

She hesitated for the barest of second and then nodded. "Yes, please."

I climbed out and offered her my hand. She blinked in the afternoon sun, her eyes watering again, but she forced them open while glancing around. The sand gleamed brightly, but it was broken up in this area of the country with scrub brush and the occasional Carob tree. The river was still high, the rainy season not long past, and it gurgled fresh and clear down from the western mountains. To the east, the smaller rises of the hills and valleys made it hard to see where the sky met the horizon. An ostrich ran by, his feet thumping a steady rhythm against the earth.

Inara gasped. "It's beautiful!"

"The ostrich or the land?" I asked as I guided her to the edge of the Nagar.

"Both." Tears that I suspected had nothing to do with the sun filled her eyes. "It's been ages since—" she cleared her throat and forced a smile to her lips. "It's a wild and beautiful land here, Dhamar."

I couldn't help the grin that blossomed at her using my first name, and I acknowledged her comment with a nod. "Yes, it is."

She dipped her bare feet into the water and giggled, wiping away the lingering tears on her cheek. "It's so cold."

I scooped a palm of water from upstream and took a refreshing sip. "It's good water, too. Pure and fresh."

Inara mimicked me and laughed again. "Oh, it's delicious!" She took a few more mouthfuls and then patted her stomach. "Very good."

Maybe it will be possible to hear that laugh every day, I thought, the wildly elusive feeling called hope beginning to bind itself around my heart. *Today has been a good start, at least.*

But would it last? I offered Inara my hand as she scrambled over the slick rocks and back to the shore. She didn't pull away as I led her toward the litter.

After she had climbed inside, Zahir handed me a sack. "It's got bread, cheese, and some dried meat."

"Thank you," I said as I turned to follow my wife.

"Be careful, my ameer." Zahir grabbed my arm. His brows were lowered with worry. "She's...broken." He shook his head. "I know your propensity for broken and hurting souls, Dhamar. But she's not like your lion cub. In fact, she's probably more dangerous. A cub injures your body. A woman? She can easily wound your heart. That's not something that's easily mended."

"I'm aware." I fiddled with the strap on the sack. "But she's my wife now, Zahir. It's my job to fix her."

"No, Dhamar. You cannot fix anything."

I sighed. "I know. But I can help, yes?"

"I suppose. Just—be careful."

"When am I ever not careful?"

His eye roll made me laugh as I climbed back into the litter to eat lunch with my wife.

Inara was sitting on the far side, away from where I had been sprawled earlier. Her fingers played with the hem of her kameez, her eyes focused on her hands. I cocked my head to the side, studying her. "What's wrong?"

She flinched. "It's your turn to ask a question."

I chuckled, glad she wanted to continue our little game. "All right, but first, food." I held out a roll from the sack. Our fingers brushed as she took it, and I couldn't ignore the tingles that worked up my arm at the contact. She electrified me, set every nerve on high alert. This hadn't happened with any of the other women I had married.

But you didn't want a marriage with those other women. You were only trying to save them. This one? This one you want to love.

With a soft exhale, I popped a piece of cheese into my mouth, chewing slowly as I tried to decide what to ask and watched Inara nibble on her roll. "What's your favorite flower?"

Her eyes flicked up to me, looking blue in the purple tinted light. "I like jasmine."

"You smell like it." I bit my tongue and focused on the piece of meat in my hand. She didn't need to know that. That was a personal thing, something I wouldn't know if I hadn't been so close to her the night before. The memory of holding her gnawed at me, taunted me. I could do it—take her as my wife. But then I would be no different than my father. I slammed the door to my heart, locking it away. Until she wanted me, it would stay in that cage. I couldn't risk the consequences of letting it loose.

"Honey and jasmine were in the lotion Omar made us wear whenever we were on the block. He said—" She trailed off, pressing her thumb into the roll. "Never mind what Omar said. Despite all of that, I still think the flower is lovely. And the smell isn't—it isn't horrible."

Foolish question. "Your turn."

Inara looked up, staring at me for an uncomfortably long moment. Then, with a quiet whisper, she asked, "Why did you pick me?"

The vulnerability in her eyes, her tone, pricked my heart. This meant something to her. Something that could strengthen or shatter whatever tremulous foundation we were setting. I needed to answer correctly. Why *had* I picked her? Why had I promised to honor the vow I made to love, honor, and cherish her as far as she would let me?

It had taken three elite Markets to find Inara. I had searched the two in Mordova before arriving in Rana, my last hope of finding the right woman to marry. I had been feeling less than ecstatic when I'd been introduced to the women by Omar. But then Inara had looked at me—with her whole head, not just her eyes—as I entered. And in that moment, something had sprung to life inside of me. Whether it was Nicar's prompting, the beginnings of something I dared not name, or simply my own foolish hope that she would be different, it had been enough to draw me closer. That bit of boldness from Inara had made me hope that she would stand with me in my undeclared battle with the council and my father. Perhaps she was brave enough to face their prejudice and cruelty. Maybe life wouldn't be so lonely if she were able to stand and not cower.

Clearing my throat when I realized I had been lost in thought, I met her gaze. I couldn't say all that. It would sound like the rambling of a crazy person. So instead, I said, "I picked you because you are different from all the others at the Markets. You looked at me as you rocked back and forth, daring to defy what the Market decreed. You were bold and—" I wasn't sure how to end my train of thought. "There was something different there that wasn't in the others, something uniquely you."

"I suppose you should thank Saif, then." She pressed another finger into the roll. "He encouraged me to be myself."

"Are you being yourself now?"

Inara glanced up from her mutilated food. "Is that your question?"

"Only if that's yours." I smirked as she scowled. "That's up to you. If you don't want to answer that one, I have another question."

"No, I'm not being fully myself."

"Why?"

"You already had a question. It's my turn." Color bloomed in her cheeks, and she stared down at her roll for a moment. When she looked back up, Inara's face had taken on a mischievous look, and I found myself completely captivated. She didn't have to answer why she wasn't being herself. I'd discover that on my own.

"What is your question, my wife?"

"What is the palace like?"

I blinked, and she ate a bite of bread with a triumphant smirk. "That's your question? You'll see it for yourself in a few hours."

She dipped her head, even as she reached for the cheese and meat I held out to her. "Yes, I am fully aware of that. But I'd like to know it through your eyes first."

I scratched at my jaw. "Do you do that a lot?"

"Do what?"

"Live vicariously through others?"

"There wasn't much of a life to be had the last six years. It was that or go crazy." She shrugged her shoulders. "But you need to answer your question now."

I smiled, though it felt pinched at her admission. Six years she'd been locked away. Six years without fresh air and sunshine. I leaned back on my elbows, willing to tell her whatever she wished to know, whether that was about the palace, my life, or any place in all of Taletha.

She inched closer, stretching out against the side of the litter but her face was level with mine. Not a part of her made contact, but her eyes seemed to bore into my soul, touching a piece of me crushed long ago by my father and his steel-like hold over my life—or so I had thought. She woke me up from a sleep that I hadn't known I was in.

And it scared me.

Clearing my throat, I asked, "Where should I begin?"

"Outside." She sighed, her eyes breaking the spell as they slid closed. "Tell me about the gardens."

CHAPTER SEVEN

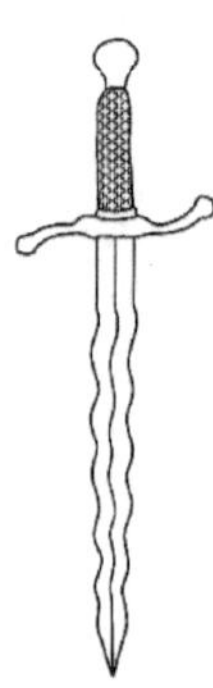

Inara

Talking about the palace felt safe. It was simply us talking about home, my new home. I hadn't had a home in years, not since Momma died. I kept my eyes closed as Dhamar described the gardens. I tried to picture them, but it was harder than I thought. My memories of home were buried, scabbed over by years of ignoring them. It was my defense against pain; an attempt to keep from hurting.

But it didn't work, because now they felt hazy, like a dream of a dream. The longer Dhamar talked about the flowers and plants, the pools and green grasses, the harder it was to remember, to grasp the tendrils of my life before. A tear snaked down my cheek, and I let it.

Don't let me forget it, I prayed. *Momma and our little garden, laughter and love. Don't let the pain of my past take anything else from me.*

I forced myself to focus on Dhamar's voice again. "There are winding paths and a fountain that my father runs during the rainy seasons. We have millions of flowers and trees. I know we have jasmine as well as acacias and blood lilies, though don't ask me about what else we have." There was a smile to his words, and I bit the inside of my cheek to keep from sighing.

It was hard to hate him, to be angry that he was carting me off as wife number five without a speck of remorse. Though, why he picked me at all still felt strange. His reasons didn't feel like enough. Rejection still pinched that tender part of me that wanted to be valued, seen as special and worthy of being chosen. Of being loved. But that was a hope not worth holding onto. He was an ameer, a man with power and prestige. He could pick any woman—still could by law— and I was merely the means of appeasing the council and his father. The pain that came from unshed tears tightened around my throat, and I rolled away from Dhamar.

"Are you all right?" Dhamar asked.

"I'm fine." My words came out clipped, but I didn't try to hide it.

If he could tell I was lying, I didn't care. Curling onto my side, I wanted nothing more than to dissolve into a puddle of tears, but the years of hiding my emotions meant that I couldn't let him see my hurt. My pain was mine alone to bear. If I let him get closer—let anyone get near—it would only result in more heartache, and that wasn't something I could handle. Not again.

Dhamar was a smart man and kept silent as the litter swayed up the road. I could hear the sounds of people and animals moving along outside. The pungent smell of barnyard wafted through the thin linen of the canvas, but it smelled familiar, like a warm hug from a friend you hadn't seen in ages.

The tightness in my throat grew to an uncomfortable ache. I took a shuddering breath as the sounds faded, though the scent remained. As I let my eyes slide closed, the memories associated with the smell of animals, manure, and hay slowly sprang to life. A prayer of thanks for those memories touched my mind, and I grinned sleepily.

A hand grasped my shoulder, startling me from the past. I sat up quickly, scrambling to the side with a small yelp of fright.

Dhamar had his hands raised when I looked up, a sheepish smile on his face. "Apologies. Didn't mean to startle you."

"Please don't—" I shivered, the memories of men and their wandering hands still too fresh in my mind. "It's all right. What's wrong?"

"I was going to ask you that."

"Nothing is wrong. I'm fine. I told you that. Please don't ask me again." I curled back on my side. So much had happened in the last twenty-four hours. My thoughts couldn't seem to catch up. My head pounded, and I wanted to sleep for a million years, preferably in a bed of my own.

"We're nearly home." He hesitated before holding out his hand to me. "Please, Inara. Tell me what's wrong."

"Everything. How can you not see that?" I sat up, fire flaming in my chest as I glared at him. "Nothing in my life has ever been right, and I don't know what to think or feel, and it hurts." I turned away from him as I kneaded my fist over my heart. "It hurts, and I'm scared."

"I know. I wish I could take it from you." Dhamar sighed and ducked his head. I hated him a little more for the humility rolling off him. He didn't get to be humble. He was supposed to be cruel and inflict pain. Though I didn't want to endure it, it would almost be easier if he only used me to satisfy a need, to get his heir, and then left me be.

The litter stopped and lowered down before the curtain parted. Zahir nodded toward Dhamar. "Ameer, the malek is waiting for you in his chambers."

"Only the malek?" Dhamar asked, and when Zahir nodded, I watched with undesired fascination at the change that swept over Dhamar. His spine stiffened, his shoulders rolled back, and every nuance of his face hardened. A shiver snaked down my spine as he ducked out of the litter and offered me his hand.

"I was hoping this could wait." His voice was as cold as a desert morning. "But it looks as if Father wants to greet us."

His father. The man who would have forced us together last night if Dhamar had been less honorable. If I weren't concerned for my life, I would have dared to march up to the malek and punch him in the nose. But the best vengeance, I knew, was not in lashing out. Rather, it was in standing tall and not letting the malek walk over me. I had done the same with every man who had entered the Wife Market. I hadn't kissed them back, hadn't run my fingers over their bodies, hadn't played their game. Now I would do the same. I would carry myself as an amira in every form of the word and remain by Dhamar's side. No, I didn't want to be here, but I was going to live as if I did.

I dropped to the ground and glanced up at the sprawling limestone palace. Part of it had been whitewashed, standing out against the blue of the sky and the intensity of the sun. Three red domes stood at equal intervals along the lower buildings, intricate lattice covering the tops. Upon the center one, a blaze of gold against the blue sky, was the swooping swallow—the sign of royalty. My gaze traveled to the two sets of steps that curved up to the horseshoe shaped arch. It led into the middle dome, into the heart of the place that I would call home. A glance over my shoulder showed a wall of limestone that matched the palace with one large wrought iron gate at the very center. It clanged closed with an echoing finality as I took Dhamar's hand and held fast.

His eyes flicked from our clasped hands to my face as I mirrored his stance—shoulders back, spine straight, face hard—and said, "I'm ready."

His lips twitched, but nothing else cracked his veneer as he replied, "Yes, you are."

The icy mask I always wore when on the Wife Market block slid into place, and I didn't let it waver as Dhamar guided me up the left set of curved steps to the large arch that led into the palace. My palm felt sweaty in Dhamar's grip, the high collar of my kameez choking me as my throat tightened. The round entryway was airy and light. Mosaic tiles of red, yellow, and orange wove a circular pattern on the floor. With its top painted gold, the high, domed ceiling kept the foyer cool.

A servant—dressed in nothing but flowy black salwar and red vest—stepped forward and bowed to my husband. "His most excellent ruler, exalted Malek Nadar, awaits your arrival, Ameer Dhamar."

"I am aware. Thank you, Yusef."

I was surprised that he knew, let alone used, the name of the servant, but I didn't have time to dwell on it. Dhamar's hand tightened in mine as he guided me down the gilded halls.

On our left, the wall alternated between whitewashed and un-adorned limestone, giving the hall a light feeling. Tapestries hung along the tan walls and swayed gently from the wind that blew through the open right side of the hall, where pillars broke up the portico and patio beyond. Gardens filled the spacious courtyard that was dozens of yards long. Sycamore trees sat along the far side, their branches reaching up and over the open wall. A fountain stood in the center, singing merrily as flowers, bushes, and trees grew in an organized chaos all around it. It felt peaceful, serene in a way I longed to feel within. It almost brought back to life the memories of the little garden I had tended with my mother.

I slowed as we neared the end of the portico, not ready to leave the life that was teeming in that garden.

"I will show you the garden after we speak to Father," Dhamar said in a whisper.

Deciding to trust Dhamar, and not really wanting to discover the consequences if we angered the malek quite yet, I continued through the passageway.

The simplicity of the halls fell away, becoming more and more ornate the farther we went. Swirling tiles lined the floor, reds and blues so busy in design that it made my head ache. Tapestries now lined every inch of the walls, and on the pillars were etchings of bloody battles. I was only too thankful when we reached a set of double doors. However, the knowledge of who lay beyond them made my stomach lurch.

The top of these doors sloped into a point, and like the pillars, had etchings of battles on them. The one that caught my eye had a man in a turban, holding aloft the severed head of a man with a long beard. I winced when Dhamar knocked against the head. It felt wrong, somehow, dishonoring to the dead.

The doors groaned opened. Another manservant stepped back as we strode in. With each step we'd taken down the hall, Dhamar had grown stiffer and now felt ready to snap. A quick scan around the room showed cushioned seats, a low table piled with food, and a single round window on the far wall. The pattern of the colored glass in the pane danced along the ground, captivating my attention until I breathed in. That single inhale filled my nose with the suffocating scent of the myrrh incense that was burning somewhere in the room, and I struggled not to cough.

At last, my gaze landed on Malek Nadar himself. He sat on one of the plumpest cushions, hands folded atop his rotund paunch. His black hair was streaked with gray, and his long gray mustache matched his downturned lips. "This is her?"

He's not even going to greet his son? I tensed, my dislike for the ruler already quite high.

"Yes, this is Inara, my wife." Dhamar practically spat the last word, despite his face remaining blank. "I have obeyed the orders you and the council commanded."

Though I had only been married to him for a day, I could tell he was hiding from the man before us. He never looked his father directly in the eye, never relaxed.

"You did it then?" a new voice asked, and I caught sight of a wiry man with gleaming onyx-colored eyes. He leaned forward, plucking an olive from a golden bowl on the low table before him.

"Married her, Lord Shaeen?" Dhamar asked, a bite in his voice.

Malek Nadar rolled his eyes as if Dhamar were a simpleton. "Did you consummate your marriage?"

I didn't think it was possible, but Dhamar braced further, as if ready for a hit. Stepping out from behind his arm, I bowed low, tucking my leg under me, and lowering my head. "We did, your majesty." Heat flooded my face at the blatant lie, and I kept my head down so the truth wouldn't shine through.

Dhamar hadn't let go of my hand, even with me practically on the floor at his feet. Gently, he tugged me up. His voice held derision as he asked, "Didn't your little witness come tell you?"

"Yes, but we like making you squirm." The malek's cold brown eyes locked onto me and I met his scrutiny head on. His mustache twitched, and he turned back to Dhamar. "I have a servant for her. She'll prepare her for the wedding tomorrow. You won't see her again until then, so it's time to say goodbye."

The malek's beady gaze didn't waver as Dhamar turned to me. He leaned close, too close, and mouthed *forgive me* before kissing me.

I placed my hands on his chest ready to push him away, but one of his hands slid to my waist as the other cupped my cheek. I gripped his tunic, my mind not processing what was happening as he deepened the kiss, lingering over my lips as if they were a fine wine by which he was intoxicated. I froze in place, needing to pull away but rooted to the ground by the gentle way Dhamar's kiss held onto me. It searched, pressed, yearned, but I couldn't return it, couldn't for the life of me move. After a long, breathless moment, he leaned back. No emotion showed on his face, but his eyes flicked to my lips as if he were contemplating kissing me again, as if exploring my lips had been enjoyable. I stepped back, the spell he had on me broken for the moment, and drew in a deep breath to clear my foggy head.

A slow clap sounded behind us, and I glanced over Dhamar's shoulder at Lord Shaeen. He met my gaze, his lips tipping up. "Good show."

Nausea rolled. The man was sick. I didn't doubt that he would have been at the Wife Market, watching Dhamar and me if he'd had the chance. I would have to keep my eye on this lord.

"Yes, quite the display." The man that was now my father-in-law took a bite of kamoon, the jelly dribbling down his chin.

"May I escort her to her room, Father?" Dhamar's hand was still on my waist, and he drew me closer.

"Yes, yes. Then come back here. We have had some—developments."

"With the tribesmen?" Dhamar's shoulder slumped.

The tribesmen of Šeri?

The malek nodded. "Yes, and we must discuss a plan for that. Meet us in the Council Chambers after you've said good night."

"Yes, Father." Dhamar turned and grabbed my hand, dragging me from the room and back down the hall.

We hurried back by the courtyard and through the foyer. Dhamar ducked down another wide hall and up a large flight of marble stairs. We strode down a passage with an intricate railing on the left-hand side and doors with different motifs etched on them set every few feet on the right. His pace was exhausting me, and I finally pulled free. He kept on for a few feet, so lost in thought that he didn't even notice my hand was gone from his. He abruptly halted and turned back around. But it was as if he were looking through me, to some distant point that I didn't have the vision to see or understand.

Easing forward a step, I asked, "What's going on? Is everything all right?"

"No. Nothing is all right." His gaze finally found my face, and he leaned down to let his forehead brush mine. "I don't know what he's after, keeping you from me today and most of tomorrow, but I—"

Dhamar closed his eyes, his body trembling once before he eased back and continued down the hall.

I hesitated to follow, instead pressing my hands to my flaming cheeks. What was happening? Why was I nervous around the man I was already married to? Arguably, I had only been his wife for a day, and while we had shared a bed last night and a kiss today, he was still nearly a stranger. Yet why were butterflies taking flight inside me every time he touched me or looked at me?

Because he was tender and thoughtful last night. He's been putting your needs first since you exchanged vows yesterday. He chose you after years of rejection. He is caring and gentle and an astonishing kisser.

I shook that final thought away, my throat tightening once more as I caught up with Dhamar. He turned the knob of a door that was painted light blue, knocking once before stepping through. With a sweeping gesture, he bowed slightly, and he said, "Your room, my lady."

I gasped, turning in a slow circle. An enormous bed sat in the very center of the room. Plush white blankets and pillows covered it, a gauzy canopy trailing all around to keep out the insects. A day couch, with cushions on the ground beside it, was along the left wall. A vanity and about a dozen ferns and other plants were situated on the right. The room itself was completely whitewashed so that it glowed in the late afternoon sun that poured through the lattice-covered window.

Breathless, I turned toward Dhamar. "Is this mine?"

"Yes. The amira's suite." He pointed to a door I hadn't noticed on the far side of the couch. "That leads to our common room, and my room connects on the other side.

One room was all that separated us. I felt my smile falter. While he had been considerate yesterday and today, would tomorrow change that? Who would stop him? Not his father, not the councilmen, not Zahir nor even Saif. If he wanted me, he could easily take me.

Dhamar didn't seem to notice my silence. "Father will have guards at the doors tonight to ensure we don't see each other until the official wedding tomorrow." He scowled.

Will he miss me? I shook my head. *Of course not. He barely knows me. All he'll miss is the chance to have me in his bed.*

But even with those thoughts, I eased a bit closer, gesturing around the room. "This is more than I ever thought I'd have when I thought about marriage."

"You deserve the world." Dhamar clasped my hands, swaying a touch closer. "Especially after all you went through in the Wife Market."

I ducked my head. "You bought me. I deserve only what you wish to give me, my ameer."

He tucked his finger under my chin and raised my face to meet his. Unlike before, I didn't flinch away, meeting his gaze to see if I could find the truth. Did he want me, the woman he didn't even know yet? The me I hid from everyone, even myself at times. She was messy, raw, vulnerable. She was weak and scared, the little girl who huddled in the corner while her father beat her mother.

I swallowed, and his eyes followed the motion down my throat. Still, he didn't speak, only let his eyes drift back up to my face. Leaning a bit closer, his breath caressed my cheek. The air stalled in my lungs, all my thoughts fixating on one thing: was he going to kiss me again? Would it be real this time? Would I dare to kiss him back? My heart sped up. His last kiss had been heady. My legs went weak at the thought of what it would mean to truly kiss Dhamar.

His nose brushed mine, and his lips had barely skimmed my own when a knock sounded. Dhamar swore and flung open the door.

"What do you want?" he snapped.

I tucked my hands behind my back, my lips tingling even from that brief contact, and watched as a maid stepped in. She wore a plain, yellow kameez with a sash about the middle. Her curly black hair was pulled back and was covered by a kerchief of light blue, though a few strands still trailed around her temples.

"Out," she dared to order Dhamar. He glanced at me with a strange longing in his gaze before he obeyed the servant's orders.

"I am Hafza, your maidservant." She bowed after the door clicked shut. "What would you like me to call you, Amira?"

"Inara is fine." I fidgeted with the sleeve of my kameez. "All of this has been...a bit overwhelming."

Hafza smiled, the hard expression she had given Dhamar evaporating as she gestured toward the vanity. "I'm sure it has been. I have been the maidservant for all of Ameer Dhamar's wives, and every one of them has come in with that look of shock on her face. Though between you and me, I must say I've never seen Dhamar quite so reluctant to leave a wife before."

A blush stole its way up my neck.

Hafza chuckled, picking up a brush as she began to detangle my hair. "We shall prepare you to be the most stunning bride Taletha has ever beheld. You shall win the ameer over completely, and perhaps"—she lowered her voice to a conspiratorial level—"even silence the malek and that wretched council of his."

I gaped at her in the mirror's reflection. She was bold indeed to talk about the malek and his council in that way. But Hafza only laughed and winked before going back to my hair with a renewed gusto.

Chapter Eight

Dhamar

I braced my hands against the banister of the patio, trying to cool my simmering temper before having to face my father and the council yet again. Five days had not been long enough. Usually, I went months without having to see and endure them. Now it had been less than a week and I was being summoned to the overly tight and warm room again. I rubbed at my chest, breathing deeply of the eucalyptus and jasmine that swirled on the warm breeze. It blew pieces of hair against my forehead as I squeezed my eyes shut. It was unreasonable to withhold my wife from me tonight. We were already married. Separating us was just another way to control me. Although, it shouldn't matter that I was apart from her tonight. It was unrealistic to crave being near Inara. We had been married for twenty-four hours. That was it. I didn't know *her*. I knew her beauty and a bit of her mind, but her heart and body were still hers. I hadn't earned them or the right to caress the tender parts of her that she held close. I wasn't sure I ever would.

No, you shouldn't think that. I forced myself to inhale, hold, then release before I strode toward the council chamber. Yes, Inara was making me fight for every inch of progress in our relationship, every touch, every look, every word. But I was finding that I liked it. I liked that she wasn't just handing herself to me. There was a lock on her heart. To reach it, I needed the key she clutched in her fisted hand. But I would get it, I would find a way. I wanted Inara, every bit of her mind, body, and soul. This time I was willing to fight for what I wanted. *And it will make my eventual victory so much sweeter.*

The council doors banged behind me as I strode up to the throne. I fisted my hand over my heart before taking my spot standing beside the throne. Someone had lit the incense that Father had in his room, and in the already tight quarters, it was suffocating. I coughed, using the sleeve of my kurta to muffle it.

Two of the six council men were missing, and unfortunately, they were the levelheaded ones. Sitting on their cushions were the Lords Arqa, Shaeen, Hakeem, and Mulazim. I resisted the urge to tug on the collar of my kurta and instead, clasped my hands behind me.

"We all know the reason we are gathered." Father swirled the goblet of wine in his hands, a sour look twisting his already scowling face. "The tribesmen have attacked and slain a number of our border guards while Dhamar was off finding his bride."

"Which Market did you get her from, ameer?" Shaeen asked, a curl to his lips. "She looks entirely too northern to be a proper amira. If you're interested, I'd gladly take her off your hands. You can have my daughter, an appropriate Talethan bride."

"I went to three Markets, Lord Shaeen," I gritted out between my clenched teeth. "The two elite markets here and then the best one in Rana. It was only in Rana that I found the bride I'd been searching for. So, excuse me if I am not interested in your daughter and am quite happy with my choice in a wife."

Shaeen shut his mouth, the click audible in the silent chamber.

"So, there is a backbone in there after all." Father chuckled. "But Shaeen is right, boy. She is awfully northern."

"She is my wife. You let me pick, and she is the one I chose." I scratched my jaw once before letting my hand fall to my side. "Now, back to the possible war at hand?"

"Yes, yes." Father cleared his throat and glared at me as if it were my fault the conversation had veered off course. "Šeri is attacking, and our only viable course of action is, of course, to retaliate and show them the might of our armies."

Arqa nodded, his words slow and languid, as if he were in no hurry to finish. "We will more than likely have enough men to quickly rout the scum with little resistance."

Likely have enough? I shook my head. We needed better odds than that to warrant a full-fledged attack against the Šerian nation.

"We are certain that the men of Mordova are equipped for such an attack?" I asked.

Father struggled to sit up from the slouch he'd been in on his throne. "Are you suggesting that the enemy is stronger than the might of *my* kingdom?"

I stifled a sigh. "No, my malek. I would never even insinuate that." *Even though it is quite possibly true.*

Mordova—and as a whole, Taletha—had grown comfortable and lazy. We allowed the pirates of the North Sea to protect us from the lands to the north and east—despite their being little to no threat east of us—while the Šeri tribesmen protected us from Doray, the country that lay in the far south. The west held our most loyal supporters. But spread out as they were, it would take weeks to rally the full force of the Talethan army.

"By my calculations, we still would outnumber the basic bulk of the Šerian warriors." Arqa tipped his head back, staring up at the ceiling. "I do not believe we have much to worry about."

"And if you can't rout them that quickly?" I asked, feeling rest-less agitation. The pictures of war that riddled the palace walls played within my mind. Blood, death, loss—so much loss. My people would lose their lives, Mother's people would lose theirs, and for what? A few animals and stolen grain.

"Oh, not us. You, ameer," Hakeen bellowed and clapped his hands. "You will lead us to victory!"

Panic clawed at my throat. "What are you talking about?"

"As ameer of Taletha, it is your duty and honor to lead your men into battle." Father grinned, and it was more terrifying than his frown ever was. "You shall have your three-day feast to celebrate your marriage, and then you shall be off!"

"And what about the heir you want so badly?"

"Your bride will be waiting, keeping your bed warm for when you return." Shaeen rolled his eyes. "Or are you that eager to bed this foreign one, Dhamar?"

"Watch your mouth, Shaeen. I am still your ameer, and she is your amira. You will not speak ill of my wife!"

Once again, the chamber grew eerily silent—enough so that I could hear my ragged breathing and the sputter of the incense stick.

"He was only jesting, boy." Father cleared his throat. "Go, you have a war to prepare for."

"May I see Inara tonight, Father?" I asked.

"No. Save that energy of yours for tomorrow, Dhamar." The waggle of his brows did nothing to ease the churning of my stomach.

"You better hope I don't die," I muttered under my breath as I turned and moved toward the doors.

Shaeen's chuckle followed me as I walked past him. "You won't die, ameer. You have the luck of Nicar on your side. She certainly blessed you with that bride you bought yourself."

I didn't dignify that comment with a response. Throwing back my shoulders, I strode out of the room with as much poise as I could manage. The door clicked closed, and I slumped against the wall with a groan.

"Ameer Dhamar?" I blinked up to see Zahir.

"They're sending me to the border." I scratched my jaw as I straightened and began to move down the hall. "I really don't want to go."

"You're usually clawing to get out of the palace," Zahir said as he fell into step beside me. "What changed?"

"Not what. Who." I glanced at my friend. "They want me to go after the celebration is complete. It's not fair to leave Inara here, alone, four days after arriving. And then Lord Shaeen—" I shook my head. "It's like leaving her in a den full of vipers."

"Your wife is mighty, my ameer. I have a feeling that throwing her to the wolves—or the vipers as it may be—might make her stronger still."

I mulled those words over in my mind as we reached my room. Would Inara survive here? Had I dragged her from the Market only to throw her into a worse and more dangerous life? Shaeen's comments about her beauty, about our marriage, sent my heart racing. He'd set his sight on *my* wife, and I didn't like it in the slightest.

My eyes fell on the light blue door, *Inara's* door. Longing welled within me. What was she doing? Was she comfortable? Was she thinking about me as much as I was thinking about her?

Probably not the last one. I sighed.

Saif's gaze flicked in my direction from where he stood guard by her door. "Do you have a message for the amira, my ameer?"

I opened my mouth for a moment before clamping it closed. "I will in a moment."

Ducking into my room, I was halted by the golden body of Gamil—my lion. He purred, his large size knocking me off balance as he rubbed against my legs. Laughter slipped out as I tumbled onto the rugs with a *umph* of impact.

"You overgrown kitten." I laughed as I rubbed my fist against his forehead. His purrs vibrated my body, and he pressed his nose against my cheek. "I missed you too, Gamil. But I have a mission. I will love on you later."

Pushing him away, I quickly found a quill and parchment. Dipping the nib in the ink, I hesitated. Did I dare explain what was about to happen in a simple message? I didn't want to worry her, although knowing how she felt about me, it might bring her some relief. Still, it felt like a delicate conversation, and one best saved to be shared in person. Then there was Lord Shaeen. I'd have to warn her to be careful, but again, it felt like a message to share face to face.

So instead of everything I wanted to say, I scratched a short note of what she needed to know. Closing it with my seal—two scimitars crossed behind the head of a roaring lion—that no one but the recipient would dare open, I stared at it for a long moment, questioning everything I'd scrawled inside.

Shaking away my doubts, I signed my wife's name with a flourish. Her name was as beautiful as she herself was, and I was half-tempted to trace it with my thumb if the ink was not wet. I shook my head. What was wrong with me? I was becoming a sentimental sap but somehow knowing that Inara was mine made life...different. She made me want to be a better man.

But how do I be a good husband?

I let the question roll around my head as I stepped back into the hall and handed the message to Saif. I didn't release the letter until he met my gaze. "Thank you."

He seemed taken aback by that, his mouth opening and closing before he nodded. "Of course, my ameer."

With that, I returned to my room. I paced from my bed to the window, my hands clasped behind my back. Nervous energy coursed through my body, needing to be expelled, but how? The person whom I most wanted to see was sequestered away in her quarters, and I couldn't disobey the word of my father, no matter how displeased I was by it.

Gamil hit my leg with his head, and I sighed, settling onto my cushions to rub his mane and bury my nose in it. He was warm, and his purr rumbled through the room. It was strangely comforting after the week I had endured.

Had it really been less than a week since being ordered to wed? In some ways, it felt like years had passed. The highs and lows of the past twenty-four hours were enough to make me want to weep. I wanted desperately to talk to my wife, to make sure she was settling in all right, that Hafza was treating her well. While I truly had no doubts about Hafza—I trusted her nearly as much as Zahir—was Inara comfortable with her?

I groaned, my head thumping against the wall. Gamil growled and rolled onto his back, his large head resting in my lap as he waited for me to scratch under his chin.

"Overgrown house cat." I chuckled, stroking his honey-colored fur absentmindedly.

A knock broke me free from the unending worry and anxiousness of my thoughts. But Gamil would not let me up from where he'd effectively pinned me.

"Enter!" I called.

The door creaked on its hinges, and my mother walked in. Her light brown eyes darted all around, checking for any threat as she let the door close behind her. She wrung her hands, not moving further in until I invited her with a wave of my hand.

Lenna, rania of all Taletha, was a sad sight to behold. She reminded me of an animal that had been beaten into submission. Any loud sounds made her jump. Her eyes held dark circles beneath them, and she currently sported a bruise along her jaw. It was anyone's guess as to what had happened to make my father hit her. The signs of abuse likely riddled her body and that realization had me grinding my teeth together. If I were braver, I would have stood up to my father long ago for the pain he had inflicted on my mother over the years of their marriage. But any act of rebellion on my part would only mean further pain for her. And that was not something I could stand the thought of.

"Mother." I greeted her as she sat beside me before gesturing to Gamil. "I'd greet you properly but as you can see, my pet has other ideas."

The lion chortled, a gravelly sound in the back of his throat, and stood. Shaking himself, he padded on silent paws to his bed in the far corner of the room, yawned—which revealed all of his teeth—before falling into slumber.

I leaned over and gave Mother a kiss on her cheek. "What brings you by?"

"Your marriage?" She smiled, and it was the first one I'd seen in years that actually went to her eyes. "Is it true?"

"Did Father give you that?" I brushed my finger lightly over the mark, and she flinched. "Mother, what else did he do?"

"Nothing that will kill me." She clasped my hand and moved it to her lap. Her wavy black hair—so like mine in texture and color—held more gray than I remembered. But then, Father rarely allowed her to come see me, and it was hard to make myself visit her when I knew he would inflict physical pain on her later. Father had never denied me permission to see Mother, but I also knew it displeased him.

"You need to—"

"I need to hear about this woman!" Mother smiled again, a dimple appearing in her cheek. I was thankful that most of the features I had inherited had come from my mother. It helped to look in a mirror and see her rather than my tyrannical father, gave me hope that I wouldn't become like him.

"She's...wonderful." I returned the squeeze she gave my hand. "I'm truly not worthy to call her mine."

Mother hummed a sound of disagreement. "No one will ever be good enough for my son in my eyes. You are a blessing from Nicar to me, Dhamar, a single star in a sky of darkness." She patted my arm. "You see yourself as unworthy of this woman? I see myself as unworthy of being your mother. So perhaps this woman is a blessing from Nicar to you like you are one to me."

"I'm unworthy of such a blessing. I can't even protect my own mother." My eyes stared pointedly at the bruise. "I was foolish to bring a treasure like Inara into this place."

"Her name is Inara?" When I nodded, Mother's eyes began to shine again. "Do you know what her name means, Dhamar?"

"No." Names held meaning, everyone in Taletha knew that. Often, a parent picked a name as a blessing to their child. My name meant *searcher of truth,* and I tried to do that in everything. Mother's name meant *lion's strength,* of which she had an abundance. Though she had suffered much at the hands of my father, she always came out stronger. But Inara's name I didn't know. "What does it mean, Mother?"

"It means *shining light.*" Mother knelt, tipping my head toward her when I tried to turn away. "You had no choice but to marry, and I believe Nicar sent you this woman to be your helper, a light when you'll need it the most."

"I'm going to war," I whispered, and Mother sat back hard. "When?"

"After the three-day celebration." I rubbed the back of my neck, resting my elbows on my bent knees.

"Against Šeri?" she asked, though she likely already knew the answer. When I nodded, she sighed. "I feared this day would come. They are a hard-headed people. They never forget and rarely forgive."

"What am I to do? Either way, I lose this war. How can I fight against a people I consider my own?"

"You do what you must do to survive, Dhamar. Although—" Mother leaned against me, a soft sob slipping out "—I am so tired of simply surviving."

I tightened my arms around her. "We survive so that someday we can live."

"But will that day ever come?" she asked in a whisper. "For twenty-six years I've survived, survived your father, survived watching you being raised under his thumb, survived being away from my family. I'm ready to live."

My heart broke hearing those words. I wished, not for the first time, that I could take that pain for her. But I was bound as much as she, a prisoner to the malek's every whim and fancy. I pressed a kiss to the top of her head.

"Keep surviving, Mother. I will see that someday, somehow, you get to live."

"And you—" she sat up, wiping at her cheeks, and waving a finger under my nose "—you treat that wife of yours as a jewel, a treasure. You are not your father! Don't be a boar nor a bear. I will not have it, Dhamar! I will not—" Another sob caught in her throat, and she curled into me like Gamil, crying out all her fear and pain on my shoulder.

When she finished, she stood, wiping at her eyes and giving me a final hug. "I'm sure your father won't let me come to the wedding, so I wanted to give you this." She pressed a small wooden box into my hand. "It is the one thing I was able to hide from Nadar the day he married me."

I shook my head. "I cannot take this."

"No! You will." She closed my hand around it, her eyes hard. "You and your amira will bring peace to our lands, Dhamar. You will. I—I will see it done. And this," she shook our clasped hands and the box, "is a promise that I stand by you. I love you, Dhamar, and I am so proud of you."

I nodded, not trusting my voice. My father had never said those words to me, though I longed to hear them. I strove to do what he asked as far as my conscience would allow. But it was never enough, never what he actually wanted. To him, I would always be a failure of a boy, a disappointment. But to hear my mother say she was proud soothed a bit of the ache that stabbed at me. Her praise was worth far more than Father's would ever be.

"Thank you, Mama." The old endearment came off my tongue easily. Father hated it and forbade its use once I turned five. But when it was just my mother and me, I used it, just to see her smile.

She pecked my cheek, then patted it before turning and leaving.

Darkness had fallen now, and with a sigh, I sat the box on my table. The talk with my mother had done little to settle me, and I began to pace once more, waiting for my wedding day and then...war.

Chapter Nine

Inara

I stared at the three pools of water that Hafza led me to. Steam curled up out of the middle one, and I longed to slip into it. The scent of eucalyptus and lavender lay heavy in the muggy air, and water trickled down the rock walls, plinking in unsynchronized beats against the tile floor.

Hafza steered me toward the first pool. "Dunk yourself five times in that one."

"In my clothes?" I asked, fingering the buttons of my kameez

Hafza huffed a sigh and batted my hands away. She undid my buttons and then tugged my kameez over my head. "You can shuck your own salwar. Hurry up!"

I couldn't help but smile at her bossy attitude. It had only been an hour, yet I could already tell I would be well taken care of by this servant. She was quick to laugh and to listen. She was steady, something I appreciated greatly in my rapidly changing world.

Hafza picked up my dusty clothes and gestured to the pools once more. "After you wash five times in that one, you can soak in the middle pool."

I nodded and stepped into the water. My teeth clenched at the cold that seeped into my skin. A hiss slipped out, and I wanted nothing more than to turn and dive into the middle pool. But I knew dirt from the journey was caked on my face and in my hair. While Dhamar and I had both been in the litter, dust had made its way past the canvas and onto us.

With a gasp, I dunked my head into the frigid water. Shivering, I came up and promptly dove in again. I scrubbed my scalp with my fingers, though they felt stiff and shaky.

Three more quick dunks, and then I stumbled up the steps and into the warm pool. My chattering teeth echoed in the bathing room as I slipped beneath the water. The heat soothed and caused my body to ache as it chased away the cold. I groaned with pleasure. This was much better.

I soaked, letting the warm water wash away the dust and weariness from the journey and the stress from the past few days. But the heat couldn't erase my thoughts.

Tomorrow, I would marry Dhamar again in front of the entire city of Mordova. The Great Temple of Nicar stood right outside the palace walls. It was large, ornate, and could seat hundreds of people. Hafza had told me that the council would be there; I would be forced to meet them and their wives. People would expect me to be the ever-poised amira, a vision of the grace and beauty of Taletha.

What would they do when they met me and saw the fair features that had always been a mark against me? Would Dhamar regret choosing me as his bride once the gossip started? I groaned, ducking beneath the warm water. I was tired of second guessing myself, weary of wondering what he was thinking and feeling. Why were relationships so challenging? I'd never been particularly good at them. Father was always angry, Mother always sad and scared, and I had played mediator between them—with varying degrees of success.

Then there was my betrothed. That disaster was the last thing I wanted to think of now. I didn't want to *think* at all. So instead, I closed my eyes and began to hum a song Mother used to sing to me whenever I had a nightmare. It was a song about a desert knight rescuing a beautiful genie. They fell madly in love with each other, and the genie granted the knight three wishes. First, he wished that they might always be together. She granted it, and the two were bound by a red cord of fate, destined to always be beside one another.

Next, he wished that they would always be true to one another. The wish was granted, and they had eyes for no one save each other.

Finally, he wished her free—not to wed him, but to experience all that life had for her. With the words just past his lips, the genie's shackles fell away. Free to do as she pleased, she chose to marry her knight. And because the knight had so selflessly wished her free, the Jinn of the Genies declared that their love would be legendary—it would never be forgotten and would outlast the end of all time.

I had just finished the final refrain when Hafza returned, towels and a bundle of clean clothes in her arms.

"What were you singing?" she asked as she set the items aside.

"*The Knight and the Genie.*" I smiled wistfully. "It's a song my mother used to sing to me. It's beautiful, don't you think?"

"If you are fond of gallant acts, I suppose." Hafza winked at me. "If you are, Dhamar is the man to be married to."

I blushed, and she laughed. The sound echoed around the chamber and brought a levity to my heart that I hadn't felt in years.

"All right, Amira, into the last pool," she commanded.

I eyed it suspiciously. "Is it freezing cold, too?"

She chuckled. "No, it has mineral salts and a number of oils added to it."

"How are they kept warm?" I asked as I climbed out of the middle pool and into the third. It wasn't quite as warm as the second pool, but it didn't set my teeth to chattering either.

"There are hot springs beneath this area of the palace." Hafza lathered something sweet smelling into my hair, tipping my head into a bowl and using cold water to rinse the concoction from it. "It warms these two pools."

"And the cold one?"

"Ice from the eastern lands. They keep Taletha steadily supplied."

I let her finish scrubbing my scalp, eyes half closed from the relaxing massage. Hafza had me lather with all manner of soaps, varying in scents from lavender to frankincense, then dunk three times in the pool to wash away any lingering suds. She held open a fluffy towel that I gratefully stepped into before wrapping my hair in another to dry.

"Unwrap the towel from around your waist," she said.

I obeyed without a murmur, and she tugged a plain silk shift over my head.

She looked me over one final time before motioning for me to follow her back to my room. Saif snapped to attention when we reached the door. Hafza didn't hesitate as she strode past my guard, but as I moved to enter, he stopped me by extending a sealed piece of parchment my way.

"I was asked to give this to you." He pressed it into my hand, eyes flicking up and down the hall.

I glanced at him. "Who—?"

He pressed a finger to his lips. "Best read it and see."

With a nod, I ducked into my room. My hands shook as I turned the parchment over to look at the seal. It was a lion head between two curved swords. I traced it with my finger, nerves swirling in my chest about what the letter might contain. I thought I knew who it was from, but why would he write to me? What did he want to say that couldn't wait until tomorrow? I broke the wax and unfolded the single piece of parchment. It took several seconds for my bleary eyes to focus on the words written in a neat script.

Dearest Inara,

I'm sorry for the way my father and Lord Shaeen treated you today. It was deplorable, and I wish I could say I was thoroughly shocked. But, alas, it is who they are.

I greatly wish to see you. Tomorrow feels an eternity away. I miss seeing your smile. Strange how something so simple can mean so much already. Your beauty renders me breathless, Inara, and I'm a blessed man to call you mine.

Though I cannot promise what our future holds, I will fight for a good one if it means you'll be standing by my side when it's over.

Forever yours,

Dhamar

I bit my lip, my heart fluttering at the words. Rereading the letter once more, I folded it and slid it beneath the pillows on my bed. My ears rang as my mind replayed the events of the last day.

Dhamar choosing me from Omar.

Dhamar protecting me from the leering eyes of the priest.

Dhamar being gentle and patient at every flinch and fear of mine.

He's blessed to call me his? I'm blessed to have a man like him. Tears pricked my eyes. Was it worth it to let my guard down for Dhamar? Was he truly a good man, or was it all an act?

Your beauty renders me breathless. The words of the letter rolled through my mind, and I blushed. It shouldn't matter that he found me pretty, but it did. For my entire life, I was almost beautiful, almost perfect, almost enough. For him to tell me he found me beautiful, it smoothed a healing balm over a tender part of my heart that I hadn't let myself acknowledge in years. I smiled as I stared down at my pillows.

Hafza stood by the vanity, watching me. A smirk appeared on her face as she waved a hand in a circle. "If you're finished swooning over your love letter from the ameer, there's food over here. While you eat, I'm going to brush out your hair, do some henna on your arms and feet, and then lather you in lotions before sending you to bed. You need to be well rested for tomorrow."

I settled myself on the stool, and began to eat cheese, olives, figs, and bread as Hafza brushed my hair. She picked up a small section of my hair, starting at the end and working up to the roots. Slowly she brushed, piece by piece, while I picked at the food. A million questions welled up inside of me, and finally, one spilled forth.

"What is Dhamar like?" I hurried to explain when Hafza raised her brows at me in the mirror. "I know what I've seen, but a man can hide his true self for some time." I dropped my gaze to my lap. "Is he really as perfect as he appears?"

"No man is perfect, Inara." She paused in her brushing to consider my question. As she began again, she said, "Dhamar is truly a kind and gentle man, but he is also an over thinker. I think that's why he struggles so much with his father and the council."

"I sensed a bit of that when I was introduced to them. But the way you said that, are you thinking of something specific?"

"I am." Hafza gently worked at a knot, her words as soft as her fingers. "His father is a cruel man. He enjoys his power and uses it to satisfy his...desires." Her face took on a red hue. "Dhamar is not the malek's only child, but the only one he acknowledges. He has a room full of women he claims as his property. Be thankful, my amira, that you are married to his son."

"Dhamar hasn't...he isn't like that?"

Hafza smiled at my reflection in the mirror. "No. In fact—" she gestured to herself "—I was his first wife."

My mouth fell open, and Hafza tipped her head back with a laugh.

"And you're—you don't mind serving me?" I asked. If it had been me, I would have been irate to be serving the new wife of Dhamar.

But Hafza shook her head. "He married me, and I think he truly believed that he would grow to love me. Men like Dhamar are taught all their lives that they'll pick a wife from the Market, that their wives will serve, satisfy, and love them. But you and I know the truth." Her voice dropped to a whisper, her eyes growing distant. She was in another time, another place. "We know that it's a painful reality, waiting, never knowing who will walk through the doors, what they will or won't be. Perhaps we had love, only to lose it the day we were sold to the Market. Perhaps it was a safer place than where we came from. Perhaps it's different for every person who steps through the doors." She still held a lock of my hair, but the brush hung limply in her hand.

I understood what she was saying. My life hadn't been one of blissful ignorance. I'd known loss, pain, betrayal. I had love once, only to discover how fickle it truly was. Men said one thing, lived another, and it was a rare thing indeed to find one whose words and deeds lined up in harmony. In some ways, the Wife Market had felt safer than my home.

But it was still a form of slavery. Omar owned my body and sold me to the highest bidder.

Now you belong to Dhamar. He can do with you whatever he wishes. Just like Father. Just like Jamal. My breathing came short and erratic as memories I wished to forget pushed to be recognized. Phantom pain raced down my back, and I held a hand to my throat as I struggled to rein in my panic.

Hafza adjusted her grip on the brush. Her voice brought me back to the present, to the soft stool and her gentle fingers untangling a knot in my hair. "To answer your question, my amira, I don't mind serving you. Seeing Dhamar so happy, that is a gift. He tried with me, but it wasn't the right match. He's content and wants to be near you, Amira. That letter? That is a small stab at the malek and the council. They're keeping you apart tonight, and yet Dhamar dared to write to you. You should take it as the highest form of flattery that he's willing to push like that."

Was it really that hard to fight against the malek and the council? They seemed to have such a hold over Dhamar, but how? He was the ameer, the future malek of all of Taletha. Surely, they had to respect him, enough to want to secure the royal line by having him marry and produce an heir. So why was my husband so obedient to them, even when he disagreed?

There is much I have to learn about this life.

I bit my lip, deep in thought, as Hafza finished brushing my hair and ran her hand one final time down the back of my head. Rolling up the sleeves of my nightdress, she drew detailed flowers on my hands and feet with henna, swirling vines creeping up my wrist and around my ankles. After it had dried enough to not worry about smudging the designs, she wrapped clean cloths around it and then smiled at me. "All right, to bed with you."

"Hafza." I twisted my fingers in the skirt of my nightgown. There was one final question I had to ask, something I needed to know before I vowed to be Dhamar's wife a second time. "Dhamar said—he told me that he didn't…" Heat flamed in my cheeks at the mere thought of this question. "He said he never had marital relations with any of his other wives. Is that true?"

Hafza smirked at my discomfort. "That's right. He barely touched me, never kissed me. He was so worried about my welfare that he often ignored his own basic needs. He is a good man, Inara. You truly can trust him to do what's best for both of you."

I ducked my head, guilt gnawing at me. It was true, Dhamar had done nothing to warrant my distrust. But he was capable of pretending, just as Jamal had. Once my best friend, it hadn't taken Jamal long to brandish his lies about my life. Promises quickly made and then broken over and over. He had said he loved me, would take care of me. Yet when the sun rose on my secret, he had run away. I couldn't endure another betrayal.

I crossed my arms over my chest, shoving down the pain as I rose and moved to my bed.

"Amira Inara, one final thing, and then I will retire." Hafza twisted her fingers together, looking more uncertain than she had all evening. "I know the Market wounded a part of you. It seems to injure all who step through its shadowed doors—one way or another. But Dhamar, he truly is a respectable man. He cares deeply, and if he falls in love with you, it will be passionately and without holding any part of himself back." Her throat bobbed, and it took her several seconds to continue. "I may not be his wife any longer and I was never meant to be. But he did rescue me from that pit, and because of that, I care for him. I'm not asking for you to love him. I'm not sure any of us Market brides fully understand what love is. But, please, don't hurt him."

Her eyes, so dark in the dimming light of the room, shone with the sheen of unshed tears. Her passion for Dhamar struck me deeply. She knew him better than I did, and of all the people here, she had the most reason to loathe him. My head spun with all of the information I had been given that day, and all I could do was nod and whisper, "I'll try, Hafza."

She bowed her head before turning and leaving my room. My hands shook as I pulled back the blankets on my bed and curled into a ball. The earthy, grassy smell of the henna was strangely comforting, giving the tears permission to fall like two nights before. I curled on my side as they trailed down my cheeks. Fear, relief, and worry shadowed my soul even as darkness enveloped the room, both crowding out the light.

The cooing of doves from outside my window filled my room as I stretched to wakefulness. The sun shone through the colored glass, painting the white walls a kaleidoscope of colors. I stared at it, not quite ready to rise and face my second wedding day.

A strange ecstasy blended with terror and filled my heart. I wanted to laugh and cry at the same moment and settled instead for burying my face in a pillow and screaming. Why were my mind and heart so befuddled? Couldn't I pick an emotion? I was already married to the ameer. He said he wouldn't leave me, and it wasn't like I had a choice either way. I was his to do with what he wished. And today he wished to marry me again.

Hafza entered my room, bustling to the vanity. After arranging a few jars in a particular order, she glided over to a narrow door where she pulled out a number of undergarments and laid them over the foot of the bed. Opening the main door, she exchanged words with someone on the other side. With a click, the door closed, and Hafza was by my side.

"Time to rise, my amira. It's your wedding day!" I tried to smile, but my panic must have bled through, for Hafza clasped my hand in hers. "I promise, it will all be fine."

I let her words carry me to the vanity. With deft hands, she unwrapped and wiped off the henna. Then, she began to braid my hair and pin it back into an elaborate style of tiny braids and twists. She settled a diamond maang teeka against my forehead and flung my veil over the left side of the mirror for after I was dressed.

Spinning me away from the mirror, she brushed a sparkling powder on my eyelids and used a black pencil to line my eyes. A dab of pink colored paste was rubbed on my lips, and a light pink powder on my cheeks.

"Time for you to see your dress." Hafza glanced around and then rolled her eyes. "If that ridiculous servant ever brings it. Wait a moment, please."

She hurried out the door, and I snuck a glance at myself in the bit of mirror that was visible under the veil. I looked strange. My blonde hair had rarely been done up before, and it drew the eye to my long, slender neck. The added cosmetics only accentuated how very different I was from my fellow Talethans. But I was one of them. My heritage was here, and whether or not they wanted me, I claimed them. I loved them, even if they never chose to love me.

The longer it took for Hafza to return, the more anxious I became. Rising to my feet, I hurried and grabbed the letter out from under my pillow. I smoothed it out against my leg and let myself reread it. The last part had my traitorous heart skipping a beat:

Though I cannot promise what our future holds, I will fight for a good one if it means you'll be standing by my side when it's over.

Did he mean that? Did he really want me at his side? I wiped away a blasted tear. *No, no softening. You're bold, but you're also hard. You can't let him in. Your heart is a mess, and if he saw it, he'd turn and run. Just like Father and Jamal. Just like your brothers.*

The door clicked open, and I turned away from the mirror as Hafza slipped back in, a bundle of sparkling white fabric draped over her arms.

"Honestly, this is ridiculously lavish." She spread it over the bed. "It also weighs a ton."

I stared at the stunning kaftan. Golden thread held sparkling jewels over all of it. They were twisted into intricate patterns and pictures. A gauzy sash, festooned with jewels along the hem, was attached to the left shoulder, and it draped down across the bodice.

"It's breathtaking." I motioned to the veil. "It seems a bit plain in comparison."

Hafza scoffed. "That's only because Dhamar will remove it before the feast. This has nothing to do with you, Amira, and everything to do with how it makes Malek Nadar and the council look to the other officials of Taletha."

"So, this whole thing is another political statement?" I asked.

"Ah, she is learning." Hafza added more pink powder to my cheeks where my tears had ruined her earlier work. "Yes, as Dhamar's wife, you've become another pawn for them to move around their game board."

I bit the inside of my cheek, trying to cool the simmering anger I had toward the malek and his council. I didn't like how they controlled my husband, and I was already tired of being a pawn. I wasn't about to let them control me a moment longer than necessary.

Hafza dabbed perfume on my neck and behind my ears. It smelled like jasmine. It was strangely comforting, as it brought to mind Dhamar's comment in the litter about how I smelled like my favorite flower.

Why does that make my heart flutter? Why should I care that he noticed?

The bells in town rang the noon hour as I stepped into my wedding kaftan. It was heavy, as Hafza warned, but it also fit me perfectly. It hugged my waist, flaring out the further it fell to the ground. The train stretched a few feet behind me. The sleeves clung to my arms and ended at my wrists. A row of pearl buttons marched down my back, and Hafza spent five minutes doing them up.

"That should be fun for Dhamar tonight," she muttered.

"Please don't talk about tonight." Heat flamed in my cheeks at the thought. He'd shown compassion on our first wedding night. But if he wanted more tonight, there was nothing I could do to stop him. Did I even want to stop him? Did I want to stand by his side, as he asked, and be the wife he needed?

I pressed my hands to my cheeks, and Hafza raised her brows at me in the mirror. But she thankfully didn't say anything more as she settled the comb of the veil into my hair before draping it over my face.

"Perfect. You are gorgeous, my amira." She turned me around, and I couldn't believe that it was me in the mirror's reflection.

Tears flooded my eyes. "I've never—looked like this before."

"You will render them speechless." Hafza squeezed my arms, her chin resting on my shoulder. "The malek himself will be green with envy that you are his son's."

I am Dhamar's. Don't forget he owns you. I fisted my hands against the folds of my skirt and drew my shoulders back. Yes, I was

Dhamar's. Yes, he might take more than I wanted to give. Perhaps he was even cruel at heart. But it didn't matter because I was the amira he had chosen. Like it or not, it was time I started acting like it.

Chapter Ten

Dhamar

I stalked the length of the common room, then paced back. The bells chimed an hour past noon. My high collared kurta choked me, and I tugged at it. The cream color of it hadn't been my choice, and I wasn't certain what the diamonds and golden thread woven across it were meant to prove. Thankfully, the matching salwar were free of embellishments, and the cuffs hugged my ankles. The fabric was loose enough to rub against my skin as I paced, heightening my anxiety.

"You are going to wear yourself out if you don't sit." Zahir's tone held a trace of humor. "Honestly, Dhamar, you're already married to the woman. Why are you so nervous?"

"Because this is a statement of some kind." I wrung my hands. "Father and the council must have something planned with all of this."

Zahir chuckled again. "Yes, they want to parade you around the people to ensure that you stay married to this girl. They want a secure line. You told me this yourself."

"But there's something else." I scratched my jaw with one finger. They always planned three steps ahead to ensure everything went *their* way. Father didn't care who he hurt along the way, not even his wife and son. The thought rankled now, leaving me helpless and fearful for my bride. Helplessness was a feeling I hated. I'd felt it enough to last me the rest of my life.

"Well, I shall stand by your side as well as the amira's. Saif and I will prevent any disturbances from becoming calamities." He gestured to the low table in the center of the room. "What is that?"

I scooped up the box from Mother, opening it and staring at the giant ruby surrounded by tiny diamonds. Zahir whistled when he caught sight of the ring, but the look on my face kept him from saying anything further.

I still didn't feel like I deserved to present Inara with this ring. Mother's one treasure from Šeri, her one tie to her homeland. Fingering the slender, golden ring, I took a deep breath. She wanted me to give this to Inara, so I would. I would vow anew to love and protect her, and it would all be all right. Father and the council would be happy, and I would win Inara's heart.

Just breathe and be strong. I pried my eyes open as I snapped the case closed and slipped it into the pocket of my salwar.

Turning to Zahir, I said, "Thank you for standing by me, my friend."

The older man smiled. "You will be a wonderful husband, and once you win her heart, you will be two of the greatest rulers Taletha has ever seen. Of that I have no doubt, my ameer."

I clasped his shoulder in thanks, but secretly wondered if he was right.

The Temple of Nicar was filled with people. Turquoise and black tiles were pressed into the red stone walls, creating diamond patterns along them. Further up, beams crisscrossed against the ceiling. In between them were painted different patterns in the same colors as the tiles. Golden vases filled with jasmine and sprigs of tamerice lined the steps up to the altar, while matching shallow bowls held floating purple lotuses and desert roses. Blending with all the floral, was the heady scent of frankincense waiting to be spread at the start of the ceremony.

I wiped my slick palms against my tunic before clasping them behind my back, my eyes glued to the ebony doors on the far side of the room. The priest stood at my side, hands folded within the wide sleeves of his yellow robes. He was younger than the market priest, and his eyes shone with undisguised curiosity as he studied me.

"What?" I asked somewhat testily.

"I'm just curious why you're marrying this one so publicly." His voice was high and whiny, grating on my already frayed nerves.

"That is between me and my *wife*."

His teeth clacked as he snapped his mouth closed.

The low murmur of voices drew my gaze to the doors once more. There stood my bride. Inara glided forward, hands at her sides as she stared straight ahead. Her dress shimmered in the dusty light from the large round window at my back. The maang teeka sparkled through the veil as she drew near and ducked her head, hiding her eyes from me.

As the priest began his opening liturgy—sounding only slightly less bored than the priest from the Market—I reached under Inara's veil and tipped her face up. She flinched, though it was less violent than the other times I'd let my fingers brush her skin. I itched to tear the veil away, but that wouldn't be possible for a while yet. Instead, I let my knuckle trail across her cheek, spreading my hand out as I ran it down her arm and clasped her hand. Swaying closer, I whispered, "You look stunning."

Her eyes flashed, her jaw tensing when she asked, "Do you like your investment, my ameer?"

There was that question again. She'd implied something similar on our first wedding night—that she was mine to do with what I wished. Did she think I *owned* her? Because that was the furthest thing from the truth. I refused to let her entertain such an idea. My father treated my mother little better than a dog. *My* wife would know that she was my partner and friend. We would be a team against the storms of life.

But you never told her that, never gave her a reason to think otherwise. Already I was failing at my duties as husband. There had to be a way to show Inara that I cared, that I was willing to try and be a good husband, even if I wasn't sure what that looked like.

The priest turned to me. His black eyes went hard as he extended the dagger and asked, "Ameer Dhamar, do you swear by blood and blade to love this woman to whom you are pledging yourself? Do you promise to cherish her, body and soul, until the day Nicar ushers you both into her heavenly dwelling?"

This was the moment I was supposed to say the typical vows every Talethan man said on his wedding day. But with my realization that my wife thought she was my property, I knew I had to say something different. I gazed at Inara—her chin high, her eyes cast downward—and said, "I swore that two days ago. So, I make a different vow to Inara today."

A murmur started through the crowd as I lifted Inara's veil before the traditional time, brushing a thin strand of her hair behind her ear as I did. Her eyes glanced up at me, her lips parting in surprise.

The priest's mouth dropped open for a split second before he caught himself. "Ameer Dhamar, this isn't done!" he hissed.

"But perhaps it should be." I took the dagger, sending him a withering glare. He stepped back without further argument.

"Inara of Mordova." I pricked my finger, letting the blood pool on my finger as I stared deeply into her eyes. They looked sea green today, bright and clear. "Yes, by blood and blade, I pledge my loyalty. By my body and soul, I swear to cherish you. But today, I also promise that my words will be flavored with kindness,"—I pressed the blood onto her chin, below her quivering lips—"I promise to love you with all my heart,"—I rolled my finger in a circle below her collarbone, above her heart—"and I vow to serve you, my *partner* in life, until there is nothing left for me to give." And with a final flick, I swiped my finger across her brow. "This I vow from this day on, forevermore."

Inara's throat bobbed as I turned the dagger toward her. The priest cleared his throat and said, "What vow do you have in return?"

"I—nothing so eloquent." Inara ducked her head for a moment before lifting her gaze to mine. Her voice was surprisingly steady as she said, "Dhamar, ameer of all Taletha. There is not much I can give you, not much I possess to show you my loyalty and devotion." She pricked her finger, staring at the bead of blood for a long moment. "But this I vow to you. I vow to stand by your side, hand in hand," she clasped my hand and smeared a circle of blood on the back of it, "and I vow to speak the words you need to hear." She pressed a dab against my jawbone, below my ear. "And no matter what comes our way, I promise that I won't abandon you. As long as you want me, I am yours."

Something hot flashed in her gaze, a sort of challenge before she turned to face the priest, who spluttered for a moment before saying, "Well then. I suppose that in the sight of these witnesses, they are bound by the vows they have spoken. By the word of our law, they are one. Tonight, they shall be bound by flesh. What is joined this day, let no man break. My ameer, you may now seal this vow."

A steady clap echoed through the temple as we turned toward each other. I removed her veil completely, signifying that she was wholly mine to cherish. Clasping her hands, I leaned in and kissed her.

It was more restrained than the kiss in Father's chamber had been. With people watching, it wasn't the time for intimacy. But that didn't slow the fire that spread through my body at her touch. Her hands settled on my shoulders as she hesitantly returned my kiss. Shock had me pausing for a single, breathless moment. Then I cupped her face with both hands, desperately wanting to deepen our kiss, to linger over the feeling of her returning the tender bud of affection that was growing in my heart for her.

But my wife had more presence of mind, easing back with a warning on her face for my eyes alone. We turned and bowed for the people present. Then, we strode out the door and toward the gate. Guards surrounded us, keeping the people back as we moved down the road.

"This is...different," Inara said, her eyes wide as she eased a step closer.

"We're nearly to the palace." I turned her toward me. "A kiss for the crowd?"

"A kiss for the crowd or you?" Her lips twitched but the rest of her face remained blank.

"Both." Feeling daring, I wiggled my brows.

That earned me a smile and a small laugh. "Fine."

"You kiss exceptionally well," I whispered before claiming her lips with mine. The crowd cheered. A few people whistled, and Inara laughed nervously as red bloomed in her cheeks. I spun her, clasping her hand tightly as I pulled her through the gates and up the stairs.

The council trailed behind us, all waiting to meet their new amira. I didn't release my grip on her hand as I made introduction after introduction while standing in the foyer. Lord Shaeen lingered overly long by Inara's side. His onyx eyes trailed down her body, and I found myself wrapping a protective arm around my wife's waist.

Couple after couple filed in. Besides the council, other Talethan officials and officers had been invited, as well as the lords and ladies of Rana. Two hours passed in a blur, and Inara all but sagged against my arm as the final member entered the feasting hall.

"Do you do this often?" she asked, hiding a yawn with the back of her hand.

"Not all that often. Father is not the best host." I offered her my arm which she took.

"We have three days of this?" At my nod, she groaned. "This is the worst form of torture."

"We don't have to spend all our time at the feast. After tonight, we might not want to enter unless we need to eat."

"Is it that bad?"

I raised my brows. "The wine flows freely when the malek hosts a celebration. Trust me, tonight and possibly the noon meal tomorrow will be enough celebration for us."

Inara shivered as we paused before the doors. The conversations were loud, the laughter even more so. I felt my wife shift at my side, her hand tightening on my arm. I wanted to reassure her that it would be fine. She wouldn't be leaving my side tonight, but I wasn't sure that would soothe her nerves.

"You look especially stunning today, my amira." I turned toward her and leaned in close. "You have shown me that Nicar does indeed bestow good gifts."

"Dhamar, I—"

She was interrupted by the servant announcing us. "His esteemed royal highness, Ameer Dhamar of Taletha, and his new bride, Amira Inara of Mordova."

Polite clapping followed us as we stepped through the doors. The marble floor gleamed in the candlelight. Dancers in sparkling tops and flowing silk skirts spun with scarves, the bells on their ankles matching the beat of the drum as the oud, ney, and mizmars players bestowed a thrumming melody to the space. Inara stared at the dancers, her lips pressed thin.

"What's wrong?" I whispered as we moved toward Father and our seats of honor on the far side of the room. They were padded with white cushions and blankets. Sparkling beads of silver, gold, and diamonds cascaded down the wall behind us, catching the flickering light and casting rainbows all around.

"Who are they?" she asked, nodding her head toward the dancers.

I watched them for a moment, noticing how certain officials and lords leered at the women. One lord even dared to tug one from the dance and out a side door. Nausea climbed up my throat, stealing my appetite. Now I understood Inara's disgust.

"I'll deal with it."

We reached our seats, and after I helped Inara to situate her voluminous gown, I quickly signaled Yusef over. "The dancers. Send them back to the harem."

Yusef paled. "They are here by order of the malek, Ameer Dhamar. To...entertain."

"They are upsetting the amira." I set my hand on Inara's knee. "Please ask my father if they may go until after we retire."

"Of-of course, my ameer."

"I'm sorry, Inara." I dropped my voice to a whisper after Yusef retreated to my father's side of the table. "It's the best I can do."

"Do we have to stay long?" Inara asked, turning her attention from the dancers. She already looked exhausted, her shoulders hunched and eyelids drooping. "I know it's the night to celebrate, but—"

I shook my head. "The feast, our dance, and then we can retire."

"Dance?" Her face paled to match her dress. "I can't dance. Not if it's like—" she gestured toward the women who were blessedly filing out the side door.

"I promise, it's not. Just follow me, and it will be fine, my love."

She slanted a glance my way at the endearment but didn't reply. Food was soon before us. Spiced lamb, stacks of kamoon and barazek, hummus with fresh vegetables, and many other rich and flavorful dishes.

But Inara barely touched any of it. Her hands fidgeted with the beads on her gown, her eyes darting around at all the people with a growing dread in the depths of them.

"It's almost time for the dance," I whispered in her ear, daring to peck her cheek.

She leaned back, but a ghost of a smile danced on her lips. "If I stomp on your foot or make us trip and fall, you were warned beforehand."

I chuckled. "Give me a chance to prove myself, Inara. I think I can keep us from calamity."

She shook her head and took a sip of her wine.

"Amira!" Lord Shaeen stumbled up to our table, clearly drunk despite the early hour. "Such beauty has never graced the halls of this palace! Our ameer is a lucky man indeed."

"Blessed, Lord Shaeen. Nicar has seen to bless me." I curved my arm around Inara and tugged her closer, protectiveness welling up as Shaeen leaned across the table.

His breath reeked of wine, and his eyes appeared glazed. "The offer still stands, Dhamar. I would gladly take her off your hands, and you can have my daughter as your bride." He gestured over his shoulder where his daughter danced with another young woman. Her orange kaftan revealed far more skin that I cared to see.

I turned back to Shaeen, jaw tense as I said, "As I told you, Lord Shaeen. Inara is my wife, and I am quite happy with her. Your daughter can find a match of her own. Perhaps selling her to the Market would be good, since you can't find her a match without bribing the husband-to-be."

Inara began to cough, taking a sip of her wine. But I caught the flash of a smile on her lips as she did so. It brought me a strange sense of satisfaction to have been the cause of that smile.

Lord Shaeen turned a peculiar shade of red, spluttering as he did.

"Excuse us, Lord Shaeen. It's time for our dance." I held out my hand to Inara and guided her to the open center of the room. The tables created a circle around it, all eyes on us as I placed my hands on Inara's hips. "Place yours on my shoulders," I guided.

She swallowed, her eyes darting around the room as the ney began to play a haunting, lyrical melody. I slowly swayed to the left, spinning her with me. Her hands shifted, her gaze meeting mine as I drew her closer then away and spun to the right.

"Is this it?" she asked.

"Until the music picks up the pace. Then, our left arms will cross over each other's chest. Our right hands we'll hold up in the air. We'll spin to the left. Then two claps, switch to our right hands crossing, and spin to the right."

Her eyes rounded, but I didn't have time to reassure her. The drums began to steadily pick up the tempo, and I crossed my arm over her chest, spinning in three rotations.

I stepped back, clapped twice and then moved closer to my bride. She looked up at me as I swung her to the right, her eyes glowing with—was it pleasure?

The dance repeated the slow turns, followed by pulling Inara in and then out. Her eyes stayed on my face, watching me as I guided her through the steps. The music rose in a crescendo then stopped.

Light applause sounded, and we bowed.

I turned to Inara and smiled, my arm curving around her waist as I led the way back to the tables. "You were wonderful. Was that really so hard?"

"No. Following your lead is easy, my ameer." Her cheeks flamed red, and she dropped her gaze to her hands.

I resisted the urge to sigh. Try as I might, she was still terrified of me and more frustrating still—I had no idea how to earn her trust.

CHAPTER ELEVEN

Inara

I was panting by the time we reached our seats once more. The dress felt ten times heavier than when Hafza had slipped me into it that morning. My head pounded from the noise bouncing around the feast room. I wanted to curl into bed and sleep for a day and a night.

*Except...*I glanced up at Dhamar, who's eyes scanned the room with a narrow squint. He stood behind me as I picked up my goblet and sipped more of the spiced wine. But even that churned in my stomach, threatening to make me ill. The touches, the glances, the kiss at the ceremony. It all felt too big, too much, too fast. Would he ask for more tonight or simply take it?

My throat tightened as Dhamar slipped his hand into mine and pulled me to my feet. The guests all stared at us again, and I swallowed my rising panic.

"Thank you all for joining us in celebration. The time has come for my bride and me to retire, but feel free to enjoy the hospitality of the royals of Taletha."

A cheer went up along with one suggestive whistle as Dhamar steered me through a curtained off doorway and down the hall. My heart thundered in my ears, so much so that I barely heard the footsteps of Saif and Zahir as they followed behind us.

The long hall to our rooms felt far too short, and suddenly we were before Dhamar's red door.

Turning to Zahir, Dhamar ordered, "Make sure we aren't disturbed until we request breakfast."

"Yes, my ameer." Zahir bowed.

Dhamar turned to Saif. "Please guard the amira's door. Both you and Zahir will patrol to the common room door and back tonight. No one should enter this hall without you being aware."

"I will not fail you, my ameer." Saif fisted his hand over his heart and inclined his head before striding to his post.

"Come." Dhamar pulled me in, shutting and locking the door behind us.

My legs shook as I took in his room. It was darker in tone than mine with more burgundies and browns. Surrounded by black netting, his bed sat in the middle of the room. A desk stood along the left wall instead of a vanity, while cushions and a low table like the ones in my chamber were in the corner closest to the door. Carpets with diamond-shaped patterns littered the floor. But what had me stepping back with a strangled cry was the giant cat that pawed forward, giving a growl of warning as he did.

"Inara, this is Gamil. I rescued him as a kit, and he bonded to me." Dhamar laughed as the lion bumped his large head into his side and growled for Dhamar to scratch him behind the ears. "He's a big kitty cat, aren't you?" I couldn't form words as Dhamar ruffled the dark orange mane. Gamil purred as he continued to rub against Dhamar playfully. My husband glanced up at me. "Here, give me your hand."

It took every ounce of courage I possessed to extend my hand and pet the beast. Gamil purred, glancing up at me with big doe eyes as I stroked the soft fur around his face. He butted his head at my stomach and purred harder.

"He likes you." Dhamar smiled, eyes sparkling in the faint candlelight. "You have that effect on people, my amira."

His amira. I ducked my head, focusing on stroking Gamil instead of meeting my husband's gaze. Nerves swirled in my stomach, and I was again speechless when Dhamar's hand landed on my arm.

"You don't have to fear me, Inara. I'm not your master."

"You bought me." I flinched at that ugly truth. "You want me to bear you children and that's it."

"No," he stated firmly. "That's not it." He sighed and stepped away, running his hands through his hair and down the sides of his cheeks. "What I vowed today, I meant. You are my partner, my wife, and we will work together. It's a partnership, in every form of the word."

His hand reached out, palm up, like he had in the Market the day he chose me. I turned away, crossing my arms over my stomach.

Though I didn't fear him quite as much as I had the day we first met, I wasn't ready to take his hand again. To work with him meant letting him in and that terrified me still. When it was clear I wasn't going to take it, Dhamar let his hand fall to his side with a sigh. "But I can't hold both sides together, especially not in the next few weeks."

"What's happening in the next few weeks?"

I turned back around quickly enough to watch Dhamar's shoulders slump. He sank onto the bed, burying a hand in his curls as he rested his elbow on his knee. "My father is sending me to the border. The tribesmen are growing restless, attacking the border villages. They killed a guard, and now the council wants me to show them our power. It's foolish."

I dared to sit beside him. "In what way?"

"They outnumber us. Badly. If the council would wait a few weeks, we could rally more of the men from Taletha. No one in Taletha particularly cares about the tribesmen and their warring ways. If they war amongst each other, no one minds as they only hurt themselves. But since they're attacking border villages and towns, we can't allow that. I understand, but engaging with less than our best is just plain—" He waved his hands in the air. "They're also my mother's people, and I don't care to be the one attacking people that are family."

I shifted, uncomfortable with this line of conversation. "So, you're leaving...?"

Dhamar stared at the ground. "In two days."

Two days. I had only two days to get to know this man who was my husband, to learn about my new home, and then I would be alone once more.

"We're hoping a surprise attack will shake the tribesmen enough that I can come home quickly." Dhamar rushed on, not waiting for my reply. "I don't like this plan. I think there are ways to resolve this without war, but the malek's word is law, even for his son."

As much as it hurt, I was beginning to understand that this was the man I had married. He followed orders, bending them if it went against what he believed was right, but he still followed through. I rested my hand on his arm. "This is the life I married into. I will simply have to get used to it."

"I'd much rather stay here with you, Inara."

Stay with me doing what? What do you expect of me? I lurched to my feet. Dizziness threatened to make the room spin as the hot, heavy gown pressed down on me and a wave of confusing emotions flooded through me. I swayed, and Dhamar's arm wrapped around my waist. I hadn't noticed him stand, but now he was close. The scent of eucalyptus and sandalwood clung to him, a heady aroma that was distinctly masculine and fitting for my husband.

My hands pressed against his chest, and I struggled to form the words I needed when his hand, which was splayed against my back, tightened and pulled me closer.

"I want to change out of my kaftan," I whispered on a breath.

"Of course." He didn't move, but his grip lessened. "Are you going to need help with it, or will Hafza be there?"

"No, she has the night off." I stepped fully out of his embrace and smoothed trembling hands against my gown. "I will need help with the buttons."

He nodded and followed me through our dim sitting room and into my chamber. Hafza had left a lantern burning on the vanity, lending a soft glow to the room. I stepped over to the vanity and unhooked the maang teeka from my hair with trembling fingers. I could feel Dhamar edge closer, startling when his hand cradled my hip.

"Is this all right, my amira?"

The question sent that strange fluttering through my chest, and I barely managed to nod.

Dhamar continued, "I forgot to give this to you at the ceremony. I think we quite flustered the priest by changing the vows."

"*You* flustered him." My voice still sounded breathy, and I cleared it as I turned, my hands pressing against his chest once more to keep from falling. He didn't move his hand, his thumb rubbing against my side in slow circles. "You're doing it now, to me."

"Am I?" His voice was low, nearly a whisper. "Good."

I leaned against my vanity, thoughts spinning. This was too much, too soon. I wanted to be near him, craved it, to a small degree. But after stolen glances, brushing fingers, lingering looks, this amount of contact was like drinking a goblet of the oldest wine in the cellar—far too intoxicating for my own good.

"Wh—" My voice cracked, and I cleared my throat again. "What did you forget?"

In his free hand, he held up a small wooden box. The lid was open, and a beautiful ruby ring sparkled inside.

"Is that for me?" I glanced up and caught his slight nod. "No, my ameer. That's too much."

"To be honest, this is my mother's ring. She wanted me to give it to you to bring our families together." He leaned closer, his dark brown eyes level with mine as he whispered, "But even if it wasn't hers, nothing is too much for you, my wife."

A rush of emotions I couldn't name had tears pooling in my eyes. The longing for safety—comfort for my body, heart, and soul—had me curving my arms around his waist and leaning my cheek against his chest. A tear leaked out of my eye, but I ignored it. His hand on my waist eased up, circling against my back, and he simply held me for a long moment.

"Will you wear it," he asked, "and with it remember our vows tonight?"

"Yes." I leaned back and let him slip it on my left hand. It caught the lantern light, flashing brightly. "Thank you, Dhamar."

He smiled softly. "May I kiss you?"

"No." Free of his hands, my head cleared, and I pushed him back with a nervous smile. "But you can unbutton this kaftan so I can change."

"All right." He chuckled, his eyes sparkling. "It does look rather heavy."

"That's an understatement." I turned my back on him, and an irrational urge to run shot through me as his hands settled at the top of the kaftan. Right then, I was vulnerable. He could do whatever he wanted to me. I moistened my lips with the tip of my tongue as his hands set to work at the top of the dress. His finger brushed the nape of my neck, and a shiver raced down my spine. As he progressed, he touched nothing but the buttons, fumbling his way down the dress. His breath tickled the baby hairs on the base of my neck, and my throat tightened.

He's being so gentle, so kind. I vowed to stand by him, and that means being what he wants me to be. But what does he need? What does he expect of me?

Dhamar swore. "This many buttons should be a crime. They are so blasted small."

"The price of fashion, apparently." I giggled nervously even as some of the tension unraveled in my stomach.

He joined me in my laughter, meeting my gaze in the mirror as he smiled. His laughter died, and he pointed to the blood on his cheek. "Perhaps we should wash that off."

My heart pinched at the thought of erasing the visible sign of our vow so soon. The vows we'd said meant more than just the rote ones of the traditional ceremony. We'd chosen the promises we'd made today, and somehow, that made them more precious and sacred. My fingers trailed across the circle on my collar. "I don't mind leaving it be a while longer."

"You don't?" He raised a brow as he went back to the buttons. "I thought you would find it all..."

"I know the customs of our people." I bristled, angry that he'd assume I didn't value Taletha's traditions. "I *am* Talethan, Dhamar."

"Did I say you weren't?" he asked.

"No, *you* didn't. But others always have. My hair, my eyes, my skin. I inherited it all from my mother."

"And you're beautiful." His finger trailed down my spine, light as a feather, and I shivered. "Your buttons are undone."

Neither of us moved. I couldn't find my voice or the strength to do anything but stare in the mirror at Dhamar. His finger trailed up and down my spine twice more before he cleared his throat. "Get changed. Then come into my room where we can talk."

Talk. That was all? Or did he mean something else entirely?

Despite my buzzing mind, I did my best to not think as I stepped out of the kaftan and into the white shift that Hafza had laid out. I tightened the strings at the neck, but it still showed more than I liked. I didn't want to give Dhamar any ideas. This may be our second wedding night, but it wouldn't be any different than two days ago. I would make sure of it. Grabbing one of my blankets, I threw it over my shoulders before kicking off the tapestry slippers and padding across the cool stone floor to Dhamar's room.

The door was open, and through it I watched him throw his kurta over the chair at his desk. His olive skin looked a shade darker in the shadowy room. The muscles on his arms rippled as he sat on the bed, leaning on his elbows as he had done in the litter the day before. *He is a very handsome man*, my racing heart told me, and I swore in my mind. Yes, he was handsome. But my heart wasn't ready for this.

As if he sensed me, he glanced up, smiling as I tiptoed closer. "The gods have seen fit to send me a pretty angel tonight."

"No flirting this evening, my ameer," I reprimanded as I eased onto the edge of the bed, though I found the comment rather sweet.

"Tonight, of all nights, is a night to flirt." He raised a brow. "Unless you have something else in mind?"

I shook my head so fast my neck hurt.

"I thought so." He chuckled. "So, whose turn is it for a question?"

CHAPTER TWELVE

Dhamar

It was pure torture, sitting next to Inara and keeping my hands to myself. I remained on my elbows, watching my wife pick at the hem of her nightkaftan. Her hair was still pinned up in the little braids, and the lantern light added to her allure.

"You go first," she whispered, keeping her chin to her chest. My fingers twitched to tip her head up, but I fisted them and turned to stare up at the ceiling instead.

"Tell me about your childhood," I requested. She had made a few passing remarks about her life before, and I wondered what it truly was like.

Gamil padded over, resting his chin on Inara's knee. She ran her hand over his ears, more comfortable with the lion than she'd been when we'd first entered my rooms. Her stroking started him purring as she began to speak. "It was just Momma and me. Father was a sailor and took the boys out on the sea for months at a time. He only came home a couple times a year. When Momma died, he had no use for me. Better to make some coin than to be burdened with a daughter." Her tone was cold as she spoke about her father. She buried her nose in Gamil's mane, her shoulders rising and falling several times before she turned back to me. "What was yours like?"

I sat up, crossing my legs, and turning so I could face her. "Not much better than yours, I'm afraid."

"I suppose I did paint a rather bleak picture. It wasn't all bad." Her eyes met mine, looking blue in the dim light. "Momma and I had fun together. She had this little patch of courtyard. It was probably the size of the bed. But we loved flowers. Her favorite was the tamerice bush, as pink was her favorite color. I loved the jasmine flower." She smiled, relaxing a bit as she stroked Gamil. "There was a small desert rose bush that had the prettiest magenta tipped flowers. We loved that garden. The feeling of the dirt between our fingers, the sun warming our hair and cheeks. It was the one place where I could be a little girl, and she could be my mother. Not—" She swallowed and shrugged. "But when Father was around, things—changed."

"I'm glad you had a place that was yours. Especially since it seems that your father was..." I hesitated. "Neither of us has the greatest example of fathers, it seems."

"We'll simply have to make sure our children do." She glanced sidelong at me, a hint of red in her cheeks. "And from the little I've seen of you, I think you will make a good father, Dhamar."

She thinks I'll be a good father? Heat flared in my chest, and I wasn't sure how to reply. How could such a small comment mean so much coming from her?

"But now you must tell me about what you used to do as a child. Did you get into trouble?" She smiled, and it helped me to relax.

I leaned back against the pillows, tucking my hands behind my head and staring at the red tiles on the ceiling. "Remember the fountain in the courtyard?"

"Of course." She smiled at me. "You still have to show me that, since you did promise."

"Tomorrow." I grinned back, and her head ducked once more. "Continuing on with my story. It was the height of the summer, and the fountain was off to conserve water for important things—like man and beast." I scratched my jaw, pausing for the drama of it. "Well, I was ten, and one of the gardeners was wrapped around my finger. I convinced him that Father wouldn't mind in the slightest if we turned the fountain on for the day, allowing me to swim in it."

"You didn't!" Inara laughed, the action softening the lines around her mouth and setting a sparkle dancing in her eyes. Gone were the haunting shadows, and I found that I wanted to make her smile appear as often as I could.

Rolling to my side, I propped my head in my hand and whispered, "I most certainly did. Father gave me a sound scolding for wasting water, but I was dripping and cool, and so I bore it like the great man I thought I was."

She laughed, shaking her head. "You only received a scolding?"

"Yes. That may have had something to do with catching Father dipping his feet in it afterwards." I shrugged as she laughed again. "As I said, it was a particularly hot summer."

"I think I remember that summer." Inara settled against the pillows, her legs curled up beneath her. Gamil wandered back to his bed beneath the window, bored with our talk.

"How old were you?" I asked. While her papers at the Market had said she was twenty-two years old, some owners lied to get rid of the women in their care. Older women were said to be younger. Younger women were made up to look older. No one truly knew, sometimes not even the women themselves. If Inara's age were true, she should have been seven when I performed my fountain prank.

"I was nearing my seventh year, I believe." She squinted, tipping her head to the side. "Or maybe my eighth. Time has little meaning to me anymore."

Good, she's not much younger than me.

"But I recall that summer specifically. It was an unbearable one." Her smile disappeared, tears shining in her eyes as she remembered. "Father came home, sick from being on his ship. The boys too. It was vomit and fevers, and me tending them all in the unbearable heat."

"Your mother—"

"Had to work." She shook her head, her voice dropping to a whisper. "And it was not the type of work that a seven-year-old should have known about."

If her mother was northern, there weren't many businesses that would hire her for respectable jobs. I could only imagine—and didn't even want to do that—what her mother would have had to do to support her family. And what kind of man was her father, to allow her mother to do such work at all, but especially with a child at home?

"I'm so sorry, Inara." I reached over and clasped her hand in mine. "No one should have to bear that, let alone a child."

A few strands of her hair curled around her cheeks. They made me want to undo it all, run my fingers through the silky tresses, feel the softness of her skin beneath my fingers. I leaned back, forcing my gaze to the ceiling again as I fought my traitorous thoughts.

"It was what it was." I heard her take a sharp inhale, but her voice was steady when she asked, "Do you have more stories of your childhood?"

"It's not my childhood, but would you like to hear the story of Gamil?"

"Oh yes! What was it like taming a lion cub?" She inched a bit closer. Close enough for me to see her face from the corner of my eye.

Fabulous. Simply fabulous.

"It was a day like any other. I was taking my charger, Zaid, out for a run across the open wilderness. He gets restless if he's penned up for too long." *Much like me.*

"Well, we were flying across a particularly open patch, cliff faces on either side, when we heard this...mew is the best word to describe it, though it was raspier than a kitten. I reined in Zaid, and we listened. I knew that lionesses rarely abandon their cubs. Their mothering instinct is strong, and they'll even allow cubs that aren't their own to suckle. But this cub sounded weak. So before searching, I watched for a lioness in the grass. Seeing none, I warily began to search for this poor creature."

"You weren't worried she was still hiding, watching?" Inara had settled down against the pillows as I talked, pulling a blanket over her lap.

I shook my head. "Not very. It had been at least a quarter hour, and Zaid wasn't prancing. He has good instincts and has saved my life more than once.

"We searched, and there, in a dense pack of grass, was one surviving lion cub. He was incredibly weak, barely able to cry at all. The only way I had heard him was because his faint cry had echoed off the cliffs around us. I quickly tucked him in my cloak, and we rode for home. I was able to help him suckle goat's milk from a rag, and Gamil has been with me since that day."

"How old is he, then?" Inara looked around me toward my purring lion on his throne of shredded blankets and pillows.

"He's three. He's fully grown and will live until about twelve." I smiled over at him. "He's been a good friend, especially when the days of being ameer grow lonely."

"I—I would like to be friends." Inara's words, whispered as they were, struck me in the chest like an arrow.

Turning back around, I sat up and grasped her hands in mine. "I want that too, and more if you'll let me, Inara."

Her eyes widened and then darted around. "I—if that's what you wish."

I swore and tore a hand through my hair. Was she still thinking of herself as my property, as a possession to do with as I pleased?

"Inara, please listen to me. Hear me. You are precious to me, and precious things are meant to be treasured. I will not touch you as a husband until you want me to. Or rather, until you ask me to." I cupped her cheek, pressing my forehead against hers. "As long as it takes, I will win your heart, my amira."

"It's locked up rather tightly," she whispered, and I felt a tremble shudder through her.

I smiled, easing back from her once more. "I'm good at finding hidden things. Gamil is proof of that."

Inara laughed, a bit breathlessly. She turned her head away, a yawn that she tried to stifle with her hand escaping.

I chuckled. "Am I that dull?"

"No. It's just been a long day."

It had been. My eyes felt gritty, and a dull throbbing pounded in my temples. But I wasn't ready to say goodnight. She was like water in the desert—refreshing and reviving. I hadn't realized how dry and parched my life was until she'd been poured into it. I wasn't ready to let her go.

"Stay here tonight?"

She stiffened, her eyes darting from my face, to my hand, to the pillows behind us. "I—"

I squeezed her hand. "I made a promise, Inara, and I keep my word. Please, stay with me tonight. We only have a few days until I have to go, and I want to spend that time with you, even in slumber." Pain ripped through me at the thought of leaving her here without my protection. Father and the council could command her to do whatever they wished. Saif would be here, but he, too, would be under orders, and Mother was too scared to stand up to anyone to help Inara. My only comforting thought was that for the next two days, I would be at her side. I would teach her all the tricks needed to live in the palace of Mordova. How to survive being an upright royal in a world of underhanded politics.

I released her hand and rubbed my face. "Go to bed, Inara."

She stood but hesitated by the edge of the bed. "I'll stay, if you truly wish it."

Yes. "What do you wish?"

"I wish to remove the pins from my hair." She stared at the floor. "And then we will see."

Trying to hide how much those words hurt, I nodded. "Go."

After she disappeared through the door, I pulled back the blankets, knowing she wouldn't come back. She was as timid as a gazelle. The slightest movement startled her. Any comment of her beauty and grace had her flinching away.

I sighed, moving to wash the blood—Inara's blood—from my hand and cheek. It felt symbolic of my failure, somehow. I'd vowed to protect her, cherish her, but I couldn't even come close without her panicking. Perhaps that wasn't my fault, but it still hurt.

Wanting tomorrow to come quickly, I blew out the lantern and climbed into bed. The soft mattress gave beneath me, revealing how sore my muscles were. It had been a long, tense day. Exhaustion had my eyes slipping closed, sleep teasing the corners of my mind.

It vanished the moment the mattress shifted, and cold toes brushed my own. I rolled to my side. Inara was curled on her side, her back to me. The blankets were fisted in her hand, drawn up under her chin. Her blonde hair cascaded across the pillows, glowing in the moonlight that poured in through the window.

I shifted, and she shivered.

"Are you cold?" I asked.

"A little," she whispered.

I scooted closer, but still didn't touch her. This moment felt fragile. One wrong move, and she would run back to her room, leaving me alone in the dark. Pulling my arm out from under the sheets, I let it wrap over her, keeping the blanket between us.

"Is this all right, my amira?"

She shivered again as I pulled her back against my chest. Beneath the blanket, I could feel the rise and fall of her chest, her heart beating as rapidly as my own.

"Yes," she whispered.

I would take it. If this was all she could give me, I would embrace it, embrace her. If I had learned anything about her during our talking, it was this—her heart had been trampled in many different ways. It was torn to shreds that I knew I couldn't piece back together. But despite all of that, I knew I wouldn't—couldn't—stop fighting for her love. I would do almost anything for a sliver of affection, a piece of her heart.

With Inara wrapped lightly in my embrace, I wasn't certain I'd be able to fall asleep. But with the sound of Gamil's purring, Inara's steady breathing, and the warmth of her body next to mine, I soon drifted off into a dreamless slumber.

CHAPTER THIRTEEN

Inara

Something was wrapped around my waist.

I jerked awake, panic clawing at my throat as I rolled away from whomever or whatever was holding me. The blankets tangled around my arms and legs, causing my breathing to become short and sporadic. Reaching out a hand to balance myself, I was greeted with nothing but air.

Blinking, I stared up at the red ceiling and a half-asleep Dhamar peering over the edge of the bed.

"Did you—" He smacked his lips together and roughed his hand over his face. "Did you just fall out of bed?"

I groaned and covered my face with my hands as the memories of the day before rushed into my mind. The wedding, the dancing, how I'd fallen asleep with Dhamar last night.

"Inara? Are you injured?" The bed creaked, and then he gently pulled my hands away from my face. His brows furrowed as he looked for some sign that I was hurt.

"Nothing but my pride, and I didn't have much of that left to begin with." I forced a smile as I pushed into a sitting position. "That was a rather rude awakening."

He chuckled. "It was indeed. Shall we try again?"

"Of course." I smoothed my hands over my nightkaftan. "Good morning, Dhamar."

"Good morning, Inara." Something sparked in his eyes, and I looked away as he asked, "Did you sleep well?"

"Very." I smiled, realizing it was true. Though I had been terrified of climbing into bed with Dhamar, scared that he might take back his promise, once his arm had settled about me, I'd quickly fallen into slumber. He made me feel safe and secure. Perhaps I was even beginning to trust him? Turning toward him, I asked, "And how did you sleep?"

"Quite well. You blessedly don't toss and turn." He stood and offered me his hand. "I've heard that can make or break a marriage."

I smiled as he helped me to my feet. "Where did you hear that?"

"Zahir. Although he may not be the best choice when it comes to advice on women since he has yet to marry."

A laugh slipped out, and Dhamar's smile widened enough to make his dimple appear. He squeezed my hand before dropping it.

"Go dress and then meet me in the common room. I'll see that breakfast is brought up for us."

"Thank you." My heart warmed at his tenderness, at the simple tasks he was willing to do. Who was this man that was so considerate of my needs, and how had I been so fortunate to marry him?

"Inara?" I paused by the door, turning to look over my shoulder at Dhamar. His voice grew husky as he said, "Thank you for staying with me last night."

Heat climbed into my face, and I dropped my gaze to my bare toes. "You are my husband."

"Yes, but you didn't have to do it. There is a reason for the separate rooms."

I looked up at him, but he was staring at the bed, a peculiar expression on his face. "Are *you* all right, Dhamar?"

He startled, as if he'd forgotten that I was there. "No one besides Zahir has asked me that question in ages."

Feeling a tiny bit bold, I stepped closer. I linked my pinkie with his, the back of our hands brushing. Tingles shot up my arms like fire against parchment, and I nearly pulled back from the contact. But I didn't. Rather, I gazed up at Dhamar, my heart aching at the loneliness I was just beginning to see in the depths of his gaze. His fathomless brown eyes, as deep as the Eastern Seas, seemed to pull me in. The sorrow, the pain. He was as broken as me, yet in a way I didn't understand.

"Have you been honest with Zahir?" I asked, my voice a bit scratchy as I stared into his pain-filled face.

"No. I'm the ameer. I have to be strong."

That made my heart ache even more.

"It is not weakness to admit you're not fine, my ameer." I dropped his hand and moved to the door. "I think that sometimes it takes the strongest people in the world to admit they're not all right."

The door closed, and I hurried to my room. I moved to the narrow closet and found a burgundy kameez. Pulling it and the matching salwar on, I then brushed my hair and twisted it into a braid over my shoulder. I looked in the mirror. The sun pouring in through the window caught the ruby in my ring. I held it up, twisting it to and fro to let the light dance across the walls. It truly was stunning. The ruby had been cut into an oval. The gold around it had been fashioned into a ten-point star, each point holding a small diamond. It was beautiful, elegant, and fit my finger perfectly.

I didn't deserve it. Once he knew of my past, of my broken mess of a life, he would run. I was tainted, and unworthy of a man like Dhamar, no matter how much I craved him.

A knock sounded on the door to the common room, and when I opened it, I found Dhamar standing there. He smiled at me, taking me in as he said, "You look beautiful this morning, my amira."

"Thank you." I tried to smile, but it felt brittle.

Once he knows the truth, this beautiful daydream will be over.

Dhamar guided me to a low table and helped me sit on the cushions. The food spread before us was copious. Hummus and foul dip sat next to a platter of pita bread. Falafels with steam still wafting from them made my mouth water. The air held the tang of garlic and herbs, and my stomach rumbled loudly.

Dhamar picked up a piece of kamoon, the jelly thick on it, and placed it on my plate. "Your stomach says it's starving."

"Only because I barely ate a thing yesterday." I chuckled and bit into the soft bread with a groan of contentment.

Dhamar laughed as he placed a few falafels on my plate and a scoop of hummus. Suddenly, he froze, a look of horror flashing across his face. "You do like all this food, yes?"

I nodded, my mouth too full of kamoon to answer. His shoulders relaxed, and he went back to serving the both of us. I watched, fascinated by this man who was so gentle, yet so strong. Though he disagreed with his father and the council, he was still respectful. Though he was my husband, he didn't demand things from me that I wasn't comfortable giving—even if it was his right to do so. Dhamar was a noble man.

Dhamar glanced at me as he chewed a bite of pita and foul. "What are you thinking?"

"May I ask you a question?"

"Is it your turn?" A teasing glint was in his gaze.

I tossed my braid over my shoulder and leaned in towards the table. "It is now."

Dhamar laughed before gesturing toward me. "Ask away, Amira."

"It's—personal."

He raised his brows at me. "You may still ask it. I am your husband, after all."

"Will you—tell me about your mother?" I asked. "She wasn't at our wedding, was she? If she was, I didn't see her."

A dark look crossed Dhamar's face as he glowered down at his plate of food. "No, Father forbade it."

"He wouldn't let your own mother attend your wedding?"

Dhamar's head snapped up, that mask of cold and stone sliding into place. "He forced me to marry, then had a witness watch as I made love to you, Inara. And the fact that he wouldn't let my mother come to our wedding surprises you?"

His bluntness had me clearing my throat and dropping my gaze. I had touched upon a tender topic. Dhamar's anger wasn't directed at me, I knew, but it didn't lessen the sting of his words. I ran my fingernail along the edge of the table, trying and failing to think of what to say next.

I cleared my throat again. "Never mind that question, my ameer. Let's talk about something more pleasant."

I shoved a bite of hummus and pita into my mouth as Dhamar sighed. "Forgive me, Inara. My temper wasn't directed at you."

"I know," I hurried to assure, "but it appears that this is a topic for later."

"We don't have many chances for later." He wouldn't look at me. "There is much you need to know before I leave for war."

My food turned to ash on my tongue, and it took everything in me to swallow. I pushed the plate away. "Later. Please, Dhamar."

"All right. But it will be discussed later." He turned back to me, a softer expression on his face now. "I want to know—need to know—that you're safe while I am away."

"Is the palace that terrible of a place that you worry for my safety?" I ran my fingers over the collar of my kameez. "This is your home."

"This is not a home, Inara. It's the place I live. A home is a place where one goes to love and be loved. The palace has never been very good at supplying that." He reached across the table and squeezed my fingers. "But I will see that no harm befalls you."

"You cannot promise me that, Dhamar." I turned my palm over so that our hands were clasped. "You can try, but something may still happen."

"Then I will do my utmost to protect you, my wife." He raised my hand to his lips. "Nicar as my witness, I will try."

The words warmed me nearly as much as the spiced wine in my goblet, and that was a touch worrisome. Dhamar had found a chink in my armor, a hole in my cage, and try as I might, I couldn't seem to push him out anymore. I wasn't sure I even wanted to.

"So, my mother." He cocked his head to the side, spilling his black curls over his forehead. "You really wish to know more about her?"

"Yes, but not if it's going to upset you." I nibbled at an apricot.

"It won't." He smiled, but it didn't quite reach his eyes. "I already told you that my mother is a daughter of Šeri."

I nodded.

Dhamar scratched at his jaw, his gaze growing distant. "She married my father when she was sixteen, and they had me eleven months later."

"That quickly?" I began, but my husband's sigh had me snapping my mouth closed.

"My father takes what he wants. Willingly or unwillingly, he always gets his way." Dhamar's arm curled across his chest. His eyes still appeared glazed, and I knew he was caught in some memory.

He likely didn't realize he was cradling his ribs, protecting his chest in a gesture I knew all too well.

"What has he done to you, Dhamar?" He still clasped my hand, and I squeezed it, easing closer. "Does he hit you?"

"He used to." Dhamar hissed, pulling free and picking up his goblet. "But I'm stronger and quicker than he is now. Now he only attacks me with his words."

Like ordering him to marry me. I looked down at my half-eaten plate.

"I'm fine. I survived." His voice held a lightness I knew was forced. He was trying for normalcy, and as I had been the one to broach the subject, it was my duty to redirect the conversation.

"What's your favorite food?" I asked.

"I think it's my turn to ask a question."

"But I simply must know this answer." I smiled, interlocking my fingers and resting my chin on them. I fluttered my lashes like I'd seen a number of girls at the market do, trying to look as utterly ridiculous as possible.

Dhamar laughed, low and deep and real. It stole my breath. More beautiful than any music, it rumbled through the air and into my chest, making my heart ache to hear it again.

Dhamar shook his head, still laughing, though it wasn't anywhere close to those first peals. "If it will make you stop with the—" he gestured to his eyes and shook his head with another laugh "—then I will gladly tell you my favorite food."

I had already stopped so I motioned for him to continue.

"It's manakeesh."

"Why?"

"It's heavenly." He smirked when I rolled my eyes. "I like it with some lamb, tomato, onion, cheese. With a bit of olive oil and za'atar underneath it all..." He let his eyes slide closed as he licked his lips and rubbed his stomach with a groan. "It's simply—"

"Heavenly." I laughed when he cracked one eye open. "I'll admit, I've never had manakeesh like that. We only ever had it with cheese when we could afford food at all."

Dhamar dropped his hand, his face going serious once more. "You should have never had to go without, Inara. No one should."

"I'm sorry, my ameer, but there are far more of your people starving than you realize." I sighed. "But there really is only so much you can do. Some people choose it, expecting the malek and the council to help and complaining when they don't. Then there are those who truly need help but are too prideful or scared to accept it." That had been my mother. Often, I would suggest we go to the temple and seek help. She always said no. Now I wondered if it had anything to do with her occupation. "And then there are those who accept charity or work to improve their situation as much as they can. But there will still be poor people, people who are hungry. Do what you can, but don't blame yourself for it all. You are one man, one crown. To change the direction of a nation will take time, my ameer. Don't ruin yourself trying to change it all at once."

I bit my lip and ducked my head, unsure of where those particular words had come from, or why I'd felt brave enough to say them at all. I wasn't important; I had officially been an amira for a whole twelve hours at most. Why would he care about what I had to say?

"What do you suggest I do, Inara?" Dhamar asked, surprising me.

"I—stop the war, first." I met his gaze. "Win it, stop it, do whatever you must to keep the bloodshed as low as possible."

"I would have no bloodshed." His jaw tightened before he sighed. Without warning he stood, grabbing my hand, and pulling me to my feet. "Let's go."

"Where are we going?" I asked, surprised when he interlaced his fingers with mine.

He turned, a mischievous grin on his face as he said, "Exploring."

Chapter Fourteen

Dhamar

I wasn't certain where I planned to take Inara, only that I wanted to get her away from our rooms. The longer we were there, the harder it was to keep myself at a distance while I continued to earn her trust. It pleased me to see the emerging confidence in her, her willingness to ask me questions, to speak truthfully with me. She was the bold lioness I'd glimpsed—somehow—at the Wife Market.

Perhaps Nicar did show me something. I scratched my jaw as Inara and I strolled down the hall.

"Where are we going?" Inara asked again.

I tsked my tongue at her. "No, it's my turn to ask you something. You've already asked two questions this morning, and I haven't had a chance to ask you anything."

"You're right. You haven't." She swung our clasped hands for a moment before catching herself. She straightened and began to glide beside me like the rania she'd be someday. "Ask me anything."

I asked the first thing that came to mind. "What's *your* favorite food?"

She giggled. "I offered to answer any question, and that's what you pick?"

"I'm a simple man." I shrugged, and she laughed again.

"I would have to say chocolate covered dates." She licked her lips with the tip of her tongue. "They're what I consider heavenly."

I chuckled, liking this light and easy banter between us.

"Now it's my turn!" Inara looked up at me, her eyes nearly sea green in the morning light shining in from the balcony on our left. Her braid slapped her back with each step we took down the hall and I swung our clasped hands in time. A look of shock flitted across her face, quickly replaced by a tentative smile.

"Ask your question." I nudged her with my shoulder.

"Have you decided where we're going yet?"

"Wherever you wish!" I gestured dramatically, bowing at the waist. "I shall be your guide for the day, m'lady. Where do you wish to go on this fine morning?"

"The courtyard!" Her grin grew, and I found myself matching it. "And do you happen to have a library?"

"We do indeed. And I will gladly show you both."

We kept our hands clasped as we wandered down the stairs and out to the courtyard. Inara hurried forward, tipping her head back towards the sun as she dropped down onto the fountain's edge.

"Oh, I've missed this." She sighed contentedly as I lowered myself next to her. "The sunshine, the bird songs, the flowers."

I breathed deeply, the floral perfumes and freshly turned earth filling my senses. "I must admit, I don't spend nearly enough time out here."

An idea sprung to my mind. There was a place I could take Inara tomorrow where it could be just the two of us, where we could talk and enjoy our final day together before war and separation stole into our lives. I swallowed the anger in my chest. Why Father was insisting on this war was beyond my understanding. A peace summit could accomplish just as much. But no, the malek demanded bloodshed, death, and war.

"Ouch!" Inara pulled her hand from mine, a worried divot in her forehead. Only then did I realize how tightly I'd gripped her hand.

"Forgive me." I buried my face in my hands and rested my elbows on my knees, rubbing my face roughly before clasping my hands beneath my chin. "I'm just thinking."

"About?" Inara turned toward me, her fingers trailing through the cool water of the fountain.

"Nothing pleasant."

I gasped as Inara splashed the water at me, an impish look on her face. "That is not a proper answer."

"You do realize I have the fountain at my disposal as well?" I asked, trying and failing to hide my smile.

"I am well aware of that fact, yes." She cupped her hand, waiting. "Now answer me: what were you thinking about?"

I pressed my lips into a tight line. Inara rolled her eyes and flung another handful of water towards me. Darting around the fountain, I waited for Inara to chase after me before scooping a palmful of water onto her. She shrieked, laughed, and then returned the gesture. Around we went, laughing, shouting, and playing. My heart soared to hear Inara's laughter. I felt her icy shield beginning to melt and reveled in the fact that she was comfortable enough with me to let down her guard.

Inara sat, panting and laughing, on the edge of the fountain. Rivulets of water chased each other down her cheeks. Loose strands of her hair clung to her temples, and a rosy hue tinted her cheeks. She still smiled, her eyes crinkling in the corners, and all I could do for a long moment was stare at her in wonder

"Are you going to sit?" She patted the space next to her.

I complied, my gaze still on her. My hands settled on the warm stones, not touching Inara's, but available if she decided to grab hold. I wanted her to reach out for me, to make an effort to show me that she wanted this as badly as I did.

"Now, please, Dhamar. Tell me what you were thinking about earlier." She brushed one of those loose strands of hair off her temple, and my throat tightened. She was a vision, beautiful and fragile while simultaneously being as bold and wild as a lioness.

"Do you really wish to know?" I found myself asking, shoulders hunched as the weight of responsibility began to press down once more.

"Yes, I do. You're my husband, and I vowed to stand by your side. To do that, I must know what's bothering you."

Her words from earlier that morning came to me.

It is not weakness to admit you're not fine.

"Truthfully?" I stalled, hoping she would let me be.

But she didn't. She simply watched my face as she waited, not saying a word.

"Truthfully, I'm scared of this war. Whether Taletha wins or Šeri, I will lose. There will be bloodshed on both sides. These are my people, Inara. *My* people. I want to protect them all, and I don't see how I can."

I leaned forward, my elbows on my knees, and hung my head. The crushing weight of failure pressed harder still, and I groaned, burying my face in my hands.

Inara sighed, and I nearly jerked away when her hand landed on my back, rubbing in small circles. "It will be all right. It has to be."

Nicar above. I couldn't think with her hand on my back. With the smell of her jasmine and honey lotion catching on the breeze and overwhelming the garden's floral scent, I struggled to breathe. Everything else dimmed around me as I focused on the woman at my side.

Clearing my throat, I stood and offered her my hand again. "Enough of this sadness. Let me show you the garden."

Inara's smile didn't reach her eyes, but she let me pull her to her feet. We were still damp from our water fight, but Inara wrapped her arm around mine as we strolled among the beds of flowers. She pointed to many of them and told me their names, or some memory she had with them. I kept silent and listened, my heart filling with joy the more I heard her speak.

"Which flower is your favorite?" Inara asked as we reached a small building at the back of the courtyard.

"Jasmine." I said too quickly.

Inara's brows rose, her mouth rounding in a tiny *O*. "Any reason?"

It reminds me of you. I shook my head, gesturing to the building when words failed me. I held the door open, and Inara entered. The walls were made of a thin netting attached to a wooden frame. Flowers and bushes of all kinds were crammed into the tiny space, and butterflies danced from flower to flower. White, yellow, red, and every other color imaginable appeared to be painted on their wings, and the soft flutter of them was loud in such a small space.

Inara spun in a slow circle, watching as the butterflies flew around her. A small board of oranges stood in the far corner, butterflies all over the half-spoiled slices. Inara knelt beside it and held out her finger. A butterfly with dark blue wings tinged with light blue and yellow climbed onto it, his wings slowly opening and closing.

"How beautiful." She crooned. She looked at me and smiled. "They're lovely!"

"We're fairly proud of the butterflies. They replaced the doves Father brought out here when I was younger." I winced at the memory of that particular day.

If Inara noticed my flinch, she didn't say anything. Instead, she turned back to the butterflies, exclaiming over their wings and the sheer number of them.

As we left the building, she threaded her arm around mine and leaned closer. "Thank you for that."

"Of course. We'll go to the library after the noon meal. We may want to change though," I brushed a bit of butterfly dust off her cheek. "We're still a bit damp."

Inara laughed, a sassy smile pulling up one corner of her mouth. My heart tripped, and I knew right then that I was beginning to fall for the woman I called my wife.

I was attempting to fasten the last button on my royal blue kurta when a gentle knock sounded against the door to the common room. Cursing my spiking heart rate, I called, "Enter."

Inara stepped through. She now wore a silk kaftan of aquama-rine, a lace overdress with twisting flowers and tiny pearl beads over top. The diamond maang teeka sparkled against her forehead as it had the day before, and her bare feet poked out from beneath the swirling skirt as she walked toward me.

"How do I look?" She spun like she had our first morning as husband and wife. She looked stunning then, but now she was breathtaking.

"As you told me not to flirt with you, I shall refrain from commenting." My now sweaty fingers slipped yet again on the button, and I barely stifled a curse.

"Here, let me." She stepped closer, and I struggled to keep my hands fisted at my sides. Her long blonde hair hung in loose waves around her shoulders and carried the scent of roses. Long, tapered fingers brushed my chin and throat as she secured the final button on my collar. My breath hitched as she laid her palms against my shoulders and smoothed out the wrinkles, before running them down my chest.

"You look quite dapper. The red salwar pair nicely with your kurta." A bit of color stole into her cheeks, and she moved to step away.

Quite by instinct, I wrapped my hand around her waist. "And you, my wife, are the most breathtaking creature in all of Taletha."

She hummed thoughtfully, her lips twisting in a ghost of a smile. "And here I thought we weren't flirting today, my ameer."

I grinned down at her, drinking in her nearness. If this was love, I could grow quite used to it, to stolen moments, just the two of us, laughing together and teasing one another. To waking up with my wife cradled in my arms, close and wanting me. Life would be bliss if Inara was always by my side.

My thoughts were interrupted by Inara's stomach growling insistently. Gamil sat up, his head cocking to the side as he stared at us. Inara giggled, and I followed suit, chuckling at the comical expression on my pet's face.

"You would think I hadn't fed you this morning."

Inara rolled her eyes, though her smile was still in place. "Chasing you around the garden built up quite the appetite. You're faster than you appear."

"I shall claim that as a complement." I offered her my arm, which she took as we walked out into the hall.

Zahir and Saif fell into line behind us, a comforting shadow as we made our way back to the banquet hall. I paused before the doors, trepidation churning in my gut.

"It's going to be...disturbing, Inara." I rubbed the back of my neck. "The parties get out of hand. Drunkenness and—"

"I have seen more than you know, Dhamar." Inara's face turned cold. "I know what men and women are capable of, and I can bear it."

You shouldn't have to. With a nod, I stepped through the doors.

The lanterns had been extinguished, and even with the sun shining through the red drapes that led to the balcony, the room was dim. A stuffiness—sweat mingling with the wafting remains of food—clung to everything. Men were draped over scantily clothed women, soft snores echoing through the large room. Exhausted servants lined the wall, waiting for the nobles to wake and demand more food and drink, a different woman to enjoy, or a place to relieve themselves.

It was disgusting. My arm snaked around Inara's shoulders as I found the area where the noble lords of Taletha lounged. Noble indeed. One of the girls from the harem sat in Shaeen's lap, nuzzling her nose against the married lord's neck. His hands played against the bare skin of her back and stomach. The sight was enough for me to see red. Shaeen was an example to the people, a man who should have been respected for being upright and just and good. Yet, here he was, taking advantage of a young woman who had no choice, who was forced to entertain, forced to do whatever the men of the court ordered of her. It was wrong and evil, and I had half a mind to say those very things to Lord Shaeen and the others who had girls *entertaining* them.

It was only Inara's hand on my arm that kept me rooted in place. Today was about her. About us. There was no use making a scene, especially when Father wouldn't back me.

Where is Father?

When my eyes found him, I wished I hadn't searched. There he was, pressed into a corner with a concubine in his lap, her legs wrapped around his waist. He was kissing her, oblivious to anyone and anything else.

Bile coated my tongue, and I stiffened, no longer hungry for anything but justice. But one thought of my mother had much of the fight draining out of me. Fighting this battle would only bring more pain to her door. And what of Inara? I was leaving the day after tomorrow. To start anything now would only hurt her.

"Perhaps we should take our meal in our room?" Inara asked in a hushed whisper.

I shook my head. "We have to make an appearance today, at least. Better now than tomorrow when this will be much worse."

"Worse?" Inara's voice cracked. Perhaps she hadn't seen as much as she claimed. "This looks like a den of ill repute."

"And you've been to such a place before?" I asked as we skirted around a couple of partygoers who were passed out on the floor. "There are many more layers to you than meet the eye, wife."

"It was not for my enjoyment, I assure you." Her face grew stoic, and I bit back another jest. There was no point starting a conversation like that now.

We reached the head table, and the servant hurried to greet us.

"What would the ameer and amira like to eat?" he asked, a bit breathless and nervous.

"Inara?" I asked.

"Manakeesh with tomatoes, onions, lamb and..." She furrowed her brows. "What else did you say you put on it, Dhamar?"

I smiled, chest swelling in pleasure by her wanting to try my favorite dish. "Cheese, of course, and then olive oil and za'atar underneath."

"Yes! That sounds divine."

"Very good, my amira." Inara's face went blank as the servant bowed to her before he turned to me. "And you, Ameer Dhamar?"

"I'll have the same. Also, bring out some chocolate covered dates."

"Of course, Ameer." He bowed again, and then hurried through the door that led to the kitchen.

I lowered myself next to Inara and tried not to look at the spectacle that was the royals and lords of Taletha.

"Are they always like this?" Inara shifted closer to me, her hand clamping tightly around my own.

"Whenever there's excessive wine involved, yes." I squeezed Inara's hand back. "But I try to stay away from it all. It's been a part of my life since I was old enough to be introduced to the court."

"When was that?"

More sourness filled my mouth. "Ten years ago, when I was fifteen. They had a big celebration. At that age, I was old enough to ascend the throne should something happen to the malek. There was wine and an extravagant feast. During the course of the feast, they brought out this young girl. She'd just been bought to be a concubine. *Fresh* was the word they used. They wanted me to—" I shook my head, and I dropped my gaze to the table. "That was the first time I lied to avoid my father's will."

"Fifteen?" Inara's grip tightened.

"She was so scared; shaking like a leaf and babbling uncontrollably." Her fear was the reason I'd married Hafza as quickly as possible when I turned eighteen. If I were married, I wouldn't have to endure women forced on me. Oh, they tried. But I refused, claiming I was happy with my wife. Little did they know, I never slept in the same room as Hafza, never touched her. Three years later, we were no longer married, and she had a job as a maid—far too feisty for Father and the council to want her.

Four brides later—four rescued women—and Inara was here, holding my hand and lending me her strength. I turned my hand over as the servant returned with the platters of manakeesh and the bowl of chocolate dates.

Inara plucked a date and held it out toward me. "These are the biggest dates I've ever seen!"

"Yes. Quite large." I lowered my head and bit into the dessert she offered. Heat spread down my limbs and desire stirred in my chest as she gasped in surprise. Mentally I chanted, *Stop, stop, stop,* as I plucked the other half of the fruit from her hand and nodded in agreement. "And very delicious."

Inara smiled, color blotching her cheeks, before she turned and cut into the manakeesh. She closed her eyes, chewing slowly as she hummed in contentment. "This *is* divine."

"Told you so." I bumped her shoulder with mine, and quietly we went to work on our noon meal.

But all the while, my mind was busy thinking of impossible scenarios while my heart longed for the trust and love of the woman at my side more with each passing minute.

Chapter Fifteen

Inara

Dhamar was wound tight as we ate, the slightest sound causing him to stiffen more. It set me on edge, too. The Market had been bad, but at least we had guards. The owners of the elite Markets hadn't wanted their wares damaged, so they had kept hold of the men entering to a small degree. Here, however, the room reeked of cruelty and evil. The men did whatever they pleased, and a few cries of pain reached the table where Dhamar and I sat.

I forced myself to finish my manakeesh. Dhamar was right, it was delicious, though my stomach rebelled at the food as the deplorable revelry continued around us. If we had been in our rooms, it would have been a far more pleasant meal all around.

Popping a date in my mouth, I reached out and squeezed my husband's hand. He looked down at me, and I could see the war in his eyes.

"Let's go to the library. We made our appearance here, and the servants can relay that we came since no one is paying us much mind." A yelp echoed in the room, and I squeezed my eyes shut, memories I didn't want to remember coming to light. "Please, Dhamar. Let's leave."

Without a word, he threaded his fingers with mine, and we stood. I couldn't help but notice that he had barely touched his food. Was he, perhaps, as disgusted by this as me? Guiding me around the edge of the room and out the door, he relaxed as we strode down the hall.

"I'm sorry," he said after a few minutes. "No one should have to endure that."

"Least of all you." I leaned closer. "Honestly, I'm—astonished by you."

He glanced down, a skeptical look on his face. "Why?"

"You've endured that for years." A shiver snuck down my back. "I wouldn't have been strong enough to face that scene over and over again."

Dhamar's lips pressed thin, and he shrugged.

A strained silence settled over us as we walked. I wanted to understand more about this man, what he'd faced at the hand of the malek and the lords. But prying meant I would have to share as well. Share the truth about my past and the pain inflicted on both my heart and body.

My chest tightened, memories pushing for recognition. I laid a trembling hand over my heart as Jamal's leering face stared down at me. Pressing me in a way that made me seem unloving if I didn't agree.

Tightening my hold on Dhamar's hand, I buried those memories. I wouldn't think about them, not now. Instead, I turned my attention back to the man at my side and the narrow door we were stopping before.

"Is this it?" I asked, underwhelmed by the plain brown door. Nothing ornate or sparkling adorned it, and a plain curved handle led the way in.

Dhamar's lips quirked up. "As with many things, it's not what's on the outside but on the inside that counts."

He reached out, and the door ghosted open on silent hinges. A single lantern hung right inside, a scribe snoozing beneath it. His snores echoed around the dimly lit room, and every so often, a mumbled word slipped out.

"Bahis?" Dhamar shook the man's shoulder.

He startled awake with an exclamation of, "Not while there's still breath in my body!"

I stifled a laugh and pressed my hand to my lips.

"Beg pardon, ameer." Bahis rubbed his fingers in his eyes. "I don't get many visitors, and I certainly wasn't expecting your highness this day."

"My wife wished to visit." He pressed a hand against my back. "She is interested in our great library."

"Ah, Amira Inara." The portly little man clasped his hands behind his back and bowed at the waist. "It is a pleasure to meet you."

"Thank you." Heat flared in my cheeks. I still wasn't accustomed to people bowing and showing me respect.

"Shall we, Bahis?" Dhamar reclaimed my hand as the scribe nodded enthusiastically. Turning to me, my husband said, "There is no better guide of the Great Mordova Library than Bahis. We are in good hands."

In the shadow of the lantern light, I caught Bahis ducking his head at Dhamar's praise. "Head Scribe Daris is more learned than me, my ameer."

"Perhaps." Dhamar agreed, then lowered his voice for my ears only. "But Bahis has helped me find scrolls time out of mind. He is always in the library, while Daris is more often at my father's beck and call."

I nodded my acknowledgement, but my attention had been captured by the towering shelves of the library. They stood almost twice as tall as Dhamar. Ladders leaned against them, so that the scribes could climb up and pluck scrolls from the top shelves. And how many scrolls there were! Rows and rows of them. The dusty scent of the room was punctuated by the fragrance of ink and parchment filling the shelves.

Words were painted on the walls above the scrolls, swirling script that said:

For the pursuit of knowledge, we yearn. For the quest of wisdom, we strive. For the love of the people, we endeavor to accumulate both.

"How beautiful." I pointed to the words when Dhamar raised his brows toward me. "I love that message."

"If only the malek adhered to it." Dhamar sighed before forcing another smile to his lips. "But yes. I want to be that kind of ruler; one led by wisdom and knowledge because he loves his people."

"We've only known each other a short time, Dhamar, but I can already tell that you are that ruler."

Another forced smile appeared. "I'm striving for it."

Bahis turned around sharply to face us and pointed to the shelf on our left. "This is the history of the maleks, going as far back as the founding of Taletha." Walking backwards, he gestured to his right. "And that is the section for scrolls on the cultural advancements of our people."

"Of which there haven't been many," Dhamar leaned in to whisper, making me giggle.

"Over there, is the section that houses the records of the wars and conquests of Taletha." Bahis waved as we turned the corner. "And my favorite section is the one on Nicar and her great acts for our people."

"Do you have any of the poets and stories?" I asked.

"Of course. That is along the back wall. That happens to be Ameer Dhamar's favorite section as well." He winked. The act startled me so much that I backed up into Dhamar's chest. My husband caught my arms, keeping me from falling onto the ground.

"Bahis, stop flirting with my wife." Humor lit the words, and I blushed.

The scribe turned red as well. "Oh. Beg pardon. I didn't mean to—"

"I'm jesting." Dhamar's hands rubbed on my arms. "Bahis is right. I do enjoy the epics and songs of our people."

Following Bahis to the back, I found a low table with a second unlit lantern and a few scrolls on top. A lounging couch sat against the wall, a blanket draped over the back.

"Here are the scrolls you asked for the other day, my ameer." Bahis clasped his hands behind his back and rocked forward and backwards. "Is there anything I can get for you, my amira?"

I glanced up curiously at my husband. "Anything Dhamar suggests."

"How about the epic of Kaan, the first king of Taletha?" Dhamar scratched at his jaw. "It's one of my favorite tales."

"Of course! Of course!" Bahis began to mumble as he riffled through the scrolls. After a moment, he withdrew a scroll and brandished it like a sword. "Here it is!"

I took it from him, smiling. "Thank you, Bahis."

"If you need anything, I shall be by the door." He bowed to me, then Dhamar, before trotting back down the aisle.

"What a funny little man." I laughed softly as Dhamar's hand settled against my back again and guided me to the couch.

"He is." Dhamar sat, and I settled next to him. "But he is loyal and upright. A model of the library's creed."

"To pursue knowledge, quest for wisdom, and acquire both for the people?"

"Exactly." He adjusted his position, his arm settling along the back of the couch and around my shoulders. "Is this all right?"

"Perfectly." I snuggled down against the cushions with a small smile before unrolling the scroll and jumping into the story of Kaan.

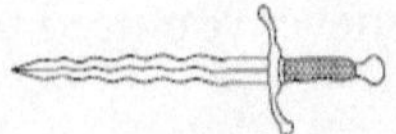

"Inara?" Dhamar's voice broke through the scene of battle, of Kaan raising the war cry as trumpets echoed over the field of victory.

"Hm?" I blinked, meeting Dhamar's sparkling gaze in the lantern light.

"Are you ready to return to our rooms for dinner?" His fingers brushed my shoulder, and I shivered.

"Of course." I glanced down at the scroll. "May I bring this with me, or must they remain here?"

"Bahis and Daris prefer they remain in the library. However, leave it on this table, and I'll inform Bahis that you'll return to finish the story later."

"Thank you."

Rolling up the scroll, I set it beside Dhamar's. We rose and walked hand in hand through the shelves back to Bahis.

Dhamar explained about my scroll as I surveyed the room one last time. There was a strange comfort in being around words. The stories within felt like familiar friends, a hug and a smile on parchment. This was a place I would return to soon.

"Thank you for everything, Bahis," I said after Dhamar finished. "This is a lovely library."

"The pleasure is all mine, Amira." Bahis bowed yet again. "I shall gladly welcome you whenever you need to escape into the written word."

"Flirting, Bahis." Dhamar's lips quirked, and I dared to elbow him in the ribs. He chuckled, that low rumble that sent my heart into my throat. "I echo my wife in my thanks."

"Anytime you need assistance, you only have to ask, my ameer."

We walked back to the rooms in silence. Holding his hand was becoming more comfortable. Being in his presence was easy rather than fearful. His smile and laugh brought forth my own. His sorrow made my chest ache.

Be careful, my head warned, but my heart tip-tapped its excitement in the question of *what if.*

What if I let myself fall in love with Dhamar? *What if* he wanted to love me? *What if* my past wouldn't ruin what was beginning to form?

We reached the common room, and I stepped in as Dhamar asked Saif to order food before the guard went to spend the evening with his wife. I bit my lip as I stepped into my room to change into more comfortable clothes. The purple kameez and green salwar made of the softest cotton felt light against my skin, and I sighed as I dabbed a bit of perfume behind my ears.

Did I dare tell Dhamar about my past? What would he think of the truth—that I was not as pure and innocent as he thought?

My hands shook, and I balled them into fists as tears pricked my eyes. I hadn't asked for it, but it didn't change my reality. I had been manipulated and told I wasn't worth it if I didn't allow it. That I was a disappointment.

Hands settled on my shoulders, and suddenly it was *him* all over again. I jerked away, my breathing short, my vision blurred. My hip smashed into the corner of the vanity, and I fell into the wall, my legs turning soft as I slid down to the floor.

"What's wrong?" Dhamar's voice broke through the ringing in my ears, but I couldn't speak past the terror that had my head spinning and my pulse racing.

Dhamar tipped my chin up, his brow furrowed before he scooped me into his arms.

Irrational panic had me squirming. "Put me down," I choked out. "Please, put me down."

"I will. But on your bed." He settled me against the blankets and pillows. I pulled my knees to my chest. I was safe; I knew that. Yet still my breathing was erratic, and my thoughts fuzzy.

"Is there anything I can do?" Dhamar's weight settled on the edge of the bed, and I tipped toward him.

"No. I simply need rest." I squeezed my eyes closed. "I'm sorry."

"You have nothing to apologize for." A blanket was draped over me, and Dhamar's hand smoothed my hair out of my face. "I'm sorry for startling you."

"It's not your fault. It's mine."

"Well, that I don't believe." His words were as gentle as his hand against my brow, both an attempt at soothing me. It didn't work.

It conjured memories of pain and fear. Desire tainted with dread. Would every touch, every intimate moment with my husband, be shadowed by my past? By mistakes I'd rather forget?

"Sleep well, Inara." He pressed a kiss to my temple, churning my already sour stomach. "I will see you in the morning."

"Good night, Dhamar." The door clicked closed. Emotions raged, and my tired brain couldn't sort them: desire and longing, revulsion and fear, love and safety, worry and despair. Tears trailed down my cheeks as I rolled to my side.

I'm sorry you married me, Dhamar. You deserve someone so much better.

Chapter Sixteen

Dhamar

A scream of pure terror jerked me from my sleep. Launching to my feet, I stumbled through the common room and into Inara's without a thought. My wife thrashed against the blanket, a sheen of sweat glowing in the moonlight.

"Inara?" I edged to the bed as she whimpered.

"Please stop! Stop! I don't want it!"

Her words pierced my heart. Was that toward me? Or some phantom haunting her sleep? I reached out and grabbed her hand, squeezing it. "Inara, wake up. It's only a night terror."

She gasped, her breathing so short I thought she might hyperventilate. Then she groaned as if in pain.

"Is she all right, Ameer?" Zahir stood at my side, his forehead wrinkled with worry. "What is plaguing her?"

"I don't know."

I winced as Inara screamed, "Stop!"

"Inara, you must wake up." I cupped her cheek, feeling helpless. But at my touch, she stilled. Her whimpers stopped, and she leaned into my hand. Eyes fluttering open, her breathing leveled out.

"Dhamar? What happened?" Her hand rose to her throat, and she winced. "Oh, I remember."

"I shall return to my post, if the amira is unharmed?"

With a nod from Inara, Zahir fisted his hand over his heart and left.

"What was that?" I asked, adjusting my seat on the bed.

"A nightmare about—the past." Inara shivered violently and whimpered, "It was horrid."

"Would you like me to stay?" I asked.

"Yes. I—I feel safe with you near, Dhamar." She squeezed her eyes shut. "Somehow."

I eased beside her, and she curled away, putting some distance between us. It shouldn't have upset me as much as it did. Turning away is what she'd done since I chose her in the Market, was testament to some hurt within her. But it still ached. I wanted to be close to Inara. To have her confide and trust in me. To be what she needed when she was hurt.

With a silent sigh, I covered her with the blankets before curling on my side of the bed, tucking the blankets around me too.

"I'm here if you need me, my amira."

"Thank you." Her voice was a soft whisper, choked with tears. I swallowed my desire to fix it, and instead rolled away from my wife.

While Inara had no trouble collapsing back into her slumber, I was wide awake. I laid on my back, hands folded behind my head, and listened to Inara's now steady breathing while her tortured screams of panic still rang in my ears.

Stop! No, I don't want it!

What was haunting her? What about her past was so horrible that it tormented her?

I rolled to my side staring at Inara's rising and falling back. I wanted her to trust me. Yes, I needed an heir to keep from having women forced upon me. To appease my father and the council. But it was more than that. Being with Inara the past three days had awakened something deep inside of me. Deeper than the fleeting attraction I'd had with Hafza, and the primal protection with my other three wives. She made me want to be better, to fight, to rise up and show her what a true man would do for those he loved.

But are you a man? Father's voice bounced around my head, churning my stomach and confusing me more. *A man takes what he wants, places his mark on what is his. If you want this woman, claim her as yours.*

I slammed my hands against my ears, shaking my head faster and faster. I knew the truth. That wasn't love. That was greed and lust and control. Inara needed to feel safe and Nicar above, I would see that she was kept safe. She had been hurt by many—of that I was certain. I would not add to that list by forcing myself on her. Slowly, I would coax her. Like an easily startled desert stallion, I would persuade her to trust me. Even then, I wouldn't do anything without her asking.

Mother's voice spoke in my mind now. Softer and gentler than Father's, she whispered, *"You made a vow, Dhamar of Taletha. See that you keep it."*

I will. My eyes drooped closed, my gaze still on Inara's back. *From now, until the stars go dim.*

Something soft tickled my nose. Prying my eyes open, I found that Inara had rolled over and was now curled against my side. Her soft hand rested against my chest, her head tucked under my chin. I didn't dare breathe, could barely think with her next to me—let alone touching me. I swallowed, wondering what propriety dictated of me. Hadn't I just decided that I wouldn't push her? And while this was her doing, she was asleep. She wasn't aware of what was happening any more than I had been until just now.

Get up. Move. Leave her to rest. My mind screamed. But as much as it ordered me up and out, I couldn't make myself move.

Inara stirred before mumbling, "Good morning."

"Good morning, my amira."

"Did you stay here last night, Jamal?"

I froze, that singular name running through my head faster than a charging camel. *Jamal.*

"Who is Jamal, Inara?"

Her eyes popped open, and she sat up, her hand pressing against my chest. Her hands flew to cover her mouth. She appeared so panicked and upset that I wasn't sure if I should push it.

"I'm so sorry, Dhamar." Her eyes wouldn't meet my gaze as I sat up, tucking my legs to my chest.

"Who is Jamal?"

"It's someone from before the Market."

A strange heat tore through my limbs, and a gnawing worry that I wouldn't be good enough for this lioness at my side pounded against my temples and chest. Forcing a lighthearted tone to my voice, I said, "Should I be jealous of this Jamal?"

"You shouldn't." Inara turned away, swinging her legs over the edge of the bed so that her back was to me. "Not unless you're planning on walking out on me, too."

She stood and moved to her wardrobe; our conversation obviously finished.

"I'll change and have breakfast brought up." I stood and stopped behind her. Her back straightened, her head tipped down. I leaned closer to brush up against her back. "Thank you for letting me stay with you last night."

"Thank you for coming to help." She swayed back. "Though I wish you hadn't needed to. I should be strong enough to not deal with this anymore."

"I believe someone told me it's not weakness to admit we need help." My hands clamped around her shoulders, and I gently rubbed at the knots I felt there. "I'll gladly help you whenever you need it, my wife."

She pressed a hand against mine, her thumb circling tenderly. "I know."

I didn't push, but I waited until her hand fell back at her side to drop mine. "I have somewhere to take you after we eat. Will you be up for it?"

"Yes." She smiled up at me weakly. "I'll see you in a moment."

I pressed a quick kiss to the top of her head, before turning and hurrying back to my room.

After asking Zahir to order us breakfast, I dressed in a burgundy kurta with gold salwar. I tugged a white vest over it all, smoothing my hands against it to settle the trembling as I stepped into the common room.

Inara stood uncertainly in the doorway, shifting from foot to foot in a yellow kameez with light green salwar underneath. A light purple sash was draped over her shoulder, and she played with the hem of it as she watched me step closer.

"You look like a spring morning," I said as I picked up her hand and pressed a light kiss to the back of it.

"And you look quite regal." She patted my chest before tugging me gently to the cushions.

A plethora of fresh fruit covered the table. Warm samoon sat on two plates with mugs of steaming coffee next to them. I helped

Inara sit, and then picked up my mug. "We already know how we slept, don't we?"

Inara chuckled, eying the mug suspiciously. "What is this?"

"This is coffee." I raised my brows when she gave me a blank expression. "You've never had coffee?"

"No. What is it?"

"It comes from beans grown in the south near the border of Šeri. We grind them and then pour boiling water over them."

"Beans?"

I chuckled and took a long sip. "Delicious."

Inara sniffed it, then took a sip. Her face screwed up, and she stuck out her tongue. I laughed, passing her a small pitcher of cream and a bowl of sugar. "Try this."

She poured in the cream and then a spoonful of sugar. Once she finished, she took another hesitant sip and then smiled. "Now this is good."

We lapsed into silence as we ate and drank, giving each other tentative smiles and glances across the table as we did. It was a comfortable quiet, one punctuated with ease and companionship.

After wiping my mouth with a napkin, I pulled Inara to her feet. "I have something to show you."

I clasped Inara's hand as I led her down the hall and out into a narrow walkway between the palace and the wall. Our shoes scuffed against the brick lined path, the only sound in the cool morning air. This walk, her fingers entwined with mine and the soft huff of her breath, felt terribly intimate. More so than even our first kiss. This was a part of my life that few knew about—not even my mother. Zahir knew of my hiding place, but only to guard me from a distance. Sharing this with Inara was important, though I didn't fully understand why. I needed to do it, if for no other reason than to show her I trusted her.

"Where are you taking me?" she asked, glancing back over her shoulder, her lower lip caught between her teeth.

"It's a surprise." I winked when she turned back around, and her mouth rounded into a perfect *O* of surprise, giving me no small end of satisfaction.

I led her up to a small crevice that was hidden in the sandstone wall. Angling my body through the small opening, I kept hold of Inara's hand. She followed after me, carefully wiggling through so as not to snag her kameez. She blinked as we stepped into the sun. It bathed her in a radiant glow, and I found my heart stalling as she let go of my hand and spun in a slow circle.

"Oh, Dhamar." She folded her hands and pressed them under her chin as she drank in the sight before her. "It's a secret garden!"

I nodded. Smaller than the courtyard garden, it was no less full of life. There were tamerice trees in full bloom, their pink blossoms delicately blowing in the slight breeze. The purple-tipped desert roses, pristine white jasmine, and bright red blood lilies were clustered in small groups beside the brick pathway that curved in an oval around the green-tiled pool. Purple and white lotus flowers bobbed merrily in the water while the fountain at the center gurgled merrily, seeming as pleased by Inara's joy as I was.

On the far end of the garden, beneath two sprawling sycamore trees, sat a bench. A small cage with a few doves sat off to the left, and they cooed happily in the early morning sunlight.

Inara spun around again and clapped her hands. She turned to me, smiling radiantly as she said, "Oh, it's absolutely lovely!"

"I thought you might like it." I returned her smile, pleased when she took my extended hand. "When you spoke of the gardens last night, I thought it was time I showed you my hidden one. I like to come here when I need to get away and be alone."

"Do you come here often then?" she asked, stepping closer as I led her toward the bench.

"Not as often as I'd like," I admitted as we sat. "My father and the council see that I'm kept fairly busy." Bitterness leaked into the words, and I bit my tongue to keep from saying anything further. I didn't want to ruin our last day together by complaining about the one thing I couldn't control, no matter how hard I tried.

Inara braced her hands on the bench and leaned forward, making it so I couldn't see her face. "What does your job as ameer entail, exactly?"

"Paperwork." I teased, bumping her shoulder with mine before leaning back against the wall and crossing my arms. "But mostly it's obeying my father and the council's every whim. Though, I'm supposed to be learning how to lead this country once my father is gone. How to care for the people."

That realization was a burden that pressed hard against my chest. I would someday be responsible for the people and the land of Taletha. That's what the malek and the ameer were meant to be, the caretakers of the people. But somewhere along the line—whether it had been my grandfather or his father or even the malek before that—we had lost sight of that role. Ruling had become about what we could gain, what power it gave. It weighed heavily on my mind that I couldn't change it.

Inara tipped her head toward the caged birds. "Do you see those doves?"

The abrupt change of subject had me blinking rapidly. "Yes. What about them?"

She leaned back against the wall, a thoughtful purse to her lips. "I think we're both a little like those birds."

"In what way?" My heart tripped a beat when her shoulder brushed mine.

"They're caged. Hidden behind bars that confine who they truly are. What they're capable of. They can't fly, their song is sad, and they're...trapped." She paused, her finger rubbing the hem of her purple sash. I thought about her words. My heart ached just thinking that she felt hidden away and trapped. Yet it resonated within me, as well. My father stifled me, belittled me. I was a pawn in a game, and no matter how I tried to maneuver myself, I always ended up where he wanted me. I hated it. But I was stuck in the cage with no way of obtaining the key.

Inara sighed deeply, her head tipping to the side and settling against my shoulder. Every thought flew from my mind as my senses filled with my wife. Her sweet scent, the pressure of her head against my shoulder, the rise and fall of each breath.

We sat that way for what felt like hours, but was probably only a few minutes before Inara whispered, "I don't want to stay caged any longer. I'm tired of being sad and forlorn. No, I want to soar." Her arm slipped around mine, hugging it closer. "Soar with me, Dhamar. Where will we fly to?"

"Wherever you wish," I whispered, pressing a kiss to the top of her head. She didn't flinch. Rather, it almost felt like she leaned closer. We sat in silence again, listening to the bubbling fountain, the cooing of the doves, and the breeze as it rustled the branches.

And I knew then that I had never been more content in my life.

Chapter Seventeen

Inara

Dhamar's hand tightened on mine as we strolled back toward our room. I still hugged his arm close to mine, uncertain what he was thinking after last night.

The nightmares pressed heavy even in my waking hours, and though I tried to act normal and happy, I was terrified to fall asleep. Jamal haunted the edges of my reality, and I hated him more for it. I should be happy with Dhamar. He was a good man, fair and gentle, but every moment in his presence brought Jamal forward once more.

You don't have to do this, Jamal's voice hissed. *But I'd like you more if you did.*

I eased closer to Dhamar as a shiver coursed down my back. I tried to think about the secret garden, of his hand in mine, of the scent of eucalyptus and sunshine that clung to his clothes. Anything but the living nightmare that had become my mind.

"What would you like for dinner?" Dhamar asked, breaking into my panic.

"I don't care." I fidgeted with the hem of my sash, trying to calm my rapid heartbeat and choked breathing.

"Is something wrong, Inara?" He hesitated near our doors, and I pulled him forward, not ready to talk about my past nor my nightmares.

Once we were sequestered in our rooms, and Dhamar had instructed Saif on whatever fare he wanted for dinner, he turned back toward me.

"Are we going to talk about last night?" he asked, crossing his arms over his chest.

"It was just a nightmare, Dhamar." I sat among the cushions, staring at the swirling pattern of a burnt orange pillow to keep from meeting my husband's gaze. "You already know my past is not beautiful or nice."

"But it's part of you." Out of the corner of my eye, I watched him shove his hands through his black curls. "Regardless of the ugliness or nastiness, it made you who you are, Inara, and I swore by blood and blade to cherish you."

"You wouldn't say that if you knew, Dhamar." I swallowed the tightening in my throat as he knelt and clasped my hands in his.

"Yes, I would. I made a vow to you. Have I broken it yet?"

I shook my head, tears rolling down my cheeks as I closed them, unable to meet Dhamar's gaze.

"*You* are who I chose from the Market. I know my past doesn't allow for much trust, but Nicar above, Inara, I won't leave you."

"Why?" I blinked as I looked up at him. "You told me I was different. But why would you want different?"

"It takes a very special person to survive the courts of Mordova." His hand reached up and tucked a strand of my hair behind my ear. "And you've risen to it these past three days, my darling."

I shook my head but didn't pull away as his finger traced my ear. I let myself get lost in his deep brown eyes, let myself enjoy the pressure of his hand against my cheek and his fingers twined with my own. He was so gentle with me, treating my fragile heart like a priceless artifact in the treasury. Dhamar leaned closer, and I thought—just for a moment—that he might kiss me. And the strange thing was, I wanted him to. I wanted to feel the press of his lips against my own, let him tangle his fingers in my hair. Tipping my chin up fully, I met his gaze.

"Inara?" His voice was gruff, his eyes drinking me in as he continued to caress my cheek with his thumb.

"Yes?"

"May I—" A knock sounded on the door, interrupting whatever Dhamar had been about to say. He eased back. "If that's one of the guards, I'll kill them."

I laughed breathlessly as Dhamar strode to the door. It wasn't a guard, but Hafza. She sailed in with a steaming tray of shawarma and pita bread. A few servants followed behind with bowls of chocolate covered dates, faloodeh in frosted glasses, and baklava. One carried two silver goblets and a pitcher of spiced wine, which he poured for us.

"What word from the banquet room?" Dhamar asked, though his tight jaw and clasped hands made me think he didn't really want an answer.

Hafza finished arranging the trays on the table before straightening. "All I will say is I am glad I'm serving you and the amira."

Dhamar nodded once, his eyes dropping to the ground as he moved to sit across from me at our table.

"Anything else, my ameer? Amira?"

When Dhamar didn't reply, I shook my head. "Thank you, Hafza."

"Of course. Have one of your guards come fetch me if you think of anything you need." She bowed and then shooed all the others from the room.

I began to serve us both, though Dhamar continued to stare at his hands.

"Does the revelry of your father and the council bother you so much that you won't even speak to me now?" I asked, trying for lightheartedness, but failing. Dhamar raised his gaze to meet mine, his eyes holding that stony, detached expression that meant he was hiding. I wasn't certain when I had started to notice that look, or how I had identified it as hiding, except that I well understood it. I had my own way of coping, of hiding, and perhaps it was that common factor that drew me to Dhamar more than any man I'd known before.

"It does bother me, and I'm sorry I stopped talking." He smiled, but it barely turned up the corners of his mouth. "This wasn't how I wanted our last evening together to go."

I bit into a piece of baklava, enjoying the nutty sweetness and the flakiness of the pastry. "What did you imagine, my ameer?"

His expression warmed, and his dimple flashed for the barest of moments. "More conversation with my beautiful wife. Making her laugh and smile so that I can remember it during my time away."

"You do make me smile." My stomach tightened, and I dropped my gaze to my plate of food. "It's been a long time since someone has been able to do that."

"What makes you smile?" he asked, finally picking up his pita and shawarma.

"The gardens." I couldn't help the grin that sprang to life on my lips. "And babies—animals and otherwise."

His brows shot up, and my cheeks warmed.

"And a good story can bring a smile to my face," I finished rather weakly before shoving a chocolate date in my mouth.

"Well, I shall endeavor to ensure those will always be around to make you smile. Especially when I am not here."

We lapsed into the same silence we had shared at the morning meal, and it remained unstrained. It was the silence of two people who were growing comfortable with one another. Would we lose all that when Dhamar left for war and battle and bloodshed? I nearly choked on my bite of food, and I pushed my plate away with a bit too much force. It bumped into my goblet, sloshing some of the liquid over the brim and onto the table. I stifled a curse as I blotted it up with a napkin.

Dhamar eyed me curiously but was wise enough to not ask. Instead, he stood to his feet. "I must pack. Will you come with me?"

"If it is what you wish." I followed him into his room and sat on the edge of his bed while he moved around, gathering items and placing them in his pack.

Why did it frustrate me so much that Dhamar was leaving? I'd lived for six years practically alone, animosity on all sides. Saif had been my sole companion, and I would still have him after my husband left. I would be fine.

But what would happen to me if Dhamar didn't return? What if he died in this pointless war with Šeri? Would I be shoved into the harem, to be petted, pawed, and worse by Dhamar's father and the lords of Taletha? I shivered at the mere thought. I would rather die.

"Do you have to go?" The question slipped out as my thoughts whirled, and I didn't take it back.

Dhamar paused, the kurta he was packing half-in, half-out of his pack. His shoulders hunched as he whispered, "You know I must. The malek's word is law, Inara."

I was growing weary of that excuse. I crossed my arms, an argument brewing in my chest. But Dhamar was leaving for war the next day, and I didn't want this night to end in a fight between us, especially when there was a chance he might not return.

He finished folding his kurtas and salwar into the pack and slid the straps closed. Then he just stood there, staring at it.

What if he doesn't come home? The thought wouldn't leave my mind. If Dhamar left and didn't return, it would be just like my father all over again. And my brothers. And Jamal.

Suddenly, the room was too hot, heavy with the panic that he would leave and die, trampling what little of my heart I'd given him over the last three days. I stood, turning toward the door that led to my room and the safety to let my guard down.

"Inara." Dhamar grabbed my arm, halting my escape.

I stiffened and tried to pull away. My chest heaved as anxiety clamped its claws around my lungs. But Dhamar didn't release me. Gently, he turned me around to face him.

"Please, let me go." I gasped as he moved his hands up and down my arms, breathing in measured breaths until I mimicked him with equal calmness.

"Inara, this isn't what I want to do. Please understand that."

"I do." I tried to convince myself of those words, even as I said them. "I'm simply worried."

I bit my lips, staring at the gold stitching on his burgundy kurta. Why had I said that? He didn't need to think about my worry. He needed to only be concerned about living. About coming back to me and continuing to build our relationship. Whether that was a friendship, a marriage, or love, I truly didn't care. I just wanted to know I was safe and cared for.

His voice dropped to a husky whisper. "What are you worried about, my amira?"

"You're leaving." His hands began to rub up and down my arms again and tears flooded my eyes. Hot, angry tears that had me struggling to free myself from his grip. "What if you don't return, Dhamar? What will happen to me? I can't—I don't want to live without you. Not now that I have you. I can't—" Not thinking about it, I flung myself at him and buried my face against his chest. "I don't want you to leave me. So many people have left. Please, stay with me."

His arms tightened around me, and he rocked gently from side to side. I'd never felt so safe as I did in that moment cradled in Dhamar's arms. His scent enveloped me, a soft reminder of how close we were. Physically, at least. My heart knew a chasm still lay between us. Both of us were trying to bridge it, but for every board we laid, it felt like two or three were pulled up.

A soft sob slipped past my lips, and I tightened my hold on Dhamar. He couldn't leave. Not yet. Not when our thin connection was just beginning to strengthen. War and death loomed on the horizon, and I wasn't sure we were strong enough to endure it together, let alone apart.

But he was leaving—leaving me, leaving us. And it terrified me to no end.

"Please don't cry." Dhamar pressed his cheek against the top of my head. "I will try and return within a week."

"A week?" I sniffed. "You swear it?"

"Nicar's armies couldn't keep me away longer." He tipped my chin up, his thumb caressing my jaw. "I will return to you, Inara. Leaving, whether in death or by choice, is too painful a thought to even entertain."

He pressed a gentle kiss to my forehead, his hands settling against my waist.

"You can't decide when you're going to die," I snapped, trying once again to pull away. "Death chooses you."

Memories of my mother, weak and delirious, flooded through my mind. The stench of her body, the blood around her legs, was seared into my memory like a brand. Her glazed eyes, so like my own, looking but not seeing me any longer. I trembled, taking a step away from Dhamar.

"I'll be careful, my darling." He moved after me as I retreated, pinning me against the closed door. His eyes smoldered with the same heat as before dinner. It made my heart trip over itself and sent a thrill through me. He stroked my cheek with his index finger as he whispered, "I wonder, does this worry mean you care for me? Just a bit, perhaps?"

"A small bit, yes." A gentle smile bloomed on my face, and I looked up at him. He was so close I could feel the rise and fall of his chest, and strangely, it didn't fill me with dread. Rather, anticipation sent tingles shooting down my arms and legs.

"Enough for me to kiss you?"

My mouth went dry. "I—yes, Dhamar."

His head dipped down painfully slowly, inch by inch, as if giving me the chance to change my mind. His nose brushed mine, and he braced a hand by my head as the other drew me closer. My breathing grew shallow.

His lips were but a hair's breadth from mine, but still he hesitated. "Are you certain, my amira?" It was such a soft whisper, a kiss in and of itself. He wasn't taking, he was offering. I could refuse or accept what he was holding out to me. The gift of him and his tender love. And while I knew I wasn't ready for all of it, I was ready for this moment.

Without reply, I turned and pressed my lips to his.

We hadn't kissed since our second wedding, and I had forgotten the headiness that was kissing Dhamar. He'd been restrained the first two times, but this was an invitation for more. I lost myself in his kiss, in the feel of his lips exploring mine, of his hands against my waist and back. Gently, he pressed me against the wall, his kiss moving from my lips to my cheeks and then my neck. He hit the soft spot between my ear and my jaw. I gasped, a memory I wanted to forget springing forward, and I turned away, bumping against the bed in my haste.

"I'm sorry." I pressed my trembling fingers to my swollen lips. "I just...that was..."

Dhamar smiled, that dimple appearing in his cheek. "Yes, it was..."

I swallowed, trying and failing to shake away the old memory. "I'm sorry."

"You apologize so much, Inara." He stepped closer, and when I didn't recoil, he came to sit beside me. "You have no need to apologize for what isn't your fault."

"But I flinched away from you." Hot tears of frustration filled my eyes. "I don't want to do that."

"There may always be times you flinch away. You were hurt deeply by people. That doesn't simply vanish. I understand that things happened to you that I will never be able to comprehend. And that's all right. I care for you, Inara. All of you, including your trauma and pain. There is never any need to apologize for that."

There was no displeasure in his gaze when I looked up, but I was plenty disappointed with myself. Why had I remembered *that* moment with Jamal right when my husband had been kissing me? Jamal had left me, Dhamar was here.

For now.

I tried to banish the negative voices. I picked up Dhamar's hand and kissed the back of it. "I don't deserve you, my ameer."

"Nicar blessed us." He reached up and tucked a strand of my hair behind my ear. "No matter what the future holds, that much is true."

Tears blurred my vision, and I leaned against him as I struggled to regain control.

"Would you like to stay here tonight?" Dhamar asked, squeezing my hand. "In case you have more dreams?"

How did he know? I nodded, feeling vulnerable and depleted.

Dhamar pressed a kiss against my forehead. "Go ready yourself for bed. I'll be waiting here for you once you're ready."

I nodded, my face feeling puffy from my tears, my lips still swollen from his kiss. I hurried to my chambers, shedding my clothes and leaving them in a pile on the floor. I slipped into my nightgown and hurried back to his room. My hands trembled, uncertain what I wanted to happen tonight. More kisses? Curling against his chest and listening to his heartbeat? More than that?

Dhamar sat on the bed's edge, head in his hands. His back bowed as his elbows rested on his knees. I climbed onto the bed and crawled to him, wrapping my arms around his middle and laying my head on his back. It felt far too intimate, but I didn't want to pull away either. I was his wife. He needed me tonight as much as I needed him.

Dhamar turned and wrapped me in his arms. He pecked my lips before whispering, "Are you ready for bed?"

I wasn't. I knew dreams would come tonight. Dreams of things better left buried.

But I was with Dhamar, and he wouldn't push me, I knew. I was safe with him. So, with a nod, I slipped beneath the covers. Dhamar pulled me close, his body curved around mine as he held me against his chest. Somehow, despite his earlier struggles, his breathing soon leveled out in sleep. I listened to it. Perhaps it was wrong, staying this close when I knew my heart was still too shattered to give to anyone. It may have been selfish, but I needed Dhamar near me. Needed to be in his embrace as much as I needed air.

And so, I let him hold me, scared of what it meant for tomorrow, but not brave enough to face tonight alone.

CHAPTER EIGHTEEN

Dhamar

There was nothing as glorious as waking with Inara wrapped in my arms. Her hand rested over mine, tucked against her stomach as we slept. Blonde hair tickled my nose, and I let myself bury it into her soft locks, breathing in the rose scent of her soap.

Inara stirred, rolling over and laying her cheek against my chest. Slowly, her eyes fluttered open, bright blue in the early morning light that filtered in through my window. She looked up at me, smiling slightly as she whispered, "I didn't have any nightmares last night."

"No, you didn't." *How can she be rumpled and half asleep and still be the most beautiful woman in the world?*

"I consider that a good sign." She tucked her hand against my hip, and it took every bit of self-control I possessed not to lean in and claim her lips. She tipped her face up to mine and smiled. When I didn't move closer, Inara lifted her brows in question. "Are you going to kiss me good morning, or must I do it?"

"I didn't want to scare you," I said, relaxing when she smiled.

"Kiss me good morning, husband." Her voice caught. "You're leaving today, after all."

I cupped her cheek and pressed my lips to hers, trying desperately to not think about leaving her. Kissing her awoke a host of pictures of what our future could hold: Late nights together in bed, early morning kisses, long walks in the gardens, watching as Inara's belly grew round with our future children, snuggling a tiny bundle in one arm as Inara slept in my other. Joy and laughter, sorrow and tears, hope and despair, nothing seemed out of reach with Inara at my side.

I deepened our kiss, pulling her closer as my fingers tangled in her hair. How long could I stay here, with her, before I had to leave for the border? What would happen if I didn't go? They wanted an heir, and I wanted to give it to them. Wanted to give myself to Inara in every way. But after yesterday, her flinching away from my kiss alone, I knew she wasn't ready.

With a sigh, I pulled back, pressing a few pecks against her cheekbone and forehead. "Good morning, my beautiful amira."

Inara smiled. Her cheeks were flushed, her lips swollen from my kiss. I swallowed the temptation to taste them once more and sat up. Lifting my arms over my head, my back popped as I swung my legs over the bed's edge. Inara's arms snaked around my waist, and her cheek pressed against my spine.

"Stay," she whispered.

"I can't." I swore under my breath. "But as I said yesterday, Inara, I will return to you. By blood and blade, I promise to stay alive and return to you."

"In one piece?" she chuckled, but it cracked with a sob at the end.

I laid my hand over her clasped ones, breathing in deeply as I whispered, "Yes, darling. In one piece."

She shivered, but I felt her nod before she released me. "I'll let you get dressed and then I'll see you to the front gate."

"We can eat first."

I caught the wan smile she sent me. "I don't think I'll be eating much today, my ameer." And with that, she floated out the door and into her room.

I dressed in my black kurta and salwar, tugging on leather boots that I only wore when heading into battle. In the last war to befall Taletha, I hadn't had to fight. General Beeran had kept me at the rear, saying eighteen was too young for me to be at the head of the charge. It would be different this time, I knew. Father wanted me to lead the fight, to crush the Šerian people and show them the might of Taletha.

The might we don't actually have.

I growled as I picked up my scimitars and shrugged them onto my back. My fingers shook as I tried to fasten the straps, memories of screams and the scent of blood tinging the edges of my mind.

"Dhamar." Inara's voice jerked my head up. She stood close enough that I could reach out and cup her cheek if I wished. Her blue-green eyes studied me, and her brows lowered as she batted my hands away to fasten the straps herself. Once she finished, she gripped them and pulled me closer. "You stay focused. You stay alive. You come back to me."

Then she kissed me, up on her tiptoes, hand against the back of my neck. As quickly as it started, it was over. She slipped her hand into mine and guided me to the door. "Do you need some food?" she asked.

"No." *I need you.* I blinked at the realization. Inara had crashed into my life a mere five days ago, and already I wanted her by my side every moment of every day. But I had to go. *The malek's word is law.*

Zahir and Saif snapped to attention as we stepped out of the door. Zahir glanced between us before clearing his throat. "The malek has spoken with me, Ameer Dhamar."

His tone was unsettling. "And?"

"He has ordered me to stay here when you go to war." Zahir looked about as pleased with this order as I felt.

"Is he trying to kill you?" Inara hissed, her eyes going wide when all three of us turned to her. "I apologize. I shouldn't have said anything."

"No, you have every right to speak, Inara." I squeezed her hand in reassurance. "I was wondering the very same thing."

"Regardless of his motives, I have to obey." Zahir cleared his throat. "I vow to protect your wife until my last breath, Dhamar."

I clasped his shoulder. "Preferably, keep both of you alive until the war is over. I promised Inara that I would return as soon as I am able. A week, at most."

"That's only one day at the border." Zahir raised a black brow. "Won't your father—?"

"He may question it, but I truly don't believe we have enough warriors to push back the tribesmen if they're as numerous as I think they are. Mother said—" I cut a glance at Inara, who had grown rather pale at this conversation. "Never mind what Mother said. I will return within a week to collect reinforcements."

"Of course, Ameer." Zahir slapped his fist over his heart, and Saif—who had remained silent through this exchange, mimicked him.

Our group moved down the hall and out into the courtyard. Men rushed around, saddling desert mounts and collecting provisions for the encampment. General Beeran nodded his head and strode toward me as a stable boy handed me the reins to my stallion, Zaid.

"We shall be ready to mount up in about ten minutes, my ameer."

"Thank you General. I would like you to ride on my right hand when we depart."

Beeran's brows shot up. My right-hand side was Zahir's usual spot, and the general looked over my shoulder at my guard before nodding once. "It would be my honor, Ameer Dhamar."

He bowed his head and thumped his chest before turning to bark orders at the knights.

I clasped both of Inara's hands in my own. My heart ached to be leaving her. This wasn't how I wanted the start of our marriage to be—me forced into war and her left at the mercy of my father and the council. "Stay away from Lord Shaeen. Avoid contact with any of the councilmen, if you're able. Don't approach my father unless he requests you."

"I promise." She squeezed my hands. "I have both Zahir and Saif at my back. And Hafza. I'll be fine." She smiled, but it wobbled when she swallowed. "Just come home soon."

Home. Perhaps, with time, the palace of Mordova could become a home. Because home was wherever Inara was. Whether here in the palace, the slums of our city, or a tent in the desert, if I had Inara, I was home. She held my heart, I realized with a start. And with it, she had the power to break me or raise me up into something I hadn't dared dream of before.

I leaned down to kiss her, but right as my lips were about to caress hers, I caught sight of my father striding down the steps. Settling for a quick peck that left a confused look on Inara's face, I turned and swung up onto Zaid.

"Don't let the amira out of your sight," I ordered our guards. "One of you is to be with her at all times."

"Of course, my ameer." Zahir bowed his head.

Saif nodded. "I swear it. We'll guard her with our lives."

Inara's jaw twitched at that, but she clasped her hands before her as she watched me.

"Dhamar!" Father's voice boomed around the courtyard. "By the might of Nicar, crush the Šerian scum to dust! Show them that Taletha is mighty, and if they wish for war, it is war we shall bring."

I clenched my hands around the reins, not wanting to respond. But then I caught sight of Mother behind him. Her shoulders were hunched, her head ducked, as if she were hiding from everyone. What had he done to her over the course of the wedding celebration? I could only imagine, and it sickened me.

Swallowing the lump of anger in my throat, I turned back to Father. "I shall attempt to end this conflict with as little bloodshed as possible. If I find that they outnumber us, I shall return to Mordova for reinforcements. I suggest you have them ready, Lord Arqa."

The lord bristled at my command, but I didn't wait for a reply. Tugging on Zaid's reins, I wheeled him around and nudged him forward. General Beeran fell in on my right and together, we led the march for the Šerian border.

CHAPTER NINETEEN

Inara

With a growing dread in my stomach, I watched Dhamar thunder away. As much as I had enjoyed spending my days with him, life in the palace still felt far from certain.

Zahir stepped up to my side as the dust settled. He placed his hand lightly against my arm and leaned closer. "Might I suggest a strategic retreat, my amira?"

"Hm?" I glanced up at him, and he gestured with his head toward the malek and his lords, who were watching me with undisguised disdain.

"Oh, of course." I smoothed my hands against my salwar and moved toward the far set of steps.

"Inara! A moment, girl." The malek's voice felt like fingernails against glass, and my teeth ground together as I heard him following me.

"Beg pardon, Malek Nadar, but I am not feeling well."

"Miss Dhamar already, hm?" he puffed out as he grabbed my arm, wheeling me around to face him. His breath was still coated with the putrid smell of wine, his eyes bloodshot.

"Something like that, yes, your majesty." I tried to tug free, but his grip tightened painfully.

"Hm." His eyes raked over me, studying me like all the men at the Wife Market had done. I bristled, straightening up and catching Zahir's eyes. His brows were lowered in displeasure, and his hand clasped the hilt of his scimitar as he glared at the malek. The malek sneered. "What does my son see in you?"

"Why don't you ask him yourself?" I asked as innocently as I could manage. But deep-seated contempt rested in my heart. I did not like the arrogance with which Malek Nadar carried himself. While the way Dhamar had spoken of him already had my hackles raised, I found the way the malek was treating me and talking about his son most distasteful. "Will that be all, Malek Nadar?"

He gripped my chin, forcing my face toward him. "One last thing, girl. Dhamar may be your husband, but you both answer to the malek of Taletha. *Me*. If I speak, you obey. My word is law, and everyone is subject to it. Understand?"

I yanked my chin from his grasp, balling shaking fists at my side. Zahir was at my side now, angling himself between the malek and me, but I didn't cower. I raised my head high and met Nadar's gaze head on. "I understand perfectly, my malek."

He nodded as if satisfied then turned and toddled off.

Bile rose in my throat, and my legs shook. I grasped Zahir's arm, and Saif hurried to my other side. "Are you all right, Inara?"

I nodded. "My room, please?

"Of course, Amira." Zahir hustled me forward, and I gratefully leaned against his supporting arm.

The malek's words had shaken me. Dhamar had warned me that the palace wasn't safe, but only now did I realize how dangerous it truly was. The malek could order me to do anything—anything at all—and I would have to obey him or lose my life.

Am I brave enough to fight him? I wasn't certain of the answer, and that scared me.

We reached my door, but I shook my head. "Will you two come sit with me in the common room?"

My warbly voice must have conveyed how fearful I felt because Saif was already nodding. "Of course, Inara."

"It's not proper, Saif." Zahir halted Saif by grasping his arm, his brow furrowed. "We shouldn't enter the amira's room without the ameer present."

"I am inviting you," I insisted. "And if it would make you feel better, I'll call Hafza with some tea and coffee." Zahir opened his mouth to argue, but I grabbed his hand, tears pushing at the corners of my eyes. "Please, Zahir. I don't wish to be alone today."

He sighed, his forehead losing some of the wrinkles as he nodded. "Saif and I will remain outside the door until Hafza arrives, all right, Amira?"

"Yes." A weak smile graced my lips as I inhaled shakily. "Yes, that is fine."

I stepped into the common room, and Gamil lumbered out from Dhamar's room. He paced around the table and headbutted my side, a growl of displeasure emanating from his chest.

"I miss Dhamar, too." I lowered myself to the cushions and rubbed my face into his mane. Gamil began to purr and stretched out on his side as I continued to stroke him.

Why did I miss Dhamar so much already? He'd scarcely been gone an hour, and yet, it felt like days. Perhaps it was my encounter with the malek coupled with the unknowns of the next week, but I wasn't as eager to be alone as I would have been a mere three days before.

A light rap sounded before Hafza sailed in, her light green kaftan swirling around her legs. "I was told you needed some cheering up!" she said brightly, her smile firmly in place.

Saif and Zahir entered behind her, the latter taking up his place by the door with crossed arms and a displeased expression on his face.

Saif lowered himself next to me and gripped my hand with his large one. "I'm sorry you had to deal with the malek alone, Inara."

Hafza nearly dropped the mug she'd been pouring tea into. "Inara, you faced the malek?"

"Yes." I curled my free arm around my stomach.

"Oh, you poor thing!" Hafza wrapped her arm around me and leaned her head against my shoulder. While our intimacy was not strictly appropriate for a servant and her amira, in that moment I was simply a woman thrown to the wolves too soon, afraid of failing before she even had a chance at succeeding.

I choked back a sob. "I can't do it. I can't do *this*." I gestured around the room with a grunt of frustration. "I'm not an amira, and I never will be."

"You are more of an amira than any other woman I've ever seen here in the palace," Hafza argued. "You're graceful and kind. You've not yelled at me once since I started serving you. You also make our ameer smile and laugh. He didn't do that often before you. Isn't that right, Zahir?"

The guard started, surprised to have been addressed. But he smiled at me and nodded. "He is more himself with you, Amira. He's strong, but that strength is also his weakness."

"A weakness?" I asked.

"A person can only be strong for so long." He eyed me for a moment. "As I'm sure you know, eventually the weight becomes too much. It cracks even the sturdiest of foundations, and if the foundation is already shaky?" He clapped his hands together. "If Dhamar appears weak, it's because he's been strong for too long."

I dashed at a tear. "I miss him already. How is that possible?"

"Because you're falling in love," Hafza said as she finished pouring the drinks. Without waiting for an invitation, she grabbed Zahir's hand and dragged him to the table. "Sit. I won't hear a word of argument, Zahir! You're drinking some coffee with the rest of us—or tea like the amira."

Saif chuckled. "I'd listen to the woman, Zahir. She's quite persuasive."

"By the sands, don't I know it!" He shook a finger at my maid. "You forget I dealt with her when Dhamar first married her. I'm the reason she didn't murder the ameer in his sleep."

Hafza snorted. "Having you stand guard in the common room didn't deter me."

"What did?" I asked, cradling my teacup in my hands. The golden band around the hourglass cup was warm to the touch, and I traced the pattern with my thumb as Hafza winked at me.

"Dhamar's sweet personality of course. And I may have watched him practicing in the training arena. He's quite strapping without a shirt on."

Saif's mouth fell open, revealing a half-chewed piece of baklava, while Zahir rolled his eyes at Hafza's comment. But I felt a strange surge of jealousy at my maid's words. Dhamar was my husband, but Hafza had more history with him. She was married to him first, after all. I set my teacup on the table and traced the lip of it with my index finger, trying to tamp down the emotions that sprang to the surface far too easily since my weddings.

"Can we talk about something else?" I asked.

Hafza raised her brow but nodded. "What would you like to talk about, Amira?"

"Anything. Whatever you desire."

Hafza began to talk about her siblings—what she could remember from before the Wife Market. Saif chimed in with stories about Ranya, her siblings that they cared for, and his life as a married man. But Zahir said very little.

"And what of your life, Zahir?" I asked as I bit into a barazek.

He raised his narrow brow at me. "What does the amira wish to know?"

"All you wish to tell me." I smiled and was rewarded with the barest of grins in return.

"I met Dhamar when he was a lad of five. I was fifteen." He steepled his fingers, meeting each of our gazes as he told his story. "I was simply a squire sharpening my scimitar in the shadow of the stable. While I sat there, I overheard a plot by two of the malek's servants to assassinate the malek's son. Well, I didn't have the authority to approach the malek, but neither could I let the ameer perish at the hand of those rogues. So, with the permission of the captain of the guard, I was stationed in the ameer's suite without anyone else knowing."

"What happened?" Saif asked, his chin cupped in his hand as he sipped his coffee.

"Nothing. Neither the first night nor the following." Zahir shrugged, but a light danced in his eyes. "Well, a week after I heard the plans for the assassination, the men appeared. I fought and killed one and scared the other off by slicing his forearm. I was wounded in the process, but I saved Dhamar's life. Even after I foiled the assassination, I still followed the ameer around. He asked a million questions about my presence, but he didn't mind me by his side. When the captain suggested to the malek that the ameer needed a bodyguard, I was assigned the task. I've been his constant shadow ever since."

"Why did they want to kill Dhamar?" Hafza asked.

"I never discovered the reason. Perhaps they were upset at the malek. It wouldn't be the last time they targeted his son. I've saved Dhamar's life many times since." He shrugged again and took a bite of baklava.

He didn't say it arrogantly, or with any measure of pride. It was just a fact. He had saved Dhamar over and over. The mere thought of Dhamar being targeted, of death hanging over him like a cloud, sent my heart into my throat.

"Is it common for them to want the royals dead?" I whispered.

Zahir looked at me, his expression softer and kinder than I'd ever seen. "For the malek and Dhamar? Yes. But I am certain that once Dhamar ascends to the position of malek, things will change. He is a good man. He wants to do right by his people—to protect and serve them like the malek of a nation ought. Do not fear men wanting to hurt you, Inara, but rather, encourage your husband to stand strong and fight for what he believes in."

"I'm not sure I have that kind of power, Zahir." I looked at my hands clasped in my lap. "But I will try."

"That is all we ask, Inara." Hafza clasped her hands over mine. "You are a strong woman. Stronger than me. I wasn't brave enough to fight for a happy ending with Dhamar. But I believe you have what is needed to fall madly in love with your husband."

I think I'm halfway there already. I rubbed at one of my temples and forced a smile. "I suppose we shall see."

Zahir and Hafza exchanged a look. When I turned to Saif, he still had his chin cupped in his palm, and he grinned at me like he knew some great secret. A blush rose in my cheeks. How did they seemingly know me so well?

I poked at the baklava on my plate. *And what am I going to do with all these strange emotions? I'm not brave enough for this.* I squeezed my eyes shut. *Not brave enough at all.*

Chapter Twenty

Dhamar

Zaid tossed his head as I reined him in. His black mane stuck to his sweat-slicked neck. I scrubbed my sleeve across my own sticky forehead and sighed. Only one day of travel and already my heart longed for Inara, her touch and comforting smile. I wanted to wheel Zaid around and fly home to her.

But I couldn't. I glanced over my shoulder at the mass of men behind me. Though they were a paltry host compared to what they could have been, I was responsible for them. It galled me that the tribesmen had more: more men, more experience in the desert, more prowess with warfare. Father and the council should have known better. We were riding into a massacre. And once again, I was helpless to stop it.

I fisted my hand around the reins, turning to General Beeran at my side. "We will make camp here. Send scouts to study the route and report any enemy activity they spot."

"Aye, my ameer." He saluted and shouted orders to the men as they began to swing off their horses and bed down for the night. But my body was too tightly coiled to rest. Anger flared in my stomach, worry in my chest, and I found myself pacing a few dozen yards away from the rest of the men.

I hope she is finding peace, I found myself thinking, imagining Inara curled on her bed. I hoped she wasn't suffering from nightmares, from memories of her past and the man Jamal. Anger at him stabbed through me, though I had no idea if it was a righteous fury or pure jealousy. Yet I couldn't seem to expel the nerves from my heart. For the first time in twenty years, Zahir wasn't there to talk to. I was alone.

I tipped my head back. The stars blinked in the vast blackness. Always constant, always guiding. With them staring down at me, I felt a bit of my loneliness and anger slip away, and as it did, the realization struck me that I would return to my wife. I hadn't come so far only to lose her now.

Nicar, be with us all until the stars go out.

My stomach settled, my muscles relaxed, and I rolled into my blankets with a peace I couldn't explain settling the war within.

We reached Šeri three days after we left Mordova. The grayer sand of our wilderness—with the scrub brush and cacao trees—fell away to the bright, golden sand of the Šerian desert. I couldn't fully explain the thrill I felt at seeing my mother's homeland. My heart swelled—and then dropped into my stomach when I realized that I would spill blood on this sand before long.

"Ameer Dhamar." General Beeran trotted over on his dappled mare. "Permission to speak?"

"You have it, General. There is no need for such formality here." The man had been the one to train me in the art of the sword, bow, and spear when I had been the tender age of eight. I was now nearly on par with him, something I took a small bit of pride in. While Zahir had trained me up in the ways of a man, General Beeran had trained me in the ways of a warrior.

"There is an encampment on the next rise with close to two thousand men, not counting the women." General Beeran shook his head. It was common knowledge that many of the women of Šeri were trained to wield the bow, if not a sword. Because of the wild desert in which they lived, it was important for them to be able to protect themselves.

I scratched at my jaw. "They out number us two to one. We need more men."

We hadn't gathered the fifteen hundred men Arqa had promised. We only had a thousand. Maybe. Looking out over the endless desert, I could picture the enemy's men marching over the dunes, banners waving in the wind, as they cut us down like the wheat in the fields around Mordova.

"Yes." Beeran rubbed the back of his neck. His graying black hair lent him an air of wisdom, which he truly did possess. "But you can't go back without proof. They'll never listen to you."

"You mean they'll listen to me with proof?" I couldn't help the derision that slipped into my tone. "That would be the day, General."

Beeran smiled sadly and clasped my shoulder. "You will be a good malek, Dhamar. I'm trusting you'll live long enough to prove me right."

He turned and strode back to our tents. Bile coated my tongue. Yes, I was meant to be the next malek, but I didn't want it. I couldn't do it. They'd expect things of me that I wouldn't do. There were problems in our land I wanted to fix that the lords would not endorse. Could I truly lead an entire nation? The thought felt suffocating.

I stared out over the sands, watching as the sun kissed the horizon. The heat rippled against the hot sand, giving the illusion of water. And with that view, my heart pinched once more.

Today, peace reigned in the land, but it was as false as the water rippling across the sand. The sun would rise, and red would coat the golden, leaving death and destruction in its wake.

And you are helpless to stop it. I clenched my hand around the strap of my sword belt and waited for the morning.

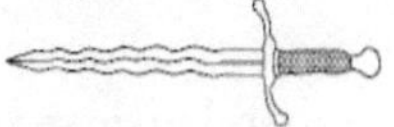

Battle was horrific.

I swung my scimitar, ducking beneath my opponent's attack to slam my blade into the soft flesh of his stomach. He cried out, his hand clutching at the blood streaming from his middle as if that could slow his inevitable death. He stumbled backwards as I plunged my second scimitar into his heart. There was no time to process that I had just ended a life, as another tribesman was on me with a howl of rage.

Flecks of blood—both mine and the enemies'—coated my hands and clothes. Screams of pain and anguish echoed over the hills, the ground littered with lives lost. A metallic taste tainted the air, coating my tongue as I plowed forward, cutting down people as if they were nothing more than chaff on the wind.

You're a monster, I thought as I withdrew my weapon from yet another chest. The fighting had lessened, the tribesmen falling back into the desert to lick their wounds. *We're slaughtering each other like sheep. Could I have stopped this?*

General Beeran limped over to me, a splotch of red coating the leg of his salwar. "They're retreating."

"For now." I swallowed, wiping my scimitars on the small patch of grass that had made it through the battle unscathed. "How long until they regroup?"

"A week at most." The general grunted, swaying on his good leg.

I clasped his shoulder, holding him steady. "You need a healer."

"I'm fine." He waved his hand at me. "I need to tend to my men."

"Let me." I squeezed his shoulder. For all the death dealt us that day, I couldn't handle losing Beeran. "You get your leg tended to before dealing with anything else. Now that we have proof that they're stronger than we first thought, I will return to the palace to try and speak reason to my father and the council."

General Beeran raised a brow but didn't speak the obvious—that trying to get to that particular group of men to see reason was about as likely as changing the direction of a charging rhino.

A healer took command of the grumbling general while I walked through the carnage of war. With every step, my strength ebbed, worn down by the blood and ruin all around. My heart ached, and I crumpled to my knees, digging the palms of my hands into my eyes. My father had caused this. He had demanded war, and the result was loss. So much loss on both sides of the conflict. It wasn't that I was squeamish; gore did not bother me. But this senseless violence towards people I considered my own? That made me want to never see food again.

I'd been gone a week now; the battle had lasted off and on for three days. How we had managed to hold our ground that long, I didn't know. But I had broken my promise to Inara.

A liar and a murderer. I wanted to scream, punch at the air and go to war with Nicar herself just to make sense of this day. *Why?*

"Ameer Dhamar?" A soft voice spoke, and I turned to see a young boy standing a few feet behind me.

"Yes?"

"This message came for you." The boy extended the folded parchment, his eyes flicking around at the bodies sprawled across the sandy ground. His face paled, and his throat bobbed.

"Thank you." I took it. Who was writing to me? I dropped my gaze to the parchment, and my heart leapt at the sight of my seal keeping the letter tightly closed. Inara had written.

After checking in with the captains, I received the death count that had my stomach turning sour once more. Over a third of our men had been lost. If Šeri regrouped and attacked within the week, we would be utterly annihilated.

I strode back to my tent after that. There was nothing left to do but let the healers tend those they could and make the ones they couldn't as comfortable as possible. My muscles screamed at me to rest, but as I lowered myself onto my mat, I broke the seal on Inara's letter.

Dhamar,

I know you said you'd be back within a week, and it has only been two days since you left. But something in my heart knows you need a bit of home. Of peace.

I inhaled sharply, dashing at a stubborn tear that leaked from my eye at the memory of plunging my sword into a fellow man.

I slammed a steel door over those memories, and instead, focused on my wife's swirling script.

The palace isn't the same without you here. I take all my meals in my room, as Hafza informed me that's what the malek and rania do. I've also returned to the library. Bahis fawns over me, and I think if I wasn't already your wife, he would have proposed by now.

I chuckled at that, picturing the doting scribe bringing whatever scrolls and parchment Inara wanted to her side.

Zahir and Saif are obeying your every order and one of them is always nearby. Thankfully, I am used to that from Saif. I even managed to make Zahir smile a number of times already.

I could easily imagine my stoic guard bestowing a small grin to Inara over something she said or did. He did it with me, too, though they were always few and far between.

I shouldn't wish it, but I'm ready for your return. I'm not certain how to navigate this world, not without my ameer. If you're not at my side, I am not an amira. But you are fighting for the safety of our people, for peace. And I am proud of you for that. I only wish there were something for me to do while I wait.

I am not certain how to end this letter. We all anticipate your victorious return, my ameer.

Always yours,

Inara

I pressed the parchment to my nose. It no longer held Inara's scent, but my memories did. Jasmine sweetened with a hint of honey. Recollection gifted me with her smooth skin beneath my fingers, her startling blue-green eyes. Her soft voice, quiet strength, and steadying hand. I craved her presence and needed her to reassure me it would be all right, that killing wasn't the thing I would die doing.

Home. I needed home. Not the palace, not the gardens with the sweet flowers and butterflies, not even my room with my lion and bed. No, home had become a person. Her kiss, her touch, her smiles and laughter. When they surrounded me, I was safe. Comfortable. Myself. When I was with Inara, I was home.

Nicar above, see me home. Please, help me get home.

CHAPTER TWENTY-ONE

Inara

Ten days. Dhamar had been gone for a week and a half after he promised a week.

And now the malek had summoned me.

I smoothed my hands over my kaftan, the silver embroidery scuffing my hands as I fidgeted with the light blue material. The malek had ignored me for the most part after he'd cornered me the day Dhamar had left. But he had called me to the council chamber, and now my stomach threatened to heave.

Zahir trailed me today, three steps behind, hand resting on the hilt of his scimitar.

Stopping at the banister of the garden, I leaned against it, face upturned to the warm sun. I'd spent many hours out in the courtyard, and the sun had warmed my pale complexion to a faint tan. It was my safe place in the uncertainty of the palace and the vile men that shadowed her halls. My hands trembled against the railing, remembering the scene of our wedding celebration: Pawing hands, wandering lips, women who had to let the men do whatever they wanted. My stomach heaved, and I pressed my hand against it, willing it to settle.

"Amira? You need to go to the council," Zahir warned in his low voice.

"What will they do to me, Zahir?" My voice pinched. "Dhamar told me to stay out of their way, and if I go in there—"

"They wouldn't dare lay a hand on you, Inara." Zahir stepped to my side, resting his hand on my shoulder and gesturing to himself with the other. "You need to believe that Dhamar is protecting you, even while he's away."

"You can't go in that room with me, though. Can you?"

"No, but if you shout, I won't hesitate to break every rule to ensure your safety." He raised a brow, and the corner of his mouth tilted up. "Do you believe that, Amira?"

I nodded, throwing back my shoulders. Keeping them taut and my head high, I strode down the corridor. Inwardly, I was trembling, but I wouldn't let it break the icy mask I'd donned. No, I would be the Talethan amira of ice. Cold and hard and unshakable.

A door with battle carvings appeared. Three times as tall as the doors to the malek's private chambers, they were a daunting sight. I straightened further, pressing my clasped hands against my stomach as Zahir knocked. As the door swung open, I closed my eyes to calm my nerves one final time.

I opened them as I stepped under the doorway, nearly crying out in relief at who I saw standing beside the malek's throne. Dhamar looked up, his black hair a shade lighter with the desert dust clinging to it. His eyes warmed as he strode forward and wrapped one arm around me.

"I missed you," he muttered against my hair.

I couldn't respond, my throat clogged with too much emotion as Dhamar eased back.

"Good show, Amira." Shaeen clapped slowly, his leeching smile on his lips. "You almost make it believable that you care about this pathetic excuse for an ameer."

Dhamar stiffened.

"Leave the boy alone, Shaeen," Lord Mostafa—at least, I thought that was who spoke—ordered. He offered a kind smile in my direction before glaring at a different lord who sat across the room. "It's not his fault Arqa failed to gather the numbers he promised."

"As if I can control the speed by which the men of this worthless city organize themselves!"

The lords began to shout, shaking fists and leaping to their feet in agitation. I stepped closer to Dhamar in terror that bloodshed might come from this fight. With his arm curved around my back, he guided me through the chaos to the throne, where his father slouched, chin in hand, watching the arguments erupting in his council room.

"Can this meeting wait?" Dhamar asked.

Malek Nadar blinked and looked us over, smiling suggestively. "Yes, yes, go bed your wife. I'll send messages to our supporters to start rallying more men since you apparently weren't strong enough to destroy our enemies the first time. You'll leave tomorrow with those men."

With every sentence the malek uttered, Dhamar tensed further. His arm was still around my shoulders, but it suddenly lacked the warmth of moments before. Without a word, he turned us toward the door and strode out. Zahir closed it behind us and stood to the side, watching.

"They're a bunch of—" Dhamar uttered a word that had me flinching as he pulled away to brace himself against the wall.

Zahir stepped between us, whispering something to Dhamar. My husband slumped against the wall before drawing a deep breath. He turned to smile at me, though it didn't reach his eyes. "I'm sorry, Inara. That's not how I wanted our reunion to go."

I shrugged, twisting my fingers in front of me. Something about my husband was different. He was colder, closed off in a way that he hadn't been before, despite all the abuse he'd suffered at his father's hand. "Did you get my letter?"

"Yes." His face softened at that, and he pushed off the wall to clasp my hand in his. "It came right when I needed it most."

"Good." He stood toe to toe with me and I had to tip my head back to see his face. He cupped my cheek, but I pushed him back with a tsk of my tongue. "I would love to kiss you, my ameer. But first, you need to bathe."

He grinned, pressing his lips to my forehead despite my squeal of protest. "As you wish."

"I'll have dinner sent to our rooms. It'll be waiting for you when you return."

Dhamar started, staring at me with the most peculiar expression on his face.

"What?" I asked after a prolonged silence.

"You called them 'our rooms'."

I blushed. "Aren't they?"

"Yes, I just—" He trailed his fingers across my cheek. "I've missed you, Inara."

I smiled. "Go bathe."

He nodded and strode down the hall. It was then my turn to slump against the wall. Emotions rose and fell like the wind within me, exhausting me to no small end. Largest of all was my worry, because my husband was home once more. And I wasn't entirely certain what he would expect from me this evening.

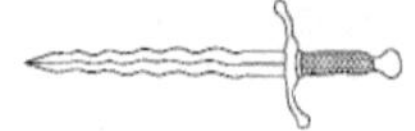

I hurried back to our rooms and changed into the navy blue kameez I'd worn on my first day as Dhamar's wife. My hands shook as I did up the front. Why was I so nervous?

Because what if tonight is the night? What if you decide it's time? Are you ready to be Dhamar's wife?

I bit my lip and turned to the window, wringing my hands as I stared out. I'd missed Dhamar dreadfully. More than I ever thought possible. He'd been on my mind since the moment he left. It wasn't just safety from the malek and the council that I had missed. Rather, it was Dhamar's smile, his laughter, his gentle embrace. I'd missed my husband the *man*, not just my husband the ameer.

Was my heart softening toward Dhamar? Was I willing to let him in and show him the darkest secrets I'd kept close for so long?

Hafza entered, scattering my thoughts as she smiled at me. She dragged me over to the vanity and pushed me onto the stool. "Let me do your hair. Then, I'll go fetch some food for your dinner."

I shook my head. "Thank you, but no. I'm going to keep my hair down tonight."

"Of course, my amira." Hafza wiggled her brows.

I ignored her implication. "Can you have the cook prepare manakeesh with lamb, tomatoes, onions, and extra cheese?" My cheeks heated when Hafza raised her brows. "It's Dhamar's favorite food."

"I'm pleased you know that, Amira." Hafza nodded before scooting out the door to get the meal ready.

Smoothing a trembling hand against my kaftan, realization struck that tonight *was* the night. After our meal, I would tell him about my past and he would either accept me—flaws and all—or turn me away. But I had to tell him the truth.

With a steadying breath, I marched into the common room. Dhamar wasn't there yet, and I forced my body to relax as I went to stand by the round window. My husband was home. What was I hoping for when he walked through that door? Did I want him to kiss me or simply hold me? Did I want to fall asleep curled up beside him like I had the night before he left?

No, it's safer to be alone. Even if he knows the truth, I'm not ready to be his wife, am I? The memory of waking in his strong embrace sent my heart leaping into my throat. *That* hadn't been a bad thing. Dhamar was my shelter to rest in.

But if he wanted more tonight? He'd witnessed war—blood, death, and destruction—and wouldn't he want the comfort I could give?

My breath caught in my chest when I heard the scuff of a foot against stone. I turned toward Dhamar's room. There he leaned against the doorframe, his black curls wet against his forehead. His arms were crossed, and the action pulled the red fabric of his kurta taunt against his muscular arms.

He looked good. Very good. My throat tightened as I forced my feet to carry me closer to him. I stopped an arm's length away, and he tipped his head to the side, a curl falling into his eye. "May I kiss you now?"

"If you wish."

His lips twitched. "Only if it's what you wish."

My bare toes curled with anticipation at the thought of his lips pressing against mine. The memory of our previous kisses had me swaying closer, my words breathless as I whispered, "I do."

Dhamar smiled, his hands settling on my hips, guiding me closer. "Are you certain?"

I nodded and then he was kissing me. Slow and deep, searching and a little bit desperate. I snaked my arms around his neck, leaning even closer. I never wanted this moment to end.

Dhamar leaned back from my mouth, his nose brushing mine as he tugged my body closer still. "Nicar above, I missed you."

I smirked. "I'm not sure I believe you."

He growled, his eyes sparking with challenge. "Let me show you again."

"If you wish." I laughed as his arms tightened, and he kissed me once more. Only this time, the kisses trailed from my mouth to my jaw, from my jaw down my neck. I gasped as he hit the soft spot below my ear, but this time I didn't flinch away. He froze all the same, his nose brushing my neck.

"I'm sorry. I forgot." His voice was gruff as he straightened and pressed one final kiss against my forehead.

"I—I think it's time for dinner." I pushed against his chest.

He relented, offering me his hand. "Of course."

I let him guide me to the table as a knock sounded on the door. Hafza sailed in, an army of servants bearing trays following on her heels. They spread the platters onto the table, raising the lids and letting the savory aroma of meats and herbs escape.

"Anything else, Amira?" Hafza asked.

"No, thank you."

She bowed and then retreated out the door.

I turned to Dhamar, who was staring at the table with an unreadable expression on his face. I tucked my hands behind my back, fidgeting with my fingers.

"You remembered," he said at last.

"Remembered what?" I rocked onto the balls of my feet and back.

"That I liked manakeesh."

"Of course, I did. You're my husband." *And it's only been two weeks since you told me.*

Dhamar turned and pulled me into his embrace. It was so sudden that I wasn't sure what to do with my arms. This shouldn't have been that important. Yet here he was, hugging me so tightly I could barely breathe, over manakeesh.

"Thank you," he said at last. "Father hates manakeesh and never has it for meals."

I cupped his cheek, forcing him to meet my gaze. "Then we shall have it all the more often." Dhamar looked about ready to kiss me again, so I gestured to the cushions. "Sit, and I will serve."

He sat cross-legged on the cushions, watching me as I cut into the manakeesh and placed it on his plate. With every dish, he thanked me, his smile softer and warmer than it had been mere minutes ago.

I sat, and we began to eat. Dhamar was silent, and it quickly grew to an uncomfortable level. It bothered me. Before he'd left, the silence had stretched in companionable comfort. What had changed in the last ten days to alter even our silence? I cleared my throat and asked the first question to appear in my head. "How was the border?"

He choked on the sip of wine he'd taken, coughing as he swiped at his mouth with his sleeve. A blank look shuttered his emotions from me as he stared down at his goblet.

"I'm sorry, I shouldn't have asked," I hurried to say, feeling foolish. "Of course, it wasn't good, I just—"

"No, you have every right to ask." His brows pinched. "It's only that it was—it was horrible, and I don't want to relive it."

"I understand." The memories of the Market whispered around my mind and then Jamal followed, his gaze leering over me, his lips and hands wandering—I shook my head. "Mine may not be of war, but we all hold memories we'd rather forget."

Dhamar looked up, his expression softening. "Perhaps sharing them would be healing."

"Perhaps." I dropped my gaze to my hands in my lap. "But I don't think now is that time."

Later. After dinner. You're going to tell him, Inara. You have to. I gripped my fork as I tried to calm my breathing.

Dhamar sighed and cut another piece of manakeesh. "I wish we had more time."

I halted, my cup of wine halfway to my mouth. "What do you mean? You're not going back, surely."

"I have to." His shoulders slumped, and he wouldn't meet my gaze. "You heard Father. Tomorrow he wants me to take the new recruits and the reserves to the border."

I set my goblet down and squeezed my fork tighter, feeling the metal cut into my hand. "You are his heir. It's ludicrous to risk your life like this!"

"The malek's word is law."

That phrase snapped the restraint on my barely stifled temper. I slammed my fork onto the table, letting the anger pulse in my chest. It wasn't just anger at the malek, but my frustration at being stuck where I could do nothing. I couldn't save myself from Jamal, I couldn't save Mother from her illness, and now I couldn't save Dhamar from the war. I leapt to my feet. "Why don't you tell your father and the council that their plan is foolish? That risking the Ameer of Taletha for a *border war* is—" I waved my hand and growled. It was stupidity beyond words, and judging by the flashing rage in Dhamar's eyes, he knew it too.

"They listen to no one but themselves," he snapped.

"It might help if their ameer dared to stand up to them."

"You don't think I've tried?" Dhamar flinched. "That has never ended well for anyone, Inara. I don't recommend it."

"Of course, you don't. You don't stand up to anyone. Not me, not your father, not the council. Not even that priest on our wedding night." Dhamar's jaw set, but I wasn't done. A floodgate had broken, and the words poured far too freely. "Oh, you fake it well. Bend their rules just enough to get what you want. You say your father is too stubborn to listen to anyone but himself and his council. Perhaps that's true. Yet you are doing the same things as him. Manipulating and twisting situations and people so you get what you want. You're so scared of becoming your father that you're standing for nothing, and in doing so, you're becoming him."

"Don't say that." Dhamar's voice was low, almost too controlled as he rose to his feet and met me glare for glare.

I shook my head. "Why not? You do fear him. You have never given him a reason to respect you. You're letting him turn you into him."

"I am his son. I must follow his orders, like them or not." With every word, Dhamar stalked closer. I backed up until I hit the wall. Dhamar leaned close, not feeling like my safe place any longer. Something lay in his gaze that I couldn't name, something he wasn't saying about my accusations. "You've only been here two weeks, Inara. You know nothing. Beyond that, you are my wife, and you will submit to and obey *me*."

My heart shattered at the stoic look on Dhamar's face, but I kept my shoulders back, words frosty. "And what are your orders, Ameer Dhamar?"

"Get out of my sight." He growled, turning away to shove his hand through his hair. Without a backwards glance, he strode into his room and slammed the door. I turned on my heel and did the same.

Slumping against the door, tears burst from my eyes. I sobbed, tucking my legs to my chest. That had not been how I'd envisioned our dinner going. I had planned on being the wife who was sweet and kind, so when I told him the truth, he would still want me, despite my past. But no, I had to speak my mind. Why had I said anything? I should have kept my opinions to myself, been the silent, submissive wife I was supposed to be.

But he made me feel safe. Secure enough to make him furious at me. I angered him enough for him to wield his authority over me. His ownership. I swallowed the lump in my throat and pushed to my feet, tottering to my bed to bundle under the covers. Warmth seeped into me, but the ache remained.

I didn't want Dhamar angry at me. No, I wanted him to say everything was fine, that he'd talk to his father. That he wouldn't turn into a monster like the malek—one that threatened me when he thought no one would notice. I wanted Dhamar to stay here with me where it was safe. No more battles, no more playing with death. I wanted his strong arms and solid chest. Forehead kisses and meals together.

I want it all, I thought as my eyes closed. *I want to lay the truth before Dhamar and have him choose us. Because I will fight for what we have, no matter the cost. But will he?*

Chapter Twenty-Two

Dhamar

I paced the length of my room, Gamil's tail flicking lazily as he watched.

"Who does she think she is, saying I'm like my father. I'm nothing like my father." I shook a finger at Gamil. "It's insulting, that's what it is."

Gamil chortled and hid his face between his paws.

"I'm not my father." I tore my hands through my hair, feeling warm and agitated. I tugged off my kurta, throwing it onto the ground before flopping onto the bed. I closed my eyes, but that didn't take away the memory of my wife's face as I'd pinned her against the wall. Fear had flashed in her eyes at my outburst. She'd shrunk back for the barest of seconds before straightening, but when she had, gone was the softness I'd grown to love over the four days we'd spent together.

I killed that. I buried my face in my pillow, hot tears of frustration forming in my eyes. Maybe I was more like my father than I cared to admit. *All you know how to do is destroy what you love.*

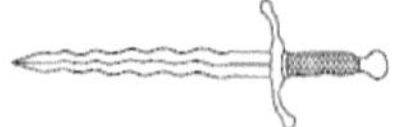

Blood sprayed the battlefield, rolling in unending waves. Screams echoed around the hills, continually growing louder with each swipe of my scimitar. Man after man fell from my blade. My hands shook, longing to drop the weapon, but it was as if the metal were seared to my palms. No matter what, it was stroke after stroke, blow after blow. I was born for this, born to destroy everything I cared about.

Then *she* was there. Inara. Her blonde hair blew in the breeze. Her words slapped at me as she stalked closer. "You don't stand up to anyone. You fake it well. Bend their rules just enough to get what you want."

Stay back! I cried out, but my words only bounced around my mind, didn't escape past my lips.

Panic clutched my chest as nearer and nearer she came. My sword was a blur, and all I could focus on were her sharp words. "You say your father is too stubborn to listen to anyone but himself and his council. Perhaps that's true. Yet you are doing the same things as him. Twisting things so you get what you want. You're so scared of becoming your father that you're standing for nothing, and in doing so, you're becoming him."

Scared.

Scared of being your father.

Stand for nothing.

Scared and stubborn

Scared. Scared. Scared.

My blade didn't stop. It cut through all the men surging forward until I was before Inara.

"You're scared of yourself. Of becoming the very thing you fear most," she said, her eyes boring into me with a dare in them, a condemnation. My hands shook. She hadn't said that earlier. No, it was my own tortured mind. Reminding me that I was failing. Failing as a husband, as a son, as an ameer.

And then, without my permission, my sword plunged into Inara's chest with a spray of red. She gasped, and her beautiful eyes rolled back into her head as she fell to the ground.

"No!" I screamed, sitting up in bed with my chest heaving.

"Ameer?" A pounding sounded on the door. I was shaking, chest aching, and I couldn't get the words out. It felt as if the blood were coating my hands, my face, and I grabbed the blankets to wipe furiously at the phantom sensation.

"We're fine, Zahir. I'm here with him." Inara stood beside my bed, moonlight spilling across her slim frame as she hesitantly stepped closer. Some peace washed over me at her being near, until the accusatory memories invaded my head again.

You're scared of yourself. Of becoming the very thing you fear most.

Some of that guilt must have shown on my face because my wife dropped her voice to a whisper. "If you want me here, that is. Do you want me, my ameer?"

The phrasing of the question pricked at my already tender conscience. Pain laced her words, and it was my fault. My fault she felt unwanted and unloved. I inched over and pulled back the covers. My hands still trembled, as did my voice when I said, "Yes. I'd like you here with me."

Her fingers twisted together in front of her, and she didn't move. I swore under my breath, swinging my legs over the bed's edge. I eased closer to her, clasping her cold hands in mine. "I shouldn't have—lashed out the way I did. I hurt you."

"I could have been gentler." Her eyes met mine, and tears shone in them.

"Sh." I pressed my forehead against hers before pulling her onto the bed. She squirmed for a moment, twisting so that her head rested against my chest. I tucked her under my arm, before tugging the covers around us. I stilled as warm, wet tears trailed across my chest as Inara curled against me. I'd made my wife cry. My anger and frustration were the cause of these tears. My throat closed off, and I hugged her tighter. "I'm sorry for my words, Inara."

She shook, her sobs silent as she wrapped her arm around my waist. "You're leaving again."

I pressed my lips together, not sure what she wanted me to say. As much as I hated it, there was no choice in the matter. I had to go. Rebelling would result in pain for Mother and Inara. Father would lash out, heads would roll, bruises would form. Retribution from the malek was steep, and it wasn't a price I was willing to pay. Not when it meant Inara and Mother would be hurt.

"Please, don't leave me again." Her words struck me harder than any sword. I hugged her tightly.

"I wish I could stay," I whispered, my voice hoarse.

She stilled, her tears glistening on her cheeks in the moonlight. "What was your nightmare about?"

Now was not the time for *that* discussion.

"Nothing. It's better now that you're here."

She snuggled closer. Perhaps we should have stayed awake and dealt with what laid between us—with the truth of her words, of my fear, of whatever had caused Inara's temper to flare when it hadn't before.

But in that moment, I simply wanted to cherish my wife, cradle her close and breathe in the scent of jasmine and honey that wrapped around us both as we drifted back to sleep.

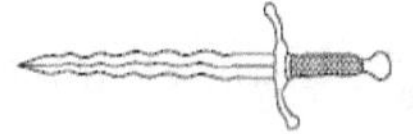

No more nightmares plagued me that night. Rather, they were dreams of the future. A little girl with Inara's blue-green eyes and my black curls and a little boy who looked just like me. Inara was wrapped in my arms as we watched them play in the garden. Giggles and shrieks echoed off the sandstone walls, and I smiled, tugging my wife closer as I pressed a kiss to her forehead.

"This is what I always dreamed," Inara whispered, her arms enveloping me as she smiled up at me. "Everything I never thought I'd have."

I tried to answer, say it's what I wanted, too, but my mouth wouldn't move.

Inara rose onto the tips of her toes, her gaze searing me with its intensity, and when her lips were a hair's breadth away, she whispered, "You have to fight for it, Dhamar."

I awoke to an empty bed. Inara had already slipped out, though the spot where she had been was still warm. Tugging the sheet to my nose, I inhaled slowly. Yes, it still held her scent.

With a groan, I forced my body from bed. Both of my dreams lingered over me. Fear mingled with hope as I dressed in a plain kurta and salwar—black to match my mood. How was I supposed to fight for what was impossible? As long as Father lived, there'd be no peace. No joy or laughter would echo down the halls.

You have to fight for it, Dhamar.

I wasn't strong enough. If something happened to either Inara or Mother, I would never forgive myself. Though, they would tell me to fight. But I couldn't when it meant risking their love.

I found myself fidgeting with the hem of my kurta as I strode toward the common room. I paused, staring at my hand. When had I started to do that? I growled, uncertain why the habit made me so angry.

Inara startled from her place at the table as I stalked in, nearly upending the piece of samoon she'd been spreading jelly on.

"You started without me, I see." I flinched at the tone in my voice. It wasn't her fault my dreams taunted me—not entirely. I shouldn't have let them get such a grip on me, mess with my heart and head. They were simply dreams. They meant nothing.

Yet, the stories of old talked of Nicar speaking through dreams. Was this her way of trying to get my attention?

Inara set her bread on her plate and met my gaze. "You were sleeping. You also cried out in your sleep again last night, and I thought you could use more rest."

"Why did you leave?" What was wrong with me? Why was I being so difficult? None of this morning's foul mood had anything to do with Inara. Yet she was here, and so to her my anger was directed.

"I was hungry." Inara's eyes narrowed. "Are you going to come eat?"

I sighed and sat across from her. Crossing my arms, I stared at her, waiting to be served. Inara's jaw locked as she went back to her bread. Finishing with it, she set it aside and met my gaze. "Would you like something, my ameer?"

"Food."

"Then ask for it."

My temper flared. She may have stayed with me last night, but I wasn't going to take this. Ignoring the warning bells that said I was being unreasonable, I pushed to my feet.

"Dhamar." She rose too, her icy mask in place. "I won't let you become *him*. You aren't him. And—"

I strode to the door, slamming it once I was on the other side.

Both Saif and Zahir jumped, pretending they hadn't been eavesdropping. They glanced at each other before Zahir followed behind me, leaving Saif to guard my wife.

"My stubborn, mule-headed wife can't keep her mouth shut," I muttered under my breath as I stomped into the courtyard. Once there, I paced around the fountain.

"My ameer, why are you so upset?" Zahir asked after a long moment of me raving and stalking.

"Because—because—"

"Could it be," Zahir asked, drawing out the words, "that Inara is correct about you and your father?"

I glared at my guard. "Not you, too."

"It is only a possibility, Dhamar." Zahir shrugged, hand still clamped around his scimitar. "I've noticed what Inara sees as well. You try to be strong, to not give in to their demands, but the way you do it is by bending whatever rules they give you. Is that really standing and fighting?"

I raked my hand through my hair. Was Inara right? Was that why I'd flown into a temper? I didn't want her to be right. I desired to be different from my sneaking, conniving father. But what if, in trying to please both sides, I was really becoming just as deplorable? My chest ached. I had just stormed out on my wife. She didn't deserve for me to yell at her like that, to be that mad over her simply stating the truth.

"I'll speak with her after I report to the council." I trailed my fingers through the water, remembering our water fight and laughter on a day that felt an eternity ago. "Do you think I ruined everything?"

"Not everything." Zahir chuckled. "I know the amira has been missing you. It may take time to win her trust again, but I believe you will."

"You mean I had it to begin with?" I sighed when he nodded. "I made a mess of this."

"Yes, you did." Zahir chuckled again. "Why do you think I'm a confirmed bachelor?"

"Because you're too busy serving me to look at women."

"Except for threat assessment." Zahir nodded solemnly.

I groaned and roughed my hands over my face before dragging my feet toward the council chamber. My shoes scuffed against the stone floor of the palace as I walked down the corridor. I felt exhausted. My nightmare-fogged brain wanted nothing more than to turn back around and flee, to go to Inara and beg for her forgiveness for my petty actions. Tell her she was right, and I was afraid.

Afraid of death and dying.

Afraid of becoming Father.

Afraid of failing.

Failing the kingdom.

Failing my loved ones.

Failing myself.

Instead, I strode into the council chamber.

From the bleary looks on all the lords' faces, I wondered if they'd even left the day before. The stuffiness felt overpowering, and it took everything in me not to bolt from the doorway.

"Get in here, Dhamar!" Father's eyes swept over me as I strode forward and bowed. He grunted. "You look like hell."

I didn't respond.

"Well, time for your report." Shaeen eyed me. "How bad was the border?"

Bad enough for nightmares. "As I said yesterday, it was war. There's nothing grand nor spectacular about it."

Arqa grunted. "Well, end it, and get back home."

"What if I can't?" I ran a hand through my hair. "What if winning isn't what we're meant to do?"

"You want to lose?" Father all but roared, launching to his feet faster than I thought possible with his girth. "We're not laying down and letting them win!"

"Is that what I said?"

"You insinuated it!" Lord Hakeem roared, slamming his meaty fist into his palm. His jowls quivered, and his bulging eyes raged.

"I simply meant that maybe we should see why they're doing this. Why are the Šeri tribesmen attacking Taletha after all these years? If they wanted, they could have attacked us twenty-seven years ago."

"We don't listen to aggressors," Yamin snapped.

I balled my hands into fists. "We attacked *them*."

"Yes," Father said lowly, catching the attention of everyone else in the room. "And I will continue to do so until they surrender or are eradicated."

"Father—"

"Do you hear me? Either they surrender, or every one of them dies."

I stared at the man who'd helped give me life. While he had once been a decent father, he no longer seemed to hold a shred of love or compassion in him at all. "These are Mother's people, Father."

"Good riddance, then," Shaeen spat to the side, and everyone else followed suit.

My chest ached with sorrow as I bowed my head. "When do you want me to leave?"

"As I said before, you're leaving today."

I nodded and turned. My limbs shook as I all but stumbled out the door and back to my room. I locked both my door and the door to the common room as guilt gnawed at me. Inara's words taunted, racing through my thoughts like desert hares.

You're afraid.

You're afraid of becoming your father.

Then the dream voice spoke, echoey and disjointed. *You're scared of yourself. Of becoming the very thing you fear most.*

I tore my hands through my hair with a growl of frustration and slammed my fist into the pillows on my bed. I was failing. At being an ameer, a husband, a son. It pressed like a weight against my chest, sharper than a blade and more painful than flames.

I can't face Inara now. She's right—I'm a coward. Perhaps I should let someone else be her husband. They would undoubtedly be better than me.

Packing my bag without really seeing what I threw in, I strapped on my swords, only fumbling once when I remembered Inara's deft fingers helping me the last time I'd left.

But there would be no send off today. No kiss goodbye nor warm embrace. I scratched Gamil's head when he bumped into my leg and gave one final glance at the door that would lead me to Inara. Then, I turned and left—striding back to war, and blood, and death.

Chapter Twenty-Three

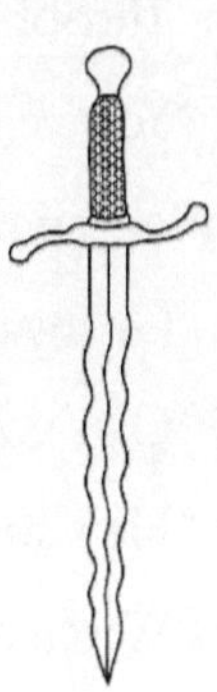

Inara

My cheeks burned with anger as I heard Dhamar leave his room. I peeked out of my door and watched as he walked away, his swords strapped to his back, his bag at his side. Everything in me wanted to call him back, to beg him to stay. I would be a better wife. Quiet and submissive. I wouldn't argue. But if that were true, that meant letting him walk away.

And I couldn't promise that. I wanted to see him grow—grow into a good man who loved fiercely and fought for what was right. This war wasn't right, and I knew it. Dhamar knew it, but he had to want it enough to fight for peace.

My vision swam, and I pushed out the door, heading the opposite way Dhamar had stalked. Wandering for a few minutes, I finally decided on the secret garden. I slipped in and heard my guards follow. The sun was high, warming everything to an unbearable temperature. I sprawled out on the bench beneath the sycamore trees, letting the rays that filtered through the branches soak into my skin. If I burned, at least I'd be feeling something other than the throbbing ache in my heart.

"You've chosen sulking, I see." Saif's voice felt like sand in my shoe—sticky, itchy, and entirely unwanted.

"Go away."

"Can't. Ameer Dhamar's orders, remember?"

"He's suffocating even when he's not here. Fabulous."

"Wait a minute!" Saif knocked my feet to the side and sat beside me on the bench. "Yesterday, you couldn't wait for him to come home. Today, he's suffocating. What slipped my notice?"

The biggest fight I've ever had with anyone in my life. The breaking of a heart that was just beginning to soften. The death of my dream for love.

I closed my eyes. "We had an argument."

"And?" Saif snorted. "Ranya and I fight all the time. Sometimes even daily. It's part of having a relationship. Being close means you step on each other's feelings now and again." Saif chuckled. "And sometimes you grind each other to a pulp. Marriage isn't easy, Inara. It's a messy, dirty, get-in-the-grime-and-dig kind of work. Sometimes it takes tearing down our carefully constructed walls in order to fall more in love."

"He doesn't love me." I crossed my arms over my chest and shivered. "He made it very clear that I'm his property."

You're my wife. You will submit to and obey me.

"No, Inara." I cracked open one eye to see Zahir leaning against the tree behind Saif. "He cares about you more than you realize.

That's why he was so angered by what you said. Truth tends to hurt."

"But what if—" I swallowed and closed my eyes again. "We've been together for four days in total, and already we've hurt each other. Maybe we're just..." *Wrong for each other.*

"Amira." Zahir's tone was the sharpest I'd ever heard; I sat up, startled. He dropped to his knee, clutching my hand in his. "Please don't give up on him. Don't stop pursuing that joy you felt. Keep fighting. Love is not an emotion. It's an action. And like all actions, it takes training. Training in patience and kindness and gentleness. In humility and forgiveness."

"Sounds terrifying," I whispered.

"It is." Zahir's small smile slipped onto his lips. "Why do you think I have no wife?"

I laughed, wiping away a tear that had snuck its way out of my eye.

"But you will succeed, Amira. You only have to dare to fight for it. Dhamar rescued your body from the Wife Market. But only *you* can choose to free your heart and soul from bondage."

He straightened and began to patrol the courtyard. Saif stood a few feet away, close enough to jump to my rescue if I needed, but far enough to give the illusion of privacy.

I stretched back out, closing my eyes as the first wisps of hope began to form in my heart.

If I wanted to be free, that meant telling Dhamar the truth. The truth about Jamal and me, about my father and who he was, about the Market and all that entailed.

For all my talk of bravery and fighting, this particular battle seemed insurmountable. I wanted to reach the goal—a marriage of love and choosing—but was it worth the risk to my heart? Would Dhamar still want me, even after he knew the truth?

I want to love again. I sighed. *And to do that means to let go of my fear and take a leap of faith.*

I groaned as Hafza smeared aloe against my burnt cheeks.

"Honestly, why Zahir and Saif didn't bring you inside is beyond me." She rolled her eyes as I hissed against the cooling sensation of the ointment. "Foolish men."

"I wouldn't have come in anyhow."

Hafza huffed a breath, a loose strand of her tightly coiled hair fluttering against her forehead. "Then you're just as foolish."

I wasn't about to tell her the pain felt good. For a few moments, it distracted me from the fear and aching in my chest. I had made up my mind to tell him about my past. But how was I to wait for Dhamar to return? I needed to talk to him, to figure this out. If what Saif and Zahir said was true—if love was an action and took work—then sitting and waiting wasn't possible. An idea churned in my mind, making my stomach flip and my hands shake.

"Hafza, can a person request an audience with the malek?" I asked.

Hafza jerked, glancing at me with wide eyes even as she continued slathering my arms with aloe. "You want to go to the malek? Alone?"

"Of course not." I shook my head. "I'd take the guards."

"It's still dangerous. He is dangerous, and he'll probably have you go before him and the council."

Meaning no Zahir and Saif. And disobeying a direct order from Dhamar. I swallowed, twisting my fingers around each other. "I'm aware of the dangers, but—"

I couldn't explain it. The sudden need to make things right with Dhamar choked the words from me. This courage wouldn't last. Overthinking would snuff the life from it, drag it back to the dark corner of my heart and bury it. The daring was there now, and I would embrace it. Had to embrace it. "Hafza, I must speak to him."

"Then I'll speak to his manservant." Hafza wiped her hands on a towel and shook her head. "I just hope you know what you're doing, Amira Inara."

I hope I do, too.

A few days later, I held one of my kaftans on my lap, adding some embroidery to the cuffs. Hafza had said she could do it, but the isolation and waiting were making me anxious. The needle and thread, the constant in and out motion of it through the silk fabric, and the creation of something beautiful, it all helped distract me from the loneliness and worry. It also soothed my heart that skipped a beat each time I thought about my husband off fighting people he considered his own, in a war he didn't wish to win.

Because either way, he'll lose. My heart pinched, and I bowed my head. *Nicar above, protect him. Help me reach him and ask him to forgive and love me before it's too late.*

A knock sounded on the door, and Saif poked his head in. "Rania Lenna is here to see you, Amira."

Dhamar's mother? I blinked and nodded. "Show her in."

Saif swung the door open, and a timid woman slipped inside. She wore a veil over her head which matched her vibrant red kaftan. It made her appear pale even though she had the same olive complexion as her son. Her eyes, a greenish brown, darted all around as Saif shut the door. She'd barely crossed the threshold, her posture was rigid, and she wouldn't look at me.

"Rania Lenna, it's a pleasure to meet you." I sat aside my work and moved toward her. "Won't you please sit? I can send for some tea."

"No, no. I'm fine." Her voice was light and airy, as if she were having a hard time breathing. "I—I shouldn't be here. If Nadar finds out, he'll—" She shivered.

He'll what? My fear and anger flared again. The malek clearly scared this woman half to death. *And you said Dhamar was like him.*

Ignoring my guilt, I clasped Lenna's hands and dragged her to the cushions. "I'm glad you've come to visit. You are my mother-in-law, after all." I smiled. "But I sense there's a specific reason you're here."

Lenna started, her eyes going wide before she looked away. "Yes."

I waited, but she didn't seem like she wanted to share. With a small huff, I stood and went to the door. Saif raised a brow at me, and I shrugged, as puzzled as he was at the appearance of the rania. "Will you please get us some tea?"

"Of course, my amira." Saif turned to leave, and Zahir moved to stand in his place. His carefully stoic face gave no hints about his thoughts.

Shutting the door, I strode back to my cushion. "All right. The tea is on its way. Now, please tell me why you're here."

Lenna smiled slightly. "Now I can see why Dhamar chose you. You have a strength to match his."

My heart flipped at her assessment. "I think I'm only now discovering my strength, Your Majesty."

"Please, call me Lenna." Her shoulders relaxed, though her eyes still darted around like a cornered animal. "I'm sorry for this strange visit. I've wanted to visit you since Dhamar brought you home, but every time I asked Nadar to come, he forbade it." Her lower lip caught between her teeth, and she looked away again.

"He doesn't know you're here, does he?" I asked, trepidation at what that might mean making it hard to swallow.

"No." Lenna sighed, a bone-weary one that heaved her whole frame. "And if he discovers that I'm here, he'll make me pay." She shook her head. "But I won't regret it. You deserved a proper welcome, and I didn't get to give it to you."

"I don't hold it against you." I forced a smile to my lips. Lenna was putting herself in danger, and if I had learned anything about Dhamar, it was that he wouldn't approve of that.

Lenna smiled, and I realized then how young she truly was. The malek was at least in his seventies. Lenna looked no older than forty. Bile rose, and I sucked in a breath.

"Do you have any questions about my son?" Lenna asked, smoothing her hands over her legs.

The light rap of Hafza at the door saved me from answering right away. My maid swept in and deftly laid out the tea things, allowing me to sort through which question I needed to know the most. I nodded in thanks, and she sailed back out the door.

"This may seem too personal," I began after I poured our drinks. "But has Dhamar ever stood up to the malek and the council?"

Perhaps it was something I didn't want to know—didn't deserve to know. But it had shaped the man I was married to. It was part of who Dhamar was. To start tearing down the walls, as Saif had told me to, I needed to know.

Lenna sighed again, and this time it was tinged with sadness. "Yes. Once, when he was about sixteen. He then had to watch his father..." Her words cut off, and she inhaled an uneven breath. "He had to watch his father abuse me."

"*Abuse* you?" I laid a hand against my chest, the ache intensifying to a painful throb.

"Yes." Lenna's eyes were glassy when they met mine. "In the worst ways possible."

"He—" I shook my head, the lump in my throat choking any further words.

"If he doesn't stand up to his father, Inara, it is because he is scared of it happening again. Or worse," she reached around the tea things and clutched my hands in a surprisingly strong grip, "seeing it happen to you."

The tears that had been coming far too frequently as of late flooded my eyes. "So, he's going to war with the tribesmen to protect us?"

"Yes." Lenna leaned back, picking up her cup of tea and cradling it in her palms. "He isn't scared for himself. In fact, if it was him being abused, I think he would have stood up long ago. No, Dhamar's fear is that his father or the council will hurt us."

"I suppose I've not helped that, then." My shoulders slumped. "We had an argument about it, actually."

Lenna's lips pursed. "You didn't know. No one fully does. Dhamar likes to hide his pain. He likes to be strong. And he is.

But admitting we need help is not a source of weakness. I think sometimes it takes more strength than we realize."

"I told him that very thing." My throat closed off when I realized the hypocrisy of my own words. I didn't trust anyone, not fully. My heart was mine, and I tightened my hold on it with each hit I suffered from those around me. What would it take to release it, to trust someone enough to let them help me heal?

"Inara, I heard you wish to speak with the malek." Lenna's voice drew my attention from my thoughts. "What do you wish to speak to him about?"

"I—I want to go to the border to speak with Dhamar." I twisted my fingers together. "It's a matter that cannot wait for his return."

"Then you should just go," Lenna stated.

"Go? Without permission?" That sent a whole new level of panic through me. I didn't even know where the Šerian border lay, let alone how to get there.

"If you approach Nadar and ask, he will use it to his advantage." Lenna's voice dropped to a whisper. "If Nadar knows how much you care, he will use it to destroy you. Trust me, Inara. Just go to Dhamar."

"But—" I swallowed, a new worry wriggling to the forefront of my mind. "Will Nadar hurt you?"

"Perhaps." Her face paled, and she leaned back. "But if this means I get to aid my son in finding happiness, then it will be well worth it."

"Dhamar won't think so." I knew that in the depths of my soul. "And neither do I. Your pain will not help us be happy, Lenna."

She smiled sadly. "Maybe not. But if you feel the urge to go, then go."

I mulled over Lenna's words. What would Dhamar want? And what about my heart? Could this conversation wait? *But what if he doesn't return?* I squeezed my eyes closed, clasping the teacup to my chest and breathing slowly to stem the panic that wanted to erupt. "If it's truly that dangerous to approach the malek, then I can wait. If only to keep you, our mother, safe."

Tears filled Lenna's eyes. "How did Dhamar find you?"

"I don't know." Setting aside my tea, I knelt before Lenna. "But I thank Nicar above that he did. He saved me. Now it's my turn to save you both."

Lenna smoothed my hair back. The gesture brought a flood of memories to mind: Momma, brushing my hair by our fireplace, singing a song softly as she did so. Momma, dabbing my forehead with a wet cloth when I was ill. Momma, her face pale as she grew weaker and weaker with the disease she'd contracted while working, and me, wiping at her sweat-slicked face and brushing back the wisps of her gray-blonde hair. A tear snaked down my cheek, and Lenna wrapped her arms around me.

"I'm thankful for you, daughter."

Daughter.

With that word, something I hadn't realized was shattered began to piece itself back together deep within me. It wasn't immediate, was not an instant fix. But it was a start. It gave me hope that I could heal—and perhaps this was the first step.

CHAPTER TWENTY-FOUR

Dhamar

My thoughts beat in time with Zaid's hoofs as we thundered over the wild land of southern Taletha, three days after leaving Mordova and Inara behind again.

You ran away from your wife.

Coward.

You can't stand up to your father and the council.

Scared.

You're trying to outpace your own mind.

Afraid.

I growled, urging my stallion forward. The dust flew behind his heels, and he leaned his neck forward, as if that might increase his speed. I could hear the pounding of our company behind us, another five hundred men.

Not enough.

Scrubbing my sleeve across my sweat-soaked forehead, I reined in Zaid. He puffed and stamped the ground—agitated that we had stopped our race. But I could see our camp on the horizon. I wasn't ready to enter; not ready to face more death and destruction, and not ready to admit that Inara was right—I was afraid.

Afraid of failure. Afraid of yourself. Afraid. Afraid. Afraid.

"Take Zaid to camp," I thrust his reins at one of the recruits and turned to walk away.

"Ameer Dhamar? What are we to tell the general?" His voice quavered the slightest bit, and I almost turned around. Almost guided them all into the camp.

But instead, I said, "Tell him I'm on a walk."

"Ameer—"

"You have your orders, soldier!" I barked, hating the tone of my voice. "See that you follow them."

He fisted his hand over his heart and then kicked his horse into motion. The other soldiers—some who had trained with me all those years ago—shot me peculiar glances as they cantered forward.

Shoving my hands through my hair, I moved toward the crest of a dune. It overlooked the Šerian encampment, and I stood there, staring down at the pitched tents. Nerves clenched my gut at the sheer number of them. This was going to be a slaughter. The tribesmen also had reinforcements join their numbers while I was away. Now they easily had three men for every one of mine.

Coward. Afraid. Scared.

I gripped the straps of my sword belt and forced myself to breathe.

"Ameer Dhamar?" General Beeran strode to my side. He gazed down into the valley with me, a strained expression on his weather-beaten face. "What are you doing here?"

"Here on this crest, or here in the middle of what will surely be a slaughter come morning?" I scoffed and shook my head, refusing to meet the general's gaze. "My father and the council *ordered* me here."

Beeran clasped my shoulder and sighed. "I can send you back with a letter requesting more men still. Arqa has to know this is madness, regardless of whether or not he states it to the rest of the lords."

I shook my head. "They're fools. All of them."

"Perhaps." Beeran raised one of his bushy brows. "But there's more to this sour mood of yours, my ameer. Something at home you need to attend to, perhaps?"

I stiffened, hating that Beeran could see through me so clearly. "I can't go home. Father will still say I'm shirking my duty."

"I'd rather keep you alive, Dhamar." Beeran's words echoed my own dark thoughts.

"Death would be easier," I admitted sullenly.

"Now that is the coward's way out. And no matter what the council or your father says, you are not a coward."

Coward. Afraid. Scared.

"I am, though. I ran from my wife." I choked out the words, not able to look at the steady general. "I don't stand up to my father and the council. I bend to their whims and only push back enough to appease my own mind. Isn't that the coward's way out?"

"Bravery doesn't mean you never cave to cowardice. It's what you do afterwards that matters." Beeran sighed. "My wife died a few months back, son. I would do anything to have one more minute with her. I don't want you riding into war with regrets. Nor do I want you leaving your amira with any."

His words hit the core of what was bothering me. I was sorry for how I'd stormed away from Inara. She was my reason for wanting to return to Mordova at all. But that didn't solve my immediate problem. "I don't want to face my father."

"Perhaps not." Beeran smiled. "But you will, one day. You are, after all, *not* a coward."

He turned and left without another word. I gazed back over the rows and rows of tents in the distance and the small shadows of men and women trailing between them. I scratched my jaw, a different voice ringing in my ears.

Destroy them all.

My heart shuddered at that. I couldn't. They weren't just the *tribesmen*. They were the people of Šeri—my mother's people. My kinsmen. Even the thought of turning on them more than I already had made my stomach sour.

I glanced down the other side of the hill at my men. They were also my people; I was their ameer and future malek, the man responsible for leading them. Father might not take that duty seriously. He might recline in his room, gorging himself on women, wine, and fine food. But I wasn't my father.

You're afraid of yourself, Inara's dream voice rippled through my mind as if it skimmed across a mirage. I rubbed my temples, exhaustion telling me to simply give up.

Because yes, I was afraid. Terrified that I would become the very man I loathed. Lazy and weak. Cruel and prone to violence. But how could I remedy that? The only way to stop a war was with—

I paused, an idea taking root in my mind. It was foolhardy, dangerous, very likely to fail before it even began. But I couldn't shake it. The peace I'd felt my first night on the warpath settled over my mind and heart. *This* was what I had to do.

"There are ways to prove strength that have nothing to do with war," I whispered aloud. Could it get me killed? Perhaps. But better to die doing what was right than to spend another minute bending before wrong.

I unclasped my swords, turning to look back at my camp one final time before dropping them onto the sand.

Nicar above, keep me safe. Keep my wife safe. Let us all be reunited when this is over. Don't let this lead to more death and pain.

My heart thundered like Zaid's hooves as I strode toward the Šerian camp. I clasped my hands into fists at my side, refusing to let them shake.

Coward.

No, I was doing what was right. This was right. Peace still lingered over my heart, and I prayed to Nicar my whole walk to the camp.

So focused was I on approaching, that I failed to notice the figures coming toward me on my left until the humming of steel against steel rang out.

"Halt! Who are you?" a low tenor asked, halting me in my tracks as the prick of a sword pressed into my neck.

"You don't know who this is, Emre?" A light laugh followed and a woman, shrouded in the shadows of the setting sun, sashayed around me. Her layers of skirts swirled round her feet, and she smiled, her teeth bright against her tan skin. "This is the ameer of all Taletha, and we've captured him."

Chapter Twenty-Five

Inara

After that first meeting, Lenna came to see me more often. She returned the day after our first tea sporting a bruise on her cheek. Neither of us made mention of it. We both knew the truth, and it didn't need to be spoken aloud. It broke my heart, the pain she kept silently inside. But she was determined to come and see me, despite what she suffered at her husband's hand.

Today, we walked along the walls of the palace. Zahir patrolled before us, and Saif behind, keeping us relatively undisturbed from the normal guards' rotation. I linked my arm around my mother-in-law's as we strolled. The sun was not quite at its zenith, and it bathed the city below in its light. As much as I hated Mordova for what it had done to me, there was a strange beauty to the city of my birth. Around the eastern wall, six white-stoned domes reached toward the sky. The closest was nearly against the palace wall. While they were smaller than the palace, they were still mansions compared to the mud brick homes around them. Arches of marble glinted behind the stone walls—testament to the wealth of those inside. Thieves had better beware, for the owners of those mansions had the means to control the scum of Mordova, and they would.

At the apex of the mansions' domes were crests, similar to the swallow crest atop the palace. From where we walked along the wall, I caught sight of a lion's head, a crescent moon, and a star.

"Which lords lives there?" I asked Lenna, pointing to the crests.

Lenna gestured to the house closest to the palace. A lion's face roared down at us. "Lord Hakeen lives there. He's a great beast of a man and enjoys roaring out his opinions over everyone else in the council room."

I couldn't help chuckling at that, remembering the thundering lord from my brief moments in the council chamber.

"Then the moon is Lord Mostafa. He's a peaceful man. When he speaks, everyone listens."

"Even Lord Hakeen?" I asked in a conspiratorial whisper.

Lenna smiled. "Even him. Then the star is for Lord Shaeen. The guiding light of the council, or so says he."

"You don't think so?"

"The man is insufferable." Lenna's eyes widened, and she glanced around before lowering her voice. "I shouldn't speak ill of the council. But they guided my husband and son into this war, and that I cannot abide."

"You do not agree with the war?" Hope bloomed in my chest. Perhaps Dhamar was more like his mother, calm and caring. I had seen glimpses of that man, but with our argument still fresh in my mind, anxious thoughts of a marriage like Lenna's had plagued my nights. What if I told Dhamar the truth, and I became little better than a toy to him—like Lenna was to Nadar?

"No." Lenna's hazel eyes grew melancholy, and her voice softer still. Her hand tightened on my arm. "The tribesmen are my people. I was a daughter of Šeri, and while I've grown to love the people of Taletha, my home is not here with them."

"I cannot imagine being so far away from the land of my birth." I patted Lenna's hand, gazing out over Mordova as I did. "People often assume I belong in one of the northern lands. But I am not from there. I am a Talethan." I pointed at the area of the city I had grown up in. Even from where we stood, I could see the lines stretching between the buildings, colorful rugs and tapestries waving in the warm breeze. The slums were quite near the palace. It had loomed over us, mocking our pitiful existence each day. Never as a child had I dared to dream I would be living here, the wife of the ameer of Taletha. "That's where I lived. Most of those houses are falling apart. Most of the one room hovels hold far too many people. Mine sometimes held eight."

"You had eight people in one room?" Lenna turned a little green when I nodded. "How did you survive?"

"I almost didn't. If my mother hadn't worked as—" I swallowed the word. I hadn't even told Dhamar about this part of my story. But Lenna wanted to embrace me as her daughter. She had earned the right to know about my life. And I would tell Dhamar. Eventually. "My mother worked as a prostitute to help us keep the house. Father was often off on the seas with my uncle and five brothers.

He never sent home any of his—bounty. Mother did what she had to do for us."

"Oh, Inara. How horrible." Lenna leaned her head against my shoulder and tightened her grip on my arm. "While I cannot imagine what life was like for you, I do wish I was more like your mother. I wish I protected the ones I loved no matter the cost."

"Well, it cost Mother her life." I laid my head on top of Lenna's as we both looked out over the sparkling city. "Maybe you need to learn to stand up for what you care about, but I cannot be upset that you haven't. Selfishly, I am very glad you're here with me."

Lenna sighed, lapsing into silence.

My heart pinched when I thought about my words. If Dhamar had stood up to his father, would he be alive now? Would Lenna? Was I wrong when I pushed him to fight back?

I quickly changed the subject. "Besides being your homeland, what do you love about Šeri?"

"The rolling, golden sands and the small oases that dot them. The endless blue sky that touches the horizon for miles and miles. The brightly colored tents of my people that you can see over the hills. Traveling miles and miles on the desert horses as the sun warms your skin." Lenna breathed in slowly before exhaling in a giant whoosh. "Oh, Inara. There is nothing like the freedom of the desert plains."

As she spoke, desire welled up within me, nearly suffocating me in its grip. I longed to see the beauty of the land that Lenna loved so much and could picture it all. The endless desert and sky, retreating to oases, the freedom that it offered. It seemed impossible. But her passion told me it must be true, must be real and lovely and beautiful.

"Perhaps, once the war is over, we can visit. I would love to explore your desert, my rania."

"If we are to ever visit, it would be once *you* are rania, my dear. Nadar would never allow it while he yet breathes."

Her voice hitched at the end, and I wrapped my arm around her waist. "That is a fight we'll have to face once Dhamar returns home. He'll know how to get us there."

Lenna smiled, but it failed to reach her eyes. "If you say so, daughter. I'll trust the faith you have in your husband."

"He's your son, Lenna."

"And I have failed him." Her shoulders slumped once more. "I never showed him how to stand and fight for what is right and good."

But he shouldn't have to fight his own father. I swallowed the bitterness on my tongue. The more I learned about the malek and his ways, the more loathing and hate raced through my veins at the mere thought of him. He was an evil man, cruel and cold. He took what he wanted without thought of the repercussions. And if Hafza was to be believed, he murdered—both body and soul—without a thought.

And you accused Dhamar of being like him. I pressed a hand against my chest, tears threatening my vision. *Nicar above, how wrong I was.*

"It's never too late to help him learn," Zahir said, startling us both.

"What?" Lenna asked in a whisper.

"Teach Dhamar how to fight for life and love." Zahir rolled his shoulders in a casual shrug, his eyes scanning the city below. "He loves to learn, my rania. While it may be hard for you to understand, you haven't failed him. His five marriages have saved women. He's waged a silent fight against the malek for years. He may not be bold yet. But it is within him, waiting. All it needs is to be coaxed out." His eyes flicked to me, a small smile on his lips. "And I believe we have what is needed to bring it to the surface."

"Perhaps we do." Lenna smiled at me, and this time, her eyes sparkled with the light of hope.

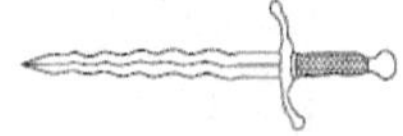

I sat, curled upon the couch in the library. The scroll with the story of Kaan lay on my lap, but my mind wouldn't focus on the text.

Dhamar had now been gone for another two weeks. It wasn't as if I were counting, I kept telling myself. But, in truth, I was. Dhamar was my first thought when I woke, and my last before falling asleep. I longed to talk with him, tell him what I knew, what I desired. *Him.* I wanted him. Wanted a marriage not only of friendship and cold, mutual respect, but one that contained love, caring, and a burning desire to fight for one another.

Will he want that once he knows the truth? I hugged my arms around my waist.

Bahis trotted toward me, his arms filled with scrolls needing shelving. He always seemed to be near when I retreated to my library sanctuary, but not in a predatory kind of way. I didn't fear him. Rather, he was a presence of comfort between dusty shelves and ink-filled scrolls.

"Bahis, I have a question." I set aside my scroll and leaned back, pressing my hands into the sofa cushions.

"Yes, Amira?" He cocked his brow but continued with his work.

"If you learned something about someone that was—less than flattering, how would you react?"

He paused, looking up at the ceiling. His eyes darted to and fro, as if he were reading something, before he turned toward me. "Do I love this person?"

"Possibly. At the very least, you like them." I fidgeted with the tassel of my shawl.

"If I merely liked the person, I would tell him it was a mistake. If he was apologetic, then it wouldn't matter to me. But if I loved the person," he sat beside me and waited until I looked him in the eye, "then even if he was unrepentant of that unflattering truth, it still wouldn't matter to me. Amira, if Ameer Dhamar loves you, then your past won't matter to him."

"But I—I'm not who he thinks I am." A tear leaked out of my eye, and I stubbornly dashed it away with the back of my hand. "I'm tainted by my past."

"Aren't we all?" Bahis laughed, low and deep and surprisingly pleasant despite his nasally voice. "Amira, there isn't a human alive who doesn't have to live with mistakes and decisions of the past—whether theirs, their parents, or even their grandparents. You are not unique in this. If the ameer loves you..." He shrugged, letting the rest of his statement hang between us.

That was the crux of the matter. Did Dhamar love me? What did love mean for us? Did I love Dhamar enough to bear my heart before him, with all its shattered pieces and past regrets, and trust him not to smash it further?

I rubbed at my chest, setting aside the scroll and standing. "Thank you, Bahis."

"Of course, Amira." He bowed, his smile pulling up the corner of his mouth. "My library is open to you whenever you wish. As is my council." He winked and then returned to his task.

Once I left the library, I wandered toward the courtyard. My thoughts whirled, and my tired mind wanted only to curl into bed for a nap. But I was supposed to meet Lenna in the gardens today, and I couldn't leave her wondering where I was.

The bells in town chimed ten tolls as I stepped over to the fountain. Lenna hurried to my side. The pale-yellow kaftan she wore fluttered around her, but I barely noticed that, for her eyes were wide, and when she reached my side, she gripped my hands tightly.

"They're calling for you," she whispered in a strangled gasp.

"Who?" I stared at her.

Her trembling hands told me the answer before her words.

"Nadar and the council." Her voice shook as tears filled her eyes. "He—he has news from the border. Oh, Inara—"

Dhamar.

My heart dropped to my toes as I released her hands. Was I too late? Had I tarried too long to build something beautiful with Dhamar? Something worth fighting for? Disregarding all propriety, I hitched up my kaftan and ran. Footfalls sounded behind me, proof that Zahir and Saif were still trailing after me, as always. I careened around corners, ignoring everyone in my single-minded goal to find out what happened to Dhamar.

I flung the door to the council chamber open, the heavy thing slamming with a resounding crash against the wall as I strode in. "What's happened to my husband?"

Nadar wasn't on his throne like normal. Rather, he paced before the tiled chair, his hands clasped behind his back. He glowered at me. "Do try to show some respect, *Amira.*"

I had to force the scowl off my face as I bowed, fist over my heart. "Beg pardon, my malek. I just—"

My eyes flicked to the man standing before the small dais, hands clenched behind his back. His tan face was lined with wrinkles, his hair streaked with more gray than black. His jaw was tight, his chest-length beard quivering from the tension.

"General Beeran, this is Amira Inara." The malek waved his hand toward me. "I called for her since this affects her standing in the court."

"Pardon?" I interlocked my fingers to keep them from trembling. "I'm sorry, Malek Nadar, but what has happened to Dhamar?"

"He's been captured by the tribesmen," Lord Shaeen said in a clipped voice. I wasn't certain where the anger was directed—he glared at the general, but the words were pointed toward me. "We're still unsure how they seized him, but the šefe of the tribesmen is now demanding that he marry his eldest daughter."

The blood drained from my face. "Surely Dhamar won't agree."

"He will." Nadar turned toward me. "And you're going to be the one to tell him to do it."

"What?" I stepped back, heat flaring in my face.

"Yes, Amira." Shaeen stood and paced around me. My stomach rebelled as I remembered the Market. The block. The wandering hands, sour breath, and leering eyes. "You will go and tell that pathetic excuse for an ameer that he should marry the Šerian scum's daughter. That man has no sons, and their *culture*," he sneered at the word, "allows women to inherit the title of šefe. If Dhamar marries her, he will be the leader of both Taletha and Šeri."

"He's married to me." I struggled to keep my voice level, my gaze fixed on the malek rather than the leering man pacing around me. "He is my *husband*. This council made quite sure of that."

Shaeen grabbed my face, pinching it roughly in his hand, and leaned so his nose nearly brushed mine. No one in the room moved—I was certain no one breathed. Shaeen whispered, "You are a woman. You will obey the decisions of men or suffer the consequences."

I tore away from the lord, heat flaring through every limb. "I obey one man only, and that is Dhamar. Not you."

"Watch yourself, girl." Nadar turned as red as the blood lilies in the garden. "You may be an amira, but this council is still above you."

"Besides," Shaeen sneered once more, "Dhamar is a worthless, stupid boy who let himself get captured by the enemy."

Nader nodded, a scowl etched on his face. "Indeed. He has no sense. I wouldn't doubt he let himself get caught, the coward. He's too much like his mother."

"Do not speak of him that way!" I snapped, fury making my limbs shake. Shaeen stepped back, his black brows rising in surprise. A leering smile spread over his face as he raked his eyes over me once more. His tongue touched his lips, and I nearly gagged. Nothing would have pleased me more than to erase that look from his face.

"Amira, you are very close to spending the night in the dungeon." Nadar crossed his arms over his ample girth and glared at me.

"Then keep from slandering my husband's name." I took a step closer to the malek, every muscle tensed for a fight as I said, "Dhamar is not worthless. He means everything to me. He overflows with compassion and kindness, and that does not make him weak. He sees those around him as valuable which is more than you and your council have ever done, oh Malek. He is good, gracious, and brave and I—" I fisted my hands at my side as the words caught in my throat. Did I dare utter them? I had felt it for weeks, this burning desire to claim Dhamar in my words and actions. But when the chance arose, would I run away again? Was I truly the coward I had called my husband? I swallowed and dared to meet the malek's cold eyes, drumming up the courage to whisper, "I love him."

"Sentimental nonsense." Lord Shaeen's tone was thick with scorn as he stalked closer. His fingers trailed over my cheek. "No, Dhamar will divorce you like all the other women and marry Šefe Aydin's daughter."

I flinched away from his clammy fingers and met the malek's gaze. His cold brown eyes watched me, then he waved his hand dismissively. "So says the malek."

And the malek's word is law.

My stomach turned. I dared a glance at Beeran, who's tan face had gone pale.

Lord Shaeen gripped my chin, forcing it up to meet his cold gaze. "And when he does, you'll join the other women in the harem. Imagine what fun we could have together, Inara."

I pushed his hand away. "I would rather die."

Malek Nadar stepped up to me and grabbed my wrist. His grip tightened as he leaned over me, his eyes cold as he hissed, "That can be arranged. Soon, you will be ours."

He gestured around the room to the other lords. Many appeared bored, as if this was a common occurrence at their meetings. I didn't want to imagine how many of the young women in the harem had been brought here, the acts that had been performed for the enjoyment of these twisted, corrupt men.

The revulsion must have shown on my face, as the malek's grin turned feral. "Beeran!"

"Yes, oh, my malek?" The general's voice sounded hoarse.

"Take the amira, and leave at once. She'll tell Dhamar of our decision. The consequences if she doesn't...well, she won't enjoy them."

A shiver worked down my spine as Beeran bowed. "Of course, my malek."

"And Lenna," the malek whispered as he turned back to me, his eyes hot with a crazed gleam. "Don't think she'll escape unscathed if you don't obey us."

General Beeran gripped my arm, all but dragging me into the hall. The whole way, the malek and Shaeen stared at me—one gaze hot with hate, the other searing me with lust.

Once the door rumbled closed, General Beeran slid down the wall onto the ground. He roughed a hand over his face. "Dhamar is going to murder the malek. Him and the rest of that blasted council."

My body convulsed, and it was only the sudden support of Saif's arm around my shoulders that kept me from falling. "He...Dhamar hasn't stood up to him in nearly ten years. Why would he now?"

"He has you to fight for." Zahir stepped into sight. His face was pinched in disgust, his jaw flexing. "We couldn't help overhearing.

Upon my honor, I'll get you to the border, my amira. But it's up to you and Dhamar to fix this mess."

"Will he even believe me?" Tears—those blasted, inconvenient waterworks that wouldn't stop—trailed down my cheeks. The fear of rejection reared its ugly head again. For six years, I had been spurned by man after man. Dhamar chose me, but since our marriage, he'd been more interested in obeying his father than working on our relationship. And while I knew it was to protect his mother and me, it didn't lessen the fear that this command could ruin everything. "I don't want to give up on us, Zahir. I meant what I said to Nadar. I love Dhamar. But if he doesn't choose us, then—"

"Then you must fight for him, my amira." Zahir leaned closer. "Fight for the love you've discovered with our ameer."

I wiped my eyes with the back of my hand, drawing myself up as straight and proud as I had day after day in the Wife Market. I was still Inara—the woman nobody wanted. But I was also more now. I was the amira of Taletha. I was Dhamar's wife. I was a survivor, a lioness in human skin, and I wasn't going to give up what was mine without a fight.

Chapter Twenty-Six

Dhamar

I could no longer feel my arms. They were stretched above me, tied to the post of a tent that was bare of all adornments. Thankfully, I had been forced to sit, legs stretched out toward the tent flap. Although, that meant my tailbone was now completely numb. I could hear the tribesmen outside, the guards pacing before my prison.

Getting captured hadn't been part of my plan. The only strategy I'd stalked off with had been to approach the šefe of Šeri to negotiate a truce. Father would kill me as a traitor, but our lands would be at peace.

"But like a fool, here you are," I muttered under my breath as I tried to shift against the sandy ground. I had far too much time to think, and my thoughts hadn't been all that encouraging to say the least. With a sigh, I leaned my head against the post with a dull *thump*.

Hopefully, it will be a swift death.

But was that what I really wanted? There were regrets littering my heart. Yelling at Inara and leaving without a word was my biggest. It kept prancing before my eyes like the dancers at our wedding.

Coward, my mind whispered.

Yes. I know I'm a coward, as big a fool of a husband as I am a man. I thumped my head against the wood behind me. *And now, I will go to the grave regretting that mistake.*

Yet, in my heart I prayed that I would somehow live, that I could make it up to Inara; win her forgiveness and her heart. I had added to the shattered pieces, and now I desperately wanted to help mend them.

Nicar above, please let me live. I squeezed my eyes shut, trying to focus on anything but my whirling thoughts and the needles stabbing into my numb arms.

A new voice joined the murmur of the guards, startling me from my thoughts. The flap opened. I squinted against the stabbing light that filled the tent before the fabric fell back into place, leaving a woman standing before me, clothed in a rainbow.

Her blue kaftan fell to her knees and had a swirling pattern sewn across it in yellow, green, and red thread. Layers of sashes—both gauzy and solid—swished around her waist as she strode around the perimeter of the tent. Her black curls were pulled into a low tail, a magenta scarf knotted over the top of her head. A string of golden coins hung around her neck, jangling with every step she took.

"So, you're the man Otac wants me to marry?" She paced around the pole, her voice familiar. "You're not much to look at."

"I'm also already married." I stiffened, tugging on the ropes I knew were secured far too tightly. *Not part of the plan at all.*

"I don't mind sharing." She knelt beside me, far too close. She purred, "Besides, I am to be the šefe someday. I wouldn't mind having an ameer for a pet."

Her fingers curled in my hair, her face inching toward mine, as if to kiss me. I leaned away from her as best I could. "I don't think my wife would like that."

As suddenly as she'd approached me, the girl sat back on her heels. "Good."

"Good?" Was I trapped in some heat-induced dream? Her sudden change in demeanor had me shaking my head. "What?"

The girl smiled, her teeth gleaming white against her tanned face. And that's when I realized who she was. The woman who'd known my title. One of my captors. "My name is Aysa, princezo of Šeri. You're Dhamar, of course."

"Of course." I shook my head, my brain starting to work once more. "Wait a minute. What was that?"

"A test." Aysa crossed her legs and smiled at me. "And you passed."

"What?" I shook my head again. "I'm sorry, I think I may have hit my head."

"No, you didn't." Aysa laughed, low and throaty. "Though, Emre might have roughed you up a bit bringing you here."

The brute of a man had thrown a sack over my head before hauling me into the Šerian camp, but I was still stuck on Aysa's flirting and near kiss.

"What is going on, Princezo?"

She dropped her gaze to her lap, where she was weaving her fingers together and then apart. "I'm sorry, Ameer Dhamar, but I had to know if you would fight this with me."

"Fight what?"

"Fight for peace." Aysa sighed, leaning back on her hands. "Otac doesn't understand that war isn't what our people need. He's angry at your father. He thinks he's been wronged, though I'm not entirely certain why."

I might have a guess. "And he thinks warring against the border villages because of that slight is a wise idea?" When Aysa nodded, I thumped my head against the post once more. "Tremendous."

"We do have a military advantage." Aysa shrugged, eying me even with her head tipped up toward the ceiling. "You can't deny we could crush your meager force right now, if we wished it."

I couldn't, and my silence was louder than any words.

Aysa leaned forward once more, brushing the sand off her hands. "But if we stand up to my father, he cannot force us to wed."

My stomach clenched.

Coward.

I ground my teeth together. No, I wasn't going to be the coward any longer. Perhaps I had felt the urge to step into the enemy's camp for more than peace. Was this my chance to prove not only to myself, but also Taletha and Šeri that I was an ameer who would stand for what was right? Who would fight for the land and people he swore to serve?

"Your father might not force us, but if *my* father receives word of this, he can order me to wed you."

Aysa stiffened. "How?"

"The malek's word is law." I closed my eyes, the words even more bitter than they had been when I parroted them to Inara. "If he demands that I marry you, I will have no choice. It's that or death."

"You claimed that you're married. Surely, he wouldn't—"

"No, he would. He would either force me to divorce Inara in order to marry you or have two wives." Bile coated my tongue. "There's no law against that in Taletha."

"That's..." Aysa's nose wrinkled, and she gagged as if there wasn't a word strong enough to express her disgust.

"I agree."

Inara. I closed my eyes and pictured her. *Am I willing to fight not just for Taletha, but for her? For us?* I remembered my hands on her hips, drawing her closer. The light in her eyes after I kissed her. The deep, pulsing, fire that spread through me whenever she entered the room. Her laughter, that zest of life that rolled off of her despite everything she'd been through. Her smell and her touch. All of that spun into one beautiful bundle that was my wife. And I knew I couldn't live without her. Was that love? Breathless anticipation, burning passion, but also quiet contentment? The knowledge that she was all I needed to make life wonderful, even if we had to wade through pain together?

"Oh, you love her." Aysa's voice snapped me back to the present.

"What?" *How many times have I said that already?*

"You love her. Your wife." Aysa gestured to her face. "You have that smile."

"Smile?"

"Yes." She giggled. "Otac gets it when he looks at Majka. It's how you know someone is truly in love."

I chuckled at her exuberance. "How old are you, Aysa?"

"I am twenty summers." She raised a slim brow. "But don't confuse my youth with immaturity, Ameer. Bandits and outlaws fill these plains. Pirates too, along the coast. You may be prince of all Taletha, but I have seen more wars and bloodshed than any Talethan man twice my age."

My heart twisted at her words. "I want this war to end."

"Me too." Her eyes, which were a strange gray color, held such intense emotion that they took my breath away. "And I'm willing to fight to bring both our peoples to peace once more."

"As am I." I smiled at her, feeling some of my tension release. The words brought a level of peace, of surety, that I hadn't experienced in weeks. This is how I'd felt when I made my vows to Inara, when I chose her in the Market.

By blood and blade, Nicar as my witness, I will fight for what I love.

"Good, we have an understanding then. I'll be back soon." Aysa stood, brushing the sand from her skirt.

"Where are you going?"

"To greet our guests." She hesitated by the tent flap. Her body seemed to slump as she looked at me. "Your amira is on her way here."

"Inara?" Panic clawed at my throat, my breaths coming in gasps of pain. "Why is she coming here?"

"Otac sent word to your malek." Aysa crouched beside me, laying her hand on my shoulder. "But I swear that no harm will come to your wife. And I will not marry you."

I looked up at her. "You swear it?"

"On the sun, moon, and all the stars."

That vow was binding—the most powerful of any Šerian vow. If Aysa broke it, it would be my right to kill her. Her father wouldn't risk her life, would he? I swallowed the panic that was still rising at the thought of harm coming to my wife.

"Aysa, your father—"

"Trust me, Dhamar." The princezo didn't flinch away. "Let me help you protect her."

My head dropped, my chin hitting my chest as I struggled within. Screams echoed in my ears, but they weren't screams of war. They were memories. Painful memories of my mother, screaming in anguish as the man who claimed to love her hit her over and over. Guards held me tight, making me watch as Father beat Mother because I had dared to question him, to say no. She suffered because of me. That was the last time I had stood up to the malek. I couldn't bear the pain he inflicted on her. And though he'd made me watch other times as he hurt her—both emotionally and physically—I still complied. Never stood up to defend her.

Watching him hurt the people I loved was worse punishment than him turning his fists, feet, and words on me.

And now Inara was riding into danger, into possible pain and torture. To suffer as my father and the šefe used her as a pawn to get what they wanted. Once again, I was helpless to protect the one I loved.

Coward. Scared. Afraid.

"Dhamar," Aysa said, drawing me from my taunting thoughts. "She'll be all right."

"I'm trusting you," I whispered. "Don't let it be misplaced, Princezo."

"I won't fail you." With that, Aysa stood and left me in the dim tent with my ever-darkening thoughts.

Chapter Twenty-Seven

Inara

"I don't think this is a wise idea." Saif shifted on his dappled mare, turning his head to look over his shoulder to where I clung to him. We'd ridden hard and fast, making the normally three-day journey in a little over one. I was exhausted, but our fear for Dhamar and what the šefe might do to him spurred us on.

"It will be fine." My breath hitched as the mare shied to the left, Zahir approaching on our right. The sunlight glinted off the sand, making it nearly impossible to see. But more painful still was the panic choking my throat. I wasn't sure what I was more afraid of—facing the šefe of Šeri or facing my husband. I rolled my shoulders, the tension in them almost unbearable. "Besides, the malek wouldn't send me here to kill me."

Zahir made a snorting sound in the back of his throat. Saif stared down at the colorful tents scattered against the sand, his broad back stiffening. Neither of them said anything. They didn't have to. I knew my words were a lie the moment they'd rolled off my tongue. But I didn't recant them. Instead, I prayed to Nicar for them to be true.

Everything within me went numb as I pressed my forehead between Saif's shoulder blades. "I have to do this. Dhamar is my husband, and I *will* fight for him."

Even as I said it, my heart flipped. Did I really mean that?

"Do you love him, Inara?" Saif asked. "Do you trust that he'll stand up for you like you are for him?"

"I—I don't know. Nearly every man I've known has betrayed me or hurt me in some way. Father, my brothers, my betrothed." My heart pinched at that admission. I wanted my words to be true. Wanted to believe that I loved Dhamar, that he loved me, and that he would fight for me. "The truth is, I don't know how to trust anyone. I'm so afraid of being hurt again."

Saif looked toward Zahir. "Sage advice? You seem to have an abundance of it."

Zahir laughed at Saif's assessment, his eyes still scanning the horizon as he said, "Amira, it's not that you won't be hurt ever again. That's impossible. But when you trust and love someone, you give them the ability to hurt you believing that they won't."

"Will Dhamar?" I whispered, afraid of the answer.

"Not intentionally. But hurt people tend to hurt others. It's part of being human."

"Then how can anyone heal?"

"Learning to listen." Zahir met my gaze over Saif's shoulder. "Listening through the pain you inflict on each other. Yes, it's hard.

It will be messy. But that's the magnificence of love. It's fighting through the chaos to reach the beauty."

I sighed. It wouldn't be easy, but I wanted to wade into the chaos with Dhamar. The past month had been the longest of my life, and I didn't want to endure another. I wanted to tell him everything—about Jamal, my father, my mother—then let him decide if I was worth fighting for. I was done holding back. If I was going to get hurt, it would be because I chose to go all in, without hesitation.

"Let's go," I whispered.

With that, Saif kicked the mare into a trot. The desert sand flew from the horse's hooves, spraying my already dirt-encrusted clothes. My kameez stuck to my back, my salwar to my aching legs. Nothing about me felt regal or royal as we reined in before a host of Šeri warriors who poured out from in between the tents as we approached.

The warriors' brightly colored clothes seemed out-of-place in the endless gold of the desert all around. Their horses pawed the ground, their large hooves beating an agitated rhythm of impatience that matched my own thundering heart. I slid off Saif's horse, my legs nearly buckling from stiffness, but I drew on every ounce of my frozen façade as I turned to face the warriors.

A young woman strode forward, her feet bare and head covered with a magenta scarf. She raised a brow as her gaze swept over me.

"Amira Inara, I presume?" Her voice was deep and melodic. It commanded attention and respect, which I sensed rolling off the warriors around her.

"Yes." I folded my hands before me, trying to straighten my aching back. "Šefe Aydin's daughter?"

"Aysa, princezo of the Šeri people." She inclined her head in a slight show of respect, the gold coins around her neck rattling.

"Where is my husband?" I hated the quaver in my voice, but worry choked me like a snake did its prey. I fisted my hands at my side and sucked in a deep breath. *Keep your wits about you, Inara.*

The šefe's daughter smiled knowingly. "He is safe, Amira. Please, follow me, and you can see for yourself."

I started forward, but Saif grabbed my arm. "No. You won't go alone."

"Your guards are welcome to accompany you," Aysa said, fingering her necklace. "As long as they leave their weapons with my men."

Saif stiffened, but Zahir stepped forward, scimitar already across his palms. "I will accompany Amira Inara, Saif. You will remain with our horses and weapons."

Without waiting for any of us, Aysa turned on her heel and marched back to the camp. I followed, thankful that Saif didn't waste time arguing with Zahir. My pulse roared in my ears, and I wanted to dart between the men standing in straight lines as their princezo strode between them. But I knew that would simply alarm them, and I needed to see Dhamar far too much to risk that.

Zahir stayed on my heels as Aysa led us to a small, brown tent. She lifted the flap and pointed to my guard. "You may check the tent for thirty seconds, then you shall remain out here while your amira enters."

My guard grunted his acknowledgement and stepped inside. Aysa counted aloud and with every second my nerves coiled tighter. I was very near to passing out when she reached twenty-three, and Zahir exited. His face gave nothing away as he moved several paces away and crossed his arms to glare at the two Šerian guards.

"Go," Aysa ordered. "I will enter in a short while."

I ducked inside before Aysa changed her mind. It took several seconds for my eyes to adjust. Slowly, Dhamar took shape. His arms were tied above his head, but otherwise he looked unharmed. I took several steps closer before stopping. What was I doing? He'd left without a word. Unresolved conflict still lay between us, thick as wet sand. Would he even want to see me?

"Dhamar," I whispered, hating the tremor in my voice as I inched a bit closer.

His head hung between his arms, which were bound above his head. He groaned. "Why are you here?"

I took a half step away at the question. Of course, he didn't want me here. He'd left me. I crossed my arms over my stomach and whispered, "I'll go, then."

"No!" He tugged against his bindings and swore. "Come here, you crazy woman."

Still nervous about his rejection, I knelt beside him. My eyes scanned him for injury, for some sign that he'd been tortured and abused, but I couldn't find a thing wrong. "Are you all right?"

"No." His eyes blazed as they met mine. "I want to kiss you, and I can't."

My throat clogged with those blasted tears, and I hurried to swipe them away before he could see. Hope welled up, but I still didn't trust his words. Didn't trust my own fallible heart. It had led me down this path once before, and that had ended in heartache and pain.

Dhamar stilled, his eyes smoldering with barely restrained passion. "Please put me out of my agony, Inara."

I let the tears slide down my cheeks as I cupped his face with my hands. "I missed you."

He leaned forward as best he could and kissed me. His arms got in the way, but it didn't matter. He was kissing me, near me, and everything felt better. Aligned in a way it hadn't in weeks. I leaned back, rubbing his cheeks with my thumbs. "They didn't hurt you?"

"I can't feel my arms, but otherwise I'm fine." His eyes took me in. "And you? Why are you here?"

I squeezed my eyes closed, leaning my forehead against his. A chasm still lay between us, but I wanted him. Needed him. Being close to Dhamar confirmed everything I thought I knew but had questioned over and over the whole ride here—I loved him.

Taking a steadying breath, I answered his question. "Your father and the council want you to marry Princezo Aysa."

A scoffing laugh slipped past his lips. "Well, then *they* are bigger fools than I thought."

"Perhaps you should, Dhamar. She might make you happier than I can."

"Nicar above, you're being foolish, too!" He pulled back. "Look at me, Inara."

I flinched at his command but rose to meet his gaze.

"I've had a lot of time to think while trapped here. And I've realized that if I had to do it all again, I would still choose you. In a million lifetimes, it would be you. It will always be you I choose." Such longing lined his eyes, a depth that even I couldn't decipher. "I'm sorry for making you feel as if that wasn't true."

"I—I love you," I whispered the admission, a sob choking the end. "When the malek said I had to make you marry the princezo, I couldn't—couldn't bear it. He said you had to, that his word is law, and after our fight, I didn't know—"

"Inara." Dhamar pulled on the ropes again, a growl of frustration rumbling in his chest. "My love, please don't cry."

I leaned my head onto his shoulder, and he pressed his cheek against the top of it as I struggled to pull myself back together.

"I'm sorry about what I said before you left," I said at last.

"I forgive you, even though you were correct." He pressed a kiss against my head.

"No, I wasn't." I sat up and cupped his cheek with my hand. "You are not your father. Not by any stretch of the imagination. Standing up to him is terrifying, Dhamar, and I was wrong to accuse you of cowardice. You're the bravest man in the world."

I closed my eyes, pressing my forehead against his again. Sweet Nicar, had I ever missed him. I wanted his hands free, wanted him to cradle me close and tell me he wouldn't leave. That he was mine forever and always.

Dhamar bumped his forehead against mine, causing me to lean back. "Inara, I forgive you for what you said. But you made me realize that perhaps I wasn't as courageous as I needed to be." I opened my mouth to argue, but he shook his head. "Will you forgive me for leaving the way I did? It was cruel and wrong. It's tortured me these past weeks."

It had hurt terribly, reminding me of people and places better left buried. But it had also forced me to choose—choose to embrace Dhamar and fight for what I wanted. To be the bold woman Dhamar had seen at the Wife Market.

"I forgive you, my ameer." I eased back, wiping my cheeks. "It's funny. Saif said fights make love grow deeper. I think I'm finding that to be true."

"I would agree with him. For I love you, Inara, more than I ever thought would be possible." Dhamar smiled, his dimple appearing, and I found myself smiling too. His gaze set my heart to racing. Nicar above, how was it possible to feel as if I was burning from the inside out?

The tent flap snapped open, and Aysa stepped in. A knife was in her hand, and I gasped, stepping between her and Dhamar. "What do you want?"

Aysa chuckled, her brows rising. "Do you want him untied or not?"

"Untied?" I eyed her, not moving.

Dhamar sighed, but humor lit his voice as he said, "I trust her, Inara. She wants to help us."

Still wary, I crouched beside my husband as Aysa sawed through the ropes holding him captive. He rubbed his arms as they fell to his sides, flexing his fingers and wincing with every movement.

"Sorry," Aysa said, not sounding the least bit apologetic as she sheathed the knife once more. It was cleverly hidden among the folds of her scarves, but the handle was within easy reach.

"How are we stopping this marriage?" I whispered, inching closer to Dhamar. He clasped my hand, threading our fingers together. Heat that had nothing to do with the stuffiness of the tent made me a bit lightheaded.

Aysa fingered a coin on her necklace. "The only way these pigheaded men seem to know how."

Dhamar stiffened, his grip on my hand tightening. "No more war."

"Of course not." Aysa smiled, and it looked a little wild in the dim light. "No, we're just going to be more stubborn than they are."

CHAPTER TWENTY-EIGHT

Dhamar

I clung to Inara's hand as we followed Aysa further into the camp. People stopped and pointed, eyes wide as their princezo strode past them with the Talethan ameer and amira trailing behind. I was thankful to have Inara at my side, but a deeper, more primal part of me—the part that feared being helpless to keep those I loved safe—wanted her far from all the danger lurking on the edge of the Šeri camp.

Her thumb slid over my knuckles, and my heart skipped a beat. Her admission in the prison tent had sent me soaring. *You are not your father.* It had soothed a wound deep inside, calmed the fears that were raging. If Inara thought I could be better than the man who'd helped give me life, then I would be. If she said jump, I would. Because I wanted to be the man she needed. Wanted. Chose.

Choose me, wife. I glanced down at her, squeezing her hand ever so slightly. *Choose me as I've chosen you.*

Aysa stepped up to a tent where a massive man stood guard. His black hair was covered with a blue-gray turban, his skin a shade lighter than the princezo. He glared at us, arms crossed over his wide chest.

"Where have you been, and what are they doing free?" He jabbed a finger at Inara and me.

Aysa rolled her eyes, her hands on her hips. She only reached the guards bicep, yet her attitude toward him made me think she knew him better than most. "My otac put me in charge of them. I can do what I see fit, Emre."

Emre growled. "If I go speak to him, he will agree with you?"

"Of course." Aysa stuck out her chin, looking all sorts of stubborn. "Now let me pass."

Emre muttered something and stalked off. I had the feeling this wasn't the first time Aysa had gotten into mischief and that this particular guard had dealt with it.

"Excuse my guard." Aysa rolled her eyes, then gestured to the tent. "This is yours until we can arrange something better."

The tent was square, the fabric a russet orange. Tassels hung from the sloping edges, gleaming a golden yellow in the afternoon sun.

"Is this yours?" Inara asked as she eyed our new lodging.

"Yes." Aysa grabbed Inara's free hand, making my wife jump at the contact. "I have sworn to Dhamar that I will protect you, and now I swear to you, Inara, on the sun, the moon, and all the stars, that both of you will leave this place alive. I will protect you and Dhamar with my very life."

"I—"

"No, Amira." Aysa shook her head. All pretenses left her face as she stared at my wife. This was the real princezo of Šeri—raw, honest, open. "Say nothing. Please, let me do this to bring peace to our people."

Inara inclined her head. "Thank you, Princezo. We do not deserve such loyalty."

No, we didn't. And I didn't deserve Inara's love, Zahir's faithful service, nor a mother who protected me as much as she was able. Yet there they were, gifts that I didn't treasure nearly enough. My breath caught as I wrapped my arm around Inara's waist, and she leaned into me. Starting now, I would fight for my gifts. Protect them. Stand up for them no matter what. Maybe I would fail, but I would fail having given my all.

"I'll bring some food for you, and some water and rags to clean up." Aysa nodded, meeting my gaze. "You have another guard outside of camp. I'll send for him to be brought to you with weapons."

I raised my brow. "Are you certain?"

"I trust you, Dhamar." Aysa's eyes flashed. "You'll keep disasters from happening."

"Thank you, Aysa," I said.

With a final nod, she glided away.

We stepped into Aysa's tent with my hand pressed against Inara's back. A pile of blankets lay on the right side of the tent, a trunk on the left. A few scrolls were stacked by a small group of pillows, and a small heating pot sat by the main tent support. Scarves were draped from the support beams, lending a coziness to the space.

Inara sighed and turned as the flap closed, wrapping her arms around my waist. "We need to talk. I have—a lot I need to tell you."

My shoulders sagged. "Right now?"

"I..." She tightened her hold, her body convulsing. "Yes. If I don't, I'll lose my courage. You need to know before you choose me fully."

"Inara, I'm not going anywhere." I rubbed her back. "Not today, not tomorrow. Never again will I walk away from you."

She looked up, her eyes a beautiful blend of blue and green. I rubbed her cheek with my thumb as I cupped her face.

"Wait until I tell you." She stepped back, out of my arms. Her chest rose and fell rapidly. It was painful to watch. She crossed her arms over her stomach and dropped her gaze. "Before the Wife Market, there was a man."

She paused, her eyes flicking to me, but I kept my gaze carefully neutral.

"His name was Jamal, and he was so sweet." Inara wouldn't look at me. "He brought Mother and me flowers and food, even though he knew what Mother was."

"And that was?" I thought I knew, but I wanted to hear it from her.

"A prostitute." She trembled, and I took a step closer. She flinched, turning away. My heart ached, but I stopped moving so I could hear her barely audible words. "She served the Priests of Nicar mostly. Our house was down the road from the temple in the lower city, and they used her frequently."

My jaw tightened, that fierce protection flaring. These were men who claimed to serve our goddess, and yet they treated vulnerable women this way?

"Jamal was over often. He brought food and treats, and with Mother working frequently, we were alone most times." Her shoulders slumped, her chin hitting her chest. "He said he loved me and that he wanted to marry me. We were practically betrothed. And so, when he asked to touch me in places he shouldn't, I allowed it. It was thrilling to be caressed, to feel his hands on my skin." She pressed a hand to her lips as a sob slipped out. "He said he loved me, that he wanted to be mine. But when he found out who my father was, he walked away."

I reached out and pulled her to me, rubbing my hand up and down her back as she cried. I kept my voice level, as soothing as possible when I asked, "Did it ever go beyond touching?"

"No." She shook her head, her voice barely above a whisper. Her hands were fisted into the back of my tunic. "But he was so intimate with me. And I feel so dirty, Dhamar. I'm not worthy of you."

"Inara." I smoothed my hand against her hair. "I'm not leaving you, my darling."

Her grip tightened as if to reassure herself that I still stood there. "I know, but Jamal—"

"I'm not Jamal." I eased back, cupping her cheek and smoothing away the tears with the pad of my thumb. "He preyed on you. Used you to satisfy his flesh. I will *never* force myself on you, my wife.

Not with touching, not with more intimate measures. We are one. To hurt you would hurt me."

She sniffed and nodded but still wouldn't look at me. "There's more. You need to know about my father. He's so awful."

She shivered and pressed her face into my chest once more. Was she that afraid of her father? Or was she still afraid that I would walk away like Jamal? I wouldn't.

But I had walked away already. We'd gotten into a fight, and I'd run away. How could she know that I wouldn't do the same again? My words were just that—words. I had to prove to her that I would stay.

"Do you remember our vows, Inara?" I asked, adjusting my grip as I started rocking us from side to side.

"Which ones?" she asked.

"The traditional ones."

"By blood and blade, I am yours. I swear to love you, serve you, and obey you as a wife ought, and to be faithful to you alone until Nicar calls us from this life."

"Do you believe that? Because I meant every word. I will love and serve you alone. You're the one I choose until Nicar calls us from this life. Whether that is twenty years or ninety, you are the one my heart longs for. No matter your past, no matter our future, no matter our relations, you are the one I choose."

Inara sniffed and nodded. "And I choose you. From this day on, forevermore."

I pressed a light kiss to the corner of her mouth. "That being said, who is your father?"

"He's..." she swallowed, whispering a name so softly I didn't quite catch it. I eased her back, tipping her chin up to look at me. But when I did, her eyes widened and she flinched, startling back as if I had slapped her.

"I—I'm sorry." She hid her face in her hands and slid down the post, curling her legs up to her chest. Her reaction startled me, and I wasn't sure what to do.

"Ameer?" Zahir's voice penetrated the tent flap. I held it open, keeping Inara in the corner of my vision. Zahir held up a bucket of water with a few cloths in it, as well as a bulging sack. "Princezo Aysa said this was for you and the amira." His brows pinched when he caught sight of Inara's hunched figure. "What happened?"

"I...don't know," I admitted, taking the items with a nod of thanks. "But I'm going to find out."

Setting the bucket and bag by the door, I squeezed the water out of one of the cloths and approached Inara. She still had her face buried against folded arms, though her tears had slowed. Laying my hand on her shoulder, I asked, "May I?"

She turned, her cheek pressed against her arms, and sighed. "Yes."

I sat facing her, our hips brushing as I leaned in and began to wipe at the dirt smudging her face. She wouldn't look at me, her shoulders shaking with every swipe of the cloth.

"Did something happen back home?" I asked, moving from her cheeks to her forehead and then to her neck.

"No, everything was—" She squeezed her eyes closed. "No, that's not true. Trust," she whispered the word. I could feel the struggle within her, and kept my mouth shut. After a few deep breaths, she dragged her eyes to me. "Your father and Lord Shaeen threatened me."

I stiffened, a red-hot spear of anger stabbing through me. "They what?"

"They said if I didn't get you to marry Aysa, then I wouldn't like the consequences. Shaeen grabbed my chin and—"

She gasped again as I tipped her chin up, looking for a bruise. Finding none, I cupped the back of her neck. "I'm so sorry I wasn't there to protect you. That snake will pay for laying a hand on you."

"You were a little tied up when it happened." She grabbed the cloth from me in her trembling fingers and began to wipe at my forehead, forcing me to release her so she could work. My hand was braced against the ground, crossing over her waist as I gazed at her. Her hands were gentle, cleaning the grit of battle and capture from my face. She slowed as she finished, her eyes flicking to my lips. "I missed you. Have I said that?"

"I like hearing it." I leaned closer. "And you said something else, too."

"Did I?" Her eyes didn't flutter shut. Our noses brushed, and she snaked her arms around my shoulders. "What did I say?"

"You said"—I pressed my lips to her ear, making a shiver work its way down her back— "that you loved me."

"I do." Her nose nuzzled into my neck, and her lips brushed my collarbone as I wrapped my other arm around her waist. "I love you, Dhamar."

"Good. Because you are my wife, and I'm never letting you go." I slowly lowered a kiss to the soft spot between her neck and her ear, giving her enough time to push away if it made her uncomfortable. But she didn't. If anything, her arms tightened around my neck, pulling our bodies closer. I had dreamed of winning her heart, of holding her close, and here we were, doing just that.

Yet, I still hadn't heard who her father was. Did it matter? My heart had Inara, my body wanted her, so was the past important?

It was, I knew. It made her who she was. Before I could love her completely, totally, this wall had to come down.

With every ounce of self-control I possessed, I eased her back. "I didn't hear who your father was, Inara."

She seemed to shrink. "My father?"

"Yes. Who is he?"

"He's—" Her eyes fluttered closed. "My father is Umar, the pirate of the North Sea."

Umar. Not just *a* pirate of the North Sea, but the most feared pirate in all of Taletha. A man who'd killed hundreds while stealing money, goods, and food from across our lands. He was known to hurt women for his own sick pleasure, capturing adults and children alike and pressing them into service on both land and sea. He was a force to be reckoned with, one that my father and the council had let thrive for far too long. He protected our soil from an attack from surrounding nations all while leaving a trail of evil in his wake.

Yes, Umar had to be dealt with. He was a sickness that needed to be purged from our land. But Inara wasn't her father, just like I wasn't mine.

"While he is an evil man, we aren't responsible for our families, my darling." I brushed my finger across her cheek, a warning to her before I raised her chin to face me. "You are uniquely you. I am me. And together?" I brushed my lips across hers. "Together, we're incredible."

"You aren't upset?" she asked, her hands pressed against my chest. "He's—"

"Not you." I shook my head. "I love *you*, Inara. And I want to be yours in more than just words. If you'll have me?"

Tears were trailing down her cheeks again as she pulled me closer, kissing me with a passion that left me breathless. Time ceased as I pulled her into my lap, wrapping my arms around her and leaning in. It was simply us. And in that magical moment, I dared to love and know Inara as I had never loved and known anyone else before.

CHAPTER TWENTY-NINE

Inara

Warm arms encircled me when I awoke. The scent of eucalyptus still clung to Dhamar, even after weeks of travel, war, and capture. It was the most wonderful scent in the world, because it was *him*. I scooted closer, feeling his chest rise and fall in his slumber. He was a solid presence at my back. One I would never walk away from, no matter what the malek ordered.

Last night, I had revealed my heart to him, and he said he'd stay. He'd seen my raw, trampled heart, and said I was worth fighting for. I was his wife, and he wanted me. Chose me.

By blood and blade, I am yours.

Dhamar shifted, arms tightening. His fingers rolled circles over my bare arms as he nuzzled his nose into my neck. Tingles raced across my skin, and I snuggled closer, pressing into Dhamar's warm chest as I hugged his arms closer.

"Good morning, my love." His voice was thick, sleep clinging to the words.

"Good morning."

We just lay there. For how long, I wasn't sure. But I wanted to savor this moment. After this, we would be plunged into ending a war, uniting Aysa's people with ours, and stopping Dhamar's father from ripping us apart.

"Ameer Dhamar?" Saif's voice came muffled through the fabric.

Dhamar groaned and sat up. He ran a hand through his curls, making them stand even more on end. I smiled, tugging the blanket up under my chin as he tugged on his salwar and strode to the door. His body was taut with frustration, but all that did was define the muscles on his arms and chest.

He pulled open the flap to talk with our guards. I let my eyes fall closed, though the bed was decidedly less warm without Dhamar at my side. Last night I had felt cherished, loved in a way that Jamal had never made me feel. I was seen by my husband, flaws and all, and he wanted me. I was safe to be myself—angry, sad, happy. It didn't matter. Dhamar loved me. I sighed, the euphoria of the moment clinging to me like the sweetest of fragrances.

"You need to get dressed." Dhamar sighed, his voice closer than it had been.

I cracked one eye open to see him crouching beside me. "Already?"

He smiled, his brown eyes warming as he stared down at me. "When did you turn so lazy?"

My brow rose. "Since I married you."

He laughed, leaning down to kiss my temple before grabbing his kurta and sliding his arms in. "I'll go see if Aysa brought breakfast."

I nodded. After he left, I pulled a fresh kameez and salwar on and brushed the dust out of my hair. Braiding it over my shoulder, I crossed my legs and took a deep breath.

While I was ecstatic about last night, fear churned in my stomach, because this was all too beautiful to last. Something or someone would come along and snatch away the love and joy I'd found. It happened every time. I didn't get happily ever after.

No, I thought with a shake of my head. *No, we will fight for it. Together.*

I yelped as a hand landed on my shoulder. Dhamar crouched before me, scratching his jaw as he leaned closer. "Are you all right?"

"What if we're not strong enough to win this?" The question came out unbidden, and I bit the inside of my cheek as I dropped my gaze. He didn't need my doubts and fears. He had to believe we'd make it through. This was terrifying enough without me muddying the waters with my own insecurities.

"I've learned something since I married you." Dhamar sighed as he settled beside me. He picked up my hand, tracing his thumb around my knuckles and down my fingers.

I glanced up through my lashes when he didn't continue. "What?"

"There are things I am willing to bend my will to. Father ordering me about, eating food that's not my favorite, going to council meetings." He gagged, and I smiled. "But there are other things that I have to fight for. Stand up to. Ending this war? It's worth whatever I have to sacrifice. But I will not kill anymore to obtain that. And Inara? I will *never* give you up."

Dhamar curved his hand against my cheek, and I leaned into his touch. It was so gentle, so tempered with love and self-control. Last night, our love had been passion and heat. This morning, it was soft words and tender touches. One wasn't better than the other. Love was sweeter when it was both.

"What about your mother?" I held my hand over his.

"I—" Dhamar dropped his gaze, but he didn't lean away.

"I've gotten to know her, you know." He looked up, eyes widening at my admission. "She came to see me often over the two weeks you were gone."

"She shouldn't have done that. Father wouldn't be happy if he knew." Dhamar buried his fingers in his hair.

"I know. And I tried to make her stop. She wouldn't listen." I bumped my shoulder into his, a tease touching my words. "She's stubborn like you that way."

He chuckled and shook his head.

"You're a lot like her, Dhamar. Tender and considerate. I'm glad she gave you that part of herself."

"I am, too," he admitted. "And while I am concerned about her, we'll cross that bridge when we come to it."

"All right." I shifted onto my knees, wrapping my arms around his neck. "We fight together, yes?"

"Yes." He tucked a strand of my hair behind my ear. "I like together."

I kissed him, a quick peck on the lips, before I leaned back and grabbed the bread he'd set aside. "Let's eat."

"That was cruel," Dhamar grumbled as he handed me a piece of cheese.

I stifled a grin and scooted closer to him. "Later, my love."

The sparkle of anticipation in his eyes warmed me to my core.

The peace of our morning breakfast didn't last long.

Aysa stepped into the tent as we finished our food, her plump lips pressed thin. "I'm sorry, Ameer. I tried to stall, but Otac is demanding a meeting with you and the amira."

"Mother always told me that Aydin was never a patient man." Dhamar sighed and pushed to his feet. Offering me his hand, he helped me up, keeping a firm grip on me as he led me to the tent flap.

"How does your mother know of my father?" Aysa asked Dhamar with a raised brow.

"I fear many of my people have forgotten the connection between our families. Not many want to admit it."

"What connection?" I asked.

"You'll see." Dhamar's cryptic response had my nerves coiling at the base of my neck. Would this end badly all around?

Aysa eyed him curiously as she led us to a large tent at the center of the camp. A glance over my shoulder showed Saif and Zahir two steps behind us, eyes darting around. They wouldn't be much help if the šefe turned on us, but their presence at my back was nearly as steady of a reassurance as Dhamar's hand in mine.

Nicar above, help us get out of this alive.

"Ready?" Aysa asked as she stepped up to the tent flap. The guards on either side glowered but didn't move to stop us. I wondered if Aysa had more sway over her people than Dhamar. Not that Dhamar lacked authority or power. It was just wielded differently. Aysa was within her people, part of their lives. Dhamar had to be above them.

Maybe we can change that, though. A million ideas for helping the lesser people of Mordova flashed through my head. Days where the ameer and amira saw to the needs of the poor and downtrodden, distributed food, and brought healers to the sick.

My thoughts were cut short by Aysa lifting the flap and gesturing us in. The tent was dim, and I had to blink several times before the shapes morphed into people. Colorful cushions were placed all around the oval tent, a man or woman on each one. It was similar to the council chamber at the palace, though this atmosphere lacked the hostility and evil that coated that room.

Directly in front of us sat a man I assumed was Šefe Aydin. A red fez sat on his head of straight black hair. An ebony staff was clutched in his hand, and the folds of his crimson robes seemed to bleed into the matching canvas of the tent. His eyes were hard as he gazed down his sharp, beak-like nose at Dhamar and me.

Aysa strode forward, bowing at the waist toward her father. "Otac, most excellent šefe of Šeri, I present Ameer Dhamar and his amira, Inara. They, too, wish for peace, as I have petitioned these many weeks. I respectfully request that we listen to them, for they have no desire for bloodshed among our people."

"As you've already welcomed the amira as a guest and released the ameer—our prisoner—I suppose I have to listen." Šefe Aydin gestured us forward. "Speak your piece, Dhamar."

"Are we not going to first acknowledge our bond, Šefe?" Dhamar asked, even as he strode forward and mirrored Aysa's bow. I followed him and did the same.

"What bond?" Aydin snapped. His fingers went white as he gripped his staff. Aysa stiffened, on alert.

"You are my mother's brother." Dhamar's palm felt slick in mine. "Or have you so quickly forgotten the sister who could do nothing but remember her childhood in Šeri?"

I blinked at my husband as the other people in the tent took to whispering. I knew Lenna was from Šeri, but the šefe's sister? Aysa's aunt? I could feel the tension in the room escalating, and it tightened my stomach muscles so much that I thought I might be ill.

Aydin's eyes hardened. "Enough!" he ordered, slamming the end of his staff against the ground. The room instantly stilled.

"My sister died in a raid by *your* people twenty-six winters ago." Aydin's gaze narrowed. "Why would you reopen such a wound, young ameer?"

"Beg pardon, Šefe, but that isn't true." Dhamar shook his head. "My father, reckless and foolhardy man that he is, did raid Šeri all those years ago. The women he had married failed to produce a male heir." A tremble shook Dhamar's shoulders, and his head bowed. "And so, when he raided your encampment, he did not slaughter all the people."

Lenna. He'd stolen Aydin's sister.

"He stole away a number of your women, but only one produced the heir he wanted. That woman is my mother," Dhamar stated with surprising steadiness. "Lenna, the Rania of Taletha, whose name used to be Adana, daughter of Šeri."

The murmurs started again, and no amount of pounding by Aydin was able to silence them. I edged closer to Dhamar as shouts for his death echoed around the tent. Were we going to die now? After everything we'd been through?

A shrill whistle split the air, and Aysa glared at those seated around us. "This is ridiculous. Dhamar has offered us a great gift. Now that I know my Teyze Adana is alive, I want even less for there to be war between our people." She gestured to Dhamar and me. "They are Šerian as much they are Talethan."

"They are not Šerian!" one man with long gray hair argued, launching to his feet. "They are the enemy! Why should we dare trust him?"

"Can we afford not to?" a soft-spoken lady with a long braid asked. "He has a trustworthy face, and I, for one, agree with the princezo. We don't need war. With summer approaching, we need a way to feed our people. We need water and pasture. Can we get that here in Šeri?"

A few voices murmured agreement, but there was still the undertow of anger pulsing on the fringes.

"Otac?" Aysa turned and stood between us and the šefe. "I have claimed the sacred vow over them. Death is not an option, unless you want me to die as well."

I glanced up at Dhamar in surprise. He nodded once, and I shook my head. I hadn't realized how binding Aysa's vow had been.

"Foolish choice, kćerka." Aydin pinched the bridge of his nose with a sigh.

"Please, Dayi." The šefe bristled at Dhamar's use of *uncle*. "Like Aysa, I have no wish for war to continue. I am willing to be the bulwark between my father and your people."

Aydin steepled his fingers, tapping them against each other as he eyed his nephew. "What guarantee do I have of this? You have no reason to swear allegiance or loyalty to Šeri. You could just as easily turn on us all. Why should I trust you?"

Dhamar shifted, his eyes flicking to Aysa. "As you can see, I am already wed to Inara. Therefore, marriage to your daughter is out of the question."

"Yes, although practices in your land would allow for it." The šefe raised a brow.

Dhamar shook his head. "I've seen what damage that does, Dayi. Nothing in me wants to inflict that on Aysa and Inara."

"Very good." Aydin leaned his elbows onto his knees, fingers still pressed together. "But then, what of your allegiance?"

Something in me stirred, a peace settling over me as the idea sprung to life. I was the amira of Taletha. This was my fight as much as Dhamar's, and while I couldn't do much to end the war, I could do this.

Releasing Dhamar's hand, I strode forward. I knelt and fisted my hand against my heart. It beat frantically. I was terrified at what I was about to do, but this was right. This was fighting with love and for love—with love, in hopes of mending what had been shattered twenty-six years ago at the hand of one selfish man, and for love that was just beginning to blossom with the man that stood at my side.

"I swear," I began, voice shaking but loud enough for everyone in the tent to hear, "upon the sun, the moon, and all the stars, that we will fight for the rights of not only Taletha, but of Šeri. By blood and blade, we will fight for peace, for unity, so that our children and our children's children can say that we are truly allies and friends."

My proclamation was met with absolute silence.

CHAPTER THIRTY

Dhamar

I wanted to leap forward and drag my wife back. Wanted to tuck her away so that no harm could befall her. Swearing to bring peace to Taletha and Šeri was foolish. One mistake, and Aydin could demand her life.

Realization dawned then; if Aydin demand Inara's death, he would be condemning Aysa as well. The princezo's vow of protection meant that Inara was safe from any retribution Aydin could attempt. I bit back a smile. My wife's vow would show the šefe that we were serious in our desire to bring about peace.

Aydin shifted his staff from hand to hand, undoubtedly trying to get Inara to squirm. But my wife had the patience and endurance to remain still under scrutiny. It was one gift the Wife Market had given her.

"Your courage is admirable, Amira," Aydin said at last. His gaze moved to Aysa. "I must speak to the heads of the tribes before making my decision. Take them back to wherever you had them and keep them there."

"Yes, my otac." Aysa bowed then motioned for us to follow her out of the tent. Once the flap fell closed, Aysa exhaled sharply, grinning at Inara as she did. "Well, I wasn't expecting *that*."

Inara shrugged, hugging my arm as we meandered back to our tent.

"Are you all right?" I whispered.

She lifted her shoulders again, not meeting my gaze.

Aysa motioned for us to enter. "I'll stand guard along with your men, Ameer. It will keep people from saying I'm not doing my duty." She winked. I was starting to like this cousin of mine. Her guard—Emre—appeared from beside our tent, not looking at all pleased with his princezo.

"Thank you, Aysa." I inclined my head and, before Emre could say anything, guided Inara into the tent. Her shoulders heaved in relief as the flap fell back across the door.

"That was—intense." She rubbed the back of her neck, not meeting my eye. "Are you—you're not upset with me, are you?"

"Why would I be upset?" I grabbed her hand and pulled her up against me. "You were magnificent. Every inch the amira I knew you would be."

"From the day you married me?" I opened my mouth to reply, but she slapped her hand over it. "And don't say yes. You had no idea what I would be like when you married me."

Feeling impish, I licked her hand. She squealed, trying to squirm out of my grasp, but I held on. "I was going to say 'no' before you so rudely stopped me. It wasn't the day I married you." She stilled, cocking her head to the side. My heart swelled with love and pride as I stared down at this amazing woman. Not only was she gorgeous beyond words, but she had a beautiful heart and a courageous soul. While I'd known that, seeing it on display was even more captivating.

I continued, "It was after our second wedding. The vows you said and our talk that night. That's when I knew I had married a woman that would rise to meet any challenge thrown her way. A woman worthy of being my amira."

Her eyes crinkled from the force of her smile, and she swayed closer. Wrapping her arms around my neck, she said, "No matter what happens, I'm glad you chose me, Dhamar."

Inara buried her nose against my chest, and I swayed with her. A tune my mother had sung to me when I was a child came to mind, and I hummed it to Inara. For a moment, it was just us.

No distractions.

No battles for peace.

No fear or anger or chaos.

It was simply us, stealing a few moments together.

Inara leaned back first, smiling up at me sleepily. "I don't think I've ever said it, my ameer, but thank you."

"For what?"

"For saving me."

"Saving you from the Wife Market?"

"Yes." She laid her hands against my chest. "But also from myself. I didn't want to be hurt by anyone again. Because of that, I had walls up and locks secured. No one was going to get close to me. But then you came." She smiled up at me, and the air caught in my lungs. "You didn't let the walls stay up, you got in the grime with me and I—" Her gaze dropped. "I don't deserve you, Dhamar. But I'm so thankful that I have you."

I couldn't speak, and perhaps that was a good thing. Actions were simpler, clearer. I cupped her face and kissed her. I lost myself in her. Her kiss, her scent, her feel. Inara wrapped her arms around my neck, her fingers trailing into my hair as she stepped closer still. Our bodies were flush with each other, and I didn't want the moment to end.

The sound of the flap opening broke through the haze of our kiss. Inara twisted toward it, trying to ease out of my hold. But now that she was mine—heart and soul—I wasn't ready to let go. I turned with her to see a very wide-eyed Saif standing in the doorway, silhouetted by the sun.

"Forgive me, Ameer, Amira." He cleared his throat and shoved a platter of fruit and cheese at us.

"Put it over there." I jutted my chin at the cushions, and he hurried to obey, bowing to each of us before running out the door.

Inara snorted and then burst into giggles. I smiled down at her, shaking my head. "Hopefully, he's learned his lesson about coming in unannounced."

"I—I should think so." Inara wiped at a tear on her cheek, her laughter subsiding. "His face was priceless."

I hummed in agreement then wiggled my brows, making her giggle again, before gesturing to the food. "Are you hungry?"

"Famished."

We settled among the cushions, eating, talking, and awaiting word from the Šeri leaders. Dusk fell, and Inara curled on her side, head in my lap. I absentmindedly stroked her hair away from her face, feeling truly worried for the first time since leaving Šefe Aydin's council tent. Would they decide our plan was a foolish one, an attempt to lull them into safety only to attack when we had the chance? Would they kill us? Risk the wrath of Taletha, as pathetic as it was?

Nicar above, was this plan doomed from the start?

"What do you dream of?" Inara asked, interrupting my spiraling thoughts.

I glanced down at her. She was staring at the tent flap, her hands tucked under her chin. Contemplating her question for a minute, I finally said, "I suppose I haven't really thought about it too much."

"Dream now." She rolled over to her back, looking up at me. "What does our future look like?"

A million images flashed through my mind: Inara, round with our first child. Mother, cradling a babe with black hair and green eyes. The love and grace we would extend to each other every day as our family grew. Then, eventually, there would be a great number of children spinning around us as Inara and I swayed together in our common room at the palace. I saw justice and virtue growing in Mordova because of us. There would be joy and hope and peace. Love and forgiveness.

I stroked her hair away from her face and whispered, "I want to fall more in love with you every day. I know it won't be only happy times. Like you said, hard times make the love deeper, more rooted. But that doesn't change the fact that I want to raise children with you. Children who know what true love looks like because they see it in us. I want laughter, bedtime stories, kisses on sticky cheeks, and embraces when they hurt themselves. All I want is to have a family with you, Inara. Whether I'm malek, ameer, or a common peasant, that is my dream."

Tears filled her eyes when I finished. "It's my dream too, Dhamar."

We were silent for a moment, and then a throat cleared loudly outside the tent before Saif called out, "Ameer Dhamar?"

"He's never going to come into our room again, is he?" Inara whispered through a giggle.

"Not likely." I smirked before saying louder, "Yes, Saif?"

"Princezo Aysa has requested you at the council tent."

"Thank you." I helped Inara sit up. "Are you ready?"

"I suppose I have to be." She smoothed out her kameez and patted her hair. "Do I look all right?"

She looked windblown and wild, bold and daring. More beautiful than any woman I had ever beheld. I wanted to stay in the tent, pull her to me, and never let go. Show her once more how very much I adored her. But I placed my hand at the small of her back with a smile. "You look stunning, my love."

That seemed to brighten her eyes and the smile she wore. "I love you."

"I know." I kissed the top of her head and guided her to the tent flap.

Aysa paced in front of our tent, her brows lowered.

"Is it that bad?" I asked, and she turned to face me with a frown.

"I've never known them to deliberate so long." She twisted the end of her hair around her finger. "I fear what they've decided."

I stiffened, but Inara wrapped her arm around my waist. "Killing us would kill his daughter. I cannot imagine Šefe Aydin would want that. And regardless, I will not stop fighting for peace. I will uphold my vow to the Šeri leaders. Whatever they decide, we will all face it with courage." Inara grabbed Aysa's hand. "Together."

Aysa glanced from Inara's hand to her face, and a smile began to appear. "I believe you are our family, whether Father cares to admit it or not. It may have passed from common knowledge, but I have heard the story of Teyze Adana many times. Enough to know that what you say is true. They never did find her body."

"If we can establish peace," I said, "I will bring her to see you. Or you to her."

"The former, most likely." Aysa rolled her eyes. "Otac will never march into Mordova willingly. Not for the first few years, at least." Aysa chuckled, but then her face lined with worry once more. "How much do you trust a father's love?"

I felt Inara stiffen right as my own shoulders went taut. What did we know of a father's love? Her father had sold her. Mine was willing to let me die or be miserable for all of my life to get what he wanted. Out of all of us, Aysa likely had the most loving father.

Will I make a good father? I scratched at my jaw as we followed Aysa toward the center of camp. Inara had told me she thought I would make a good father. That helped. But the only example I had of a father was Nadar—and he was cruel and vicious, beat his wife and son, abused innocent women for the sake of pleasure. I didn't want to be like him.

A face popped into my mind. *Zahir.* He knelt in the courtyard beside a small child who'd scraped his knee. He'd only been sixteen, but he had spoken soothing words and helped to nurse the boy's wound. *My wounds.*

Then General Beeran, training a young man of eleven to wield his scimitar. But more than just weapons, he'd taught chivalry and virtue, conduct and respect. He knocked me down while simultaneously building me up. He guided me, molded me in a way my own father never had.

Certainty settled around my heart. I may not have had a father by blood, but I had plenty in spirit. And that would have to be enough for the family I would someday have.

Because we will have a family. I squeezed Inara's hand. *A large, beautiful, vibrant family.*

The sky was ablaze with reds, oranges, and pinks, matching the tents we strode through. Torch light flickered against them, leaving eerie shadows along their patterned fronts. The air held the heavy aroma of savory meats and stews, but my stomach churned far too much to enjoy the smell.

Nicar, be with us. Grant us favor with the men of Šeri.

We reached the center tent, and my hand trembled as I moved it to the small of Inara's back. She turned to me, cupping my face in her hand and pulling it down to her. "No matter what they decide, I am thankful to be facing this with you."

"And I with you," I whispered.

Her lips curved up for the barest second and then she stepped back. With fingers linked, we turned and stepped into the tent.

Chapter Thirty-One

Inara

Lanterns now hung from the support beam of the tent. The light danced across the faces of the people within, making them appear like ghouls shrouded in shadow. I tightened my hold on Dhamar's hand as I caught sight of Šefe Aydin. He stood, his red robe billowing around him, and he held his ebony staff in his long fingers as he watched us approach.

Both Dhamar and I bowed, and I pressed my fist against my hammering heart, hoping it would remind the šefe of my vow to bring peace to both Šeri and Taletha.

Please, grant us peace, I prayed as we stood.

"You summoned us, oh Šefe?" Dhamar asked.

"Yes, I have." He scratched his jaw with his forefinger as he stared above our heads. My mouth fell open in surprise. The action was so like Dhamar that any lingering doubt about them being related faded completely. "We have reached a decision."

"And it is?" Aysa asked, shifting from foot to foot beside us.

Aydin glanced at her, face expressionless. "We have decided—" he paused, his gaze swinging around to all the family heads gathered around us, witnesses to this strange event "—to believe the word of Ameer Dhamar and Amira Inara. We do need peace. We need trade and stability in Šeri. It's something we've gone too long without."

I exhaled in relief, a small smile on my face. But Dhamar stiffened further. "While I have promised peace, you must be aware that my father will not be pleased."

"We are." Aydin nodded. "That is one reason it took us so long to come to an agreement."

"Do you have a solution for this problem, Ameer?" one of the leaders asked with a sneer, clearly not in favor of this arrangement.

"I shall ride to my father and try to make him see reason." Dhamar scratched his jaw, meeting the leader's hard gaze with an equally steely one as he dropped his hand. "It is the only logical solution outside of continued war, which neither of us wants."

"No." Aysa agreed, shaking her head so hard that the gold coins of her necklace clattered together. "No more war."

Aydin steepled his fingers, his staff cradled in the crook of his elbow. "Do you think having Aysa and myself present would help negotiations?"

This brought a number of protests from around the tent.

"Silence!" ordered the šefe's booming voice, making me ease a step closer to Dhamar. It took a moment for the grumbles to dissipate. The whole situation reminded me of the council room in the palace. But again, evil didn't ooze from this tent. Rather, respect and service seemed to be at the forefront of these leaders' hearts. A desire to protect their people and provide for them. How I knew that, I wasn't certain, but I knew I wanted that for Taletha's rulers as well.

Dhamar inclined his head. "I know it would be a risk for you, Dayi Aydin, but I do think it would show that you would respect an alliance. It will show my people that their malek and lords are the ones aggravating this—hostility." His shoulders slumped, as if it pained him to admit that. I dared to tug him closer. My cheeks heated when the motion turned the šefe's gaze my way.

"You two." His finger wagged between us. "You are stronger together."

"And how would you know that, my šefe?" a woman to his left asked, brow raised. The question wasn't coated in disdain, but rather with a teasing lilt.

"Because" — *did the šefe just wiggle his brows?* — "they remind me of us, my dear."

The woman smiled, and then I saw Aysa in her. In the curve and plumpness of her lips. In the tone of her skin and the set of her shoulders. She turned toward Dhamar and me, and the light caught her face. A thin leather band was around her forehead, a few gold coins laying against her brow. Her hair was curly and long, tied back in a tail like her daughter's. A few gray streaks were woven through the black, and the lines around her mouth and eyes were the only indication of her age.

She smiled at us. "Since Aydin has finally accepted you as family—though he would never stoop to saying so—allow me to introduce myself." She rose to her feet and stepped forward. "I am Enis, the kari of Aydin, the majka of Aysa, and the teyze to you, Dhamar." She gripped his shoulders and kissed both of his cheeks. Then she did the same to me, a small smile on her face as she whispered in my ear, "It is no small thing to marry a royal. Yet you carry it with grace, Amira."

I bowed my head in thanks as Enis released my shoulders and moved back to the šefe's side.

"Now." Šefe Aydin tossed his staff from hand to hand for a moment. "How are we to approach your father, Dhamar?"

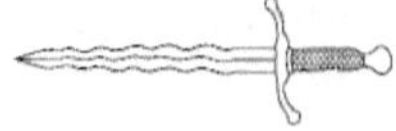

I dozed against Dhamar's shoulder as around and around the conversation went. The Šerian leaders didn't want Aydin to go near the border, but Dhamar said his father wouldn't step foot in Šeri for fear of an ambush. It was finally decided that the pocket of land in the east along the sea would keep both sides in line, especially if they set a guard limit, and Dhamar and I went forward before them to make sure there was no ambush set up for the šefe.

Discussion then turned to potential demands, how it could be ensured Nadar would keep his end of the deal. What they would and wouldn't accept from Taletha, desired trade agreements, and more kept them going as the moon rose, and the stars began to wink in the endless blackness.

"Why don't you take Saif and go back to the tent?" Dhamar whispered against my hair as Aysa and her father argued about whether wheat or corn would be a better trade for their livestock.

"I want to stay with you," I mumbled.

"You need to sleep." He chuckled. "Go to bed, and I'll join you in a bit, my love."

Perhaps he will retire sooner if I'm not by his side. That thought, along with my gritty eyes, had me rising and slipping from the tent. No one even questioned my departure, and Saif kept one hand on my shoulder the whole way back to the tent.

"Have you slept at all?" I asked, raising a brow at him before slipping into the tent. Exhaustion weighed heavy on me, but sudden worry for my guard had me pausing.

"Yes." He grinned his lopsided smile. "Zahir and I have traded off and on all day."

I paused. "I'm sorry we pulled you away from Ranya."

His smile faltered for the barest second. "Ranya will be fine. She's a strong woman. Besides, the palace has its healers and midwives. If something does happen, they will care for her until I return."

If he returned. Nothing was certain at that moment, and it made my stomach sour. I didn't want to be responsible for Ranya losing her husband and their unborn child's father.

"Inara, stop worrying." Saif sighed. "You can no more control life than I can the rain."

"I know." I did. But sometimes it felt so overwhelmingly impossible that I wished I could sink my fingers into it and drag it back to the course *I* thought was best.

"Sleep, Amira." He nudged me gently toward the tent flap. "I'll be standing guard if you need anything."

"Thank you, my friend." I turned, surprising him with a quick hug before hurrying to the pillows and blankets. Stripping off my kameez, I wrapped a soft blanket over my shoulders and let my tired eyes close.

It felt like mere seconds later when a warm, callused hand trailed down my arm before I was pulled against a solid chest. I snuggled closer, allowing the steady beat of Dhamar's heart beneath my ear to lull me back to sleep.

Chapter Thirty-Two

Dhamar

Inara smoothed the front of my freshly laundered kurta for the millionth time, her hands shaking. I pressed them to my chest. "It'll be fine."

"But your father—"

"Won't hurt me." *I hope*. My mind chose that moment to conjure the memory of six-year-old me. I had burst into my father's room to tell him about the new doves the gardener had obtained for the courtyard. My father, who was in a meeting with his general, had been enraged and dragged me into the water closet and beaten me soundly. I flinched.

"See, you're not even certain." Inara's brow furrowed with worry as she squeezed her eyes shut. "Dhamar, I don't want to lose you."

"You won't." I pressed my forehead against hers. "You won't, Inara."

If I had to drag myself—bloodied and broken—back to her, I would. We had dreams to live, hopes to pursue, and a family to build. I wasn't about to let my father steal another minute of my life from me.

"I swear to you, Inara, my wife, on the sun, the moon, and all the stars to come home to you." I wiped at a tear that was trailing down her cheek. "By blood and blade, with every breath I have left, I am yours. And I will fight with all that's in me to return to you."

"You swear it?" Her arms slipped around my neck.

"I do."

"Then seal the promise with a kiss, my ameer."

I smiled. "If you wish, Amira."

I reveled in her kiss; memorized the way her lips formed with mine, the feel of her fingers playing with the hair at the nape of my neck, the press of her body against mine. If this was the last kiss we shared, I wanted her to remember it forever.

It won't be the last, I declared, easing away in order to brush the back of my hand against her cheek. *No, we have a lifetime to live together yet.*

With that thought firmly ensconced in my heart, I interlocked my fingers with hers and stepped from the tent. Zahir and Saif fell into step beside us. I noticed people stopping to stare, but their faces were mostly open and curious as opposed to hostile. They knew we were fighting for them, for peace. It unwound one layer of stress from around my spine.

Inara squeezed my hand. "I'm riding with you, yes?"

"Yes." I pointed to the horse that Aysa was leading over. "Though I don't know his temperament."

The horse was stockier than Zaid, who was still back at our camp. He pawed at the ground in agitation as I swung onto his back. But he quickly settled as I patted a hand against his neck. Reaching down to Inara, I swung her up in front of me.

"Not behind?" she asked, already leaning against me as my arm wrapped around her waist.

"No, this is more comfortable." I lowered my head and whispered, "I get to hold you this way."

She somehow pressed closer, and I tightened my hold on her hip. "I could get used to this," she said.

I hummed, a moment of silence settling over us before I asked, "Would you enjoy a tour of Taletha once this is all over? Just you and me, Zahir and Saif." I glanced over my shoulder as Zahir trotted up to my right side.

"I promised Saif time with his wife and their child." Inara tipped her head back to look at me. "I didn't think you would mind that."

I shook my head, ashamed that I had forgotten about his wife back in Mordova. "Not at all. It's the least he deserves."

"Good." Inara smiled as if I had given her the world. And Nicar above, did I ever want to. She could ask me to leap to the moon, and I would attempt it. Swim across the seas to the northern lands, and I would try. Inara deserved it all and more. My brave, beautiful wife.

We waited atop the horse as chaos built around us. This tribe planned on following us. While many of the leaders had returned home early that morning, a number of the warriors remained.

They were worried Father would not honor the agreement I had made the night before. I hated that it was a valid concern.

As the bustle grew, I leaned forward and whispered for Inara's ear alone, "What do you think *our* children will look like?"

Her free hand trailed to her stomach. "Black hair and brown eyes, I hope."

Her response surprised me. "Why do you hope that?"

"Because then they won't be teased for not being Talethan. They will belong here, more than I do."

"You belong here, Inara. You are the amira."

"Now." I felt her sigh. "But even before the Wife Market, I was teased for being northern. For my hair and eyes, my mother's occupation, and the men that came and went from our house at all hours. All of that was why I was *northern scum*." She shook her head. "I sometimes wonder if Umar is even my actual father."

My heart pinched at the pain in her words. So much hurt still lay in her heart, wounds I would never be able to heal or understand. Zahir's warning from our first day as husband and wife was true—I couldn't fix Inara. But I could love her where she was, in the hurt and the brokenness. It might not heal what had been scarred, but it was a start.

I caught sight of Aysa and her father. Dayi Aydin looked regal. He'd forgone the fez for a bright red turban. A scarf draped over his nose and mouth. His clothes—a white kurta with a red vest and salwar—hung loose and flowing, catching the faint breeze that rustled the tents' flaps and tassels.

I nudged the horse to follow them as they began the march east.

"Do you really feel as if you don't belong here, Inara?" I asked.

"Yes." Her fingers traced my knuckles. "Your mother, Saif, Zahir, Hafza, and you see me as Talethan. But to your people and the council? They'll never see past this." She picked up the end of her blonde braid before letting it flop against her chest. "To them, I am my mother's daughter."

"Is that a bad thing?" I asked. "I know you don't agree with your mother's occupation, but it sounds to me like she loved you fiercely. She did what she had to for her daughter. Did she make mistakes? I'm sure. But she gave you life and love, and for that, I thank her."

Inara relaxed against me once more. "That's true."

"Besides, I want our children to have your eyes." My throat tightened, as I imagined little dark-haired children with blue-green eyes that held every emotion imaginable in their depths. Children with Inara's smile, courage, and spark of life that shone out of her. I wasn't sure what I wanted them to inherit from me beyond my dark curls. I didn't want them to be like me. They could be better. *I* wanted them to be better.

When I didn't elaborate further, Inara turned to look at me. "You want them to have my eyes? Why?"

"Because they're mesmerizing when they change colors."

She chuckled. "I never liked that they did that, but when you talk about them, they sound beautiful."

"They are beautiful, Inara. *You* are beautiful."

"Do you know what I want them to have?" she asked, turning forward once more as the horse charged up a dune.

"What?"

"Your smile. You have a dimple that appears when you're truly happy. And I want them to have your laugh. It rumbles around a room and warms me straight through. I want them to have your mind and wit. To cultivate your caring and gentle heart in them." She leaned her head against my shoulder and sighed. "I want them to be a lot like their father."

"They could do better, Inara."

"No, they couldn't." She threaded her fingers over the back of my hand. "You're the one Nicar saw fit to give me, therefore you're the very best man to be the father of our children. No one else can do the job."

As before, her words soothed an ache I hadn't realized resided in my heart. Perhaps there were things about me that my children would inherit that I wouldn't like. The same was likely true for Inara as well. But could she be right? Had Nicar saw fit to bind us together for the sake of our children?

"You are wise, my wife." I pressed a kiss to the top of her head, and she sighed in contentment.

As the horse trotted forward, we talked more about our future, about hopes and desires, and for the first time since I was sixteen, I dared to dream of a life outside of my father's control.

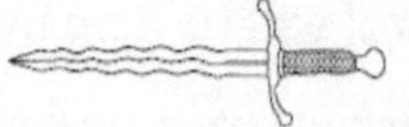

Three days later, we reached the crest that overlooked the ocean. Another tribe had tents to the southeast of the border, their colors of purple and blue a stark contrast against the golden sand all around. A gull cried, swooping low, and the surf could just be heard crashing against the sand.

My body tensed for a fight when I saw Father's encampment on the Taletha side of the border stones. The banner of Mordova snapped in the breeze that rolled off the sea, the salt and sun blending together in a scent that should have felt comforting. Instead, my stomach lurched into my throat.

Inara's hand slid over mine as it had done a hundred times since we left the Šeri encampment. She didn't say anything, just leaned against me as Aydin's white stallion trotted over to my side.

His sharp black eyes studied my father's camp. "He brought more than we agreed upon."

"He wants you to know he isn't scared of you." I scoffed at my father's ludicrousness. "Although he should be. You far outnumber us."

"And the ability to gather more easily." Aysa slipped up on my other side. Her eyes were hard, calculating. "The rest of tribes' leaders are assembling and will be here by this evening."

Good to know how much we trust each other. I tightened my hold on Inara, hating that she was in the middle of a possible conflict. I wanted to shove her into one of Aydin's tents and order Zahir and Saif to keep her there. But she would throw a tantrum, and though I never would admit it, I liked having her silent strength to lean upon. How had I survived before?

"Do your men respect you, Ameer Dhamar?" Aysa asked, shaking me from my thoughts.

"I like to think so. General Beeran does, at the very least, and the men respect him."

"Good," Aydin answered before Aysa could. "That could mean a possible victory for all of us."

"They've made a vow to the crown and will follow the malek until he's dead." I shook my head. "My father is still over us all." *And his word is law.*

"Well, I suppose it's time for us to try to make him see reason," Inara interjected as she straightened in the saddle. Her shoulders rolled back, and her spine stiffened against my chest. In that moment, she was every inch the Amira of Taletha.

I didn't miss the twitch of Šefe Aydin's lips as he nodded once. "May Nicar show you her favor."

Aysa murmured the same, and with that blessing on our heels, I spurred the steed down the hill. My heart hammered in time with its hoof beats. Did I have what I needed to face my father?

Coward. Scared. Afraid.

You stand for nothing.

You're afraid of yourself.

The words rattled around my mind, taunting me with my own fear. I couldn't do this. I was just like my father, weak and pathetic.

You are not your father. Inara's words from days before broke through the multitude of negatives, calming me as we neared the border. I wasn't Nadar, Malek of all Taletha, and Nicar willing, I never would be. I was Ameer Dhamar of Taletha and I was forging a new path. I wouldn't honor my father's legacy of corruption—rather, I would endeavor to change it all.

Reining in an arrow's length from the border, Inara pulled a white piece of cloth Aysa had given her from her pocket and held it aloft.

And then we waited. Every minute that passed heightened my unease. Father would make us sit simply to show us that he was in control. To make us sweat and crumble until he would at last grace us with his presence. It wouldn't work this time. I wouldn't let it.

"Do you think any of the lords came with him?" Inara asked, her fingers fidgeting with the white cloth's frayed edge.

"Maybe. I could see Lord Shaeen being here. Perhaps Arqa."

"And they will both side with your father." Inara's head thumped against my collar bone. "Is nothing ever simple?"

A mirthless chuckle slipped out. "Rarely. Good things take work."

"Like our marriage."

"You find that a good thing?" I asked as I watched the bustle of the men in the camp, their black salwar and vests a stark contrast to the browns and faint greens of the land around them.

"Of course. Don't you?"

"Always." I tightened my hold on her as another gust of sea breeze swirled around us, pulling the lingering fragrance of jasmine from Inara's skin and blending it with the briny scent of the ocean.

"We should move the capitol closer to the ocean," I muttered to her.

"I prefer our rooms in Mordova," she stated.

"Do you?" I asked, but Inara didn't have a chance to reply.

A cluster of soldiers moved toward us, the banner of Mordova fluttering above them. The crossed scimitars with a crown around it mirrored mine, but for the malek's crest, an eagle in flight hovered above them all. Dragging my gaze from the banner, I urged the horse forward, meeting them by the border marker. I swung off, wrapping my hands around Inara's waist and lifting her down. Her hands landed on my shoulders, and she kept them there once her feet were on the ground.

"Together, Dhamar," she whispered.

"Together."

My chest constricted as I looked over her head to where Father stood beside his stallion. Even from a distance, I could see his face was mottled red, a clear indication that he was irate. I tucked Inara slightly behind me but kept hold of her hand as we strode forward. What would he try? Would he dare do anything with so many witnesses?

Of course, he would. He wasn't afraid of anyone. He did what he wanted, when he wanted. Stealing my mother was proof of that.

That thought lent strength to my stride and iron to my will as Father stepped forward to meet us, Shaeen on his right, Arqa on his left. They glared at us as Father's voice rolled over the hills, undoubtedly echoing up to the Šeri tribesmen on the hill. "Dhamar, are you going to come here, you worthless boy?"

"You are not worthless," Inara growled, tightening her hold on my hand before stalking toward the border marker. She reminded me of Gamil, on the hunt with hackles raised to defend those she loved. Right then and there, I fell a little bit more in love with her.

"I told you before, Malek Nadar," she said, her shoulders drawing back as we reached the borderline, "do not speak of my husband that way."

"*Your husband*?" Shaeen sniffed. "Shouldn't he be marrying the princezo of Šeri?"

"No." I wrapped my arm around Inara's waist. "Inara is my wife, and I will not break the sacred vow I made to her and before Nicar."

"You did it four other times. What makes her different?" Father spat. "Nothing. She's a woman. You use them and then toss them aside."

My teeth ground. I opened my mouth to speak, but Inara stepped in. "We're not here to talk about that, Malek Nadar. Regardless of your wishes, the princezo has no desire to marry Dhamar, and seeing as how they are not *your* people, you cannot order her to do so. Together we have arrived at an alternative to bring about peace."

Father's gaze narrowed, his jowls shaking with rage. "Why should I entertain the offer of peace when I could overthrow them?"

"Because you can't," I declared. "You can't beat them, Father. To attempt it will show not only Šeri, but also your own people how weak you've become. Strength lies in knowing when you're outmatched and outnumbered." I jabbed a finger toward the hills where Aydin and Aysa stood with their men just behind the rise. "And we are grossly outnumbered."

Lord Arqa scoffed. "Nonsense. We are the strongest nation in the land."

"No. We're not." I swallowed a curse. "This is a war we won't win, and furthermore, I don't *wish* to win it. The šefe of Šeri has promised peace if we allow them grazing land for the animals. In return, they have a rare breed of desert horse and are willing to exchange two every year for the use of the land. They are also willing to exchange a portion of their flocks for corn and other items they cannot obtain elsewhere. We have also agreed to come to each other's aid if any of our enemies ever attempt to attack us, and they mentioned the possibility of rooting out the pirates in the southeast part of Šeri."

All throughout my speech, Father's face grew more and more red, and when he spoke, spittle flew from his lips. "Weak, spineless whelp! You would betray your country to the enemy?"

"They are Mother's people. *My* people! Just as all of these men are mine to lead, it is my duty to protect the Šerian people from harm." I dared to edge closer. "Even if that means I'm protecting them from you."

"You know what I can do." He growled, but the words sounded choked. Was that fear?

"I know what you *could* do. But I'm no longer the boy you ordered about and backed into a corner." I glared down at him, my courage rising when I realized I towered over him. When had that happened? He always seemed to loom over me, talking down and treating me like refuse. But love had emboldened me. Love for the Šeri people, for Taletha, and especially for my wife. I was done wallowing in fear. Boldness had me looking down my nose at my father as I said, "You are done telling me what to do. You are not worthy of my respect nor my obedience. I will not allow you to lay a hand on me, Mother, or Inara ever again."

"Or you'll what?" Shaeen challenged when Father's sputtering was the only response.

"I am not above abdicating the throne," I said, and Father's face paled. "Or I can join the people of Šeri. Perhaps I'll take Mother and my wife, and leave. Even you wouldn't be able to stop us."

The guards started to shift away, and I smiled tightly. They weren't accustomed to seeing us argue; truth be told, neither was I.

Father's breathing grew ragged. He grabbed at his chest, another choking sound slipping past his lips. He made a motion with his fingers, and I glanced behind him in time to see an archer drawing back. But he wasn't aiming at me.

"No!" I turned, plowing into Inara right as the bowstring thrummed in release.

Chapter Thirty-Three

Inara

Dhamar's body crashed into me, knocking the air from my lungs as we hit the sandy ground. I struggled to inhale, his strong frame crushing me. I reached up to push him off when I felt it. Sticky and wet, the metallic scent of blood gagged me in the faint breaths I was able to suck in.

"Dh-Dhamar?" I gasped.

He blinked at me, his gaze full of pain. "Are you—did it hit you?"

"No, you foolish man! It hit you!" I eased him off of me as the thundering of horse hooves vibrated the earth.

Zahir leapt off his mount, gazing at something in the distance before kneeling beside us. Gripping my shoulder, he forced me to meet his gaze. "Amira, you need to deal with the task at hand."

"I will not! Dhamar was just shot, and I'm staying with him." I jerked away, turning to stare down at my husband. Blood was leaving an ever-growing stain against his shoulder, the tip of the arrow just visible at its center. Tears swam in my eyes. "He needs me."

"No, you need to deal with that." Zahir pointed, and I followed his finger. The malek lay against the sandy ground with his hand over his chest. His eyes stared upward, and his body was motionless. Shaeen and Arqa were nowhere to be seen.

"What-what happened?" Dhamar rolled to his side and tried to sit up, but Zahir took that moment to snap the long end of the shaft that was sticking out of his shoulder. Dhamar hissed, sweat shining on his brow as he squeezed his eyes shut.

"You're lucky. Looks like that soldier didn't want to kill you," Zahir said.

The blood on Dhamar's tunic, the feeling of it on my hands and the scent of it in my nose threatened the contents in my stomach. "I—"

"You need to rally the men," Zahir said, his voice firm. He snapped his fingers, and Saif stepped to my side. "I will care for the ameer. You have to be strong, Inara. Saif and I know you are, and so does Dhamar."

I sucked in a breath at the encouragement shining in Zahir's eyes. Did he really believe I could be strong? I was strong before because I needed to save Dhamar. At the Wife Market because I wouldn't have survived otherwise. I hadn't been strong after Mother's death and Jamal's betrayal. It had hurt too much. And right now, my reason for enduring was bleeding onto the sand before my very eyes. I couldn't do it. I couldn't be strong this time.

Dhamar cracked open one eye and smiled, though it looked a bit delirious. "I saved you twice now."

I forced a laugh, though I really wanted to collapse into sobs. "Yes, you did."

"Amira?" Zahir raised a brow and gestured.

"Zahir, I can't," I whispered. "Not when he's like this."

"It's because he's like this that you must. Trust me, Inara. He will be fine and waiting for you at the camp when you return."

Reaching deep within myself, I grasped the sliver of courage that lay there. Though my heart lay on the sand bleeding, I turned toward Taletha and the prone malek. A few soldiers stood around him, but no one stopped me as I strode over and knelt beside him. Hesitantly, I placed a hand on his chest. I half expected him to grasp my wrist and haul me away from Dhamar. I flinched, but the man didn't move. There was no heartbeat, no rise and fall of his chest. He was dead.

"What happened to him?" I demanded.

As I rose, my sight landed on General Beeran. His hand rested on the hilt of his scimitar, and he stroked his beard as he studied the fallen malek. "I believe his heart gave out. He complained about it aching the whole way from Mordova, but he wouldn't stop or take a slower pace. He was determined to get here before his son." Beeran cocked his head at me. "Since Dhamar is injured, I believe you are now the one we will follow. Shaeen and Arqa may attempt a fight though, Amira."

"Let them try." I set my jaw, determination filling me. "Dhamar is the rightful heir, and I am his wife. We will be malek and rania, and they will submit to us or suffer the consequences."

Beeran might have smiled, it was hard to tell with his beard. "I know who shot that arrow, my amira. The man is beyond distraught. He respects Ameer Dhamar and truly did not wish to harm either of you."

"Yet, he still did," I said as levelly as I could. I fisted my hands at my side to still the shaking and tried to contain my anger at seeing an arrow in my husband's shoulder.

"Indeed, he did." Beeran inclined his head. "And he shall be punished. Ten lashes, enough to hurt, but not enough to kill."

He seemed to be waiting for my acknowledgement of the punishment, so I nodded. "Have someone gather the malek's body to be returned to Mordova and prepare to move the army out."

"Amira?" Beeran asked.

"We are upholding the agreement with Šeri. Neither Dhamar nor I want war with them, and regardless of what the council says, the malek's actions were hurting Taletha. We're done fighting the tribesmen. And if anyone disagrees, they shall be bound, gagged, and treated as a traitor to the crown. Understood, General?"

General Beeran's eyes sparked with approval as he bowed. "Completely, Amira Inara. I shall see these orders carried out. I will leave five men I trust completely to help escort you and the ameer back to Mordova once he's healed enough to travel."

"Thank you, General."

He bowed once more, turned, and began to shout orders at his men.

I allowed my hands to shake as I smoothed them over my kameez. The smell of blood lingered in the air around me, and a glance down showed that it covered the front of my kameez. My stomach rebelled, and I gagged. Saif caught my braid as I heaved into the sand, my courage spent.

After a few moments, I wiped my mouth with a grimace. "That surely demonstrated my strength."

"It's your husband's blood." Saif helped me to my feet. "I think if I were covered in Ranya's blood, I'd react the same way."

I sagged against his arm as the lingering adrenaline wore off. My head swam, and my stomach still churned despite its emptiness.

"Let's get you to camp." Saif swung into his saddle and hefted me up. My feet dangled off the side, and he wrapped his arm around my back as he gathered the reins into his hand.

I let my head lean against his shoulder. "Thank you, Saif."

He clicked his tongue, urging his horse forward. My eyes felt dry and gritty, my head ached, and all I wanted was to clean up and find out if Dhamar was all right. Closing my eyes, I tried to rest for the short ride from the border to the Šeri camp.

Saif pulled up, and I blinked blearily. Aysa stood there to help me off the horse. She tsked her tongue as her eyes swept over me. "Let's get you cleaned up and then I'll take you to Dhamar."

"Is he all right?" I asked.

"He's fine." Aysa's lips quirked as she guided me through the camp to a small, yellow canvas tent. "But you look like you're about to fall apart."

"I'm fine." But even as I said it, tears sprung into my eyes.

Aysa, ignoring the blood on my kameez and hands, pulled me into her arms. "It'll be all right, Inara. He's a strong man."

"I know, I do. I just…" How did I explain that after everything—Jamal, the market, our marriage, the war, our argument—right when life was supposed to be happy and peaceful, there was the very real chance that I could lose my husband? That a single month of marriage to him had been the most amazing of my life, even with all the chaos?

"You will get your happy ending." Aysa grabbed a wet rag and scrubbed at the dried blood on my hands.

"You don't know that." I had once thought Jamal was going to be my happy ending, and that hadn't been true. How could I know Dhamar was? If he died, I would be completely alone again. That thought clawed at my throat. I couldn't be on my own again, not after tasting the sweetness of love, hope, and peace.

"But I do. Even if something happens to Dhamar—and it won't!" She hurried to reassure me. "You have more than him in your life now. You have his mother, you have two incredibly loyal guards, and you have—" Her gaze dropped back to my hands, and her lip caught between her teeth. "You have me. My vow notwithstanding, I will gladly be your sister in all but blood."

Tears rolled down my cheeks and I let them. "Truly?"

"Yes." Aysa smiled. "I may have younger sisters, but I would gladly take an older one."

I pulled her into my arms this time, sobs shaking my shoulders. "I would love that, Aysa. Yes, I will be your sister."

Her arms tightened against my back, and I let myself cry on her shoulder. Love poured out of me for this woman I'd known mere days. Not the same love that I felt for Dhamar, and not even the type of love that I felt for Saif or Lenna. No, this love was camaraderie, fraternity, and sisterhood all rolled into an Aysa-sized parcel. It felt like healing and trusting. And I knew I would need it, would cling to it, until my dying day.

After a few minutes, Aysa leaned back, swiping at a strand of my dirty hair that clung to my forehead. "Now, let's get you cleaned up for Dhamar."

Chapter Thirty-Four

Dhamar

Pain laced down my arm, like a dozen needles slicing into my skin. Why did it hurt so much? Heat flared as a liquid was poured over my shoulder, and I screamed between gritted teeth. Sweat trickled down my temples, soaking the blanket I lay on. Or was it blood? The flashes of stars in my vision made it hard to focus on anything as someone poked at the burning pain in my shoulder.

The next thing I knew, my vision was clearing. I lay among pillows and blankets, a soft bandage cushioning both sides of my still throbbing shoulder. A fogginess clouded my mind, a result of whatever the healer had given me to reduce the pain.

I blinked, letting my eyes take in the tent. Zahir stood by the door, his eyes watching me with an unusual intensity. Despite my confused thoughts, I knew that this wasn't the tent Aysa had shoved us in before.

"Where—" I smacked my lips together. "Where am I?"

"In the healer's tent." Zahir shifted his stance but didn't step closer.

"Where's Inara?"

"She's getting some rest. She's been hovering over you all day."

"How long was I unconscious?"

Zahir rubbed his neck. "Four hours. Aysa and I had to forcibly drag your wife out of here."

My eyes were already sliding closed. My words were slurred as I said, "She's going to be angry."

"Perhaps." Zahir's chuckle was the last thing I heard before I was floating back into the blackness of sleep.

I awoke to a gentle hand smoothing my hair back from my face. I shifted, hissing as pain lanced through my shoulder. The hand pulled away.

"No," I mumbled. "Not you."

The stroking began again, the scent of jasmine and honey wrapping around me like a gentle embrace.

"Inara?" I whispered, my eyes still closed.

"I'm here, my love." Her voice sounded choked, but I could feel her. She was pressed against my good side.

"Don't go." The blackness ebbed my vision, but I felt Inara's hair brush my chest as her lips caressed my temple.

"I won't, Dhamar. I won't go anywhere."

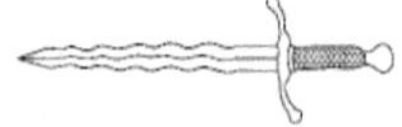

My stomach pinched and growled rancorously as I blinked awake. Sunlight shone through the open doorway of the tent, and I waited for my eyes to adjust before I caught sight of Inara standing there. Her hair was frizzing around her head, her kameez rumpled and wrinkled. Her hands cupped a mug of steaming liquid, and Saif stood just outside the flap, talking with her as she soaked up the sun.

The pain caught me then, stealing my appetite, and I sucked in a sharp breath as I reached across my body and clasped the bandage around my shoulder.

Inara turned and hurried to my side. "You're awake!"

I smiled, but it twisted as another shock of pain raced down my arm. "I'm not sure that's a good thing."

Inara's brow furrowed with concern. "Let me get the healer."

"Wait." I stretched out my good hand and grabbed the fabric of her salwar. "Just sit with me, tell me what happened. All I remember is the arrow aimed at you and jumping in front of it."

"Once you're fully healed, we're having a long talk about that." Inara's brows remained lowered, and I could see her stiffen as she remembered me diving in front of the arrow. She could be as angry with me as she cared to be. I could handle it, for she was alive and whole; not writhing in pain like I currently was. Inara settled beside me and smoothed back my curls. "I—I don't even know where to start."

"I got hit, Zahir brought me here, but what were you doing?"

"Getting the army to go back home." She continued to trail her fingers over my face. "And I had to take care of—your father."

I braced, clasping my shoulder again. "How did you do that?"

"He's—" Her gaze dropped to my chest, to the bandage around my shoulder. "He's dead, Dhamar."

It took a moment for her words to sink in. "Dead?"

"Yes."

Something shriveled inside of me. It wasn't that I was going to miss my father. Not at all. But there was a small part of me that had longed for his acceptance, his praise. For the past nine years, everything I had done I did in hopes of receiving a *well done* or seeing a gleam of approval in his eye. Instead, his last words to me had been about how insignificant I was to him.

"Dhamar?" Inara cupped my cheek. "He lied to you."

"Lied?" My mind was still on my last memories of my father. The flick of his finger as he ordered the soldier to shoot my wife. The wicked curl of his lip as he glared at me.

"You are not worthless." She let her fingers trail across my chest and rest over my heart. "You are a man who loves boldly."

"What do you mean?" I asked, holding her hand there. It was grounding, a point of contact when I felt like my world had turned upside down.

"You may have feared your father, but it wasn't fear of what he could do to you. Rather, you dreaded what he would do to those you loved if you failed to obey him. Over and over again, you stepped outside of your comfort zone to protect those you cared about. It was a little bit reckless and somewhat foolish, but it was done in love. And what we do in love, is done well."

My heart slowed its frantic rhythm as I stared at her. A million thoughts raced in my mind, a thousand feelings growing within, and none of them made any sense—save one. "When will I be well enough to return to the palace?"

"I don't know." She smiled, a teasing glint in her eyes. "You haven't let me get the healer yet."

"Go get him." I released her hand with a sigh.

She leaned over me, pressing a kiss to my forehead. "I'll be right back."

My head sank into the pillows, and I stared up at the ceiling, trying to sort through my emotions. On one hand, the relief that Father couldn't hurt people anymore clung to me like Inara's perfume. It meant I could forge a peace with Šeri that would last. I could protect Mother and Inara. As long as I lived, no one would lay a hand on them ever again.

But the other side of me was sorrowful. I was upset that Father had died and left things unresolved between us. Sad that he had been too stubborn to admit he was wrong. And my sadness—my grief—made me angry. He didn't deserve my mourning. He had beaten Mother and me. He constantly used the women in the harem, disregarding or destroying any children they bore him without a thought. He threatened Inara and tried to split us apart a month after our marriage. He was a lazy malek, unjust in his rulings. He allowed his council to dictate the laws and worried himself only with his flesh and his stomach. He was a horrible man.

A tear leaked out of my eye as my head swirled. I sucked in a breath, jarring pain through my arm. But the pain felt good. I latched onto it, letting it numb the ache in my heart until all that remained was a stone wall that nothing could penetrate.

The healer stepped in, immediately bustling over and unwrapping my bandage with deft fingers. Inara sank to my other side, clasping my hand in both of hers and settling them in her lap. I stared up, not looking at her nor allowing myself to feel anything but the pain of the healer inspecting my wound.

"I would say a day or two more of healing before he even attempts a trip to Mordova," he said at last. "It's three days there, and by the time you reach the palace, the stitches will need to be removed. Or you can remain here for a week, and we can get them out before you leave."

I glanced at Inara, who was watching me with a worried furrow in her brow. "Whatever you think is best, my love," I croaked. *But I do want my bed. Gamil. Safety and comfort. No more tents, no more wars.*

She squeezed my hand. "I think we want to return home as soon as possible."

She knew me so well. Even after weeks of separation, she somehow knew. It cracked a bit of the wall I'd wrapped around my heart. I squeezed her hand in silent thanks.

"Two more days of rest for the ameer before you leave, then." The healer smoothed a sweet-scented balm over the stitches on the front and the back before rewrapping the bandage. "I'll be back with some food. You may not feel like eating, Ameer Dhamar, but you need to keep your strength up."

I nodded, and he left.

Inara studied me. "Are you all right?"

It was so tempting to lie to her. But the words stalled in my throat. She was my wife. I could be raw and honest, and she wouldn't judge me for it. Would she?

"I don't know, Inara." A tear slipped free, and she brushed it away. "I don't know."

"Oh, Dhamar." She curled beside me, and I wrapped my arm around her waist, letting the tears fall in silent grief. "It will get better, my love."

"I know. But right now, I don't even know what I should feel."

"Feel it all." She gingerly wrapped her arm around my waist, her hand sending tingles through me as it rested against my stomach. "It's all right to not know."

"I do know one thing." I closed my eyes, relishing her warmth beside me.

"What?"

"I'm glad you're here beside me."

She inched closer, her arm tightening the barest bit. Her silent strength bled into me, telling me to feel even if I didn't understand it. She didn't care if I was confused about my reaction to my father's death. She loved me despite it.

My breathing slowed as I let the emotions play within. After a while, my mind cleared of everything except Inara's presence by my side. And with it, I succumbed to sleep once more.

Chapter Thirty-Five

Inara

The next two days passed agonizingly slowly. Dhamar was withdrawn and quiet. I sat with him most of the day, only leaving to go on walks with Aysa.

The evening before we planned to depart, Aysa and I strolled among the tents. She had her arm linked with mine, and I relished the contact.

"How is he?" she asked suddenly, breaking the quiet around us.

"Dhamar?" When she nodded, I sighed. "I don't know. Something's bothering him, but he won't talk to me about it. He's...surly, almost."

"I can't begin to imagine what he's feeling." Aysa leaned her head on my shoulder. "He's going to be malek of all Taletha. He married you, saved his country from war, and lost his father all within a month. Even if the Malek was a scoundrel, he was still his father. It must be a shock."

When she phrased it that way, my heart ached all the more for my husband.

We passed a tent where a father sat by the flap, a ney against his lips. He played a slow lullaby while his three small children sat by him, their chins resting on tiny fists as they listened with rapt attention. The mother stood in the doorway, her hand pressed against her rounded stomach as she smiled lovingly at her tiny family.

Would Dhamar and I ever know such peace? I wanted a family, children to fill the palace with laughter and life again. To hear tiny footfalls down the corridors, to see Lenna tickling a baby tummy and smiling, to have Dhamar hold me close as we watched our sons and daughters splash and frolic in the fountain and around the gardens.

Was it too much to ask for a moment of reprieve, to catch our breath before being plunged into another challenge? I leaned my head against Aysa's as we strolled.

"Pray for us, my sister," I whispered as we reached the healer's tent once more. "Pray that Nicar's healing may find us."

"I will, sister." Aysa squeezed my hands and smiled. "I see joy on your horizon. Don't give into despair, Inara. I have a feeling Dhamar will need you before this ordeal is over."

She hugged me before dancing down the line of tents.

I ducked under the flap, finding Dhamar with his eyes open, staring at the roof of the tent.

"How are you feeling?" I asked as I sat.

"I want to go home," he groused. His dark brows furrowed as he exhaled sharply. "This is ridiculous, I can travel perfectly well."

"You don't want to inflict more pain on yourself."

"A little more won't matter." He huffed indignantly, and I bit my lip to keep from snapping back.

"If this is the attitude you insist on having, I'm going to go sleep with Aysa in her tent," I stated as levelly as I could.

"You said you wouldn't leave." His eyes narrowed as he looked at me.

"I'm still your wife, regardless of where I sleep. But this peevishness is wearing on me, Dhamar." I smoothed the hair off of his forehead, grateful when he didn't pull away as he had the day before. "I love you, but even I can't tolerate that for long."

He closed his eyes, his brows scrunching. "I can't seem to control it all that well."

"Is there some way I can help?" I asked, stretching out beside him and laying my head on his shoulder. "I don't really want to go sleep with Aysa, you know."

It was good to hear his chuckle, even if it sounded half-hearted. "Help me figure out what I'm feeling."

"Grief?" I pressed a kiss to his uninjured shoulder. "Probably a bit of relief. Worry and confusion. All of it is normal."

"But this isn't normal, is it?" He looked down at me, wincing when it pulled against the stitches. "None of this is normal."

"Bahis told me that extraordinary things happen to those who are writing history." I rubbed my hand up and down his side.

Heat climbed into my cheeks as something sparked in Dhamar's expression at the contact. "We're writing history, my love."

"It doesn't make the pain go away."

"No," I said with a shake of my head. "But it does make me wonder what the future will hold."

"Less pain?" He smirked as he leaned down. Despite his moan of discomfort, he pressed his lips to mine, pulling me to him as he reclined.

"Much less." I breathed against his lips in between kisses. I savored the way he relaxed, his muscles uncoiling for the first time in two days. His hands rubbed up and down my back, and he smiled as I tangled my fingers in his hair.

Mindful of his wounded shoulder, I trailed my fingers down his neck and across his chest. In so many ways, I couldn't believe he was mine. He was gentle yet strong, meek yet bold, serious yet full of humor. I tipped his chin up, forcing him to meet my gaze as I said, "Even if there is pain in our lives, we will face it with determination, love, and joy. Because we are stronger together, Dhamar."

He traced my cheek with his finger. "I don't deserve you."

"Yet I am yours." Those words didn't grate like they once had. They brought a measure of safety and certainty that I had never known. I curled beside him, relishing his body flush with mine, and let myself get lost in his deep brown eyes with a sigh.

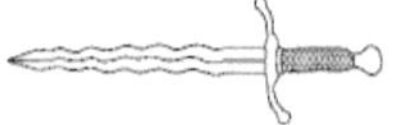

"Visit us soon," Aysa demanded, giving me a hug that stole my breath as we headed toward the group of soldiers preparing to escort us back home to Mordova.

"We will." I smiled and squeezed her hands. "So long as you come and visit soon."

"Of course." She hugged me again. "Now that we have peace, a goodwill ambassador will have to come visit. And maybe by then, you'll have a little one underfoot."

Her casual attitude toward something so personal had a blush rising in my cheeks. While I wanted a family, I wasn't certain how soon Dhamar would be ready for such a thing.

"I will see you soon, sister." Aysa laughed and bumped my hip with hers before skipping away, her bare feet leaving prints in the sand. When she came to Mordova, she would certainly shake things up. Of that, I had no doubt.

I turned back to the men, fidgeting with the strap of the bag slung over my shoulder. Saif and Zahir were helping Dhamar up into the saddle. The healer had forced him to wear a sling to minimize the amount of movement he would place on his shoulder and the stitches, but I could tell Dhamar was still using it far too much. Every movement had my husband gasping in pain. But he was determined to begin our journey home today. He wouldn't listen to any arguments—from me, Saif, or even Zahir.

"He's ready for you." Saif huffed, sweat already beading on his forehead even though the sun had just crested the horizon.

"Are you certain it's wise to have me ride with you?" I asked as I looked up at my husband, pursing my lips. "I can always ride with Zahir or Saif."

Dhamar stubbornly set his jaw. "You're riding with me."

Saif rolled his eyes but interlocked his fingers to give me a leg up.

"I'm riding behind you." I held up my hand as Dhamar opened his mouth. "And don't even try to talk me out of it. You're not moving that arm."

Dhamar growled but nodded. I gripped Saif's shoulder, placing my right foot into his cupped hands and swung up behind Dhamar. I wrapped my arms around his middle, resting my cheek against his back. He relaxed.

Worry nibbled at the back of my mind that this was too much strain on his weak body. I didn't want Dhamar to overtax himself. To lose him after everything we'd gone through would destroy me. "Are you sure we shouldn't wait?" I asked in a low voice.

"I'm sure." He ground out the words between clenched teeth, and I didn't push further. He was ready to be home, as was I. To bathe in the springs, have Hafza slather lotion over my skin, eat some warm Manakeesh, then curl up in bed together.

A small moan must have slipped out of my lips as the first two guards began to set the pace toward the border, as Dhamar stiffened beneath my hands. "Are you all right?"

"Yes." I chuckled. "Honestly if anyone should be asking that, it isn't you."

His muscles loosened, and he urged the horse after the guards. Zahir and Saif fell into line on either side of us, with the final three guards at our rear. At long last, we were finally on our way home.

I jerked awake to Dhamar moaning beside me. Sitting up, I brushed my hair out of my face and shook him. "Wake up, my love."

His eyes flew open, and he grabbed my wrist tightly. I winced but didn't pull away. His gaze darted around. After a moment, he relaxed, dropping my arm as if it burned him. "I'm sorry."

"Bad dream?" I asked as he buried his fingers into his hair.

"Yes." His shoulders slumped. "Did I hurt you?"

"I'm fine." I rubbed my wrist. He might have bruised me, but there was no way I was telling Dhamar that. He looked distraught enough.

"In the dream, you were my father. Striking out. I—" He groaned softly. "I'm sorry."

"You can't help what you dream about, Dhamar." I inched closer. "Though I wish you could dream about happier things."

"Like what?" He glanced at me.

My eyes darted around. Three of the guards patrolled the outskirts of our camp while the rest slept around the dying embers of the fire. I cupped Dhamar's chin and wiggled my brows, earning a small smile in response. He hadn't smiled a lot in recent days. "What about kissing me?"

His eyes sparked at the comment, and desire flooded me as he whispered, "I dream of a lot more than kisses when I dream of you, wife."

Heat spread through me as his hand settled on my hip. "Would you settle for kisses tonight?"

"For now." He pecked my lips. "But when we get home..."

He left his sentence hanging, and I let my imagination fill in the space as he kissed me again, letting me know exactly how much he loved me.

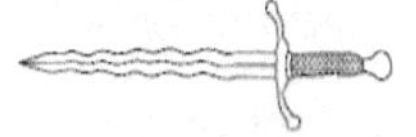

The most glorious sight in the world was coming around the bend and seeing Mordova glittering in the setting sun. I nearly let loose a sob against Dhamar's back, but his shoulders were slumped too much to worry him further. As the days of travel had trudged on, he'd gotten more and more quiet. Today, he'd barely talked at all.

It worried me, but I didn't ask if he was all right. He wasn't. I wasn't, and it wasn't my father who had died. My heart ached to take the pain from him—both physically and emotionally. For just five minutes, I wanted to grasp the elusive peace that would be a balm for our hearts and souls. I longed for the freedom to dream without the past dogging our steps. I needed to breathe, to truly relax into life, marriage, and starting a family.

I leaned against Dhamar as the horses clopped through the city and up to the palace gate. The curving steps loomed before us, sparkling white in the too bright sun. I slid off the horse and waited for Zahir to help Dhamar swing down.

Saif stepped to my side, and I waved him away. "Go find your wife, Saif."

He grinned and swept me into a surprising hug before racing toward the servants' quarters.

Zahir chuckled as he watched. "He's been able to talk about nothing else since we began our journey home."

"Do you think Ranya had her babe?" I asked absentmindedly, focusing more on Dhamar out of the corner of my eye. His facial expression hadn't so much as twitched. Worry clutched my throat. What was he thinking, and why wouldn't he talk to me about it?

"Possibly," Zahir replied in response. "But what do I know about children?"

I nodded, easing up to Dhamar and grabbing his hand. He startled, eyes glancing down to our hands then to my face. He squeezed and together we began to head for the stairs.

"Ameer Dhamar?" Zahir called out.

"Yes?" His voice sounded so weary as he glanced over his shoulder.

"I'll send for the healer to remove your stitches." Zahir's tone left no room for argument.

"Fine."

I was shocked at the venom in that one word. Whatever was bothering my husband, it went beyond the loss of his father, the nightmares he'd had each night on the road, and the pain from his arrow wound. He clutched my hand tightly as we strode up the steps to the palace, like he was afraid that if he were to let go, I would disappear. We reached the foyer, and a familiar figure stepped from the shadows.

Lenna wrung her hands together. "Dhamar? Inara? Are you all right, my children?"

"We are as well as can be expected, Mother." I wrapped an arm around her, still holding fast to Dhamar's hand. A glance at him showed his eyes misting over, though the hard look in his eyes never wavered.

"What happened, Dhamar?" Lenna's eyes wandered over her son, worry dipping her brows low.

"Father—he tried to murder Inara." Dhamar eased closer to us, letting go of my hand in order to wrap his arm around my waist. "I took the arrow that was meant for her. I saved her."

All through the explanation, no emotion showed on his face. Not in the curve of his lips nor the light of his eyes. His tone was even lifeless. I hated it. Where had my husband gone?

Did the arrow spare his life but kill his soul? I prayed not.

Lenna reached toward Dhamar, as if to lay her hands on his shoulders or chest. But she stopped short, curling them into fists and pressing them to her lips. "Where is your father? Beeran wouldn't tell me anything. He said to wait for you."

Dhamar's chin hit his chest. He didn't move a muscle as he whispered, "He's dead."

Lenna's face paled. "You didn't—?"

"No," I interjected hastily. "The healer confirmed what General Beeran thought. Nadar's heart gave out on him."

"Thank Nicar." Lenna cupped Dhamar's cheek, dropping my hand to move closer to the son she'd long been denied. "He was a horribly evil man, but he was still your father. No son should be asked to kill the man who gave him life."

Dhamar's voice shook—the first emotion I'd seen in him all day—as he asked his mother, "Is it wrong to feel nothing? To not feel relief or sorrow. Because all I feel is numbness."

He hadn't asked me that question, only told me he didn't know what he felt. While it stung to not be his confidant, I wondered if I would have had the right words for him.

Lenna let out a sob and pulled Dhamar into her arms, mindful of his shoulder. "It will come, my son. Sometimes numbness is the heart's way of protecting itself. But don't ignore what is inside of you. Keep loving fiercely and boldly no matter the pain you must face because of it. Please, my son, don't stop loving." A small smile broke through Lenna's tears. "You have a beautiful wife and many other loyal people at your side who want to help you bear this burden. I want to be there for you. Don't shut us out."

My husband's face was still stony, but he nodded. Lenna brushed back a lock of hair that had fallen in his eyes before standing on tiptoe and pressing a kiss to Dhamar's cheek. "I love you, Dhamar. I'm sorry I didn't show you that sooner."

Dhamar's eyes misted over. "I love you, too, Mother."

Then, he all but dragged me to our rooms. I couldn't help but feel that there was more to his coldness than simply his father's death. He carried himself as if the world was pressing down on him, threatening to crush him. With each step closer to our rooms, I watched his shoulders curve further and further. His back bowed, and his head dropped to his chest.

The moment the door swung shut to our common room, I planted my hands on my hips and asked, "What's wrong?"

He had his back to me, his fingers buried in his hair. "I told you. Everything feels numb inside me."

"That's not the only thing." I stepped before him, and he turned his face away. "Talk to me, my love. Like your mother said, let me help you bear this burden."

At first, I thought he wasn't going to tell me. But with a great heaving sigh, Dhamar whispered, "I'm the malek now. I am expected to rule, to lead these people."

"You will be a wonderful malek."

"No, I won't." He sucked in a sharp breath, still not looking at me. "I can barely keep hold of myself when I think about leading. The people will expect a big coronation and for me to choose my new council members or keep those I have. I'll have to make decisions about starting trade with Šeri and making certain that we don't end up in another war and—"

"Dhamar. No one expects that all at once." I pressed a hand to his chest, dipping my head to catch his eyes. "One day at a time, love. We'll have the funeral and coronation first. Then we'll worry about the rest."

Although the council may need to be chosen sooner rather than later.

"But—" He settled his hands on my hips. "Then there's us. Our family. I want to be a good father. I know what qualities I wish to have from what I've seen in Zahir and Beeran. And I know what I don't want to be because of my father. But I still don't know *how* to be a father."

And I don't know how to be a good mother. I swallowed my own momentary bout of panic. Aysa had said Dhamar would need me, and so I would choose to be strong. Be bold and brave even when all I wanted was to curl into a ball and sob. I stroked his hair and said, "I know neither of us have the best examples when it comes to family. But like you just said, we have good people in our lives.

Good attributes we want our children to see." I cupped his cheek. "What did you say to me? You want our children to know what love is by seeing us love each other?"

He nodded and whispered a hoarse, "Yes."

"Then you're already a great father, Dhamar."

I gasped as he dipped his head and kissed me. He spun me, pressing me up against the door as he deepened the kiss. I tasted salt as tears ran down his cheeks. My hands held his hips as he trailed kisses across my cheeks and jaw, down my neck. He didn't seem to mind that I was sweaty and dirty from the road.

"Dhamar." Heat pulsing through me as he claimed my lips again. It took all my will power to push him away when all I wanted to do was pull him to me and never let go. "We need to bathe, you need your stitches out, and then we need to eat."

He grumbled under his breath but stepped back. "I'm not hungry."

I raised a brow at his childish declaration, and he had the decency to redden.

A knock sounded on the door right before Hafza stepped in. "I have fresh clothes for after you bathe, Amira. Zahir asked me to send for the healer, and he'll be in your room soon, my ameer."

"Thank you, Hafza." I grinned, some of my stress evaporating at seeing my beloved maid. "I've missed you greatly during our travels."

"You mean you've missed me helping you look presentable!" Her tongue tsked as she eyed me. "Let's get you cleaned up, Amira."

I caught Dhamar's soft laugh as Hafza shuffled me off to bathe, and it was then I knew—we were going to be all right.

I fidgeted with the hem of the kaftan Hafza insisted I wear as I stood at the common room window. The pale pink material was soft, the golden embroidery across the tight bodice flattering. But it had been so long since I'd been in a gown that it felt strange. Hafza also insisted on doing up my hair.

"Trust me," she'd said. "You'll want your husband to undo it tonight."

A blush stole into my cheeks at the memory of her words.

"You look stunning." Dhamar's voice reached me a moment before he pulled me into a tight embrace.

"Your shoulder!" I leaned back, but he didn't release me.

"It's fine." He smiled, and it reached his eyes for the first time in days. "The healer took out the stitches and added more salve. I need to be careful not to do any heavy lifting for a week or so. But I hadn't planned on doing much for a few days besides enjoying your company."

The blush from moments before deepened. "I don't think I'll mind that."

"Good." He leaned his forehead against mine. "Because you don't have a choice."

I chuckled as he tugged me closer. We were still broken and hurting. There were still challenges ahead that we would have to face. But in that moment—with just me and my husband—I knew we would be all right. We had each other, a love that had survived insurmountable odds. Smiling up at Dhamar, I whispered, "Well, aren't you going to kiss me?"

He smiled, his dimple flashing. Then he was kissing me deeply, passionately. It was a kiss that I could truly drown in. A kiss that promised more. And in that moment, I finally knew what it meant to be fully seen, fully known, and completely and totally loved.

EPILOGUE

Dhamar

Three months later...

"And sign right there, Malek Dhamar."

I forced myself to not glare at Bahis as he shoved another stack of paperwork at me across the massive desk in my father's study. It branched off of the library, and he hadn't used it all that much—if the dust and cobwebs that had only recently been cleaned out were any indication.

The sun poured through the horseshoe-shaped window, casting the room in long shadows. It was a blessed sign that it was nearly time for me to return to my room for dinner.

I waved my quill at the page. "Last stack of the day, Bahis."

"Of course, my malek." He bobbed his head, reminding me of the peacocks that I had gotten Inara for the garden. It probably didn't help that the man was now always wearing greens and blues in honor of Inara's eyes—much to my wife's dismay. I couldn't help but find it humorous. Apparently, my quips about the scribe flirting with my wife hadn't been too far off.

I flourished my signature yet again. This stack was on different trade deals requested by Šeri. They had kept their end of the deal already, having sent two great desert chargers to us to signal the start of the peace.

My nerves coiled tightly as I remembered the meeting I had before my evening meal. It was to take care of the last bit of business needed to solidify my place as malek. Or rather, it was two councilmen that needed to be taken care of. Of the six lords on the council, only two had staunchly refused to acknowledge me as malek. I'd talked to Inara, and we'd agreed that there was only one way to ensure our safety. Execution wasn't to my liking—that had been Father's solution to those who disagreed. So, with the support of the other lords, it was decided that we would strip Shaeen and Arqa of their titles and land and give their homes to two men who would support my reign.

I rubbed the back of my neck. "Are the guards back yet?"

Bahis nodded. "They're waiting for you in the throne room. I was going to send you that way after you finished those papers." He gave me a look of impatience.

Pushing to my feet, I stretched my back and rolled my shoulders. My injury had healed nicely, but it grew stiff if I sat for too long a period. I sighed and stared at the paperwork. "Will this keep until tomorrow?"

"If it must, my malek." He gave a long-suffering sigh that had me smiling despite my growing trepidation.

With a nod, I strode out of the study and through the library. Before leaving, I paused in the doorway and glanced at the creed along the ceiling.

Under my breath, I vowed it as an oath to Nicar for my reign, "For the pursuit of knowledge, I yearn. For the quest of wisdom, I strive. For the love of *my* people, I endeavor to accumulate both."

Fisting my hand over my heart, I bowed my head and then strode down the hall to the throne room.

As much as it galled me to keep the four lords who'd served my father in positions of power, I wasn't willing to eradicate them all. A few still tried to undermine my attempts to remedy the evils my father had allowed to run rampant through the kingdom, but Mostafa supported me in my endeavors. He had more influence with the other three councilmen than I'd initially thought, and he was slowly swaying them to my side.

My first act as malek had been to move the tiled throne from the council room before having that room of malice sealed off completely—never to be entered again. The golden monstrosity my father only used on special occasions—like mine and Inara's wedding—had been melted down, and the gold from it was used to rebuild some of the slums right outside our palace walls into respectable homes. It had been Inara's idea, and one with which I had heartily agreed.

It wasn't the only thing she'd been right about in the last few months. The burdens of malek had come slowly after our coronation as malek and rania, which had taken place three days after our return from the border. It had been a small affair. Despite the hostilities of two of the lords, the rest of the council had been quite accommodating in my slow acclimation of duties. After a month of the most basic responsibilities, I'd insisted on taking on more. Now, I almost regretted that decision as I strode into the throne room. But the knowledge that Inara's smile would greet me at the end of this day had me settling onto the tiled throne.

"Bring them in," I ordered Zahir, who fisted his hand over his heart and bowed before opening a side door. Two guards entered, dragging a thrashing Shaeen and Arqa along with them.

"What is the meaning of this, Malek?" Shaeen snapped.

I gripped the arms of the throne, barely keeping my temper in check. "I have it from a reliable source that you threatened my wife in my absence three months ago."

"I—I did no such thing," Shaeen sputtered, but his face paled to a sick gray color.

I straightened. "I don't take kindly to liars on my council, Shaeen. Especially ones who wish to harm the woman I love."

Shaeen's eyes bulged out of his head, burning with fire. "What will you do about it, oh *Malek*?" He spat the title as if he thought it dirty.

"I strip you of your title and land. You will be allotted enough for you and your family to start again, whether here in Mordova or in another part of Taletha. You will no longer be a member of the council, and your name shall be stricken from all historical records.

So says the malek." *And the malek's word is law.* For once, that thought pleased me. "Take him away!"

Shaeen was too dumbstruck to argue as his guard escorted him back the way they had come.

"What of me, oh my malek?" Arqa had the decency to lower his head, but I still caught the rebellion in his jaw and stance.

"You were dishonest about the state of our military. It nearly cost us dearly. Your punishment will be the same as Shaeen, though your name will remain in our records. So says the malek."

Arqa nodded, his body rigid as he was escorted away.

I slumped back as the doors closed and exhaled sharply.

"Well done, my malek," Zahir said as he strode up to the throne.

"Don't call me that." I shook my head as I pushed myself to my feet. "I want to remain Dhamar to you."

"I know. But it's fun to rile you up, *Malek.*" Zahir laughed when I glared at him. As we moved back through the halls, Zahir asked, "Have you had any word from your mother?"

Inara had encouraged me to send my mother to visit her family. I was vehemently opposed to the idea until Inara had shown me a letter in which Aysa vowed Mother's safety among her people. We presented the idea to Mother who had cried, then laughed, then cried again. After we had managed to calm her, Mother had told me that she had desperately wanted to go but hadn't wanted to appear that she was abandoning me. She had left two weeks ago. We had received a letter yesterday stating she had arrived and was loving reuniting with her family. Inara had read it, smirked at me, and said, "I told you so."

I shared that with Zahir who smiled bemusedly. "Inara is a wise woman."

"She is indeed." Thoughts of my wife, who was waiting with dinner, had me hurrying down the shadowed corridors, past the gardens that Inara was taking a special interest in tending, and up to the door of our common room. I could hear the low murmur of voices, though I didn't take time to decipher what they were saying. Warmth surged through me, and I paused before the door, my hand on the latch. I had a *home*. For the first time in my life, I enjoyed setting down my work to come to dinner. I had a wife whom I desired to see happy, one whom I wanted to surprise with kisses and hugs and gifts, because she had given me the greatest thing she ever could—her heart.

I opened the door and stepped in. Inara sat by the table with Hafza, who quickly slipped around me and shut the door. Inara was stroking Gamil's large head, and her eyes lit up when she saw me. But the large cat beat her to my side. He bumped into my legs, purring as he circled them, knocking me forward and into Inara. She laughed, bracing her hands against my chest as she smiled. "Welcome home, husband of mine."

She wore a dark green kameez that made her eyes appear more green than blue. They danced as she tipped her head back, watching me. I dipped my head and kissed her, short and sweet, before my stomach growled.

She laughed, breaking the kiss. "Did you forget lunch again?"

"Perhaps." I cradled her hips with my hands.

She shook her head and stepped away. "Well, we have hummus, pita bread, and your favorite."

"Manakeesh." I breathed in the scent of herbs, garlic, and fresh bread. My stomach growled again, and this time, Gamil's ears perked up.

"Come here, Gamil." Inara shoved the reluctant beast into my room and shut the door.

"Did you take a nap with him again today?" I asked.

"Yes." She settled beside me and began to serve me some manakeesh. "How did you know?"

"You have his fur all over you." I smirked as she blushed. "But he is warm."

"He is." She traced her goblet of water, staring at her plate. I watched her out of the corner of my eye as I ate, wondering when she would ask the question that was clearly on her mind. I didn't have to wait long. "Dhamar, do you remember our conversation the other day?"

"You'll have to be more specific, my dear. We do tend to talk a lot." I chuckled. It was one of the things I loved about her. I could talk to her about anything, and she was quick to listen. She also had wonderful advice. She wasn't afraid to put me in my place or talk me down when I was enraged. Yet, she also took the time to encourage me and celebrate all my victories, big or small.

"It was the conversation about names we like." She wouldn't look at me.

"For future children. Yes, I remember that one." I took another bite of manakeesh, trying to puzzle out where she was headed with this. "What about it?"

"Did you—did you think about it afterwards? Are there any you like?"

"A few." My brows lowered at her strange questions. "Why?"

She bit her lip. "Well, we have about six months until we need to decide for certain."

I blinked. Blinked again. Then her words slammed into me like Gamil had. "You're—we're—a baby?"

Tears filled Inara's eyes as she nodded. I gasped, my head spinning. My food forgotten, I pulled Inara onto my lap. She curled her legs around my waist, arms resting on my shoulders as she laughed and cried in tandem. "Are you all right with this? Does this please you?"

"Very much." My hands settled on her hips, my thumbs rubbing the edge of her stomach. "Our son or daughter. In you."

She settled a hand against her stomach. "We're going to be parents."

I was certain that I would worry about that later. But at that moment, I was too filled with joy over the new life in Inara to question my ability to be a father. I kissed her, reveling in her soft lips before burying my nose into her neck.

"A baby." I breathed.

"Our lives are about to change again." Inara sank against me. "Are you ready?"

I sighed, relishing her as I whispered, "If you're by my side, wife, I think I could very well face anything."

The End

ACKNOWLEDGEMENTS

Sitting down to write an acknowledgement section is always a challenge. In other books, if it's over three pages, I tend to skip reading it. I don't want to drone on and on about people you don't know and likely don't really care about, but they do bear mentioning, so I'll try to keep this short and sweet!

First off, thank you to my siblings—Andrew, Abby, Alex, Allison, and Azariah—for listening to me gush about figments of my imagination. Sometimes I think I'm crazy (and maybe I am) but you're just as crazy, so that makes it all better. I love you all so much.

Thank you to my parents, Jim and Cindy, for showing me what a real life love story looks like. Your faithfulness to each other through all the highs and lows has played a large part in Dhamar and Inara's story. Someday, I hope I get the chance to love and be loved like that.

Thank you to my wonderful publisher, Quill & Flame, for seeing something in this story when it was half the length and not nearly as well-rounded. Thank you for taking a chance on me and bringing the world of Taletha to life!

Thank you to my early readers—Joelle, Victoria, Erin, Rosalynn, & Naiccole. Thank you for helping me write the first draft in a week and a half and for telling me that the characters lived rent free in your head. There is nothing more encouraging to an author than that!

To my wonderful Bookstagram community! Never would I have dared to attempt publication or even finishing a novel if it wasn't for my support system on Bookstagram! It's been such a joy to discover and promote indie authors. I love you all!

What makes a writer an author? READERS! I am so incredibly thankful for each and every one of you who picks up my books and reads them, those who leave reviews, and talk them up on social media and to their friends. So, THANK YOU for making this writer an author and for encouraging her to keep on writing.

Last but most importantly, thank You, Jesus. Thank you for the gift of storytelling, for blessing me with imagination and creativity so that I can dimly reflect how very creative You are! Thank You for the hard times I've gone through. While I wouldn't have chosen the paths I've walked, You've walked them with me so that I can help others. Thank You for Your gifts of love, joy, and hope. Without Your mercy and grace, I couldn't write a cohesive sentence. Thank You, Jesus, for it all.

ABOUT THE AUTHOR

Stories have always been part of Anna Augustine's life—whether on the page, stage, or songs. She loves telling stories that speak truth, hope, and courage into the lives of her readers. She is the author of two novella collections—*When You Found Me* and *A Love Like Ours*—has been published on *Havok Publishing* and has been in multiple anthologies including *Fool's Honor* and *Aphotic Love.* When she's not writing, Anna loves spending time with her family, snuggling with her two dogs, trying to put a dent in her never-ending stack of books, and working as a teacher's aide in a kindergarten classroom.

IF YOU WANT TO READ MORE BOOKS LIKE

BY
Blood
AND
Blade

QUILL & FLAME PUBLISHING HOUSE
HAS YOU COVERED

HEAT WITHOUT THE SCORCH

Quill & Flame
PUBLISHING HOUSE

www.quillandflame.com